WITHDRAWN

Gramley Library
Salem College
Winston-Salem, NC 27108

Harley Granville Barker

Harley Granville Barker, ca. 1910. The Raymond Mander & Joe Mitchenson Theatre Collection.

88-1704

PR
2972
.G7
D9
1986

Harley Granville Barker

A Preface to Modern Shakespeare

Christine Dymkowski

Folger Books
Washington: The Folger Shakespeare Library
London and Toronto: Associated University Presses

Gramley Library
Salem College
Winston-Salem, NC 27108

© 1986 by Associated University Presses, Inc.

Associated University Presses
440 Forsgate Drive
Cranbury, NJ 08512

Associated University Presses
25 Sicilian Avenue
London WC1A 2QH, England

Associated University Presses
2133 Royal Windsor Drive
Unit 1
Mississauga, Ontario
Canada L5J 1K5

The paper used in this publication meets the
requirements of the American National Standard for Permanence
of Paper for Printed Library Materials Z39.48-1984.

Library of Congress Cataloging-in-Publication Data

Dymkowski, Christine, 1950–
    Harley Granville Barker: a preface to modern
Shakespeare.

    Originally presented as the author's thesis (doctoral
—University of Virginia).
    "Folger Books."
    Bibliography: p. 228
    Includes index.
    1. Granville-Barker, Harley, 1877–1946—Knowledge—
Literature.   2. Shakespeare, William, 1564–1616—
Criticism and interpretation—History—20th century.
3. Shakespeare, William, 1564–1616—Stage history—1800–
1950.   4. Theater—England—History—20th century.
I. Title.

PR2972.G7D9   1986   792'.0233'0924 [B]
ISBN 0-918016-82-7 (alk. paper)

Printed in the United States of America

For my parents,
Michael and Helen Papula Dymkowski

Contents

Illustrations

Illustrations not otherwise identified depict Barker's productions.

Preface

Harley Granville Barker is generally recognized as one of the most significant figures in the history of the modern English-speaking theatre, hailed for his achievements as actor and playwright, and most notably, as director and scholar. Many of the commonplaces of contemporary theatre we owe to him: Barker established one of the first true repertory companies at the Court Theatre in the years 1904 to 1907; he insisted on the need for real ensemble playing, rather than the star system of the actor-managers; he produced plays of Shaw which for years had languished in search of performance; he proposed and planned a national theatre; he fought vigorously against stage censorship; and he restored the full texts of Shakespeare's plays to performance by abolishing pictorial scenery and slow declamation, substituting instead nonrealistic decoration and rapid natural speech.

These are just a handful of the many contributions Barker has made to our theatre, and yet surprisingly little has been written about him. Browse along the theatre shelves of any good bookstore, and you will find a number of works on Craig, Piscator, Reinhardt, and even the contemporary Brook, but you are unlikely to find one on Barker. In fact, there have been only three full-length studies published about him: C. B. Purdom's biography and Margery M. Morgan's examination of his plays, both now out of print in England, and Eric Salmon's recent appraisal of his life and work.[1] Of course, numerous articles and unpublished dissertations, as well as chapters of broader studies, deal with various aspects of his work—Barker as playwright, as critic, or as director. However, no one has yet undertaken a detailed and systematic study of his Shakespeare productions and criticism—contributions that have shaped the course of Shakespearean stage production in this century.

This book, which began life as a doctoral dissertation for the University of Virginia, is an attempt to do just that. Chapter 1 establishes the context of Barker's innovations: it outlines the state of Shakespearean production in the late nineteenth and early twen-

11

Gramley Library
Salem College
Winston-Salem, NC 27108

tieth centuries and explores the pioneering ideas of William Poel and Gordon Craig, both of whom influenced Barker. Chapter 2 is devoted to Barker's own Shakespeare productions at the Savoy Theatre from 1912 to 1914, productions that consciously intended to demolish outworn convention and replace it with a new tradition. Using promptbooks and reviews, the chapter reconstructs the productions in significant detail, discusses their contemporary reception, and evaluates their originality as well as their influence on modern staging. A comparison of Barker's *Dream* to Peter Brook's "radical" production of 1970 makes clear that Barker did indeed establish the modern tradition.

Chapter 3 deals with Barker's Shakespeare criticism in its entirety. Since Barker's written work was prolific, a detailed analysis of its place in the history of Shakespeare criticism was beyond the scope of this book. Instead, the chapter summarizes its content and development, focusing not on the *Prefaces* but on Barker's less well known articles, books, lectures, and reviews. The reason for this approach is twofold: first, knowledge of what Barker wrote provides a necessary context for discussion of his actual work in the theatre, and apart from the *Prefaces* and *Companion to Shakespeare Studies,* Barker's criticism is not readily available to readers. Second, it has become something of a commonplace to criticize Barker's later writings as divorced from stage reality, an evaluation with which neither I nor, happily, Eric Salmon agrees. To counter this misapprehension, I have simply let Barker speak for himself through extensive quotation and paraphrase. His enthusiasm for Shakespeare and exquisite sensitivity to the interplay of speech, action, and character will, I hope, encourage readers to explore his written work further, but the chapter itself aims to provide both an understanding of what Barker wrote about Shakespeare and an evaluation of its worth.

The relationship between Barker's theory and his own practice is explored in chapter 4, which deals with the *Preface to King Lear* and the Old Vic production of 1940 that it inspired; Barker himself directed its rehearsals for two weeks. John Gielgud's performance as Lear was recorded in detail by Hallam Fordham in an unpublished book, *Player in Action;* using this as well as reviews and memoirs, it is possible to reconstruct the production's significant aspects and so compare the *Preface* itself to Barker's application of it: the changes introduced by actual production illustrate his practical and sensitive approach to a text.

A few words are necessary about some usages. Barker only hyphenated his name after his second marriage in 1918; I have used the original form throughout this book. In addition, *producer* has been used interchangeably with *director,* its original meaning and one still current in Europe. Tenses posed some problems, which I have solved by using the customary present historical for literary texts and scholarship and the past for productions and reviews; thus, Lear cries but Gielgud wept. All references to Shakespeare's plays are to the Arden editions.

For permission to quote other authors, acknowledgements are due to The Society of Authors as the literary representative of the Estate of Harley Granville Barker for extracts from his published and unpublished works; to Sir John Gielgud for *Stage Directions, An Actor and His Time,* and his notes to *Player in Action;* to Stanley Wells, editor of *Shakespeare Survey,* for Hardin Craig's "Trend of Shakespeare Scholarship"; to the Folger Shakespeare Library for Fordham's *Player in Action;* to The Society of Authors and the Burgunder Shaw Collection, Cornell University Library, for Bernard Shaw's unpublished correspondence; and to The Department of Rare Books and Special Collections, The University of Michigan Library, for Barker's correspondence with G. B. Harrison and the prompt copies of *Twelfth Night* and *A Midsummer Night's Dream.*

For permission to reproduce illustrations, I would like to thank Mrs. Olive Smith for Edwin Smith's photographs of *King Lear* in performance, as well as for her kind hospitality; Angus McBean; the Shakespeare Centre Library, Stratford-upon-Avon; The Raymond Mander and Joe Mitchenson Theatre Collection; the Folger Shakespeare Library; The Department of Rare Books and Special Collections, The University of Michigan Library; the British Library; and The Society of Authors.

Many librarians have made it a pleasure to research this book, among them Jane G. Flener of the University of Michigan Library; Stephen Haste and Niky Rathbone of Birmingham Central Library; James Tyler, curator of the Burgunder Shaw Collection, Cornell University Library; Mary White of the Shakespeare Centre Library; and Colin Mabberley, curator of the Mander-Mitchenson Collection.

I would also like to thank Professor Katrin Burlin of Bryn Mawr College for teaching me to write many years ago; Mrs. D. M. Bednarowska of Oxford University for first making me think about the stage reality of Shakespeare's plays and also for suggesting Barker as a possible dissertation topic; Professor Lester Beaurline of the University of Virginia for his careful reading of this book in its earlier version and for his many useful comments; Professor Martin Meisel for helping me locate Alan Downer's correspondence with Shaw and Barker; and most especially, Professor Arthur Kirsch of the University of Virginia for his encouraging and constructive supervision of my dissertation, his generous sharing of his learning and insight, and his continuing inspiration as a teacher. I also thank the editors at

Associated University Presses for the care and enthusiasm with which they have handled my manuscript. Finally, I am very grateful to Pauline Gooderson for her unfailing help and moral support and to my parents for their boundless encouragement and practical assistance; to them this book is lovingly dedicated.

Harley Granville Barker

1
Forerunners of Barker: Poel and Craig

To say that the nineteenth century marked the nadir of dramatic achievement in England is no revelation to students of the theatre. Melodramatic potboilers, farces, and other works of little merit crowded onto the stage in unprecedented numbers. Although Shakespeare still found favor, neither an Elizabethan nor a modern playgoer would have recognized him: restoration and eighteenth-century adaptations by Cibber, Tate, and Davenant were current until the middle of the century. But even when the distortions of interpolation had disappeared, others arose to take their place.

The nineteenth century, despite its enthusiasm for Shakespeare, had no real regard for his powers as a dramatist. He was a poet, a creator of wonderful characters and interesting situations, whose knowledge of play construction was primitive and therefore lacking. Such an attitude easily justified the mutilation of his texts by actor-managers, who produced the plays as vehicles for themselves; thus, scene endings were regularly cut so that the leading actor could exit with applause, and scenes that appeared irrelevant to the plot were removed without any recognition of their place in thematic develop-ment. With the introduction of more elaborate stage machinery later in the century came an emphasis on realistic visual spectacle, and with the huge and cumbersome sets necessary for these effects came the rearrangement and omission of more scenes. Finally, the huge theatres that emerged in the nineteenth century demanded grand gesture and loud declamation, since spectators might often be as far as one hundred feet from the stage.[1]

These excesses in the cutting and staging of Shakespeare could not last. In the first place, the novelties of pictorial representation were not infinite: once the audience had seen live rabbits in the Forest of Arden it was difficult to proceed to even greater realism. Moreover, the discovery and increasing popularity of photography during the nineteenth century eventually made the painted scene appear ineffective, while the introduction of electric lighting further emphasized its inadequacies; flat painted scenery could no longer give the illusion of depth and space.[2] Clearly, reform was both necessary and inevitable.

One of the first voices to cry out from this elaborate wilderness was that of William Poel (1852–1934). Having seen an "old-style production" of *Hamlet* at Drury Lane, he complains in his diary entry for 18 December 1874 that it was

> Stagey to a degree that reduces to a minimum any interest in the characters or their fates. When individuals walk about the stage with measured steps, stand in symmetrical positions, raising their hands first to their breasts, then towards the heavens, then towards the earth, making recitals of every speech they utter, I feel sure it is fatal to all interpretation of character. I am glad a revolution has come to pass.

The revolution to which Poel refers was taking place at the Lyceum under Irving, who was moving toward a naturalistic drama along with the rest of Europe. However, Poel soon after criticizes Irving for being theatrical in another way; his diary entry for 23 February 1877 comments that "he appears to aim at creating an effect by working his scene up to a striking picture upon which the curtain may fall. This is a modern practice that I much dislike as it is sensational and stagey."[3]

The root cause of many of these abuses seemed to Poel the inadequacy of the proscenium stage for playing Shakespeare; the frame's demand for a picture to fill it not only interferes with what Robert Speaight calls Shakespeare's "poetic realism,"[4] but also distances the audience by giving them a picture instead of letting them imaginatively create one. Similarly, scenery and costumes, which grew more and more realistic as the century progressed, were sometimes painstakingly researched to be as historically accurate as possible; their effect was only to make the audience aware of anachronism and of the discrepancy between reality and its scenic representation.[5]

The Elizabethan platform stage, on the other hand, in its relative freedom from scenery and its projection of actor into the audience's midst, "acquired a special kind of realism which the vast distances and manifold artifices of our modern theatres have rendered unattainable. This was the realism of an actual event, at which the audience assisted; not the realism of a scene in which the actor plays a somewhat subordinate part."[6] Thus, by directing attention to insignificant detail, scenery distracted the spectators from the universal

Irving's production of *Much Ado about Nothing,* **Lyceum, 1882. The Raymond Mander & Joe Mitchenson Theatre Collection.**

nature and essential meaning of the plays—plays whose "dramatic construction [Shakespeare invented] to suit his own particular stage" (Poel, p. 43).

The use of elaborate sets also required frequent intervals, which interfered with the plays' continuity of action. Poel strongly argues the importance of continuity, referring to the plays themselves for evidence; no pauses should be allowed between acts or scenes, as all of Shakespeare's plays,

> with the one exception of "The Tempest," . . . are so constructed that characters who leave the stage at the end of an episode are never the first to reappear, a reappearance which would involve a short pause and an empty stage; nor, even, does a character who ends one of the acts marked in the folio ever begin the one that follows, as Ben Jonson directs shall be done in his tragedy of "Sejanus" (1616). Can we reasonably suppose, then, that a method so consistently carried out by Shakespeare throughout all his plays respecting the exit and the re-entrance of characters was due to mere accident, and not to deliberate intention on the part of the dramatist? (P. 41)

Related to this demand for continuity of action is an insistence on playing the full texts of the plays, a natural result of Poel's unusual regard for Shakespeare's skill as a playwright: "Unity of design was

Tree's production of *Henry VIII*, His Majesty's, 1910. Cardboard cutouts were used for many of the extras. The Raymond Mander & Joe Mitchenson Theatre Collection.

his aim. 'Scene individable' [*sic*] is his motto" (p. 43). Thus, Poel criticizes the Irving version of *Romeo and Juliet* on many counts. Because his heavy sets made such short scenes impractical, Irving cut Juliet's "Oh God, oh Nurse, how shall this be prevented?" speech, which to Poel marks the "turning-point in Juliet's moral nature" (p. 147). He also cut scenes that exhibit the hatred between the two houses of Montague and Capulet (p. 143) and omitted the crowd scenes that punctuate the beginning, middle, and end of the play; with this attempt to focus on the love story alone, Irving succeeded only in making it "less tragic, and therefore less dramatic" (p. 156).

Again and again, Poel emphasizes the distorting effects of omission, criticizing current acting editions for their persistent "cutting out [of] the end of scenes. . . . It is inartistic, because it is done to allow the principal actor to leave the stage with applause. Besides, it creates a habit, with actors, of trying to make points at the end of scenes, whether it is necessary or not, and this distorts the play and delays its progress" (p. 160). Only by returning to what Shakespeare actually wrote could one strip the moldy layers of convention from the plays and reveal the true conceptions underlying character; for example,

> The omission in all the stage-versions of Hamlet's lines addressed to the Ghost, beginning "Ha, ha, boy!" "Hic et ubique?" "Well said, Old Mole!" is, I think, not judicious, because it causes some actors to misconceive Shakespeare's intention in this scene. One can hardly read the authorized text without feeling that Hamlet is here shown as a young man, or, perhaps, a "boy," as his mother calls him, in the first quarto, thrown into the intensest excitement. His delicate, nervous temperament has undergone a terrible shock from the interview with the Ghost, yet, owing to the absence of these lines, our Hamlets on the stage finish this scene with the most dignified composure. (P. 161)

In fact, only by a return to the full texts of Shakespeare could one recognize the neglected dramatic concepts that underlie the plays as a whole; for example, *Hamlet* should not end, as was customary, with the death of the prince, but with the arrival of Fortinbras: "The distant sound of the drum, the tramp of soldiers, the gradual filling of the stage with them, the shouts of the crowd outside, the chieftain's entrance fresh from his victories, and the tender, melancholy young prince, dead in the arms of his beloved friend, are material for a fine picture, a strong dramatic contrast. Life in the midst of death! Was not this Shakespeare's conception?" (p. 175).

While Poel is clearly a pioneer in crediting Shakespeare with an understanding of dramatic art and purpose, his own productions, ironically, were just as apt to distort the text in order to emphasize an idiosyncratic interpretation. For example, his *Hamlet* of 1914 drastically altered the play in order to highlight its political nature: Gertrude was presented as an aged Elizabeth I, and cuts included all of the ghost, the "To be or not to be" soliloquy, and the gravedigger scene, so that Claudius became the central focus. Similarly, Poel cut *Troilus and Cressida* to emphasize the parallels between Achilles sulking in his tent and Essex departing from court in 1598.[7] Despite his own practice in the matter, however, Poel's theoretical demand for textual integrity was eventually heeded.

Deploring the declamatory style universal in his day, Poel regarded a return to Elizabethan delivery as also necessary for the intelligent rendering of Shakespeare. He finds ample evidence to support his view that Shakespeare's actors delivered their lines quickly and naturally:

> As to elocution, it may be well to recall what an Antwerp merchant who had for many years resided in London said of the English

people, about the year 1588. He then observed that "they do not speak from the chest like the Germans, but prattle only with the tongue." The word "prattle" is used in the same sense by Shakespeare in his play of "Richard the Second." In the "Stage Player's Complaint," we find an actor making use of the expression, "Oh, the times when my tongue hath ranne as fast upon the Sceane as a Windebanke's pen over the ocean." Added to this, there is the celebrated speech to the players, in which Hamlet directs the actors to speak "trippingly on the tongue." There can be no doubt, therefore, that Shakespeare's verse was spoken on the stage of the Globe easily and rapidly. (P. 56–57)

Poel realizes that although

poetry may require a greater elevation of style in its elocution than prose, . . . in either case the fundamental condition is that of representing life. . . . In the delivery of verse, therefore, on the stage, the audience should never be made to feel that the tones are unusual. . . . [O]ur actors . . . when they appear in Shakespeare make use of an elocution that no human being was ever known to indulge in. They employ, besides, a redundancy of emphasis which destroys all meaning of the words and all resemblance to natural speech. It is necessary to bear in mind that, when dramatic dialogue is written in verse, there are more words put into a sentence than are needed to convey the actual thought that is uppermost in the speaker's mind; in order, therefore, to give his delivery an appearance of spontaneity, the actor should arrest the attention of the listener by the accentuation of those words which convey the central idea or thought of the speech he is uttering, and should keep in the background, by means of modulation and deflection of voice, the words with which that thought is ornamented. (P. 57–58)

Poel elsewhere quotes Coquelin and Talma on the need to find the "key-word" of a passage, and Speaight writes that this became "the principle of Poel's elocutionary technique." He exacted a heightened form of natural intonation, paying equal attention to the contextual, semantic, rhythmical, and poetic values of the words.[8]

Poel's approach in practice was less flexible than his intention may make it appear. Sir Lewis Casson reports that Poel's "first step was to cast the play orchestrally. He decided which character represented the double-bass, the cello, the wood-wind . . . and chose his actors by the timbre, pitch and flexibility of their voices. . . ." Before rehearsals began, he decided on "the melody, stress, rhythm and phrasing of every sentence," which the cast learned by spending three of the four weeks of rehearsal sitting round a table, endlessly

repeating the "'tunes'" in a "strongly marked exaggerated form";
after two weeks or so, the play "became as fixed in musical pattern as
if written in an orchestral score." Casson recalls that Poel "used an
immense range," with the melody of one sentence sometimes covering two octaves; he adds that "when it came to *acting* and the minute
harmonies and variations that make the speech alive and natural, it
had all to be fitted into the main framework of his imposed pattern. . . ."[9] Casson judges Poel's efforts as successful, giving a "general effect . . . of swiftness and lightness, with a minimum of heavy
stresses even in strong dramatic passages," while Speaight feels he
was not in fact very sensitive to "the melodic line" of a speech
(*William Poel*, p. 198). Despite these differences of opinion, Poel's
delivery of Shakespearean speech indisputably offered an alternative to the Scylla of bombastic declamation on the one hand and
the Charybdis of monotonous conversational naturalism on the
other.

Poel's demands for a return to the platform stage, continuity of
action, and rapid natural delivery were met in his own Shakespeare
experiments. In 1879, he founded a group of "Shakespearian Students," called "The Elizabethans," to give costumed recitals around
the country; in 1881, at St. George's Hall, London, Poel produced a
First Quarto version of *Hamlet*, "the first production of a Shakespeare play without scenery and without Act and Scene divisions
since Shakespeare's time."[10] In 1893, for a performance of *Measure
for Measure*, Poel converted the inside of the Royalty Theatre into a
near facsimile of the open-air Fortune playhouse, and by 1895, his
University of London Shakespeare Reading Society had evolved into
the Elizabethan Stage Society, "with the object of reviving the masterpieces of the Elizabethan drama upon the stage for which they
were written, so as to represent them as nearly as possible under the
conditions existing at the time of their first production" (Poel,
pp. 203–4).

Poel's experiments over the next forty years were variously received, but he set before the public a dynamic Shakespeare which
gained greater and greater acceptance; on 22 July 1932, his eightieth
birthday, the *Times* leader credited him with establishing "the complete and continuous performance of Shakespeare's play [as] . . . the
rule and not the exception" on the English stage.[11] A recent appraisal of Poel's achievement suggests that his

> striking contribution to the discovery of a true Shakespeare is easy
> to mistake. It lay not in his adoption of Elizabethan dress, but
> rather in a more authentically Elizabethan regard for the play; not
> in the new rapid delivery of the verse, but rather in the permanent
> stage set which revealed the musical structure of the play; not in

Poel's production of *Measure for Measure*, Royalty, 1893, complete with onstage Elizabethan audience. By permission of the British Library.

any return to a full text, but rather in his working towards the original rhythmical continuity of scene upon scene. (Styan, *Shakespeare Revolution*, p. 48)

However, the suggestion that some of Poel's contributions are "striking" and others rather mundane misses the basic contribution that subsumes them all: that Shakespeare was an artist who fully understood the stage for which he was writing. Poel's corollary to this axiom states that Shakespeare's stage and its method are therefore intrinsically necessary to the satisfactory production of his plays; as he expresses it in his "homely image" of the foot and the shoe: "Must we cut off a toe here, and slice off a little from the heel there; or stretch the shoe upon the last, and, if need be, even buy a new pair of shoes?" (Poel, p. 121). Unfortunately, however, Poel's austere application of this corollary obscured his revelation of Shakespeare's stagecraft; his amateur productions, set in Elizabethan costume on a platform stage barren except for tapestries, seemed academic exercises: archaeological not in lavish display but in bareness.

Such criticism was leveled by Gordon Craig (1872–1966), another outstanding proponent of theatrical reform. The son of Ellen Terry and himself an actor in Irving's Lyceum company for many years, Craig nevertheless rejected, in the words of a contemporary critic, both the "ugly pedantry [of Poel] on the one hand, and [the] superfluous detail [of Irving] on the other." Craig's actual contributions to the development of Shakespearean stage production were the result of a lifetime devoted not to Shakespeare, but to a concept of the theatre itself; although his practical work gave way increasingly to theory and to experiments with model stages and designs, his visions, way ahead of his time, are now part of standard production techniques. Among his innovations was the abolition of side- and footlights in the Purcell Opera Society's production of *Dido and Aeneas* in May 1900; instead, he arranged all lights overhead on a bridge and had two "projectors," or spotlights, at the back of the audience.[12]

Craig shared Poel's contempt for the literally realistic, as he indicated in countless passages in his books: the "Realistic Theatre" merely "reflects a small particle of the times, . . . drags back a curtain and exposes to our view an agitated caricature of Man and his Life. . . . This is true neither to life nor to art"; and again, "in time realism produces and ends in the comic—realism is caricature." However, in their prescriptions for reform the two pioneers part company, Craig calling Poel's "love of the antique" irrelevant to "the purpose of the living Theatre."[13]

Craig's "art of the theatre" aimed instead to unite "action, words, line, colour, rhythm!"—that is, gesture, lighting, costume, scenery, and voice must all be molded by what Craig calls the stage manager into a consistent whole.[14] Because this art should reflect a personal vision, the director should oversee the entire production and avoid delegating responsibility, for example, to the costume, scene, and lighting designers; in fact, s/he should even disregard stage directions included by the author, since it is "part of the stage manager's task to invent the scenes in which the play [is] to be set" (*Art of Theatre*, p. 32). Craig derives authority for this declaration from Shakespeare, in the mistaken belief that he generally included no directions in his texts; Craig seems to forget that because of his double capacity as author and actor, Shakespeare would have been on hand to give verbal directions to the company on those occasions when his script gave none.

Craig visualized his perfect art of the theatre as a new art of "movement," which Bablet describes as "a single assembly of mobile forms and volumes; not one or more stage settings but a single *scene,* a *place,* capable of infinite variation; not a succession of stage pictures, but the 'movement of things' in the abstract" (*Edward Gordon Craig,* p. 121). This sense of movement was to be achieved by a revolutionary use of light and color in stage design, as well as by the use of screens to depict the "scene"; his son explains that "in place of painted scenery, [Craig] visualized scenery made of screens with two-way hinges, thus providing a plastic medium with which scenes could be composed in any shape and of any size, limited only by the size of the folds of the screens; and with the assistance of electric lights and projectors, he would colour and decorate them impressionistically." After he learned of the existence of the Asphaleia System of hydraulic lifts, Craig also posited a stage floor patterned like a chessboard, each section of which could be mechanically raised or lowered; such a stage was in fact used at the Royal Shakespeare Theatre in Stratford-upon-Avon in 1972.[15]

Craig's screens were to be manipulated imperceptibly throughout the play, without the need to lower the curtain; colored lighting would be used symbolically, or to create atmosphere, or to soften angles. Although conventional stage managers reacted to Craig's innovation with suspicion or scorn, Yeats, to whom Craig presented a complete set of screens in 1909, found them ideal for the production of his plays at the Abbey Theatre, Dublin, and even wrote his plays "into" the effects attained with a miniature set he played with while working.[16]

Craig's concept of a mobile architectural setting, "painted" with color and light, is illustrated by his early design for *Much Ado about Nothing,* produced in conjunction with his mother in 1903. In this production, Craig used five Tuscan pilasters, eighteen feet in height, whose positions were rearranged for different scenes; the spaces between them were variously filled with rows of balusters, curtains, or decorated backcloths. In this way, Craig created not only Leonato's house, but his garden and Hero's tomb as well; for a short street scene, he used only a front cloth. However, according to Edward Craig,

> the church scene in Act III . . . created the most lasting impression. . . . Against a backing of grey curtains decorated with a *varnished* pattern that sparkled in the dim light, he built a long platform, reached by four wide steps. On the platform was a great altar, crowded with enormous candlesticks. High over the altar hung a giant crucifix, part of it disappearing into the shadows above. . . . In the foreground he suggested two great columns by gathering together two clusters of enormous grey curtains. The

only illumination in this dimly lit "church" came from an imaginary stained-glass window above the proscenium arch that cast a great pool of light upon the floor below, while the distant candles twinkled mysteriously on the altar in the background. The characters were only lit when they entered the acting area which was the pool of coloured light; outside it, they too became silhouettes like the columns. (*Gordon Craig*, pp. 175–76)

Count Kessler, recalling the scene, testifies to the vivid effect produced: "Except for the curtains there was only one strong ray of sunlight, falling on the stage in a thousand colours through an invisible stained-glass window." Max Beerbohm added his own praise of the design: "By the elimination of details which in a real scene would be unnoticed, but which become salient on the stage, he gives to the persons of the play a salience never given to them before." However, the production also made music a most salient feature of the play; the program shows that Craig's Shakespeare was not very different from its predecessors in this regard.[17]

While Craig's design for *Much Ado* was obviously effective in creating the impression he desired, his sketches for theoretical productions divided critics into two camps. Many complained about his diminution of the actor, Poel among them:

His passion is for pure landscape unsullied by the presence of the concrete. . . . But the central idea of drama is man, and it is necessary that the figures on the stage should appear larger than the background. To see Mr. Craig's "rectangular masses illuminated by a diagonal light" while the poet's characters walk in a darkened foreground, is not . . . to enjoy the "art of the theatre." . . . [T]here is no room for man in Mr. Craig's world.

Poel's remarks were directed at Roger Fry, who had praised Craig's discovery of "a setting which would not only not interfere [like Poel's tapestries], but which . . . actually impose[d] upon the spectator the appropriate mood"; he found that Craig's rectangular masses and diagonal light "stir the mind to the highest pitch of anticipation" and "inspire the mood of high tragedy."[18] The two views are representative of the opposing factions.

The value of Craig's approach to Shakespeare can perhaps be best determined through an examination of his most famous production. *Hamlet,* undertaken for Stanislavsky's Moscow Art Theatre in 1908 and finally performed in 1912, was on the whole a critical success, though ultimately a personal disappointment for Craig, since his ideals had to be compromised both by the actuality of performance and by his association with a company not his own. Part of the

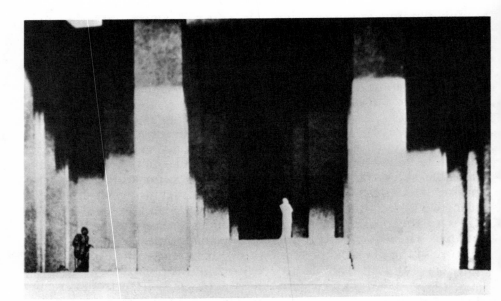

Craig's design for *Hamlet*, Moscow Art Theatre, 1909–10. The Raymond Mander & Joe Mitchenson Theatre Collection.

problem lay also in his negative attitude to *Hamlet* as a stage play—indeed, his attitude to Shakespeare as a playwright was highly ambivalent. Following the nineteenth-century Romantic tradition, he regarded *Hamlet* as poetry, not theatre, because it is only "complete" when we read it—an idea he elaborated years later: "On the stage we lose [Shakepeare's plays]," because productions "destroy that which produces those ideas [which so surround and possess us as we sit and read,] by confusing us and our other senses by appealing to those other senses at the same time."[19] He felt that "the Shakespearean play does not naturally belong to our art of the theatre" (quoted in Bablet, *Edward Gordon Craig*, p. 157), yet though "unactable, . . . [Shakespeare's plays] are the best stuff on which to rebuild the English Theatre. . ." (*Theatre Advancing*, p. lii).

Craig's increasing obsession with the dramatic potential of abstract movement renders this seemingly inconsistent attitude comprehensible: his firm belief in the "impossibility" of representing *Hamlet* or any other Shakespeare play "rightly" (*On the Art of the Theatre*, p. 285), as well as his desire that the plays be produced, stems in part from their intellectually complex nature. Craig's fertile imagination, so aware of the many possible interpretations and nuances of the plays, clashed with his principle of unity of conception and production, as no one production is capable of holding all possibilities in

tandem. And his mind, full of an ideal vision of the theatre transformed into a new art of abstract movement, understandably found
Shakespearean drama too rich to fulfill it; indeed, he told
Stanislavsky at one point that he "should even like everything to be
conveyed without words, by the movements of the actors illustrated
by music."[20]

Another problem was Craig's overidentification with the character
of Hamlet, which made him want to wrench the play into an expression of his own vision. He was happy to cut scenes and lines,
either because they did not fit his interpretation of the characters
and ideas or because he felt them unimportant. As Laurence Senelick's thorough reconstruction of the production details the distortions Craig demanded, it is enough to say here that Craig, convinced
of the vulgarity of the Polonius family, wanted to cut any speeches
making Laertes noble; he also wanted to personify what he saw as
Hamlet's death wish and to have Hamlet present on stage
throughout the play.

In addition, Craig's concentration on an abstract ideal of theatre
divorced him from stage reality. Alisa Koonen, who played Ophelia,
reports that he wanted the actors to perform impossible movements;
she, for example, was to dash headlong from the top of a huge
staircase in a swoon. Such disregard for the physical feats actors
could reasonably perform stems from their being subsumed in
Craig's idea of "scene"; Stanislavsky's assistant, Sulerzhitsky, for instance, complained about the Mousetrap's unsuccessful lighting
scheme, which made it impossible to see Hamlet but illuminated the
screens very well. Quite simply, Stanislavsky himself states that Craig
wanted "perfection, the ideal" in performance[21]—and that the ideal
of the director alone; the limitations of actual performance, whether
of budget or of human ability, both exasperated and disappointed
him. Although Craig ultimately decided that Shakespeare's plays
belong in the study rather than in the theatre, he nevertheless set
down guidelines for their performance, recommending the playing
of the entire text, the avoidance of slow scene changes, and the use
of brisk rather than drawling speech (*On the Art of the Theatre*,
pp. 281–84).

In comparing the two pioneers, it is clear that Poel's and Craig's
ideas are similar on a superficial level; they both rejected realism and
demanded livelier productions of Shakespeare's full texts. In essentials, however, they were moving in different, if not opposite, directions. Poel's contributions lay in his rethinking of Shakespeare and
his questioning of contemporary ways of staging his plays; Craig's
contribution lay in his rethinking of theatrical art itself. He, like
Poel, regarded the archaeological reconstructions of the nineteenth-

century theatre as irrelevant, but found Poel's alternative of Elizabethan-style performance equally so: it was still rigidly retrospective. Craig's vision was of a future theatre, where the conception of a creative mind could find full expression on a stage cleared of preconception; his own energies, however, were too scattered, his demands too uncompromising and idiosyncratic, to achieve this himself. Instead, he and Poel, together, succeeded in sweeping the Shakespearean stage clean, readying it for the entrance of Granville Barker.[22]

2

Barker's Savoy Productions

HARLEY Granville Barker, actor, playwright, producer, scholar, and critic, presented a series of Shakespeare revivals between 1912 and 1914 which finally "wrecked the worst conventions of Shakespeare performance." Barker's only previous Shakespeare production was a *Two Gentlemen of Verona* at the Court Theatre in 1904, which by all accounts, was traditionally staged.[1] However, his Savoy Theatre productions, beginning with *The Winter's Tale,* consciously intended to demolish nineteenth-century conventions and also to replace them with a new tradition.

The Vedrenne-Barker season at the Court Theatre during the years 1904 to 1907 had already injected new life into the British theatre. Barker aimed in this venture to lay the groundwork for a national theatre: he wanted a resident company playing a repertory drawn from the best of classic and modern plays, both British and European. Lack of time and money forced Barker to compromise with a short-run system, but the Court experiment nevertheless revolutionized the London stage: instead of a barnstorming star who arranged other players like ornaments around him, here was a real ensemble company, acting together and acting naturally, without the distraction of overelaborate scenery.

In breaking new ground, Barker gladly acknowledged his debts to the pioneers before him. In a letter to the *Daily Mail* published on 26 September 1912, he writes that Craig's 1902 production of Housman's *Bethlehem* immediately destroyed any belief he may have had about "the necessity of . . . the stuffy, fussy, thickly-bedaubed canvas which we are accustomed to call stage scenery" and "opened [his] eyes to the possibilities of real beauty and dignity in stage decoration." In the same letter, he acknowledges the influence of Poel, for whom he had played Richard II in 1899 and Edward II in 1903; from him, Barker had learned "how swift and passionate a

31

thing, how beautiful in its variety, Elizabethan blank verse might be when tongues were trained to speak and ears acute to hear it."

While the limits of Barker's indebtedness to Poel and Craig are clearly defined by his differences from them, his relationship with Bernard Shaw appears a more symbiotic one. The close association of the two during the Court years and up until Barker's second marriage was a powerful influence on both men. Though Shaw was old enough to be Barker's father (and indeed there is some belief still current that he was so), the advantages of the friendship were not all on Barker's side. Before the Vedrenne-Barker season at the Court, Shaw was a published but hardly performed playwright; with Barker's championship, he became virtually the Court's house dramatist: of the thirty-two plays presented between October 1904 and June 1907, eleven were by Shaw and firmly established his popular appeal.[2]

Obviously, a great deal could be written about the cross-fertilization of these two minds and careers, but my only concern here is to trace any influence Shaw may have had on Barker's ideas about Shakespeare. It is therefore useful to establish from the outset that Barker was no neophyte sitting at the feet of his more experienced master; in fact, he had had much more practical experience of the theatre than the older man when their friendship began.

As Barker's Savoy productions reflect some of the practices he developed at the Court, it is worth examining Shaw's claim that Barker had there "adopted [his] technique of production." Certainly, the two men had very similar methods of rehearsal, but it is difficult to substantiate Barker's supposed indebtedness to Shaw, as both began directing at about the same time and were influenced by Max Behrend's work with the Stage Society, to which they both belonged. The method they shared provides for three stages of rehearsal: first, the producer reads the play to the actors; second, the actors work through the play with scripts in hand while the producer is on stage with them; and third, the producer sits in the auditorium taking notes as the actors go through the play uninterruptedly from memory.[3]

With these external similarities, however, the resemblance ends. Shaw, who only directed his own plays at the Court, believed the producer should attend the first rehearsal of a play with "every entry, movement, rising and sitting, disposal of hat and umbrella, etc., . . . settled ready for instant dictation" ("Bernard Shaw, Producer," p. 6). Indeed, Shaw used a chessboard, the pieces representing actors, to work out the detailed stage directions he included in his plays; he claimed that any actor who follows them exactly "cannot possibly go wrong" (quoted in Henderson, *GBS*, p. 675). Shaw read the play to the company before rehearsals began so that they would get a sense of meaning and character and also "much of the actual detail of the music and phrasing of the dialogue" (Casson, "GBS at Rehearsal," p. 17); the latter seems the most important point, as Shaw feels it hardly matters if the cast does not understand the play. Whether or not the actors understood their parts, however, Shaw was determined that the portrayals should reflect the author's conception of the characters, and this was his only real concern in rehearsal. His letters to Barker during the Court years substantiate his constant preoccupation with casting, with finding the perfect actor to play a role; he has no concern with details of scenery, costume, or lighting.[4]

The difference between their approaches may be summed up by Barker's comment that productions should aim for "interpretation, not realization" of a play (*Exemplary Theatre*, p. 224). Shaw believed the latter to be possible; in a letter written to the *Times Literary Supplement* in March 1921, he complains that it will be possible to have full and exact scripts only with "a fixed and complete notation, such as musicians possess. . . ." That Shaw wants his plays to be produced exactly as he envisaged them is clear: "The notation at my disposal cannot convey the play as it should really exist: that is, in its oral delivery. I have to write melodies without bars, without indications of pitch, pace, or timbre, and without modulation, leaving the actor to divine the proper treatment of what is essentially word-music."[5] In one case, Shaw even annotated a script for an actor who understood music, giving directions about when to modulate from C major to A flat, where to place a crescendo, and other instructions (Bishop, *Barry Jackson*, pp. 28–29). It is easy to see why he believed the best director of a play to be its author.

Barker's approach, on the other hand, is a collaborative one. Throughout his writing, he insists that the producer should not impose a personal interpretation either on the play or on the actors: "To suggest, to criticize, to co-ordinate—that should be the limit of his function" (*Exemplary Theatre*, p. 226). Barker began rehearsals by reading the play to the assembled cast, mainly to give them an idea of its shape rather than to illustrate how lines should be spoken and characters played, which was Shaw's purpose. The reading was followed by discussion, which aimed at attaining, through instinct and reason, "a common understanding and a unity of intention about the play" (HGB, "Notes," p. 3); the time allowed for discussion varied with the particular circumstances of production, but ideally Barker wished this mutual study to last as long as necessary.

Barker advised actors not to learn their parts in isolation; in fact, they should not memorize their lines at all, "for the result—as with action, if the play is brought to that prematurely—is that they harden in the mind as actualities when they should merely come to it as symbols" (*Exemplary Theatre*, p. 231). When the director feels that no further discussion will be fruitful, rehearsal on stage can begin; however, the point at which discussion stops is not necessarily total agreement: as he points out in his "Notes" (p. 5), "Plays—being in themselves contests of character—may actually benefit by a tactful, regulated diversity of opinion."

Once on stage after their study of a play, the actors can begin to work out movements and gestures—and because the company will be "absorbed in the play, in tune with each other . . . their most instinctive movements will now have meaning" ("Notes," p. 4). Barker obviously does not believe in planning the production "in elaborate mechanical perfection"; the director only needs to decide "the barest skeleton of action" before rehearsals begin (*Exemplary Theatre*, p. 234; "Notes," p. 4). Cathleen Nesbitt, who played Perdita in 1912 and Goneril in 1940 for Barker, confirms that he actually put this principle into practice: "He gave his actors such freedom. He was not one of those directors who do a lot of homework with a set of puppets, and then say to the actors, 'I have you standing stage left on that line and moving stage center on this'"; he told them that "'if an actor has an emotional or mental conflict to cope with he should never have to think "Should I move there?" or "Am I in the right place here?" He should move when his instinct prompts him, not when mine does.'" The director, however, should help to stimulate the actors' imaginations, if necessary, and Barker found various ways to do so; Harcourt Williams recalls one of them: "I have known him change readings and positions from day to day, without explaining why he did it, on purpose to break down the inhibitions of some actor, and at last, out of the subconscious if you will, would emerge the right way of doing it."[6]

Many actors attest to Barker's willingness to adapt his own ideas to theirs; he saw his function as that of "ideal audience," watching "while the action of a play grows, goes its own way, not insisting on this or that—for in art as in life how many good roads to a given point there are—caring only that the roads are good, testing sympathetically step by step that the way *is* its own; that is in a sense to 'produce'" ("Notes," p. 4). While Barker believed that the director should refrain from telling the actors what to do, only pointing out what is not working, he also recognized that irreconcilable differences in approach must be solved by the director, whose job it is to weld the production into an organic whole. Consequently, Barker also took care over set, costume, lighting, and other elements of

production, ensuring that they complemented rather than interfered with the acting.

Barker's particular concern about speech reflects the tutelage of
both Shaw and Poel and also indicates his departure from them.
Like Shaw and Poel, he regarded the dialogue of a play as word
music that has to be given its proper value, but unlike them, he did
not dictate its tunes. As mentioned previously, Poel actually forced
actors to memorize the melodies he created, and he sometimes had
women play men's parts because their voices gave the effects he
wanted; Shaw orchestrated his plays for a quartet of voices like those
of the Italian operas he so loved, and demonstrated to the actors,
albeit in an exaggerated way that did not allow simple imitation, how
lines should be delivered. Despite this difference, both approaches
suggest an ideal to be realized rather than an interpretation to be
evolved.

Actors who have worked with Barker testify that his particular
concentration on speech did not extend so far. Casson writes that
while he would "demonstrate a rhythm or phrasing or emphasis," he
would "seldom give an intonation, and always with the caution that it
was given only to convey the thought, and must be made the actor's
own before use." If Barker's delivery were adopted, it was because of
his "inspired knowledge of the exact melody and stress that would
convey the precise meaning and emotion" of a line and because of
his "power of so analysing it in technical form that he could pass it on
to others."[7] The description does not belie Barker's dictum that the
director's function should be one not of dictation, but of suggestion,
collaboration, and coordination. Nesbitt adds that Barker's only bul-
lying in regard to speech was in his demand for speed and clarity.

The effects for which Barker aimed also illustrate his difference
from Shaw; as the latter often remarked, the two were as unalike in
style as Debussy and Verdi, and consequently, Shaw's constant complaint is that Barker encouraged underacting. As Martin Meisel
demonstrates in his valuable study of *Shaw and the Nineteenth-Century
Theatre*, Shaw's plays depend on the use, albeit subversive, of theatrical stereotypes—and these are the very stereotypes against which
Barker rebelled, not just as director, but as actor and playwright as
well. Their opposition is strikingly summed up in a letter Shaw
wrote to Barker in January 1908: "Keep your worms for your own
plays; and leave me the drunken, stagey, brassbowelled barnstorm-
ers my plays are written for" (GBS, *Letters*, p. 115). Their opposing
styles clashed not only on paper but in production too: Shaw came
along to the final dress rehearsal of *Androcles and the Lion*, which
Barker had directed for a month, and turned it upside down,

adding all the extravagance and exaggeration that the other had so carefully avoided. (Barker, it should be noted in fairness, did try to reflect an author's intentions in performance style; at a rehearsal of *The Man of Destiny*, he rallied the cast with the somewhat exasperated comment: "For God's sake, ladies and gentlemen, please realize that this is an Italian opera you are rehearsing!" (Henderson, *GBS*, p. 735). And his later production of *King Lear* certainly used, at least in some scenes, the grand style he had eschewed at the Court; by that time, however, the lack of such style was itself a stereotype to rebel against.)

Finally, in trying to discern the possible influence Shaw may have had on Barker's Shakespeare experiments and criticism, it is important to remember their very different appraisals of that playwright's worth. Anyone who has read the comments on Shakespeare scattered throughout Shaw's correspondence and theatre reviews will know that he attacks Shakespeare's poverty of thought and values only the beauty of his "music": "It is the score and not the libretto that keeps the work alive and fresh." Furthermore, he opposes the production of Shakespeare's plays as inimical to public acceptance of Ibsen and the new drama he so fiercely champions: "Shakespear . . . is to me one of the towers of the Bastille, and down he must come." Given his regard for the poetry, his severest censures were of course reserved for scenic productions that mutilated the text, and many of his criticisms of such productions echo those of Poel and Craig; in fact, Poel's experiments with the Elizabethan Stage Society, especially his adoption of the platform stage and the intimacy between actor and audience that it achieved, impressed Shaw with their good sense. Nevertheless, Shaw urged his actor and producer friends— Ellen Terry and Granville Barker among them—not to do Shakespeare at all.[8]

Barker, of course, did not listen to this advice. In the same letter to the *Daily Mail* quoted earlier, he voices his belief that Shakespeare "is a still living playwright and a very good one, thrilling and amusing, full of fine drama and good fun, and of an almost universal appeal . . ."—a sentiment as opposed as possible to Shaw's contention that "we have nothing to hope from [Shakespeare] and nothing to learn from him—not even how to write plays, though he does that so much better than most modern dramatists" (*OTN* 2:184). In his Savoy productions, Barker intended to show Shakespeare's plays as they ought to be performed and so prove their theatrical and dramatic worth.

Critical reaction to Barker's first revival, however, was predictable: most reviewers lamented the neglected corpse rather than rejoiced over the struggling infant; so unenthusiastic was the response that the play ran only for six weeks. However, the next production, *Twelfth Night,* met with great success and universal critical acclaim, playing to large audiences during its four-month run. By the time Barker again set critics howling with his controversial production of *A Midsummer Night's Dream,* he had firmly established his innovations as the foundation of twentieth-century Shakespearean production.[9] Barker's successful achievement of his purposes may not have been recognized by all those who saw the play during its three-month run both in London and in New York, but it is certainly clear to anyone who compares, for example, Peter Brook's *Dream* to nineteenth-century productions of the play. However, before examining the Savoy productions and their innovations and subsequent influence, it will be useful to outline Barker's general ideas about the staging of Shakespeare.

As a student of Poel, Barker had imbibed the notions of rapid speech, an uncut text, and a due regard for the "Elizabethan," but his interpretation of the latter was not the same as Poel's. In an article for *The Play Pictorial* written shortly after the first performance of his *Twelfth Night,* Barker writes about the "important . . . problem of Shakespearean scenery":

> I postulate that a new formula has to be found. Realistic scenery won't do, if only because it swears against everything in the play; if only because it's never realistic. . . .
> . . .[W]e want [a background] that will reflect light and suggest space; if it's to be a background permanent for a play (this, for many reasons, it should be), something that will not tie us too rigidly indoors or out. Sky-blue then will be too like sky; patterns suggest walls. Tapestry curtains hung round? Well, tapestry is apt to be stuffy and—archaeological.
> We shall not save our souls by being Elizabethan. It is an easy way out, and, strictly followed, an honourable one. But there's the difficulty. To be Elizabethan one must be strictly, logically or quite ineffectively so. And, even then, it is asking much of an audience to come to the theatre so historically-sensed as that.
> . . . .
> To invent a new hieroglyphic language of scenery, that, in a phrase, is the problem.[10]

Barker saw the need to keep the spirit, rather than the letter, of the Elizabethan stage; his reference to tapestry curtains above is an indirect hit at Poel's slavishly Elizabethan reconstructions. Barker instead wanted to reproduce only "those conditions of the Elizabethan theatre which had a spiritual significance in the shaping of the plays themselves." He would discard the "archaeological" bareness of Poel's stage, as well as the realism of the nineteenth-century one; the flexibility of Shakespeare's stage, not its lack of scenery, is the important point. In fact, too little scenery can prove as distracting as too much; as producer Norman Marshall explains Barker's view, requiring the audience to supply background or details that the director and designer can provide will distract attention from the actors. The result will be distortion, because it is the verse, spoken by the actors, that carries the play.[11]

Nor is scenery the only problem: how should the modern producer deal with other Elizabethan conventions, such as that of boys playing women? Which of these three alternatives should the director of *Twelfth Night* take:

> (1) use a boy to play Viola and make conspicuous what to the Elizabethans was commonplace; (2) instruct the actress playing Viola to play the part as though she were a boy playing the part of a girl and to play Cesario as though she were merely a boy; (3) play the part "straight," as Granville-Barker suggests, which will not make the Elizabethan reading possible but will at least save us from any further unnecessary distortion of the text? (Trousdale, "Question of HGB," p. 12)

As Speaight phrases the solution to this general problem, "The truth lies in proportion; in reconciling the liberty of the past with the mechanical facilities of the present without losing touch with the psychology of contemporary playgoers" ("Pioneers," p. 174). In his Savoy productions, Barker attempted this fusion of the essential elements of both past and present staging.

The outcry that followed the opening of *The Winter's Tale* on 21 September 1912 indicates just how revolutionary Barker's productions were. The stage itself was an important innovation, providing a compromise between the inescapable proscenium and the freedom of a multilevel platform. It also compromised between the "architectural or curtained" stage of the scholars and the elaborately scenic stage of the ordinary theatre (Byrne, "Fifty Years," p. 9). Barker built a curved apron out over the orchestra pit and the first row of the stalls, which measured twelve feet deep at its center and eleven feet at its sides; light gray canvas covered it. The stage proper was fitted with a false proscenium, which reduced its depth and width at the back and divided it into two acting areas. The middle one, shallow and slightly higher than the apron, was spanned by the actual proscenium arch; behind it, four steps up, was a smaller acting area containing a set scene. Proscenium doors led onto the middle and apron stages, and curtains could divide each of the playing areas, thus allowing continuous action and, thereby, a virtually uncut text.[12]

The settings likewise were designed as a compromise; in the words of W. Bridges Adams, Barker needed to "be spectacular without the help of scenery, real without realism. He [had to] out-Poel Poel, and out-Tree Tree."[13] Such a paradoxical combination may seem unlikely if not impossible, but with the help of designers Norman Wilkinson and Albert Rutherston, Barker produced stylized "decorations" that aimed to please the eye and yet provide a noncompetitive background for the action.

These decorations took two forms: front curtains and built scenes. Albert Rutherston, writing in the *Monthly Chapbook*,[14] explains that the curtains acted as

> backgrounds for the short front stage scenes . . . [and] were meant to be suggestive only of the time, place, and mood of the action that took place in front of them. There was no attempt at scenic illusion, only such colour and form being employed as were sufficient and appropriate both to the material used, and the suggestion which had to be implied. The curtains fell in broad folds, and the designs were painted on with dyes.

Each production generally had two built scenes, and these, "the main decoration," stood "on the stage proper. . . ." Rutherston explains that these sets were solid and three-dimensional, "having plan and elevation, not flat pieces of canvas painted to look like what they were not . . . [; they] attempt[ed] to give the design and plan that was demanded by the play, the charm of light and shade, line, form, and colour, which resulted from that and the mimes in front, and that alone." These abstract backgrounds, which were designed to "reflect light and suggest space" (Barker, "Golden Thoughts," p. iv), also prevented the incongruity of an actor's seeming to step out of a picture onto the apron.[15]

Barker followed Poel's and Craig's lead in abolishing footlights, using instead projectors attached to the front of the dress circle; these consisted of two center box lights, three cylinders on each side, and a light in the stage boxes, in addition to "four white arc lamps above and across the centre of the main stage" (Speaight, *Shakespeare*, p. 142). However, unlike Poel, who played with the effects of light and shadow, Barker "swept shadows from the stage as if they harboured germs."[16] Instead, he used color and pattern in both decoration and costume to achieve new dramatic effects, a point that a more detailed examination of each production will elucidate.

The Winter's Tale opened on the palace of Leontes, described by the *Times*'s reviewer as a "simple harmony of [six] white pilasters and dead-gold curtain" covering the back acting area; gold settees comprised the furniture. The traverse curtains used as backgrounds

were "green-gold . . . with flat Japanese landscapes to represent
exteriors, and with a leaf pattern design for interiors" (Speaight,
Shakespeare, p. 142). Critical reception of Norman Wilkinson's decoration was mixed, ranging from appreciation of its suggestiveness, to
admiration of its fine harmony of line and color, to outraged disapproval of its "Impressionism," lack of realistic illusion, and extravagance—criticisms stemming, of course, from lack of sympathy with
Barker's aims rather than blame for his having failed to achieve
them.[17] The most criticized decoration of the play was the "cut-out"
cottage of the Old Shepherd, with which even some sympathetic
reviewers found fault: the *Times*'s critic, calling it "a model bungalow
from the Ideal Home Exhibition," said it struck him "as a joke."[18]
This criticism partly stemmed from a dislike of anachronism that the
critic felt inappropriate—the same reviewer enjoyed other unusual
elements of scenery and costume that seemed to catch Shakespeare's
"rather wayward mood." Other reviewers were bothered by the lack
of historical definition and precision, whereas the less conventional
appreciated its appropriateness to Shakespeare's own eclecticism in a
play that unites the Russian empire, the Delphic oracle, and seventeenth-century Warwickshire shepherds in a single time scheme.

Rutherston's costumes were likewise not defined by any one
period, though they suggested the exotic East in their extravagance
and color. These costumes, whose "boldly contrasting colours . . .
[of] vivid magenta, lemon yellow, emerald green, [and] bright scarlet" Marshall describes (*Producer and the Play*, p. 156), were among
the most criticized features of the production. Unsympathetic critics
found them too bright, too eccentric, or generally unsatisfactory,
whereas even favorable reviewers regarded them as ultimately abra-
sive: Marshall's explanation that most contemporary productions
used "dull, muddy tints" provides some context for these complaints.
The *Daily Telegraph* mentioned the costumes' "gorgeous, noisy ar-
ray"; the *Observer* found them "quaint" at first, then "pleasing," and
finally "wearisome"; the *Nation* rejected the *Times*'s judgement of
"eccentricity of design—'post-impressionist' or other" but nevertheless judged the costumes "too attractive" and therefore distracting.
John Palmer, also writing a very favorable critique in the *Saturday
Review*, found the costumes somewhat distracting but forgivable in a
virtuoso production. Only the *Nation*'s critic saw that their colors
were not diffused "meaninglessly over a picture, but . . .
heighten[ed] and emphasis[ed] . . . at the point where the effect
[was] sought"; Bridges Adams confirms that the color, reminiscent
of the Russian Ballet, was especially "pure and sharp against that
unusual whiteness [of background and lighting]" (*Lost Leader*, p. 9).

Another highly criticized feature of the play was the pace at which

The Winter's Tale, Savoy, 1912. The palace of Leontes during Hermione's trial: "I appeal / To your own conscience." Leontes sits stage right; Hermione stands center stage. Shakespeare Centre Library, Stratford-upon-Avon.

The shepherds' "cut-out" cottage. Florizel and Perdita are at the far right of the photograph; Camillo and Polixenes (with masks) at the far left. Shakespeare Centre Library, Stratford-upon-Avon.

The leaf-pattern curtain of Leontes's mourning court. Leontes is seated and Paulina on his left. Shakespeare Centre Library, Stratford-upon-Avon.

"Now blessed be the great Apollo!" The disruption of Hermione's trial and of the tableau pictured previously at the palace of Leontes. Shakespeare Centre Library, Stratford-upon-Avon.

the verse was spoken. Very little of the text was cut, yet the playing time was only 165 or 195 minutes, with one fifteen-minute interval after the third act; obviously, critics had to listen to a pace very unlike that of the rhetorical delivery to which they were accustomed.[19] The critic of the *Stage*, among others, complained that he would rather hear two-thirds of a play spoken articulately and rhythmically than all of it garbled and rushed, while Barker retorted that audiences were simply not used to hearing and understanding Shakespeare's language spoken naturally (Marshall, *Producer and the Play*, p. 157). However, many more enlightened reviewers welcomed the chance to see and hear a complete and living play, rather than a butchered and recited text. Barker, like Poel, stressed a rhythmic approach to the speaking of Shakespeare's verse, but where Poel had attempted to impose rhythms on an actor, Barker tried "to persuade his actors of the values of allaying rhythm with character" (Hunt, "G-B's Shakespearean Productions," p. 46). In this production, for example, Leontes spoke quickly and Hermione slowly, a contrast both praised and criticized in the reviews: to John Palmer it was an effective method of developing character, while to an anonymous reviewer it was merely inharmonious.

Characterization and blocking also attracted criticism. Some critics regarded Perdita as too rough-and-tumble or too "common"; Leontes as "more pathological than poetic, yet . . . [giving] an intense, vivid picture of a distraught mind" (*Stage*, p. 22). The latter complaint is interesting, as it reveals Barker's success rather than failure in achieving his primary goal: "The first thing I aimed at was to get it [the play] alive at any cost" (quoted in Trewin, *Shakespeare on the English Stage*, p. 169). Such criticism betrays only a resistance to Barker's rethinking of conventional characterization. More disturbingly the *Outlook*, which printed an extremely favorable review, found the posing of the court during the revelation of Apollo's anger "pictorial rather than dramatic," revealing a "rhythm of cold design"; photographs suggest, however, that Barker used a tableau to make the disruption immediately following it even more dramatic. Barker was to be often criticized for his intellectual approach to drama, yet, as I hope to show, many of his successes and lasting influences derive from this approach.[20]

The music used in the production was also an innovation, both in kind and in function, though it received little notice from reviewers. Cecil Sharp arranged a number of English folksongs to be played by a few appropriate instruments "only when required by the poet," whereas classical compositions played by a full orchestra had previously served as general background music.[21] While Poel had led the way to the use of music contemporaneous with Shakespeare, he had still used it as accompaniment.

One element singled out for special mention was the ensemble style of playing; in Palmer's opinion, the acting shared the honors with the apron stage for the high value of this revival. The *Observer's* critic felt that Barker's production avoided the fault of "over-emphasis in the acting which leads to disproportion and the mangling of the text"—a fault avoided by the refusal to consider any player a star, an approach developed by Barker during his management of the Court. Only the *Stage* criticized the acting, and the reviewer's condemnation of it as "thin and commonplace and in some instances immature" indicates his preference for a grand, rhetorical style of playing.

On the whole, the negative criticism of Barker's *Winter's Tale* was backwardlooking, reflecting lack of sympathy with his aims and satisfaction with the previous century's scenic Shakespeare. The most positive criticisms of the production recognized not only its merits, but also its significance; John Palmer called it "probably the first performance in England of a play by Shakespeare that the author could himself have recognized for his own since Burbage . . . retired from active management," while the *Outlook's* critic stated that it "mark[ed] the first real 'revival' of Shakespeare [in our generation]—in contrast to the process of revival that consists in the heaping of a ton of bricks upon him, and leaving him for dead." Most of these enthusiastic commentators regarded Barker's adaptation of the stage as his single most important contribution. The *Observer's* felt that the apron dispelled the usual "pretence that this is not a theatrical performance of a play"—a feeling Palmer elaborated in his own review: "Gone was the centuries-old, needless and silly illusion of a picture stage, with scene and atmosphere ready-made and mutoscopically viewed. I had no illusion, and could wait receptively for Shakespeare himself to build it." In being less realistic, in eliminating what Barker called the "defensive armouring" of scenery (quoted in Trewin, *Shakespeare on the English Stage*, p. 252), the theatrical experience became more real.

Palmer felt that the stage's projection into the auditorium was responsible for the production's success in yet another way: soliloquies and set speeches were delivered from the edge of the apron directly to the audience. While the *Times* dismissed this practice (and the pipe-and-tabor music) as whimsical, Palmer appreciated that such proximity to the players made asides and soliloquies more meaningful. The reviewer from the *Outlook* added that the delivery of soliloquies from a picture stage had in fact destroyed dramatic reality and that Barker's staging had solved one of the two major problems of Shakespearean production; the other problem, the textual abridgement and long intervals made necessary by realistic

The statue scene with abstract curtain. Shakespeare Centre Library, Stratford-upon-Avon.

scenery, was now also solved both by Barker's new decoration and by the continuation of action on the apron during scene changes.

Bridges Adams, evaluating Barker's achievement in *The Lost Leader,* probably best sums up the reason for both the criticism and the acclaim showered on this production of *The Winter's Tale*:

> Everything was—to my taste—a little too much on its toes, as you might say. The challenge to tradition was too strident. I have never seen an audience more mentally alive, but that was partly because we were wondering all the time what Barker was going to do next. It was as though he knew there could be no half-measures; the public must be taken by storm or not at all—which I believe was the precise fact. Even the fantastic draperies, that took the place of Tree's front cloths and Poel's traverse curtains, came down with a defiant flop. (P. 10)

When *Twelfth Night* opened on 15 November 1912, just two weeks after *The Winter's Tale* closed, critical response was, surprisingly, virtually unanimous in its enthusiasm.[22] J. T. Grein, writing in the *Sunday Times,* thought that Barker had listened to critics of his first production in preparing the second, while the *Illustrated London*

News found it "more conciliatory" than *The Winter's Tale*. The *Times* wrote that, in this play, Barker "sets out chiefly to please rather than . . . chiefly to make us 'sit up.' There is no deliberate challenge now to the scoffer, no flaunting eccentricity, no obvious search for quaintness for its own sake. Novelty, of course, there is, and an independent, individual touch in everything." John Palmer, on the other hand, pointed out that this revival was actually no different from the first; it seems in fact that audiences and critics found themselves unconsciously won over to Barker's methods once their initial shock had passed.

For this production, Norman Wilkinson designed the costumes as well as the decoration. The major set was Olivia's stylized Elizabethan garden. At both right and left of the middle stage stood a wall-like hedge painted green, over which towered a sculpted "Noah's Ark" tree (Marshall, *Producer and the Plays*, p. 159); in front of each hedge was placed a patterned gold settee. The pink-and-black checkerboard floor led to four white steps which ascended to the back acting area. At the top stood a kind of "summerhouse"—four pink pillars with gilt capitals, supporting an arched dome; beneath this canopy, another gold settee. Staircases, each surmounted by a summerhouse, stood at stage right and left behind the hedge and tree. The promptbook for the production provides a useful sketch of the set (see illustration).[23]

Reaction to this set was mixed—the design seemed to be appreciated but the bright pink color disturbed many, among them the *Outlook*'s reviewer: "The pink pillars and walls of Olivia's summer house suggest nightmares and toothaches." Many reviewers noted the toylike or confectionery qualities of the decoration; B. W. Findon excitedly reported in the *Play Pictorial* that "the traditions of a life-time [had been] torpedoed into infinity! Every accepted canon of stage mounting thrown to the winds! For what? The quaint simplicity of a child's Christmas Toy Box." J. T. Grein grumbled that the scenery, though charming, was mistaken, for the mixture of "hideous pink with white, green, and gold" looked like "a Christmas *étalage* in sweet-shop stuff." However, most reviews stressed the beauty and delicacy of the decoration's use of color and line, finding the sets neither eccentric nor distracting. Findon reported, rather to his surprise it seems, that "bizarre though it may be, [the decoration] yet has proved an excellent background for the actors, inasmuch as it provides a pleasing relief to the eye, without disturbing the value of the author's words or diminishing the effects of the various situations: One never feels that the players are dwarfed." His last comment is interesting in light of Poel's criticism of Craig's designs.

Whether disgruntled or pleased, none of the critics noticed the

Twelfth Night, Savoy, 1912. Olivia's "toy-box" garden. At the back are Malvolio and Maria; in front are Sir Toby, Fabian, and Sir Andrew. Shakespeare Centre Library, Stratford-upon-Avon.

scenery's possible thematic motivation. Promptbook photographs show that for the last scene, the sickly-sweet garden was masked by a high white wall, with a gold-grilled, arched gateway in its center and three high-set, arched windows on either side of the gate; only the tops of the left and right summerhouses were visible. This more harmonious setting is the visual equivalent to the order and true feeling achieved at the end of the play, just as the pink confectionery of the earlier scenes reflects the false sentimentality and emotional wallowing of Orsino and Olivia when we first see them. Barker emphasized this intention by careful and symmetrical blocking; as Kelly points out, without seeing the thematic rationale behind it: "With less depth in which to play, and with much of the cast on stage most of the time, there was an increased need for the kind of control exercised by the stage directions" (p. 217). The promptbook diagram for the actors' positions at V. i. 326 illustrates this control (see illustration). Barker's use of modified sets for the same location anticipates his use of both curtained and three-dimensional decorations for Theseus's court, which will be discussed later.

While most photographs of the production show only Olivia's

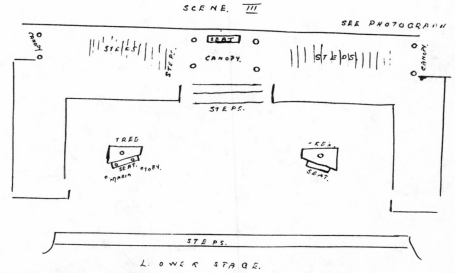

Drawing of set for Olivia's garden in Val Gurney's hand, prompt copy, p. 5. Courtesy of The Department of Rare Books and Special Collections, The University of Michigan Library, and The Society of Authors on behalf of the Trustees of the late Harley Granville Barker.

garden, it is possible to discover a few more details of Wilkinson's designs. Trewin writes that "Orsino's palace had twisted barley-sugar pillars in pink" (*Shakespeare on the English Stage*, p. 55), a detail which, if *Orsino's* is not a misprint for *Olivia's*, strengthens my previous point about the thematic use of decoration. The *Outlook's* review mentioned "softly coloured silken curtains" (as usual, the *Stage* registered a complaint about their flimsiness), and photos in the *Play Pictorial* reveal that Sir Toby's midnight revels took place around a tapestry-covered table against a tapestried background. Another photo in the promptbook shows Orsino holding court in a geometrically-patterned chair against a geometrically-patterned curtain, and Speaight speaks of the contrast between black and silver in the decoration (*Shakespeare on the Stage*, p. 143).

This playing with contrasted colors extended to the costuming, as is evident from J. T. Grein's (mostly) admiring comment in the *Sunday Times:* "a revel of boldly harmonised colours of grotesquely grandiose designs and of intense individuality." The costumes were generally Elizabethan in design with a slight Eastern influence. *Play Pictorial* photos reveal a turbaned and berobed Orsino and a Viola who finally appears in woman's weeds of vampy caftan, blousy long robe of patterned silk, and turban. Orsino wore a cloak of a "dying-sunset" color, and Antonio the sea captain stepped from an "eastern fairy-tale," complete with turban, pantaloons, curled-toe slippers,

A traditionally scenic set for Olivia's garden: Tree's 1901 production at Her Majesty's Theatre. The Raymond Mander & Joe Mitchenson Theatre Collection.

Final set for *Twelfth Night:* "I am sorry, madam, I have hurt your kinsman."
Standing in the front, from left to right, are Viola, Orsino, Olivia, and Sebastian.
Shakespeare Centre Library, Stratford-upon-Avon.

9. Duke L. of gates. Viola x's to him
Olivia gets R of gates - Sebastian x's
to her.   Seraph. Ladies Fabian
                  | gates. |
Lords
      Olivia   Mal.   Duke Viola
Seb.   o   o   o   o   Officers
  o   Antonio

A Two steps to R.C.

Val Gurney's sketch of the actors' positions following "Is this the madman?,"
prompt copy, p. 93. Courtesy of The Department of Rare Books and Special
Collections, The University of Michigan Library, and The Society of Authors on
behalf of the Trustees of the late Harley Granville Barker.

Midnight revels in the tapestried room with Malvolio, Sir Toby, Maria, Feste, and Sir Andrew. Shakespeare Centre Library, Stratford-upon-Avon.

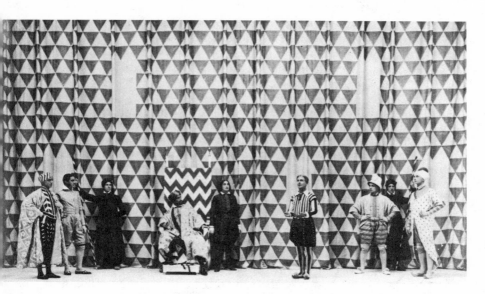

Orsino's court. Viola/Cesario stands next to the throne, while attention is focused on Feste. Courtesy of The Department of Rare Books and Special Collections, The University of Michigan Library, and The Society of Authors on behalf of the Trustees of the late Harley Granville Barker.

and pointed beard.[24] Malvolio was dressed rather like a Puritan, in somber colors and a pilgrim's hat. Viola/Cesario and Sebastian wore identical costumes for their recognition scene (kneebreeches, doublet, boots, long cloak) and sported the same pageboy hairstyle, thus making the confusion more credible. Reviewers found the costumes "less grotesque and eccentric" than those of *The Winter's Tale* as well as "more elaborate"—an interesting set of descriptions from the *Morning Post* and the *Nation,* respectively, each showing in its own way an openness to Barker's ideas in this production. Bridges Adams, however, thought the costumes were a bit too "dazzling": "Ought not one to remember more of the letter scene than the dazzling radiation of Malvolio's cloak, which drew a gasp from the women in the house when he turned upstage?" (*Lost Leader,* p. 11).

Surprisingly, in light of criticism of *The Winter's Tale,* one of the most praised features of *Twelfth Night* was the actors' delivery. The *Outlook* happily reported that the articulation was good and the speech not faster than was customary in Shakespeare's plays, while the *Illustrated London News* rejoiced that in this production poetry was not sacrificed to speed. Indeed, for the *Times,* the pace of the play distinguished the production: "The main thing about it is its 'go.' . . . [And even t]hough the people say virtually all that Shakespeare set down for them to say, they do not gabble it."

Since the text was again virtually uncut and the performance lasted only three hours with two ten-minute intervals, the pace of the verse must have been very like that of the first Savoy production.[25] P. C. Knody in the *Observer* suggested why the critical response was so different:

> We are unable to admit that in "The Winter's Tale" there was gabbling, or loss of poetry, or indistinctness. We noticed, indeed, that when the suspicions and pangs of Leontes became too complicated for verbal expression, the words came tumbling in a turbulent stream from his lips, and that Paulina in a rage spoke as women in a rage will speak. Now, in "Twelfth Night" there is no need for those particular forms of speech. . . . [T]he complete absence of torrential speech may help to dispel the notion that "gabbling" is to be a rule at all the Savoy productions of Shakespeare.

Knody pointed out in the same review that the innovative handling of the broad comedy also saved time in performance, and this suggests perhaps the major reason for the production's great success—a fresh approach to characterization. Instead of having Sir Toby and Sir Andrew played as their traditionally boorish selves (Trewin, *Shakespeare on the English Stage,* p. 55; Hunt, "G-B's Shake-

The identical twins reunited. Shakespeare Centre Library, Stratford-upon-Avon.

The resplendent Malvolio courts Olivia in the cloak that made the audience gasp. Shakespeare Centre Library, Stratford-upon-Avon.

spearean Productions," p. 47), Barker presented them as believable gentlemen: "They are human beings, these comedians," wrote Knody. So different was Toby's characterization that Palmer hoped Barker's return to "Shakespeare's original fun" would slay "the traditional drunken sot . . . outright forever." Conventional comic business was banished, and according to the *Morning Post,* the new comedy that took its place was not silly, but "natural to the situation and to the character"; for example, directions in the promptbook (p. 29) indicate that Feste hopped about like a begging dog at "By'r Lady, sir, and some dogs will catch well" (II. iii. 64). Maria was deprived of her "traditional laugh," much to the *Stage*'s annoyance, despite its admission that the laugh had been "laboured" in the past; instead, this Maria very appropriately smothered her temptation to laugh at III. iv. 5, when she remarks that Malvolio is "sad and civil," and a few lines later, when she is sent to fetch him (prompt copy, p. 53).

Barker's rethinking of character was not confined merely to the comedy. Malvolio of course was still played for laughs, but there was another side to his traditional character in this production: for Palmer, "Mr. Henry Ainley is the first Malvolio of this generation that does not seem to have walked onto the stage from some municipal museum of theatrical bric-à-brac." The *Nation* found him not a "grotesque," but a "tragic comedian," while the *Illustrated London News* added that his menial's "superciliousness . . . [was] combined with a certain surface dignity; through the austere self-command of the man there break every now and then traces of rampant vulgarity and venomous rage." The *Stage* complained in its usual reactionary way that this coldly intelligent, rather than merely conceited Malvolio was "too much in the domain of serious acting. . . . [The cross-gartering and baiting] miss much of their delicious extravagance, and the scene of Malvolio imprisoned as a madman is almost painful." This latter complaint, echoed by Grein in the *Sunday Times,* highlights Barker's concern to combine the essentials of the Elizabethan and the modern in his reconsideration of the text: the supposed madman is clearly not the simple figure of fun he would have been to the Elizabethans, and yet the pain of twentieth-century sensitivity does not completely dominate the scene either. A similar hint of this dual view is given by the *Illustrated London New*'s rather vague remark that Sir Andrew was "nonetheless Shakespearean for being modern in treatment."

Many critics felt that Viola lacked "humor," a complaint that the *Sketch* answered in its review: "The fact is that she eschews deliberately the almost traditional humour of making fun of the equivocations due to her disguise." Lillah McCarthy, who played Viola, writes that Barker insisted she play Cesario as a man (*Myself & My Friends*, p. 161); the humor, then, stemmed from Viola's convincing attempts, rather than inability, to appear masculine. The *Morning Post* commented on Cesario's being played as less feminine and more rational than usual, while John Masefield felt that the depiction, which allowed Cesario to appear gracious and gentle as well, avoided the traps both of sentimentality and of mannishness inherent in the role (*Myself & My Friends*, p. 162). The *Daily Telegraph* found that the portrayal of Cesario as "a gallant boy" led to a "delicious" duel scene and humorous interaction with Olivia. The promptbook's directions show how innovative the duel scene was. In the first movement, Viola, at a loss, imitated almost every movement of Andrew's: for instance, facing the audience and bravely throwing out the chest. In the second, the combatants ceremoniously approached each other, step by step, until they accidentally touched swords; Andrew retreated, pleased, while Viola appeared terribly nervous. The final movement involved another ceremonial approach, this time enlivened by Andrew's swinging round and nearly striking Toby and by Viola's apology for catching Fabian's sword—and especially by her gaining courage and skill. Viola fought throughout this last movement with great determination, hitting Andrew's sword three times (p. 69); the audience was left in no doubt about the likely victor if Antonio had not intervened. Clearly, the humor and fun were not missing, but were simply no longer clichés; they were perhaps also closer to the effects of an Elizabethan performance, where the equivocations of disguise, if any, would have been more focused on the boy-actor's playing Viola in the first place, than on Viola's assuming the part of Cesario.

Barker's intention to view the transvestism, this "most important aspect of the play[,] . . . rightly, with Elizabethan eyes," is made clear in his preface to the acting edition, published shortly before the opening.[26] He writes:

Shakespeare's audience saw Cesario without effort as Orsino sees him; more importantly they saw him as Olivia sees him; indeed it was over Olivia they had most to make believe. One feels at once how this affects the sympathy and balance of the love scenes of the play. One sees how dramatically right is the delicate still grace of the dialogue between Orsino and Cesario, and how possible it makes the more outspoken passion of the scenes with Olivia. Give to Olivia, as we must do now, all the value of her sex, and to the supposed Cesario none of the value of his, we are naturally quite unmoved by the business. Olivia looks a fool. And it is the common practice for actresses of Viola to seize every chance of reminding the audience that they are girls dressed up, . . . that this is the play's supreme joke.

This discussion illustrates Barker's concern to let the text direct the action. His concluding comments reflect his equal concern that the nuances of character and theme be developed by the verse:

> Shakespeare has devised one most carefully placed soliloquy [II. ii.] where we are to be forcibly reminded that Cesario is Viola; in it he has as carefully divided the comic from the serious side of the matter. That scene played, the Viola, who does not do her best, as far as the passages with Olivia are concerned, to make us believe, as Olivia believes, that she is a man, shows, to my mind, a lack of imagination and is guilty of dramatic bad manners, knocking, for the sake of a little laughter, the whole of the play's romantic plot on the head.

Barker also rethought minor roles, apparently to great effect. The promptbook shows that he took every opportunity—but no liberties—to do so; for example, in III. ii., when Sir Andrew decides that Olivia is not in fact interested in him, Barker had Fabian reassure him in response to a nudge from Toby, thus establishing a more interesting relationship between the three characters. Hugh Hunt also recalls that Fabian was "usually played by a young and unimportant actor," but in this production he "appeared as an elderly and senior member of Olivia's household[,] thus justifying his authoritative attitude to Olivia and his caution over the practical jokes played upon Malvolio" ("G-B's Shakespearean Productions," p. 47); he adds that "Feste, traditionally represented as a merry jester with cap and bells, was played as an elderly clown who was losing his power to amuse his patroness." Feste's role as entertainer, successful or not, was taken seriously: Findon reported that musical comedy star Hayden Coffin learned the virginal, pipe, and tabor for the part and sang "Old Music" arranged by Nellie Chaplin. Barker also suggested Toby and Maria's mutual fondness right from the start of the play: throughout I. iii., Toby took Maria's hand, played with her fingers, kissed her, and patted her face (prompt copy, pp. 6–7); therefore, the wager must have seemed an excuse rather than the reason for their marriage—an interpretation that reinforces the comic resolution of the play. (In Terry Hands's 1979 production for the Royal Shakespeare Company (RSC) at Stratford, the two were left at the end looking ill-at-ease and empty.[27]) Barker also helped dispel Malvolio's threats with "general laughter" at V. i. 364 ("How with a sportful malice . . .") and at Malvolio's exit; Ainley had begun to rip Maria's forged letter into little bits at line 364 and ineffectually flung them at Feste when he threatened revenge (prompt copy, p. 95).

Barker also used entrances and exits as an economical means of character development. For instance, the promptbook directs that at I. v. 221, when Olivia asks those present to "Give us [Olivia and Cesario] this place alone," Malvolio should officiously motion them to exit; just as Maria is about to leave, he should stop her and precede her out (p. 20). Similarly, when Olivia asks Maria to "call [Malvolio] hither" at III. iv. 14, Maria started to leave but Malvolio was already on his way in, anxious no doubt to test the effect of his cross-gartered yellow stockings on his putative lover (prompt copy, p. 58). The promptbook also shows how Barker tried to make the action flow smoothly and naturally; he was concerned, for instance, to make a character's appearance seem more than just a bald answer to a theatrical cue. At III. i., for example, he directed that Olivia enter at line 80 instead of line 85 and that Viola notice her at line 85 (prompt copy, p. 49); her address at line 86, "Most excellent accomplished lady," must then have seemed much less abrupt and more natural.

The rare adverse criticism of the play, apart from the widely felt distaste for pink, centered on the lack of stage illusion. The *Stage* complained that "the performance would gain immensely if it were cut off from the audience by means of the proscenium lines and if so cut off it were properly supported by scenery." Such scenery as was in the play was ridiculous; for instance, the diminutive trees, unable to conceal Sir Toby, Sir Andrew, and Fabian from Malvolio, "mock . . . the intelligence of an audience to assume that the Steward cannot see these characters." Leonard Inkster, writing a retrospective appraisal in March 1913, was bothered by the combination of the real and the abstract: "Orsino actually had a string quartette; then, had Olivia's garden really white walls and toy trees? And, when you come to it, did such people really speak in verse at all?" (p. 25). One would like to refer such critics to Dr. Johnson's judicious remarks on the credulity of an audience. However, most reviewers, far from seeing such discrepancies, were forcibly struck by the "artistic unity" and "harmony" of the production.[28]

Ironically, as Hunt points out,[29] this most successful of Barker's three productions was arguably the most challenging to his audience; paradoxically, perhaps for that very reason was it such a success. *The Winter's Tale* was "comparatively unfamiliar" to Barker's audience, and therefore, all attention focused on his innovations per se. *Twelfth Night,* on the other hand, was perhaps overfamiliar to theatregoers, and Barker's fresh and original production, challenging stale conventions and hackneyed characterizations, made the audience sit up and see the effects of his methods: the play lived again. By the time he produced *A Midsummer Night's Dream,* his methods were more accepted, and the audience more ready to argue with his use of them.

A Midsummer Night's Dream, which opened on 6 February 1914, followed the close of *Twelfth Night* by nearly a year; the most controversial of the Savoy productions, critical response to it was mixed, violent, and surprising.[30] J. T. Grein, who had called *The Winter's Tale* "an orgy of new ideas grafted on the classic soil," found the *Dream* a "revelation," Barker's "eccentricities hav[ing] mellowed into a new and definite manifestation of Art," while John Palmer's former enthusiasm for the Savoy Shakespeare evaporated; he felt "the production as a whole . . . more like a battlefield than a collaboration." Yet many other critics, like the *Observer*'s, praised the unity of a production that subordinated detail to a "poetic whole." There is a similar contradiction in Palmer's complaint that Barker's was "never Shakespeare's "Dream'" and the *Outlook*'s affirmation that the play was produced "according to Mr. Granville Barker. And, let it be said at once, according to Shakespeare."

Decoration was again by Norman Wilkinson, and again consisted of built scenes and suggestive curtains. The play opened on "a white curtain laced with frail green and gold floral lines" in an Art Nouveau design; Theseus met his court in front of it "in an austere and symmetrical tableau" (Williams, "Midsummer Night's Dream," p. 43). Barker seems to have been generally fond of symmetry, but in this play he used it to reflect Shakespeare's text; a recent scholar points out that "the court and fairy scenes are crowded, lavish and formal; the stage picture is consistently symmetrical, the choreography meticulous. Reflecting the shifts from prose to verse in the text, the blocking of the court and fairy scenes contrasts sharply with the asymmetrical movement of the worker scenes" (Barbour, "Up Against a . . . Cloth," p. 526). Another scholar notes Barker's symmetrical inclusion of Nedar among the audience of "Pyramus and Thisbe" (Griffiths, "Tradition and Innovation," p. 83). However, Barker took great care to avoid artificiality, despite his use of symmetry. (While the opening scene contained an entirely formal procession of Theseus's court onto the stage, the question of artificiality obviously does not arise in such a context.) For example, the prompt copy details the entrances of Titania and her fairies for the first mound scene (II. ii.): four child fairies entered in single file, followed by several pairs of adult fairies who ran on from upstage right; this general entrance was followed by a great deal of activity as the children ran around and up and down the mound (p. 26). The fairies' final positions, before the roundel and fairy song, are diagrammed in the prompt copy (see illustration). Thus, one can see

A Midsummer Night's Dream, Savoy, 1914. Formality in Theseus's court and in the meeting of Titania and Oberon. The Raymond Mander & Joe Mitchenson Theatre Collection.

that although the movements and positions were very controlled, they did not preclude the appearance of spontaneity; formality and symmetry were not used arbitrarily but to dignify the mortal and fairy courts and to solemnize a fairy ceremony.

The first curtain was raised to reveal a second, which hung in folds "of salmon pink silk, with steel-blue masses supposed to represent the roofs of the city" (Odell, *Shakespeare*, p. 468); a cottage door, windows, and trees were marked on it as well. Behind this hung a third curtain designed to represent the wood near Athens; it was painted green, "rising to a star-spangled purplish blue," and lights "in various changing tones of green, blue, violet, and purple" played over it (Trewin, *Shakespeare on the English Stage*, p. 58). In the center of the stage lay Titania's bower, a mound of green velvet above which hung a large floral wreath with a gauze canopy attached; the canopy's folds held tiny flickering lights like those of fireflies (Hunt, "G–B's Shakespearean Productions," p. 48). The final set was again Theseus's palace, this time "a very solidly-built affair" of seven white pillars ringed with black and silver, and "with a door at the back letting in much red light" (Odell, *Shakespeare*, p. 467); the pillars occupied the rear acting area, at the top of seven white steps. Hunt remarks on the "strong contrast . . . between the classical severity of the palace scenes and the dream-like atmosphere of the wood" (p. 48), while a more recent writer sees a further analogue between the sets and the action: Barker may have intended this change from curtains to a three-dimensional set "as a visual parallel to the stability which had descended on the characters after the turmoil in the woods"; the use of a curtain for the first palace scene may "have attempted to suggest discord between Theseus and Hippolyta."[31] Although Griffiths cannot confirm his hypothesis from the reviews or promptbooks, it seems a likely one, especially when one considers Barker's modifications to the set in *Twelfth Night*.

Reviews hardly mentioned costume, apart from that of the fairies—the biggest sensation of the production. In his review, Harold Child of the *Times* implied how these figures from "some vaguely Eastern folk lore" had dominated the play: "The mind goes back to the golden fairies, and one's memories of this production must always be golden memories." Taking his cue for this Eastern influence from Titania's and Oberon's lines about the Indian boy (Hunt, "G–B's Shakespearean Productions," p. 48), Barker here departed totally from the tradition of winged children dressed in tutus; except for Peaseblossom, Cobweb, Moth, and Mustardseed, "three in flakes of gold and the fourth in baggy trousers out of Sumurun" (*Times*, p. 8), these fairies were all adult. Dressed in exotic, elaborate costumes and with gilt faces and hands, they had hair like gold wood

Trial positions :–

Explanation :–

1. Titania. 2 Little girls. 3 Old man fairy

4 Tit's Stewardess. 5 Lady Singers 6 Male Singers

7 Male Dancers. 8 Lady Dancers.

Val Gurney's sketch of the fairy positions during Titania's lullaby, prompt copy, p. 27. Courtesy of The Department of Rare Books and Special Collections, The University of Michigan Library, and The Society of Authors on behalf of the Trustees of the late Harley Granville Barker.

The mechanicals' curtain with, from left to right, Snug, Quince, Bottom, Starveling, Flute, and Snout. The Raymond Mander & Joe Mitchenson Theatre Collection.

Titania's bower. The Raymond Mander & Joe Mitchenson Theatre Collection.

shavings, beards like golden rope, and metallic-looking moustaches. Titania sported a flamelike headdress, and both she and Oberon had a full train of followers.

The fairies were distinguished from the mortals not only by their coloring but also by their movements, which Hunt describes as "jerky" and "puppet-like" (G–B's Shakespearean Productions," p. 48). Desmond MacCarthy wrote that they looked "as if they had been detached from some fantastic bristling old clock"; they achieved invisibility by "group[ing] themselves motionless about the stage, . . . [while] the lovers move[d] past and between them as casually as though they were stocks or stones." Oberon merely had to step back, announcing "I am invisible," to be so (prompt copy, p. 23).

Considering Barker's view that "the fairies are the producer's test," it may seem surprising that he chose a course likely to focus distorting attention on them.[32] His preface to the acting edition of the play suggests that such a course, given theatrical convention, was inevitable:

I realize that when there is perhaps no really right thing to do one is always tempted to do too much. One yields to the natural fun, of

course, of making a thing look pretty in itself. [The fairies] must
not be too startling. But one wishes people weren't so easily
startled. I won't have them dowdy. They mustn't warp your imagination—stepping too boldly between Shakespeare's spirit and
yours.

Barker's use of the word *spirit* emphasizes his commitment to the
intangible essentials rather than to the letter of Shakespearean
stagecraft; the fairies had to find a new theatrical convention to
carry their original dramatic conviction.

Critical reaction to the fairies justified both Barker's hopes and
fears; they were detested, tolerated, and admired. Some reviewers
found them ungainly, dissonant, or bilious looking, while others, like
the *Nation*'s, felt they were "singularly gracious and beautiful." However, many appreciative reviewers went beyond admiration of the
fairies' aesthetic beauty to recognition of Barker's underlying intentions. The *Nation* made an oblique reference to Poel in praising a
convention "simple without the crudity and parsimony of a pedant's
attempt to be consistently archaic" (however, it also expressed the
reservation that the gold, while effective, was too austerely consistent). Desmond MacCarthy saw the production twice, disliking it the
first time and enjoying it the second, thus proving Barker right
about his "startling" figures: "When . . . your astonishment at the
ormulu fairies . . . no longer distracts, you will perceive that the very
characteristics which made them at first so outlandishly arresting
now contribute to making them inconspicuous." The *Outlook* could
not "suggest a better way out of Mr. Barker's difficulty than the one
he has taken," yet voiced "regret that Shakespeare's fairies are no
longer English [ones]"; on the other hand, E. F. S. in the *Sketch*,
while not finding them to his taste, wrote that "they *are* fairies, and
one can believe that these strange creatures are invisible to the
foolish mortals, so they give the needful uncanny atmosphere to the
piece." The fact that both positive and negative reviews were
qualified in this way shows that intellectual and aesthetic responses
to the fairies were not always in tandem.

Puck was the one exception to this handling of the fairies; no
ormulu figure from the far East, but what the *Times* called a genuine
English "hobgoblin," he was dressed in scarlet, with red berries in his
brilliant yellow hair which "stream[ed] like a comet behind him." In
a letter to William Archer dated 14 February 1914, Barker explains
that he wanted to distinguish between Puck and the other fairies, as
Shakespeare has done; the former is "as English as he can be," while
the latter are "undoubtedly foreign."[33] Consequently, Puck's costume was Elizabethan: "a doublet flounced at the waist, puffy

Barker's golden fairies, together with Helena and Hermia. Titania appears in the

top row, second from left. The Raymond Mander & Joe Mitchenson Theatre Collection.

The invisible Oberon watching the lovers' quarrel. The Raymond Mander & Joe Mitchenson Theatre Collection.

breeches, red tights and slippers," in Williams's description ("Midsummer Night's Dream," p. 45).

Although it was not the first time it was done (and many critics think it was), Puck's being played by a man in this production marked a "really significant departure from the prettiness of Mid-Victorian convention," which had made him into a kind of Ariel. Instead, this Puck was a "clowning bogey" and "buffoon-sprite," whose "antic motions" made him a "crude, deliberate patch of ugliness in a fairy play."[34] So great a departure was this from traditional characterization that the *Morning Post* wrote that Donald Calthrop "did full justice to a Puck *one does not recognize as Shakespeare's*" (italics mine).

The description of Puck as a "*patch* of ugliness" implies one other costume scheme used in the play—that of color. The *Nation's* critic himself called attention to the effects of the gold: glittering or "softened to the likeness of a shimmering cob-web," it gave the fairies "an elusive unreality when they mingled, invisible, among the parti-colored mortals." J. T. Grein also noticed that "every figure ha[d] its individual composition—from Hermia, in green, all youth and subtleness, and Helena, with the flaxen touch of Faust's Gretchen, to Puck with scarlet garments and windblown locks."

Barker's emphasis on what Styan calls a mode of "conscious non-illusion" (*Shakespeare Revolution*, p. 95) was fully realized by his exploitation of the *Dream*'s inherent theatricality. He kept Puck and Oberon, together with other members of Oberon's court, on stage throughout act III, scene ii (prompt copy, pp. 39–43) making, for the *Outlook*'s reviewer, "the mortal action . . . quite consistently a play of which the immortals are the auditors. Puck . . . , seated between us and the action, when he has not to take his visible-invisible part in it, . . . lets us know what fools these mortals be." The prompt copy illustrates how much Barker emphasized the fairies' role as audience to the mortals' "fond pageant": for instance, he had Puck enter, well before the text's stage direction at III. i. 73 ("What hempen homespun have we swaggering here . . . ?"). Instead, Puck entered after Bottom's call for a calendar at line 49, wandering around the stage and among the mechanicals (p. 34)—action that also stressed his invisibility. When Bottom spoke Pyramus's line "Odorous savours sweet" (l. 79), Puck stood on his left peering over his shoulder and then imitated his exit to the brake (prompt copy, p. 35). Similarly, in III. ii, after Oberon has anointed Demetrius's eyes and Puck has invited him to watch the ensuing show (l. 114), Puck himself played

English Puck among the exotically Eastern fairies. Oberon stands center. The Raymond Mander & Joe Mitchenson Theatre Collection.

the part of appreciative audience: he moved about, keenly watching, as Demetrius swore his love to Helena, and finally collapsed, rolling over and over in delight when Lysander repudiated Hermia (prompt copy, p. 45). By the time Helena accused the three of being in league (ll. 193–94), Puck lay on his stomach, seemingly thoroughly riveted by the display of mortal folly.

Other elements also strengthened this theatrical emphasis; for example, the use of direct address to the audience (prompt copy, pp. 6 and 31) included them in the action, emphasizing that the *Dream* was, consciously, a pageant for them as well.[35] However, the most famous device Barker used to make this point was Puck's literal "stage management of the night" (Griffiths, "Tradition and Innovation," p. 83). Toward the end of III. ii, when Oberon orders Puck to "overcast the night" so that "We may effect this business yet ere day," Barker had the two fairies nearest the center open the curtain for Oberon's exit with his train—a gesture that itself emphasized the theatrical setting. Once they were off, "Puck then [went] down C lower stage, motion[ed] for lights to go down. Then up to cloth [, bent] down and raise[d] cloth as it ascend[ed]" (prompt copy, p. 54). Puck then paced across the stage and back on his lines "Up and down, up and down," giving the audience a good idea of what was to follow.

The staging of "Pyramus and Thisbe" also heightened the theatrical nature of the production. First, Barker focused on the mechanicals as "occupied with the unreality of their play," thus providing a parallel to his own undercutting of realistic illusion in the play proper.[36] Second, the court audience "reclined, Roman-style, on green cushioned silver couches" (Williams, "A Midsummer Night's Dream," p. 47) on the dimly lighted apron stage. Their backs were to the audience, while the performance was given on the palace steps at the back of the stage—for the *Times*'s critic, an "admirable" as well as "novel arrangement," which, as Griffiths points out, solved the problem of dealing with the court audience's interjections without resorting to the nineteenth-century solution of simply omitting them ("Tradition and Innovation," p. 83). Thus, Desmond MacCarthy, who called "the performance of 'Pyramus and Thisbe' . . . the great success of the production," found that "for the first time the presence of an audience, of Theseus and his court, on the stage was a sounding-board for the fun." The court audience, not the wholly mean-spirited group they often appear, still helped to highlight the players' shortcomings: the promptbook shows that Moonshine had "dried up" and Quince was desperately trying to prompt him during V. i. 240–45. Lysander's "Proceed, Moon" at line 246 followed a long pause during which Moon hopelessly surveyed his audience; Ly-

"Pyramus and Thisbe" and the court audience. The Raymond Mander and Joe Mitchenson Theatre Collection.

sander spoke his line when Moon looked at him (prompt copy, pp. 77–78). The court audience also served to emphasize the mechanicals' peculiar attitude to dramatic illusion. Theseus, for example, jumped at Pyramus's "no, no" in the line "Which is—no, no— which was the fairest dame," obviously startled by an actor's calling such attention to a minor slip (prompt copy, p. 79).[37]

While one modern scholar admires this "novel approach to the perpetual difficulty of dealing with two competing areas of involvement," he criticizes it for making "the courtiers subservient to the performance of 'Pyramus and Thisbe' instead of, in certain ways, [its] arbiters and controllers . . ." (Griffiths, "Tradition and Innovation," p. 83). However, this seems to have been Barker's very intention; as another scholar notes,

> In "Pyramus and Thisby" Barker offers in microcosm the confusions of the earlier forest scenes. [As they enter to perform the play . . . , the workers weave their way through the pillars of the palace in a manner deliberately reminiscent of the lovers' uncertain wanderings through the forest in Acts Two and Three.] Describing a nearly perfect circle, Lion chases Thisby all around the pillars. Reducing the chase to almost pure pattern, the pillars reinforce the silly abstract geometry of it all. (Barbour, "Up Against a . . . Cloth," p. 527)

However, even this writer concludes simply that "the moving stage picture is as artificial, as schematic as the play's verse." What both writers fail to see is that the court audience of "Pyramus and Thisbe" witness a pageant very like that in which the actual audience has just seen them as actors. This parallel is, of course, also reinforced by the placing of Theseus and his subjects within the lower foreground of the audience's vision: they are physically and visually subordinate to the main action, just as their previous antics subliminally echo it. Barker's sensitivity to Shakespeare's text made him thus treat the play-within-the-play as an integral part of the composition and not as a mere "diversion"; his idea is now "a commonplace in modern criticism," as Barbour points out, "but [was] not so in 1914" ("Up Against a . . . Cloth," p. 528).

Similarly, to strengthen the audience's sense of parallel action, Barker also used a "visual motif of kneeling." Barbour notes that "at least twenty times one or more characters kneel. On at least fifteen of these occasions it is the lovers (including Bottom and Titania, Pyramus and Thisby) who kneel to one another"; at other times, "kneeling accompanies pleas for mercy" (pp. 525–26). Enough has been said about Barker's desire to emphasize parallels between the actions of court, mechanicals, and fairies; here he achieved his end by using parallel gestures.

At the end of the mechanicals' performance, none of them knew how to leave the stage, and while "not a word [was] said and scarcely a movement made," this proved as comic as any of the traditional clowning, since it took the audience " 'inside' the fun of the thing." This comment from the *Observer* points to another reason for the success of the "Pyramus and Thisbe" players, whom even the *Stage* admired—the rethinking of the traditional characterizations of Bottom, Quince, and friends. It is worth quoting several contemporary reactions to the mechanicals' depiction; they are from the *Nation,* the *Sketch,* and the *Daily Telegraph* respectively:

> [Barker] improved somewhat upon tradition by doing full justice to the weaver's bumptious intelligence.

> [The] mechanicals are not mere drolls, but respectable working men, comic merely because, like many amateur players, they attempt a task utterly beyond their reach. . . . [T]hey are entertaining in a new way—relatively, and not absolutely.

> They were permitted no divagations, or excrescences, or exaggerations, and they needed none.

Such comments show that Barker succeeded in presenting his interpretation of Shakespeare's comic intention: "Shakespeare presumably knew something about countrymen, and he made the simple discovery and put it into practice for the first time in this play that, set down lovingly, your clown is better fun by far than mocked at; if indeed apart from an actor's grimaces he had then been funny at all." Writing a preface to *The Players' Shakespeare* edition of the *Dream* some ten years later, Barker echoes this idea about Bottom's self-confidence and self-preoccupation: "This and the like of it is no foolery, but what better fun do we need?" The emphasis, he writes, should be on Bottom the weaver rather than on Bottom the buffoon. The mechanicals are not "clowns . . . in any motley sense. . . . [but the play's] wholesomely humorously human foundation."[38]

Thus, in this production, Barker cut out most extraneous business, and what he retained tended to define character and point action rather than to raise superficial laughs. An example of the first purpose can be found in "Quince's second encounter with Bottom result[ing] from an attempt to recover the property basket . . . [which makes his] confirmation of Bottom's translation depend on a concern for property rights even in the face of the supernatural" (Griffiths, "Tradition and Innovation," p. 82); an example of the second in the stage directions for Puck's persecution of the mechanicals during their rehearsal in the forest:

> Quince get R to Starvelling and both X down lower stage to L pros and hide.
> During this Flute gets LC with Snout and Puck pinches them. Flute runs round mound going up RC and down LC, twice. Puck following him round the first time. Meanwhile Snout goes up LC of mound and is met by Puck, chasing Flute. Puck trips him up and Snout rolls down and crawls round back of mound to RC, ready for his next speech.
> Bottom is rolling about C. just below mound. Flute, after going round mound twice, runs round Bot, Puck again chasing him and runs off L, followed by Puck. As soon as they are off Quince and Starvelling come from L pros. seat and run up to LC on mound and tumble over. (Prompt copy, p. 36)

As Griffiths comments, "Barker's effect . . . is intended to give force to Puck's 'I'll follow you' by embodying the situation suggested by the speech" (p. 82)—unlike, for example, Tree's staging, where Puck

> tickles Quin with wand; ditto Bot, then Snout, Starv and Snug. Then Snout again who thinking it is Star pushes him over. Star yells. Quin says: 'Sit down' Puck tickles Bot's legs 3 times, he thinking it is a fly tries to catch it, Puck buzzes, all rise and try to catch it. (Quoted in Griffiths, "Tradition and Innovation," p. 82)

However, Griffiths himself does not see the point of much of Barker's business, regarding it as extraneous as any of the traditional

Bottom translated, led on by Puck. Titania sleeps on her bower. The Raymond Mander & Joe Mitchenson Theatre Collection.

business attached to the play. In fact, whenever Barker indicates business at the same line as previous productions have introduced it, Griffiths regards Barker's as derivative, no matter how different its function and spirit may be from that of its predecessors. Consequently, he sees no essential difference between Barker's and Tree's stage directions quoted above.

It should also be noted that Puck's circular chase reinforces other action in the production—the metaphorical circle of the lovers' relationships, the Lion's stylized chase of Thisbe around the pillars of the palace, and Lysander's reaction to Helena's suspicion of a plot (III. ii, 230): he "spins round, hands to his head" (prompt copy, p. 48). These parallels demonstrate Barker's thematic approach to the play, already implied in the discussion of his staging of "Pyramus and Thisbe."

Other characters were also rethought—or perhaps thought through for the first time. The *Outlook*'s critic remarked that in Barker's production "there is an end . . . to the Demetrius and Lysander who were a kind of pair of Dromios or Antipholuses; and to the Helena and Hermia who were, quite too literally, two lovely berries moulded on one stem." Likewise, Grein admired the ensem-

ble acting that led to character differentiation rather than to caricature; Bridges Adams considers that he has "seldom seen a truer
character-pattern than that of the four young lovers . . . " (*Lost
Leader*, p. 11). The promptbook shows that Barker took care to make
the action itself more than just a crude fulfillment of the demands of
plot; for example, instead of suddenly waking to deliver his line, "O
Helen, goddess, nymph, perfect, divine!" (III.ii.137), the anointed
Demetrius slowly began to resurface from sleep during Lysander's
"I had no judgment when to her I swore" (line 134); he then sat up
to deliver his impassioned address (prompt copy, p. 44). Similarly,
the discovery of the lovers in the forest was not handled in the
simple way it might have been: Egeus shook his stick at Hermia, who
was frightened by the confrontation with her father; Helena, waking, smiled at Hermia and Lysander, and only then seeing Theseus
and finally Demetrius, was ashamed (prompt copy, p. 63). Nor did
Barker confine such thoughtful treatment to the lovers: for example, he gave a hint of Bottom's self-regard at I. ii. 79. Quince told
him he could only play Pyramus and then turned away to Snug;
seeing Snug's face, he quickly turned back to the mutinous or departing Bottom with assurance: "for Pyramus is a sweet-faced man"
(prompt copy, p. 15). Similarly, Barker managed to indicate Quince's
own doubts about his production: when Bottom announced that
their play was preferred, Quince was the only one not to clap; he
then exited very slowly after the others (prompt copy, p. 67). Clearly,
Barker took such opportunities both to develop character and to
embody the fantastic action in a more credible, human form.

Also, because the play was given "entire and [in] seriation," the
critic from the *Outlook* found that "for the first time on any stage
perhaps, the love-story [was] entirely clear and delightful," as well as
restored to its "Shakespearean proportions."[39] However, not everyone appreciated Barker's original approach to the lovers; Palmer, in
his decidedly negative review, argued that the mortals should appear
as fools from the start, as Puck would see them, yet Barker opened
the play "with just that incorrigible reasonableness which [it] cannot
endure, and was never intended to endure." Egeus argued like a
prosecuting lawyer, Hermia pleaded like a logician, and Theseus
donned a black cap "with a solemn recommendation to mercy." Even
Oberon seemed "the embodiment of comic sanity—symbolical of
Mr. Barker's clear and penetrating intelligence." Palmer ended his
review: "Mr. Barker is suffering from brains." Such criticism sows
the seeds of its own destruction. Of course it is difficult to judge
Barker's intention, but given his general sensitivity to the text and
his remarks on Bottom's comedy, one could argue that by presenting

the lovers in their own eyes, as reasonable beings, he deliberately heightened the comedy: the contrast between reality and self-delusion provides more subtle, more genuine amusement than mere farce.

In addition, Barker's staging stressed that the fairies themselves are not perfect: when Peaseblossom danced onto the stage, Puck sprang out at her, and a scimitar-wielding fairy frightened three smaller ones—business that has no relevance except to point out that the fairy world is as faulty as the mortal and to underscore the discord between Titania and Oberon. This emphasis, of course, heightened the production's thematic unity—the court laughs at the mechanicals, the fairies at the court, each group blind to its own ridiculousness. One almost wonders if the audience were meant to see its own preoccupation with realistic illusion (certainly pushed to its limit in this production) reflected in the mechanicals' same concern.

However, just as the mad mortals were invested with reason, so were the imperfect fairies given dignity and grace. The *Observer* commented on Oberon's "still and remote air . . . of a monarch who has lived for ages,"[40] while the *Times* remarked that "this Oberon, for the first time, dominates not only the scene, but the whole play, informs it with graciousness and majesty . . . and exquisite rhythmic beauty." Such emphasis on both the dignity and the ludicrousness of mortals and immortals alike must have given more depth to the solemn harmony achieved at the end of the play.

Critical opinion about the actors' delivery of the verse was divided. The *Outlook* found the "poetry . . . audible," the *Daily Telegraph* and the *Nation* found it musical, the *Sketch* found it charming. J. T. Grein encouraged potential audiences with the promise that they would hear Shakespeare's "words as clearly, as naturally, as [they] have rarely heard them before." On the other hand, the *Observer* was disappointed that the verse was not well-spoken, and the *Morning Post* complained that delivery was "rarely musical and . . . sometimes scarce intelligible." On the other side of the Atlantic, George Odell grumbled that "the verse was spoken at a rapid pace [and n]one of it was spoken well," while *Harper's Weekly* editorialized on how well Barker had taught his actors "clearness of diction." Certainly the majority of reviewers found the verse a pleasure to hear; the dissidents seemed to reflect either conservatism or idiosyncratic taste.

The text was again presented virtually uncut; examination of the prompt copy shows just how minor the few cuts and changes were: the omission of Quince's "Speak, Pyramus" at III. i. 77; the change of "odours" to "odorous" in the speeches following (a change also made in the Arden edition); the omission of the three lines after

Bottom's song (III.i.129–31); the change of "mistress" to "Mrs" in Bottom's reference to Peaseblossom's mother (III.i.179); the omission of Demetrius's half-line "No, no he'll" at III. ii. 257; and the correction of "Cavalery Cobweb" to "Peaseblossom" at IV. i. 22–23.

The excision of only four lines was a real innovation: Griffiths estimates that "no production of the play since the Restoration appears to have presented more than eight[y] percent of the text" ("Tradition and Innovation," p. 78), while Williams reports that from Madame Vestris's revival in 1840 to Beerbohm Tree's production of 1900, "interlinear cutting of the play ranged from about one-sixth to about one-third of the text" ("Midsummer Night's Dream," p. 41); clearly, Barker's production marked a great advance. Performance time was about three hours and ten minutes with two intervals—a five-minute one following I. ii and a later fifteen-minute break after IV. i. Barker himself wrote that he could not defend his convenient division of the text into three parts, and added that the play would gain from a continuous performance of two-and-one-half hours.[41] However, Barker's tripartite division made thematic sense, unconsciously discerned even by Odell who thoroughly detested the production:

> The first [part] deal[t] with the 'mortals'—Theseus and his court, Quince and the other hard-handed men: the second [ran] together without break the fairy episodes and the affairs of the perplexed lovers, as well as the transformation of Bottom; the third show[ed] all the characters again in the palace of Theseus. (P. 467)

This division of the play seems to have served the same purpose as the subordinate visual presence of the audience at "Pyramus and Thisbe"—each part set off the other and gave it deeper resonance. The first segment, showing the mortals' "reasonableness" and the mechanicals' concern with theatrical illusion, was undercut by the second, showing the lovers' illogical behavior and Bottom's literal transformation into an ass. The third united all the characters, allowing them to comment obliquely on each other and on the preceding action.

The final major innovation, as one can guess, was the discarding of Mendelssohn's traditional music, to which Barker objected because it lacked "intrinsic suitability" and also involved "the practical suppression of the lyrics." Instead, as Barker felt it to be familiar, timeless, and appropriate, Cecil Sharp again provided "old English folk-music, rather dolorous, always *piano*,"[42] and only when required by the text:

Two trumpet fanfares, two minutes apart, took the place of the familiar Mendelssohn overture. Titania's call for "a roundel and a fairy song" was answered by a round; it then led into two folk melodies that Sharp selected to fit the lullaby lyrics. "Greensleeves" was used for the Bergomask dance, heretofore omitted, and the dance was an authentic folk dance. Instead of the "wedding march," an adaptation of the ballad "Lord Willoughby" was used. An arrangement of several folk dance tunes including "Sellenger's Round" was used for the fairy finale. (Williams, "Midsummer Night's Dream," pp. 49–50)

The *Times*'s review gave a vivid picture of the Bergamask dance, which "never came out of Bergamo, but [was] right Warwickshire, the acme of the clumsy grotesque with vigorous kickings in that part of the anatomy meant for kicks."

Barker's rearrangement of the music also involved the inclusion of a song after Titania's "Will we sing and bless this place": he felt, as Williams indicates previous editors did ("Midsummer Night's Dream," p. 41), that "there is a lyric missing at the end of the play" and yet "to set a tune to the rhythms of Oberon's spoken words [would be] absurd."[43] Therefore, he tactfully added the suitable wedding song sung for Theseus and Hippolyta in *The Two Noble Kinsmen:*

> Roses, their sharp spines being gone,
> Not royal in their smell alone
>   But in their hue;
> Maiden pinks, of odour faint,
> Daisies smell-less, yet most quaint,
>   And sweet thyme true;
>
> Primrose, firstborn child of Ver,
> Merry spring-time's harbinger
>   With her bells dim;
> Ox-lips in their cradles growing,
> Marigolds on deathbeds blowing
>   Larks'-heels trim.
>
> All dear Nature's children sweet,
> Lie 'fore bride and bridegroom's feet,
>   Blessing their sense!
> Not an angel of the air,
> Bird melodious or bird fair,
>   Be absent hence!
>
> The crow, the slenderous cuckoo, nor
> The boding raven, nor chough hoar,
>   Nor chattering pie,

> May on our bride-house perch or sing,
> Or with them any discord bring,
> But from it fly![44]

Despite the controversy it raised, Barker's production of *A Midsummer Night's Dream* satisfied most demands of most reviewers, because, in the words of the *Nation's* critic, the "archaic music, the rich simplicity of the costumes, and the harmonious colouring of the scenery" favored the play's demand that actors speak the lines "with musical grace." Even more important, "upon this background the imagination could move freely."

Barker's Shakespeare productions came to an abrupt halt with the outbreak of the First World War. His subsequent work with Shakespeare was limited to writing his *Prefaces,* as well as various lectures and articles, and to supervising a production of *King Lear* at the Old Vic in 1940. These contributions assured Barker's continuing influence on the modern staging of Shakespeare, an influence that of course originated with his own productions. However, with the war's disruption of the vital life of British theatre, it seemed for many years as if Barker's experiments at the Savoy would prove to have been merely eccentric footnotes to the continuing scenic tradition. It was only after the war, when actors who had worked with Barker became directors themselves, that his ideas became firmly established as the prevailing mode.[45]

To show the true extent of Barker's influence, it will be useful to compare his *Dream* with Peter Brook's production for the RSC more than fifty years later. This production created as much sensation and critical controversy when it opened in 1970 as Barker's did in 1914, and for much the same reasons; also like its predecessor, it is commonly regarded as having "ushered in a new era of Shakespearian production."[46] Yet, to anyone familiar with Barker's work, the Brook *Dream* is clearly an inheritor of the Savoy tradition, at least in terms of its general aims and of the methods used to achieve them. Indeed, even some of Brook's most heralded "innovations" had been anticipated by Barker more than half a century before.

Rather startling, for instance, is Barker's remark of 1915:

> These modern theatres with their electric lights, switchboards and revolving stages are all well enough but *what is really needed is a great white box.* That's what our theatre really is. We set our scenes in a shell. . . . I believe in fitting [its] color tone to the mood of the drama. (Italics mine)[47]

No evidence I have seen suggests that either Brook or his designer, Sally Jacobs, knew of Barker's idea, but their decision to stage the play within three white walls reflects Barker's concern that the background leave the imagination free. Brook explains:

> Most important is that all we wanted was to make *nothingness* around the work. So the white walls are not there to state something, but to *eliminate* something. On a nothingness . . . something can be conjured up—and then made to disappear. The bare stage is a form of nothingness, but it's a joyless form. . . . The nearest thing we could find to something completely neutral which said nothing—and yet had an element of joy and excitement . . .—was a brilliant white.
> . . . .
>   . . . [W]e're making a white opening into which the imagination of the audience can pour. We're holding up a white screen, and the imagination of the audience can paint on that screen what it wants."[48]

Clearly, Brook's purpose is the same as Barker's. He rejects the joylessness of the bare stage just as Barker rejects the stuffiness of Poel's "archaeological" tapestry curtains. He chooses white walls for the same reason Barker chooses stylized backgrounds—to reflect the mood of the play and to free the audience's imagination. Only because of Barker's innovations early in the century could Brook use even more abstract decoration than his predecessor, who had to contend with a still-strong pictorial tradition. Brook's set may have seemed radically original, but it was, in essence, a clever neologism in Barker's truly "new hieroglyphic language of scenery."

Remarks by the designer support this contention. Sally Jacobs explains her decision to use the "white box" and its difference from Brook's notion of "an Empty Space":

> There's no connection with Peter's book of that name. . . . I prefer to call the set a *Contained Space*. Because to put those characters down in infinite space is not what the play is about. So, how to *contain* that space? Without suggesting architecture. Without saying: "These are Athenian walls. These are columns. That is a gallery."
>   There's just about nothing you can use that won't suggest some form of architecture. That doesn't remind you of something. Only that little box worked, in terms of a space, a contained white space. . . .[49]

Jacobs closely echoes Barker's demand for a new type of scenery, for "something that will not tie us too rigidly indoors or out" (Barker continues: "Sky-blue then will be too like sky; patterns suggest walls"). The white box is essentially Barker's solution to the problem—it is one type of nonlocalized decoration. Likewise, Jacobs's use of coiled wires for trees reminds one of Barker's stylized trees in *Twelfth Night,* while her floating-feather boa recalls Barker's mound and gauze-canopy bower in the *Dream.* Ironically, fifty years on, such innovations still met resistance: "I want to know what happened to the *mist!* . . . It says right in the text—which *I* thought got lost in all those acrobatics—that there is a *mist* when Puck puts the magic juice in the lovers' eyes! Shakespeare says that! How can *you* leave it out?"[50]

Despite this outraged viewer's opinion, Brook was very much concerned with presenting Shakespeare's text undistorted. Like Barker, he presented a virtually uncut text and impressed its importance on his cast and crew. John Kane, who played Puck, recounts Brook's advice: "'You must act as a medium for the words. If you consciously colour them, you're wasting your time. The words must be able to colour you.'" Similarly, the deputy stage manager recalls: "The thing that Brook has impressed on us is *always* to go back to the text, because that's where you're really going to find out what it's all about."[51] When one remembers the well-established tradition of mangling texts and distorting characters that ushered in twentieth-century Shakespeare production, it is clear that Barker's influence in the past seventy years has indeed been great.

Brook himself says that concern for Shakespeare's text also dictated the choice of set:

> The most extraordinary power comes from the words once the audience knows you're alone with those words and their image. I think, on the whole, we find that an audience is actually more completely involved with the play and gets more for itself, if instead of plastics and technology, they do it for themselves. . . .
> (Quoted in "Drama Desk," *Acting Edition,* p. 32, ellipsis Loney's)

This view, of course, reflects Barker's concern that nothing in the staging detract from the verse, which carries the play's meaning. Even the fairies' use of trapezes, which proved as startling as the golden fairies, was supposed to be subordinated to the text. John Kane writes:

> We made our externals extensions of ourselves, utilizing them as devices for telling our story. Only by subjugating them in this way could we counteract the tendency they had to detract from the actors and the text. (*Acting Edition,* p. 63)

One can imagine Desmond MacCarthy reacting to these acrobatic fairies in the same way he did to the bristling, ormulu figures:

"When . . . your astonishment . . . no longer distracts, . . . the very characteristics which made them at first so outlandishly arresting now contribute to making them inconspicuous." Their suspension above the stage introduced a new, credible convention of invisibility, as Barker's use of frozen movement did.

Brook, like Barker, also had his fairies present throughout much of the action. Kane recalls:

> We decided that if Spirits were omnipresent it would be impossible for them to be confined to the "Fairy" scenes. They must be available to speak the lines of Titania's fairies, but they could also be around to lower trees for the Lovers [in fact, they dangled the coiled wires from fishing poles], carry lumber for the Mechanicals and produce sound effects wherever appropriate. . . . [They] were given complete license in the early days: as a result of which, they were much inclined to pick actors up and move them about like chess-pieces [or directors?]. (*Acting Edition*, p. 57)

Such ubiquitous fairy-presence emphasized one of Barker's main points, which Brook's production also stressed: the play is "a celebration of the theme of theatre: the play-within-the-play-within-the-play-within-the-play" (Brook at the "Drama Desk," *Acting Edition*, p. 24). The set also helped to press this point; Jacobs explains that its catwalk, or gallery, made it

> an intimate acting area, which would nevertheless give us a place where the rest of the actors who were *not* in the scene could surround the action and continue to watch it. So that's how the top gallery came about. You see, the actors are never uninvolved. . . . Both on and off-stage—or gallery—areas can be seen. . . . [W]hen not in a scene, [actors] can interact in the same way the audience does. (Quoted in "Jacobs," *Acting Edition*, p. 47)

Similarly, the deputy stage manager sat on the gallery; costumed, she followed the action from her promptbook and pulled cue switches for cast, crew, and musicians ("Penney," *Acting Edition*, p. 93).

Much of the stage business also emphasized the theatrical nature of the play. For example, Jacobs says that

> the actors appear first *as actors* in their cloaks; then they drop them and begin to play their roles—to show what they can do. At the end, they drop their "costumes" and come forward in neutral white to greet the audience. They are actors again. (Quoted in "Jacobs," *Acting Edition*, p. 50)

Appropriate speeches were delivered straight out into the auditorium, just as Barker directed, and sometimes the actors actually mixed with the audience; for example, at Puck's "Give us your hands," they ran up the aisles and shook hands with the spectators.[52]

Brook also pushed to its logical conclusion the process started by Barker: the union of a new fairy convention with the inherent theatricality of the play. Charles Marowitz, critic, director, and adaptor of Shakespeare's plays, writes that

> Brook's starting point seems to have been the *"contemporary"* notion of magic. Since woodland sprites and evil fairies no longer convince, on what magical basis can *A Midsummer Night's Dream* be founded? Brook's answer is theatre-magic: A sleight-of-hand composed of scenic tricks and stage illusion, but with the mechanics laid bare for all to see.[53]

Brook himself confirms Marowitz's supposition:

> This line [about fairies and magic] which runs throughout the play cannot be presented convincingly through dead or secondhand imagery.
> How one captures this moment [*sic*] in the 20th century—. . . [and makes magic] meaningful to an audience . . .—is such a difficult and strong and clear starting point that . . . everything else—all the forms of the production—stem from having to face that question. . . . (Quoted in "Drama Desk," *Acting Edition*, p. 24; last ellipsis Loney's)

Such was the question Barker faced again and again in his productions—how to present the essentials of Shakespeare's plays in a convincing twentieth-century manner. Brook echoes Barker's recognition of the balance that must be struck between Elizabethan essentials and modern requirements: "A play is really a mass of material: thoughts, feelings, ideas, actions. The printed words are a very small part. Shakespeare's text is not what he did on stage. But the mass is still there. It's always there—and we have to find it" (quoted in "Introduction," *Acting Edition*, p. 14).

Thus, the magic flower in Brook's production was no disappointing papier-mâché replica, but the spinning silver plate of the Chinese circus, magically humming and revolving on a silver rod as it passed from Puck to Oberon—"the right device, to bring back the gasp of joy," the magic "that the familiar would kill."[54] Similarly, the fairies' use of freekas—those brilliantly colored plastic tubes that emit unearthly whistles when swung like a lasso—distinguished them from the mortals, just as their jerky movements and strange speech did in 1914. Interestingly, Brook also used unusual speech patterns to differentiate the fairies from the mortals: the famous fairy speech of II. i. ("Over hill, over dale") was divided into half-lines and even single words, spoken alternately by Peaseblossom, Moth, Cobweb, and Mustardseed.

Countless elements in Brook's production remind one of Barker's. The costumes were timeless and exotic, the loose trousers and bright satin shirts of Eastern acrobats; their shapelessness made the actors' athletic tricks both natural and mysterious, as they hid the body, its muscles and movements. Different bright colors—pink, green, blue, orange—distinguished the lovers from each other, while fluorescent colors heightened the otherworldliness of Titania, Oberon, and Puck.[55] Here, the similarity to Barker needs no pointer.

Other ideas first stressed by Barker surfaced in this production. The music director, Richard Peaslee, was struck by the mechanicals' taking "their parts extremely seriously" and found them "funnier because they were so sincere." Brook also emphasized that each group of mortals in the play is ridiculous on some levels, though he missed Barker's point that the fairies are too (a strange oversight, as he doubled the parts of Theseus/Oberon and Hippolyta/Titania). Like Barker, he bathed the stage in bright general light, without varying color or intensity, to break away from realistic illusion.[56] Moreover, Brook's was an eclectic production, "poetry, ritual, ballet and circus rolled into one."

Much more can be written about Brook's *Dream,* but it is not my intention to recreate his production in detail. Rather, I have attempted to show that even this most "revolutionary" achievement of contemporary Shakespeare production was in fact something quite different—not a break in tradition, but a validation of the aims of modern Shakespearean production first fully stated by Granville Barker in 1912. The supremacy of the text, the break from realistic illusion, the freedom from restrictions of historical setting, the need for continuous playing, the emphasis on theme, the concern to present Shakespeare's essentials in a manner sympathetic to the modern imagination—all these requirements were first posited by Barker. Even Brook's fulfillment of them differs from Barker's only in specifics, not in essentials, as the parallel statements both make about the play indicate. What to do is clear, how to do it left open.

Certainly, there have been many new influences at work in Shakespeare production since Barker worked at the Savoy. Brook acknowledges his debt to Kott and to the oriental circus, while other critics recognize the influence of Meyerhold, Grotowski, and Artaud on his work.[57] But these new influences have not changed the direction of Shakespearean staging—they have only pointed out new themes, suggested new ways of achieving Barker's goals. In truth, Marowitz's tribute to Brook's *Dream* could equally stand for its precursor:

> This is a defoliated *Midsummer Night's Dream*. Gone . . . are the terpsichorean fairies, the vernal glades, the mischievous woods. . . . The shock of dislocating the play is so great, the effect of seeing it re-assembled in a bright, hard context free of traditional associations so refreshing[,] that we are hypnotized by the very "otherness" of the creation.

This was Shakespeare's *Dream*, Marowitz adds, "but in a flashier context" ("Introduction," *Acting Edition*, pp. 11–12).

This discussion of Barker's lasting achievement once again raises the question of his much-maligned "rationalism." The *Outlook* found his posing of the Sicilian court "cold [in] design"; Inkster, as well as Bridges Adams, called him "cold and intellectual"; even John Palmer accused him of "suffering from brains" in the last Savoy production. Yet, clearly, it was Barker's intellectual approach to Shakespeare and the staging of his plays that enabled him to achieve so much. His own recognition of Shakespeare's intellect and dramatic purpose enabled Barker to strip away stale and meaningless convention so that Shakespeare's ideas could hold the stage. Those who romanticized Shakespeare as an accidental genius were clearly unhappy— and John Palmer, for all his clear-sightedness in hailing the first two Savoy revivals, seems to have fallen into this sentimental trap with the third. If *A Midsummer Night's Dream* is a mere fairy story, without purpose or reason save the beauty of the verse and the comedy of the action, then Palmer is right: the play cannot endure a "reasonableness" of presentation. If, on the other hand, modern critics are right and the play has a serious meaning, then Palmer is guilty of the closed-mindedness he scorned in other critics' reviews of *A Winter's Tale* and *Twelfth Night*. Palmer's ultimate defection from the Savoy camp reveals more about his own preconceptions of the *Dream* than about Barker's allegedly too "perfect sanity."

In thus defending Barker from his most hostile critics, I do not suggest that his productions were perfect. Perhaps his symbolic blocking and repeated gesture patterns were occasionally too transparent, his revelation of serious purpose too intense. But what exegesis is not heavy-handed compared to the text itself? The important point is that in his Savoy productions, Barker took both play and audience seriously, letting the one speak, and the other think, for itself. It is a rich legacy for which to thank him.

3

Barker's Shakespeare Criticism

AFTER the close of the Savoy productions, Barker's involvement with Shakespeare was confined to the written word, with the one exception of active collaboration in the 1940 Old Vic *King Lear*. Barker's contributions in this sphere were prolific, extending beyond the celebrated *Prefaces* to numerous articles, reviews of Shakespeare scholarship, and lectures published on both sides of the Atlantic. In them, he elaborates his ideas about the most effective methods of staging Shakespeare, often making explicit what can only be inferred from his own practice in the years 1912 to 1914.

Barker first wrote on Shakespeare in conjunction with his work as a producer; concurrently with each Savoy production, Heinemann issued the acting edition of the play with illustrations by Albert Rutherston or Norman Wilkinson and a short preface by Barker. In these prefaces, Barker explains the rationale behind each production, justifying the speed at which the verse was spoken, the division of the play, its costuming, music, and of course, scenery. Barker stresses that "these few Prefaces make no pretence to Shakespearean scholarship, as that is usually understood. They are only the elaborated notes of the producer, who must view the play, first and last, as in action and on the stage. But it is, after all, a normal way to view it."[1]

Despite Barker's disclaimer, these short prefaces do more than justify a particular production; they begin to explore the nature of Shakespeare's stagecraft. For example, Barker carefully explains Shakespeare's use of Time as chorus in *The Winter's Tale* both as a device to shift the mood of the play and as a reflection of the story's artifice (pp. 19–20), rather than attributing to Shakespeare the use of a merely clumsy but convenient device. Likewise, he recognizes Shakespeare's use of bridging scenes, a recognition implicit in his demonstrated respect for textual integrity: "The little scene of

Cleomenes and Dion returning with the oracle is a model 'bridge' from the raucous revilings of Leontes over the helpless child to the dignity of the scene of the trial" (p. 24). Similarly, Barker is sensitive to the effects of dramatic structure upon audience reaction; his discussion of the statue scene reveals that Shakespeare

> prepares the audience, through Paulina's steward, almost to the pitch of revelation, saving just so much surprise, and leaving so little, that when they see the statue they may think themselves more in doubt than they really are whether it is Hermione herself or no. (P. 22)

These three prefaces also introduce the way Barker perceives character. He discusses Leontes's jealousy vis-à-vis *Othello*, indicating that its importance does not lie in the revelation of the character's psychology, but rather in the effects for which Shakespeare aims: by presenting Leonte's jealousy as "perverse, ignoble, pitiable," by making him ridiculous and denying him dignity, Shakespeare prevents the play from slipping into tragedy and arouses the audience's expectations of a happy ending (pp. 20–21). Here, as elsewhere,[2] Barker clearly grants Shakespeare his characters on his own terms; he does not demand of them the psychological reality of characters in a modern novel, where such reality would be inappropriate to the nature of the play. It hardly needs to be added that such an attitude is far removed from the Bradleyan mode of criticism prevailing at the time.

Barker's respect for Shakespeare's purpose also involves respect for Elizabethan essentials, though not incidentals. For example, he argues that it is pointless to exclude women from the stage just because their parts were originally written for boys. However, bearing the origin of their roles in mind, it is important that women actors do not flaunt their femininity. To do so would distort the sympathy and balance of the play: "Give to Olivia, as we must do now, all the value of her sex, and to the supposed Cesario none of the value of his, we are naturally quite unmoved by the business." The comedy of the action would also be distorted, as discussion of *Twelfth Night* in the previous chapter has indicated.

The dramatic function of Shakespeare's verse also surfaces in these prefaces as one of Barker's main concerns, one that he will explore more thoroughly in *On Poetry in Drama* (1937). Barker, in writing about *A Midsummer Night's Dream*, argues that

> the secret of the play . . . lies in the fact that though [the passages of verse] may offend against every letter of dramatic law they fulfil the inmost spirit of it, inasmuch as they are dramatic in them-

selves. They are instinct with that excitement, that spontaneity, that sense of emotional overflow which is drama. . . . Even when [Shakespeare] seems to sacrifice drama to poem he—instinctively or not—manages to make the poem itself more dramatic than the drama he sacrifices.[3]

Barker here reveals his belief that drama more essentially involves the revelation of internal than external conflict or action. He repeats this belief throughout his criticism, as well as incorporating it in his own plays.[4]

Barker's next major excursion into Shakespeare criticism is his paper, "Some Tasks for Dramatic Scholarship,[5] read before the Royal Society of Literature in 1922 and published the following year. In it, he emphasizes the need for collaboration between actor and scholar: "I assume, to begin with, that dramatic art has need of the services pure scholarship can render." However, Barker finds the scholarship of his day so far divorced from the theatre that "a large part is written by people who, you might suppose, could never have been inside a theatre in their lives" (p. 17); the scholar "has often gone to great trouble to elucidate points which, if he could but have seen or even imagined the play in being—acted, that is, in a theatre, where a play belongs—would have elucidated themselves" (p. 18).

Barker is one of the first modern critics to stress the importance of performance; he warns that

drama can only be profitably considered in its full integrity. We may have, for the purposes of its service, to treat separately of its literary, its technical, its histrionic aspects. But unless, while doing so, we can still visualize the plays as completed things—living in the theatre—we shall always tend to be astray in our conclusions about them. (P. 22)

The importance of acting a play does not lie merely in the realization of the text; an equally significant element is "the effect of human association in an audience." Barker knows that emotion is as important as reason in appreciating drama, and that a skillful playwright consciously and unconsciously plays upon an audience's "senses and susceptibilities" (p. 26). He expresses his viewpoint most succinctly in the assertion that "reading a play. . . . is comparable to reading the score of a symphony and asks as much skill" (p. 37). The idea of the text as score, which is "never fully alive [until acted in a theatre]" (p. 21) is commonplace today, but was a contentious notion when Barker first voiced it; the prevalent feeling was that the ideal play existed in the text, to be imagined by the reader, while any actual performance was a poor approximation of it. Lamb's evaluation of

King Lear, for example, was still widely accepted well into this century, as reviews of Barker's *Lear* in 1940 clearly demonstrate: the critic of the *Spectator* called it a "ridiculous" play which no one should attempt to stage.[6]

Although Barker is concerned to emphasize the importance of a play's realization on stage,[7] he does not reduce drama to mere performance: "Its larger life—for I admit it has one—is the extension of that [i.e., its being acted], but never to be attained by leaving that out of account" (p. 21). He praises scholars engaged in textual and "purely historical research" (p. 20), since Shakespeare's "method may help us to account for matter" (p. 25). For example, knowing how Shakespeare would have staged *Hamlet* might offer "a key to the solution of many of the psychological, if not the philosophical, questions in the play. For Shakespeare . . . was a considerable technician— . . . he adapted his end to his means when he could not, or would not trouble to, adapt his means to his end" (pp. 23–24).

Barker emphasizes that envisioning a Shakespearean performance enables one to "separate the *essentials* from the *incidentals*" (p. 24) of the play—his first postulation of the implicit goal of his Savoy productions. He humorously explains that

> there can have been no aesthetic advantage in the fact that a gentleman might puff smoke in Burbage's face. On the other hand the intimate touch that the actor was in with his audience must undoubtedly have influenced the method of dialogue, and may have led Shakespeare to make certain demands on his actors of which their modern successors . . . remain unaware. (P. 24)

Barker's characteristic sensitivity to Shakespeare's language and to stage action enables him to make the play come alive for the reader on the page. Using *Hamlet*, Barker explains that the audience would have been unruly as well as close, and that

> This would account for a certain violence of attack which is indicated for the actor when it is necessary to capture the attention of the audience after a bustle of movement. Note the explosiveness of
>
> > "O that this too too solid flesh would melt"
>
> after the elaborate departure of the King and Queen and their attendants. Note the same sort of opening
>
> > "O what a rogue and peasant slave am I"
>
> after the amusing medley of the players and Polonius is disposed of.

On the other hand note the careful preparation by Polonius and the King for the necessarily quiet beginning of

"To be or not to be."

In a modern theatre these seem to be refinements of stagecraft. On Shakespeare's stage such things were perhaps of fundamental import. And if the modern actor and the modern scholar does [*sic*] not take account of them, he is like a musician who may be putting "forte" where the composer intended "piano" and "diminuendo" for "sforzando." (P. 25)

Clearly, Barker believes in recreating the conditions of an Elizabethan performance not in order to reproduce them per se, as Poel did in including an Elizabethan audience on the stage during *Measure for Measure,* but rather to determine the effects and moods Shakespeare intended so that these can be recaptured in a modern performance.

Barker, however, does not underestimate the difficulties inherent in producing Shakespeare successfully in a modern idiom. Just as he blames criticism for neglecting the theatre, so he recognizes the pernicious effects of ill-judged performance on interpretation; for example, the custom of having an aging star play Hamlet necessitates a matronly Gertrude out of character with the "jigging," "ambling" creature Hamlet has in mind when he attacks Ophelia, and the predominance of Canute-like Claudiuses appearing on stage obliterates the Renaissance character Shakespeare intended.

In suggesting ways around "the problem of the appropriate presentation of Shakespeare", Barker lays down no laws; he recognizes that it is "capable of no one solution" (p. 29), thus eschewing the rigid approach of scholar-directors like Poel. He poses the problem in this way:

How to present Shakespeare's plays in their integrity as works of art to a generation that cannot by taking thought—cannot with the best will in the world—transform itself into Shakespeare's audience.(P. 35–36)

His solution suggests that

bridging [this aesthetic chasm] is a matter of convenience and of compromise. What has to be decided is how far we can and must adapt our consciousness to the essential theatrical conditions of that time, and, alternatively, how far the technique of the plays will withstand adaptation to our accustomed uses without the content being in any way distorted.
. . . [W]e ought to go back as far as we can to meet the seven-

teenth century without sacrificing the spontaneity of our apprehension of the plays, and substituting for it a merely
archaeological understanding. For the technique and the content
of a work of art are properly speaking interdependent. . . .
(Pp. 29–30)

Barker adds that researches into various solutions to this problem
"should be made mutually helpful, and that each—whatever the
variety of its practice—should contribute something to the elucida-
tion of the *principles* involved" (p. 36). His emphasis on finding the
principles of Shakespearean staging again illustrates a concern to
avoid both sterile archaeological reconstruction and eccentric modern distortion of the text, a point that will be more fully discussed in
reference to Barker's review of Barry Jackson's modern-dress
Hamlet. Barker insists on the necessity of theatrical experiment inspired by scholarly research and stimulating research in return, a
necessity recognized by the current drafting of scholars into active
theatre work: John Russell Brown with the National Theatre and
John Barton with the Royal Shakespeare Company, for example. He
suggests that experiment be sometimes limited to one aspect of a
play—for instance, to the presentation of the supernatural in *A
Midsummer Night's Dream, Macbeth,* or *The Tempest,* or to the costuming of *Antony and Cleopatra*. However, Barker does not advocate a
free-for-all hodgepodge of design and interpretation; he sees the
producer's role as that of providing an "effective and *consistent* presentation of a play" (p. 37; italics mine).

In discussing the need for experiment, Barker praises Poel's productions, even though he disagreed with them "five times out of
ten": "An acute observer could be stimulated to a livelier understanding of a play of Shakespeare's by being brought to analyse his
disagreement with Mr. Poel's bold assertions than ever he would be
by the sight of a timid, haphazard staging which set out
thoughtlessly to please as best it could" (pp. 30–31). Similarly, he
admires Bradley's work: "His Hamlet and Othello seemed to me like
a very great actor's conception of the parts. . . . I can think of no
higher compliment to pay. . . . To Professor Bradley the plays are
plays and never cease to be plays" (p. 20).

Whether or not one agrees with Barker's assessment of Bradley's
criticism and of Poel's productions, his comments show what he
values in both critical and theatrical interpretation of Shakespeare.
For Barker, interpretation must be "life-giving"; that is, it must
realize "drama as a living thing," realize "the integrity of a play as
acted in a theatre" (pp. 20–21). Barker is suspicious of "aesthetic
criticism" (i.e., nonhistorical, nontextual work), because, while it can

sometimes be "life-giving," it all too often expects the plays "to turn into historical documents or problems in metaphysics" (p. 20)—a complaint still echoed in contemporary criticism.[8] While Barker admits such wider implications of drama, he refuses to let these dictate the production of a play, just as he refuses to let pictorial scenery reshape the text for stage presentation. Thus, he can admit any school of criticism as long as it does not distort the implied action and meaning of the play under consideration. His recognition of Shakespeare's variety and flexibility leads him to adopt equally various and flexible approaches to the plays, both in terms of their staging and of their wider interpretation.[9]

One of the tasks Barker assigns dramatic scholarship is the production of a new kind of Variorum edition, "one that would epitomise Shakespeare, the playwright" (p. 33). Barker hoped that such an edition would illustrate the Shakespearean practice of staging as well as record notable past performances and interpretations and modern treatments of the plays. "The weight of the editor's work," he writes, "would lie in his obligation always to exhibit the play in action, and all the material of learning he wished to assemble he should submit, primarily, to this test" (p. 33). The usefulness of his idea is suggested by the format of the New Cambridge Shakespeare, which attempts to do just this, and by the Arden editions, which now generally include the stage history of each play.

Barker's next project goes some way toward fulfilling his own prescription. From 1923–1927 he edited *The Players' Shakespeare* for Ernest Benn, producing seven volumes before the series was discontinued because of its high price of four guineas a volume (Styan, *Shakespeare Revolution*, p. 8). The texts were based on those of the 1623 Folio, with a list of significant variants and emendations included in some cases. Barker wrote a general introduction to the series, as well as prefaces to each play: *Macbeth, The Merchant of Venice, The Tragedie of Cymbeline* (1923), *A Midsommer Nights Dream, Love's Labour's Lost* (1924), *The Tragedie of Julius Caesar* (1925), and *The Tragedie of King Lear* (1927). He later revised these prefaces to varying extents, except for *Macbeth* and the *Dream*, for his *Prefaces to Shakespeare*.[10]

In the general introduction, Barker explains that he will present each play from the point of view of performance, but that he does not propose a complete production plan. Such a task would require collaboration between director, actors, designers, et al., and then actual staging would modify the blueprint—a point useful to remember later when comparing the *Preface to King Lear* with its production. Instead, Barker plans his prefaces "as the sort of addresses a producer might make to a company upon their first meet-

ing to study the play," and in order to clarify his opinions, Barker
sets out the "postulates" on which they are based."[11]

Barker's main tenet is that "the plays should be performed as
Shakespeare wrote them" (p. 44). While this ideal is evident from his
own productions, Barker here explores the ramifications of cuts:
"The question [follows] whether any omissions whatever from the
text can be justified" (p. 44). Barker advocates the excision of some
of Shakespeare's obscene jokes, on dramatic rather than on purely
social grounds:

> The manners of [Shakespeare's] time permitted this to a drama-
> tist. The manners of ours do not. Now the dramatic value of a joke
> is measured by its effect on an audience. Moreover, a joke is
> intended to make a specific sort of effect on an audience. And if,
> where it was meant to provide a mere moment of amusement, it
> makes a thousand people feel uncomfortable and for the next five
> minutes rather self-conscious, its effect is falsified and spoiled.
> And a series of such jokes may disturb the balance and alter the
> apparent character of the whole play. (P. 44)

Clearly, Barker has no patience with the kind of tampering that
turns "God" into "Heaven" and "whore" into "wanton", and he
condemns "such deodorizing of *Measure for Measure* that it is hard to
discover what all the fuss is about." Consideration of the audience
should not extend so far that it distorts the play:

> If people cannot suit their taste to Shakespeare's they had better
> do without his plays altogether. . . . Othello must call Desdemona
> a whore, and let those that do not like it leave the theatre; what
> have such queasy minds to do with the pity and terror of her
> murder and his death? (Pp. 44–45)

It is important to understand the dramatic rationale behind Barker's
comments on cutting, as he is sometimes quoted out of context to
appear a latter-day Bowdler.

Barker goes on to discuss "the fate of topical allusions whose
meaning is lost." While he sees the logic of cutting out "mere dead
wood in the living tree of the dialogue," he regards it as a dangerous
step, first, because Shakespeare's effect may still be achieved without
our total comprehension: "We have all laughed at Malvolio's reflection that 'The lady of the Strachy married the yeoman of the ward-
robe,' but not one of us could say what it means"; second, because its
application cannot be clearly delineated: "From cutting a phrase that
may offend and a line that will not be understood to excising a whole
scene that seem superfluous . . . is an enticing and a fatal pro-

gression" (p. 45). Barker outlines his own policy upon the matter.
Shakespeare, he believes, aimed not at perfection, but at vitality, and
therefore precision should be sacrificed to vitality in interpreting his
work. However, he adds an important rider to this statement:

> The plays have been so maltreated, both in text and construction,
> and we still remain so ignorant of their stagecraft, that our present
> task . . . is . . . to discover . . . what this stagecraft was. . . . To this
> end we must experiment with a play as he has left it us. It is risky
> to say, even of the smallest detail, 'This is not essential.' . . .
> (P. 46)[12]

It is doubly necessary "to discover what, as plays, [Shakespeare's
works] essentially are," because his "case as a playwright has still to be
fully proved" to producers, critics, and playgoers.

The issue of the essential nature of Shakespeare's plays leads
Barker to a related one: what is the "most illustrative method" of
staging them for a modern audience? The problem is compounded
by new emphases in the modern theatre; as Barker points out,
illusion is important, technical equipment has been developed to
enhance illusion, and so "scene-painting and lighting . . . set an
important part of the task that in Shakespeare's time fell to the
hands of playwright and actors alone" (p. 47). Manner then affects
matter, so that a modern audience may be doubly distanced from
Shakespeare's plays: both technique and substance, Barker realizes,
may be alien to them (p. 48).

To solve the problem Barker outlines several of the essential
aspects of Shakespeare's stage and suggests how the "modern stage
can conform to them" (p. 49). His first point deals with the problem
of illusion:

> Shakespeare paints a play's setting—should he think that it needs
> one—in its text, and no scene-painter by his art must discount this
> artistry. . . . Now there is surely no need to insist that realistically
> painted nests beneath undeniable castle eaves will distract the
> curious mind of the spectator just for that very short minute at the
> scene's opening [Duncan's arrival at Inverness] . . . from the
> words themselves and the speaker of them. . . . [A]ny scenic
> effect, realistic or other, which will detract from the importance of
> the actors as they begin these scenes, which will challenge their
> dominance, which will . . . set up a direct relation between the
> audience and the beauties of Inverness Castle or the cold of the
> night at Elsinore in place of the indirect relation through the
> channel of the feelings of Banquo and Duncan, Hamlet and
> Horatio, that Shakespeare has devised, must react harmfully on
> the scenes, the characters and the performance generally. (p. 49)

His discussion here incidentally points out a fundamental difference between his approach to Shakespearean scenery and Shaw's; the latter complains to Mrs. Patrick Campbell that she "might at least have made the scenepainter put in a martin's nest or two over the castle windows."[13]

In plays where "the text is a mass of scene-painting, and the difficulty [of scenery] is proportionately increased," one can find a solution in Shakespeare's own "rather subtle way" (p. 50):

> When it was a question of touching in a summer sunset or a winter night and passing on at once to enthralling matters, he was content barefacedly for a moment to call our attention to what . . . was not there. But when half the purpose of the play is to lodge us in a wood near Athens or in the forest of Arden, he either prepares our imagination by painting something which we are shortly to fancy, as he lets Puck describes Titania's bower, or he has a character picture for us some experience just past, as the first Lord and Oliver describe the wounded deer and Orlando's danger [respectively].

Shakespeare's practice should be the designer's: one should "not . . . put [the] actors into a direct antagonism with their background."

Barker also demands that "the stricter conventions of our illusionary theatre . . . not be allowed to curtail" the liberties of time and space so important to Shakespeare's plays (p. 50). Although his introduction offers no specific method of meeting this demand, Barker's stage decoration at the Savoy suggests ways in which a modern stage can be made flexible enough for Shakespeare's purposes. The sensitivity the director shows here should also extend to the timing of the interval, which should suit "the dramatic interests of the play as he finally assesses them in relation to his own stage" (p. 51).

Next, Barker discusses the importance of soliloquy and the intimacy it establishes through

> the physical proximity to the audience of the actor upon the apron stage, [and] more importantly the absence of any barrier of light or of scenic illusion. . . . As there was no illusion there was every illusion. Once grant that the man was Hamlet, the fact that you could touch him with your hand made him more actual to you, not less. (Pp. 51–52)

Barker does not offer very specific recommendations for ways to reestablish such emotional intimacy, though he suggests part of the problem may lie simply in the disappearance of the platform stage, and that here is a good case for experiment.[14] He also indicates another difficulty in actors' self-consciousness and unease when delivering soliloquies; music-hall comedians, after all, succeed in establishing real rapport with their audiences. Conversely, audiences are unaccustomed to delivery of a soliloquy in ways calculated to make them respond to it as an intimate gesture. Barker feels sure that experimentation can restore the original effect, if not the original manner: "The human ingredients of the problem have but superficially changed in three hundred years; we have only to order the others advantageously" (p. 53).

More than fifty years later, we can see that Barker was right. Experimentation with different types of stages has brought the audience into different relations with the actor; the open (or thrust) stage brings the actor forward into the audience, the small studio theatre reestablishes lost intimacy. Both, with their amphitheatrical or three-sided seating, sometimes without any stage proper, dispel the rigidly divided planes of actor and audience that the proscenium stage fosters. In turn, audiences and actors alike are now more comfortable with the convention, so that even when a soliloquy is spoken from a proscenium, it does not seem so artificial.[15]

Barker next addresses the problem of costume, pointing out that the Elizabethans had a sense of strangeness, but "no very definite sense of period" (p. 53). Sometimes, Shakespeare's practice will be suitable for the modern theatre—for example, in *Cymbeline* the Britons and Romans are supposed to be dressed in distinguishable costumes, neither necessarily historically accurate. However, difficulties present themselves with Cleopatra's "Cut my lace, Charmian," and with the hats plucked about the ears of the Roman conspirators or tossed in the air in *Coriolanus*. To Barker, the argument that "these things are trifles, anachronisms to which an audience pays no attention" is a poor one: "The actors have to speak the lines. They cannot speak them with conviction if their appearance and action contradict the words, and the constant credibility of the actor should be a producer's first care" (p. 53). A forcible reminder of the truth of this statement presented itself during the RSC's 1980 production of *Hamlet*, directed by John Barton: for several members of the audience, the reaction produced by Ophelia's death was merely bewilderment that her skimpy dress could be made so "heavy with . . . drink" that it "Pull'd the poor wretch . . . /To muddy death."[16]

In arguing for some consistency between dress and speech, Barker adds another reason to that of credibility: "The plays, one and all, are full of references to Elizabethan customs. . . . [T]he more vividly [Shakespeare] imagined a character, the more it was his instinct to clothe it with familiar details" (pp. 53–54). Thus, Hamlet and Claudius belong more to sixteenth-century England than to eleventh-century Denmark, and Cleopatra's coquetry with Antony reflects the behavior of court women of Shakespeare's time. For this reason, precise historical costumes could conflict with the conception of the characters, yet designs that ignore modern knowledge about the periods concerned could also be distracting; therefore, costuming is a matter for compromise. Sometimes, adjustment will be easy; as Barker points out, to shift *Hamlet* from 1000 to 1550 should bother no one. However, *Antony and Cleopatra* presents a different problem:

> If Cleopatra in a farthingale too dreadfully offends—well, a way out must be found. My own belief is that, submitting ourselves to the power of the play, that power being developed to the full by the cultivation of its every, of its tiniest resource, we shall have little trouble (after a first shock) in subduing our vision of it to all that was essential in Shakespeare's own. After all, we take Tintoretto's and Paolo Veronese's paintings of classic subjects with great calm. (P. 54)

Barker's suggestions have worked very well in practice. There was a successful Elizabethan *Antony and Cleopatra* at the Old Vic in 1977, as well as a recent production by the RSC which dressed the Egyptians in unhistorical but suggestive kaftans. Likewise, Trevor Nunn's highly-acclaimed *Macbeth* for the RSC in 1976 used timeless black cloth-and-leather uniforms for the Scottish warriors and a simple shift and head scarf for Lady Macbeth.[17] Period was suggested rather than defined, so that the play's trappings clashed neither with its language nor with the audience's preconceptions about the period—the precise effect Barker aims for in his criticism and initiated at the Savoy.

In summarizing his attitude, Barker suggests this motto for any producer of Shakespeare: "Gain Shakespeare's effects by Shakespeare's means when you can. But gain Shakespeare's effects; it is your business to discern them" (p. 54). He continues, replying to those who advocate a return to Shakespeare's own stage, with its multiple levels and bareness:

> Mere restoration of all this will not meet our case. We cannot quite discard the present, and, even could we, entering into the past would be a harder matter still. We should need to sit in an Elizabethan theatre as Elizabethans and be able as unconsciously, as spontaneously to enjoy the play. For spontaneity of enjoyment is the very life of the theatre and its art. This [return] cannot be. Some half-way house of meeting must be found. But let it be insisted that the further we can learn to travel back upon the road the greater profit to us. (P. 55)

As an example of traveling back, Barker assumes that the music used in Shakespearean productions should be Elizabethan and should be used the same way it was in Shakespeare's theatre.

Barker concludes with two further points. The first is another reminder that the origin of Shakespeare's roles for women demands sensitivity in their interpretation, as well as

> a self-forgetful brilliance of execution which must leave prettiness and its lures at a loss, which indeed leaves sex and its cruder emotional values out of account altogether. . . . Not that [Shakespeare] fettered his imagination with respect to the characters themselves. [His women characters] are not the less women upon this account. But all art is selection. . . . (P. 56)

Barker had previously remarked on the appropriateness of the boy-actor convention in the Elizabethan theatre, concluding that the beauty of the plays "ran a better chance of full and free expression through the medium of that pleasant artifice a boy's well-skilled interpretation could provide than charged with and coloured by the extremely personal attractions of such actresses as Shakespeare's stage would have found" (p. 55). This remark perhaps explains more about the posturing of some female actors in Barker's day than it reveals about the likely nature of Elizabethan actresses, and it suggests that if Barker were writing today he might feel no need to emphasize the point. Barker is concerned that interpretation of character reflect Shakespeare's achievement in "lift[ing] the relations of men and women to a plane" apart from the merely sexual (pp. 56–57). Written at a time when the portrayal of women's sexuality in a theatre would have been more disturbing than much of Shakespeare's bawdy, Barker's views are not substantiated today; no one, I think, would argue that our experience of Cleopatra is not intensified by suggestion of her powerful sexuality, as long as other aspects of her character are not neglected. As Barker himself realizes, Shakespeare's achievement is to show women as complete people rather than as projections of men; ironically, he points out,

> not a little of the praise bestowed—mainly by women—upon the ideal womanliness of these heroines; their freedom, that is to say, from vulgarity, pettiness, coarseness, all their moral beauty, may be counted due to this circumstance that they were parts written to be played by boys. (P. 57)

Barker's final point concerns the speaking of the verse—if it be not spoken beautifully, "all other virtues are vain." Barker argues that the "verse is meant to be spoken swiftly and yet with great variety of emphasis and tone," on the evidence of Hamlet's advice to the players. Since it should also be spoken naturally, not only must actors train their tongues, but audiences must train their ears: "Shakespeare's language has . . . to be learned before it can be rightly listened to, and playgoers must put themselves to that much trouble." Barker is also sensitive to the varieties of Shakespearean speech, recognizing that "at times . . . sound supersede[s] mere sense, the music of the lines becomes their single power" (pp. 57–58). The critics outraged at Barker's *Winter Tale* had not yet learned to listen, to understand that Leontes's "gabbling" was more expressive of his feelings than a carefully enunciated delivery, which would ensure the understanding of every word but not of the emotion.[18]

Barker's prefaces for *The Players' Shakespeare* are first drafts for his later *Prefaces to Shakespeare*. I do not undertake to discuss them individually, either in their original or revised forms; the prefaces are well-known, have been discussed elsewhere, and furthermore, such detailed discussion is beyond the scope of a book dealing with all of Barker's work on Shakespeare.[19] However, the next chapter will deal with the *King Lear* preface and its application in the theatre, and this analysis will serve as an example of Barker's approach to individual plays.

"From *Henry V* to *Hamlet*," the British Academy Annual Shakespeare lecture of 1925, was Barker's next excursion into scholarship; he revised it for publication in 1926 and again in 1932.[20] In this article, Barker moves away from a strictly dramatic point of view and discusses the development of Shakespeare's art. He stresses Shakespeare's reliance on the actor as the medium of his drama, because

> the vital quality in Shakespeare's developing art . . . lie[s] not in . . . plot . . . but in some spirit behind [it], by which it seems to move of itself; and not so much in the writing of great dramatic poetry even, as in [a] growing power to project character in action. (P. 140)

But "character in action" is a misleading phrase, for Barker seems to mean, as he later makes clear, character *as* action; he explains that "behind the action, be the play farce or tragedy, there must be some spiritually significant idea, or it will hang lifeless" (p. 146), as does *Henry V:*

> Here is a play of action, and here is the perfect man of action. Yet all the while Shakespeare is apologising—and directly apologising—for not being able to make the action effective. (P. 144)

For Barker, Shakespeare's turning point comes with *Julius Caesar,* for in this play, the author's "care is not for what his hero does, which is merely disastrous, but for what he *is;* this is the dramatic thing, and the essential thing" (p. 147). From this point on, Barker sees Shakespeare deciding that his subject is " 'the passionate, suffering inner consciousness of man, his spiritual struggles and triumphs and defeats in his impact with an uncomprehending world' " (HGB "quoting" Shakespeare, p. 149). For Barker, this shift marks Shakespeare's real achievement as a dramatist: "[His] Drama was to lie only formally in the external action, was to consist of the revelation of character and of the inevitable clashes between the natures of men. And besides, behind these there would be the struggle within a man's own nature; and the combatant powers there must be dramatised" (p. 152).

Yet emphasis on inner consciousness " 'may seem the most utterly unfit subject for such a crowded, noisy, vulgar place as the theatre' " (HGB "quoting" Shakespeare, p. 149). Barker explains how Shakespeare could achieve the expression of inner life, the expression of "things in [the characters] of which they were not themselves wholly conscious" (p. 152), through the art of "interpretative acting," an idea that will be discussed further. In addition, he developed a balance in his plays by avoiding long descriptions of external events, by using soliloquy for "intimate revelation" yet limiting its use to avoid the relaxation of tension and the weakening of structure, by writing "short-range hard-hitting dialogue," and by avoiding "passages of rock-like rhetoric." Thus, through dramatic speech, he made the actor the vehicle of story, character, and scene (pp. 152–53). In *Lear,* for example, Shakespeare "turns one character, Edgar, in his disguise as a wandering, naked, half-witted beggar, into a veritable piece of scene-painting of the barren, inhospitable heath." Similarly,

> the storm itself . . . [is] a reflection of that greater storm which rages in the mind of Lear—of anger, terror, pity, remorse—lightening and darkening it as a storm does the sky, and finally blasting it altogether. For *that* [i.e., mental] storm, as Shakespeare knows now, is the really dramatic thing; and it is the only thing that his art can directly and satisfactorily present. (P. 157)

Barker realizes that by making Lear the vehicle of the storm, Shakespeare effectively dramatizes the inner life of the man himself; he is the first critic to recognize the essentially dramatic nature of the storm, rather than condemning it for making the play unfit for the stage, or claiming that its greatness makes *Lear* a dramatic poem rather than "mere" drama.

Barker forcefully attacks the critical premise that Shakespeare's plays are not realizable on the stage (p. 161) and lays down ground rules for their successful production:

> Whether or no one can ever successfully place a work of art in surroundings for which it was not intended, at least one must not submit it to conditions which are positively antagonistic to its technique and its spirit. Such an agreement involves, in practice, for the staging of Shakespeare—first, from the audience, as much historical sense as they can cultivate without it [*sic*] choking the spring of their spontaneous enjoyment; next, that the producer distinguish between the essentials and the incidentals of the play's art. . . . But whether it is to be played upon a platform or behind footlights, whether with curtains or scenery for a background . . . this at least is clear . . .: Shakespeare's progress in his art involved an ever greater reliance upon that other art which *is* irrevocably wedded to the playwright's—the art of interpretative acting. (P. 162)

Barker, however, is quick to warn that approaching the plays from a "histrionic standpoint" may sometimes foil the scholar, since acting depends very much on tradition and tradition itself is often neglected or indifferently fostered in the British theatre; one should not expect perfection in the performance of Shakespeare's plays. Barker adds that in any case the richness of the plays does not depend on perfection but on their "fruitfulness and variety" in signifying human relations. Shakespeare's emphasis on intimacy between actor and audience puts both "upon the plane of his poetic vision," thus breaking "the boundaries between mimic and real" (pp. 163–65).

In this essay, as elsewhere, Barker is keen to establish the mutual need of scholar and actor:

> Shakespeare *did* in [his] greater imaginings break through the boundaries of the material theatre he knew, and none that we have yet known has been able to compass them. . . . But as he never ceased to be the practical playwright and man of the theatre the chances are, perhaps, that [the theatre] can [compass them]. (P. 166)

Once again he emphasizes "the art of speech made eloquent by rhythm and memorable by harmony of sense and sound" as the foundation of poetic drama (p. 167). Thus, even in moving toward a critical appraisal of Shakespeare's development as an artist, Barker returns to the theatrical implications of his findings.

"Shakespeare and Modern Stagecraft," an elaborated version of a lecture given at the Sorbonne in 1926, reiterates Barker's main tenets about Shakespearean production.[21] Once more, he stresses the need to reconcile the seventeenth and the twentieth centuries in terms of language, sense of period, presentation of women, and visual illusion versus aural appeal. He warns of the rifts between action and the spoken word which endanger the actor's credibility ("Cut my lace, Charmian" when there is no lace to cut), as well as the destructiveness of imposed consistency; for example, Iachimo is a "typically Renaissance figure" and Cloten "an Elizabethan man-about-town" (p. 709). To unite the two in a consistently Roman Britain is to destroy the life of each, just as Hamlet's depiction as a realistic tenth-century Dane would conflict with the Renaissance conception of his character. Barker advises that to this problem there is "no one solution logically and unyieldingly applicable to every play. . . . The difficulty is aesthetic; measure it then in terms of taste" (p. 710). He suggests once again that we travel as far back to Shakespeare's practice as we can "without endangering our spontaneous enjoyment of his art," which is the key to understanding it.

Barker restates his argument about women's roles in Shakespeare: written for boys, they should not be embellished with sentimentality, sensuality, "display of personal charm [or] emotional suggestion" (p. 713). The deficiency of this view has already been discussed, but Barker again makes the valid point that for Shakespeare "the stuff of tragedy and of true comedy in the relations between men and women lies *outside* the boundaries of primitive sex-appeal" (p. 713). In explaining Shakespeare's tact in writing for the boy-actor, Barker also explains how Shakespeare makes "good dramatic capital" of the convention: he often disguises his girls as boys (p. 711). In fact, Shakespeare is able to turn the limitations of the boy-actor to dramatic account for our own theatrical conventions as well as his:

> In the balcony scene, one of the most beautiful and passionate love scenes in all drama, [Romeo and Juliet] are carefully kept apart [to avoid any embarrassment to the boy-actor]. Shakespeare's artistic judgment may not have been infallible but his delicate artistic instinct seldom failed him. Even on our stage this separation of the two lovers adds a rarity of beauty to the scene. On his stage it made it dramatically possible. (P. 712)

Shakespeare also sees to it that Antony and Cleopatra "are very little together," at least "until the story takes its tragic plunge and mere sex is swamped in greater passion" (p. 712). In explaining Shakespeare's tact in writing Cleopatra's part for the boy-actor, Barker also suggests ways in which Shakespeare achieves a full realization of mythic character through a human actor, whether female or male: "The famous description of [Cleopatra] in her barge, of her beauty and wantonness[,] . . . of her sensual side is only given when the mimic Cleopatra has been absent from the stage for nearly half an hour" (p. 713). Whether or not Barker is right about the motivation behind Shakespeare's handling of such scenes, his recognition of the dramatic power of Shakespeare's tact is instructive.

Barker devotes several pages of his article to a discussion of Shakespeare's sense of place. He points out that the Elizabethan theatre did not define locality as the modern theatre does; if such definition is necessary, Shakespeare achieves it through dialogue: "Barkloughly Castle call they this at hand?" (p. 717). Barker contrasts such bare information with Duncan's meditations on Inverness Castle, having pointed out that Shakespeare's concern is never for the word-picture itself, but rather for the atmosphere it creates or for its emotional effect on the characters, and through them, the audience: "Shakespeare still has . . . but one end in view, the development of his dramatic theme" (p. 716). Thus, a realistic depiction of the beauties articulated by Duncan and Banquo would be disruptive:

> What scene painter could paint . . . better, or could better give us the calm sunset beauty which is the prelude to that murky murderous night to come? Indeed the better a scene painter did his work the worse it would be. For if his picture were beautiful it would hold our attention. And the beauty—and more important by far—the dramatic significance of Shakespeare's lines would have the less hold on us. (P. 717)

Barker concludes that place, as such, is unimportant to Shakespeare and that neoclassic precepts are irrelevant in evaluating his work:

> [Shakespeare's] stage achieved no dramatic dignity or integrity as a *place* at all. For his unities we must look to action and character development only. . . . [F]or him a play's action has a single abiding place in the minds and hearts of its characters. An essential and a vital unity indeed! (P. 720)

Barker finishes his essay by brilliantly arguing Shakespeare's case as a playwright, once again choosing the most difficult witness for it—*King Lear*. He reiterates his view of Edgar as living scenery and explains the preparatory role of act III, scene i (Kent and the anonymous gentleman): "Shakespeare artfully gives his audience the cue to the dramatic effects which are to follow, bids them to look for the old King, striving

. . . in his little world of man to outscorn
The to-and-fro conflicting wind and rain." (Pp. 721–22;
ellipsis Barker's)

Barker expands on Lear's role in the storm; he is not meant to be
"a realistic picture of a poor old man tottering about with a walking-
stick," but the storm itself: "Present us with a Lear mighty enough to
present the storm, and we have at one and the same time a Lear
capable of defying the storm[,] . . . the colossal figure of Shakespeare's imagining and Lamb's desire" (p. 722). Barker warns that if
Lear is made "realistically weak and infirm" and set against a mechanical storm and painted scenery, he will dwindle to insignifi-
cance. However, if all the audience's attention is focused on him, the
submission of "A poor, infirm, weak, and despised old man"

> shows us a Lear pathetically simple by contrast with the elemental
> fury that he has just been interpreting to us in terms of his own
> person, of his own passion, yet still colossal by association with it.
> Symbolize the very storm in his person, and in his own person he
> can stand to us, not as a mere individual, but as the very symbol of
> old age itself. (P. 723)

This symbolic presentation of Lear is then followed by the "human
simplicity of [his] reconciliation with Kent and Cordelia." Barker is
sensitive to the nuances of Shakespeare's presentation of character
and their interplay with each other, showing how the human gains
from the symbolic; he does not expect a modern consistency of
presentation or blame Shakespeare for lack of it.

Barker concludes that far from being unsuited to stage presentation, *King Lear* is "the apex of [Shakespeare's] art . . . [and] his
greatest technical achievement too" (p. 724). Staging it well would
not be easy, either in Shakespeare's time or our own, but certainly
possible:

> Great artists are the most practical and definite of men, within
> their own sphere. And Shakespeare was a supreme artist, working
> adventurously but very sanely within a medium which, crude in its
> material resource, became at his touch great in its simplicity.
> (P. 724)

Barker's faith in Shakespeare's craftsmanship is revolutionary for its
time.

Barker added a post-script to this article, in the form of a comment on Barry Jackson's modern-dress *Hamlet*[22]; its brevity makes it
possible to quote in full:

The production of "Hamlet" in twentieth-century clothing has been salutary medicine, doubtless, for people whose minds had become insensible to Shakespeare the living dramatist, who sat out the plays as a sightseer will sometimes sit through Mass in a Roman church, rising and sitting and kneeling as near as may be at the right moments, but finding it, for all that, a mass of meaningless ritual. But I cannot call "Hamlet in plus fours" more than a medicine. The twentieth century, measured by costume and manners, is farther from Shakespeare than the tenth; and we are more sensitive to the distance than were the Elizabethans. For manners (I speak of the production I saw) went with costume, though this was not altogether inevitable. And even so I should doubt the modern Danish courtier standing armed in the royal presence—even were his king a King Claudius—smoking cigarettes and tossing off cocktails. Shakespeare may well need to be shaken out of deadening ritual occasionally, but only for the sake of the congregation. There are Mumpsimus priests enough who can also best be reminded what it is all about by a sharp return to the vernacular. A dash of the ridiculous even may have its uses; as the church well knew when it let the Boy Bishop and his mumming have their fling. But a joke's a joke. And, our medicine taken, it can go back to its cupboard till next time.

Barker's implied criterion is the necessity of credibility—as he has said elsewhere, words and action must suit each other. Here, he obviously feels that modern manners, rigidly rather than tactfully dictated by costume, do not fit the play, and that even if they did, the manners portrayed would not be suitable in the particular circumstances. His criticism is interesting for the light it throws on the Savoy productions; it makes clear that Barker does not believe in novelty merely for its own sake, even though he can make a case for its occasional usefulness.[23] Yet again he illustrates his concern for the necessity of compromise between the Elizabethan and the modern: it is not enough to be provocative and original in staging Shakespeare; one must also be sensitive to the needs of the play and the expectations of the audience.

Barker's critiques of productions and of scholarly works complement his own writings on Shakespeare. In 1925, he contributed "A Note upon Chapters XX. and XXI. of [E. K. Chambers's] *The Elizabethan Stage*" to the *Review of English Studies;* these chapters deal with the staging of the plays in the theatre. While Barker admires Chambers's thorough fulfillment of the monumental task he set himself, he takes issue with him on a number of points. Chambers's inadequacies, he feels, arise from too "scientific" an approach, from an exclusion of any of the "irrational" ways of the theatre.[24]

Barker first objects to Chambers's contention that the court was

more influential than the inn-yards in determining modes of Elizabethan staging. Barker argues that the inn-yard method of staging
was dominant and far more significant than the courtly, because it
gave rise to "emotional [i.e., interpretative] acting," which in turn
made drama such a popular art: "Drama ceased to be a show and
became an emotional experience." Instead of recitation, there were
"opportunities for acting, for the vivid realising of character in
action" (p. 62). Barker deduces this development from the fact that
actors and their poetry were the drama's medium; actors and their
emotions its focus. Any aids, such as costumes and properties, were
subordinate to the emphasis on the actors themselves. If one remembers his tracing of Shakespeare's artistic development in "From
Henry V to *Hamlet*," it is clear that Barker has further reasons for his
assertion about the importance of emotional acting, which he leaves
unspoken here; however, his reliance on Shakespeare as an Elizabethan model also points to a possible weakness in his deductions:
were Shakespeare's contemporaries as capable of depicting
"character in action" as Shakespeare? If not, is "emotional acting" as
central to the drama's popularity as Barker claims?

On the whole, I believe that Barker is right. It is clear that Elizabethan drama did depend primarily upon the actor for its effects
rather than upon realistic illusion or any other aids. The physical
relation between the actor and the audience, together with the
conventions of the soliloquy and the aside, suggest that intimacy
played a large part in engaging the audience's response, in suspend-
ing their disbelief. The fact that Shakespeare achieved what perhaps
no one else did does not weaken Barker's points about the direction
drama was taking.

Furthermore, modern research has shown that structurally, the
popular playhouses do owe far more to inn-yard than to courtly
staging, for practical reasons at least. Barker too recognizes these
practical reasons; he does not believe that the Elizabethans "should
deliberately handicap themselves by setting up [only] those two
foolish doors" of the Swan drawing, when they had had the convenient multiple entrances and exits of the inn-yard for a model
(p. 70). Barker in fact criticizes Chambers for showing too much
"misguided allegiance" to the Swan drawing, and suggests that if the
scholar had actually set to work in such a theatre, he would soon
have realized its limitations as a playing space; earlier, he had commented that before dismissing it, Chambers should have set up
boards and hired a mob to test response to inn-yard staging. The
need for a theatrical laboratory, for dramatic experiment, is a theme
Barker constantly expresses, from his first calls for collaboration
between scholars and actors to the end of his career.

Barker's most forceful attack on Chambers concerns the latter's premature understanding of scenery; he points out that Chambers speaks of "'the various types of scene which the sixteenth-century managers were called upon to produce,' of 'the degree of use which they make of a structural background,' of 'a certain number of scenes which make no use of a background at all, and may in a sense be called unlocated scenes' . . . [; however,] 'they were located to the audience, who saw them against a background, although, if they were kept well to the front or side of the stage, their relation to the background would be minimised'" (p. 63). Barker retorts that a sixteenth-century stage manager would not have known what Chambers was talking about: props and locations had an ad hoc existence, the stage was simply a stage. He explains that it would be misleading to say even that Juliet carries the "scene" with her when she descends from the upper stage after the balcony scene and yet is still in her bedroom: there was no scene or sense of locality except that required by the action for immediate effect. As Barker points out time and again, the theatre does not need to be logical; the only necessity is to avoid awkwardness.

Barker sensitively discriminates between location and scene (pp. 63–66). He argues that localization by dialogue does not need scenic reinforcement: since it is unimportant, for example, whether Richard be at Flint or at Barkloughly, the audience need not see one differentiated from the other. Furthermore, precise location can actually disturb illusion; when armies fight on stage, the spectators should not constantly wonder in what part of the battlefield the soldiers are now, or where one action is taking place relative to another. As for uses of location, Barker argues that Shakespeare merely indicates it when information is necessary, while he *employs* it for effect. For example, Shakespeare does not write "Now spurs the 'lated traveller apace,/To gain the timely inn" to inform the audience of the supposed time, but to create an effect of uneasy, threatening dusk before the murder of Banquo; therein lies its importance.

Unusually for the period in which he is writing, Barker does not attribute Shakespeare's "cavalier treatment of background . . . to undeveloped stagecraft"; he argues, for instance, that in *Antony and Cleopatra*, far from being heedless of location, Shakespeare makes "locality . . . of great importance to his scheme. The whole import of the play's action lies in the contrast and clash of Egypt and Rome," and even Parthia is introduced to emphasize "that there are world affairs in hand" (p. 66). He takes issue with Chambers's assertion that in this play Shakespeare's quick shifts of location put him in danger "'of outrunning the apprehension of his auditory'" (p. 68); he rightly points out that the audience only had to listen: nothing visual

clashed with the words they heard. Only when drama moved indoors, where backgrounds could be made more effective by the use
of such aids as light, was there a move to a scenic theatre and the
possibility of visual distraction from or contradiction to the dialogue.
Such a possibility leads Barker to conclude that scenery must allow
the scene and the actor to collaborate; it should not undercut the
actor's words. Shakespeare himself is careful to achieve this balance—as Barker points out, Iachimo only details the contents of
Imogen's chamber "two long scenes" after we have seen him in it
(p. 71).

Finally, Barker criticizes Chambers for being too consistent in
interpreting the meaning of *within, without, above,* and *below* in Elizabethan stage directions, both implicit and explicit. He does not
recognize the problem, as Barker does, of talking about location
both in terms of actual use of the stage and in terms of stage fiction;
for example, Pistol may be "below," but Shallow and Falstaff are
surely on the main stage, not the upper. This stress on consistency
also makes Chambers posit a real wall for Romeo to leap over,
whereas Barker points out that the Elizabethans would have had no
difficulty in hearing that Romeo had leaped over a wall after seeing
him "vanish through a door or behind a curtain." What is important
is that what they hear does not conflict with what they see at the time;
embellishment is possible later, just as it is in the previous example of
the handling of Imogen's bedroom (pp. 70–71).

Barker's criticisms of Chambers vividly illustrate his practical approach to dramatic literature.[25] He handles each text sensitively,
trying to uncover its meaning through its stage effects, its stage
effects through its meaning. Chambers, on the other hand, sche-
matizes both the Elizabethan theatre and the plays presented in it,
reducing them to illustrations of a deduced rule. Such an approach
is too rigid, too "scientific" as Barker would say, for an art as lifelike
as drama. Barker, the supposedly overrational producer, is obviously concerned to correct the excesses of logic in bringing plays to
life.

In 1928, Barker contributed a review of W. J. Lawrence's *The
Physical Conditions of the Elizabethan Public Playhouses* and *Pre-Restoration Stage Studies* to the same journal. As with Chambers, Barker
admires Lawrence as a thoughtful and thorough scholar, yet criticizes him for a devotion to logic which leads to aesthetic quan-
daries.[26] Furthermore, he argues that Lawrence's "intensive study of
stage mechanism . . . carries with it a new tendency to discount
unfairly the Elizabethan theatre's imaginative side" (p. 233).

Barker offers many convincing illustrations to support his queries
of Lawrence's findings. Lawrence spends some time, for example,

trying to discover what the "bulk" was (see *Othello,* V.i.1) and concludes only that it was "some kind of projection from a house" whose exact nature and location must remain unknown. Granville Barker, granting the author, actors, and audience so much "imaginative accommodation," believes the "bulk" was simply any corner, recess, or pillar of the stage appropriate to the action.[27] Likewise, Lawrence believes that " 'Three sunnes [did] appear in the aire' " when called for, merely because of the wording of the stage direction (p. 235). Barker points out that promptbooks are notoriously haphazard, since they may include actual effects, notes on interpretation, the conditions at a particular theatre, and the prompter's own personal preferences in recording information: what is written in a promptbook, asserts Barker, is not "certain evidence of what actually happened on the stage" (p. 234). Thus, these three suns may only refer to something the actor pretends to see, rather than to what the audience actually does see; in fact, it would be easier to believe they actually appeared if the instructions read simply " 'Sunnes appear' " or " 'Show sunnes.' " For parallels, Barker points out that no lantern would have represented the moon when Kent says "Approach, thou Beacon to this under-globe . . ." and that Lawrence himself "rightly dismisses Macbeth's and Banquo's horses to the limbo of Dr. Simon Forman's carelessness or imagination" (p. 235). Lawrence, like Chambers, is too consistent in his interpretation of stage directions; Barker suggests that if he had only compared the notes of modern prompters, he would have learned more than he did by "tedious reconstruction of their [Elizabethan] 'remains,' " again making the point that practical experience of the theatre is necessary for true evaluation of a text (p. 233).

Barker extends this argument to sound effects; theatre terminology is always "inexact." Thus, he dismisses the noise of a sea fight, the exact nature of which Lawrence tries to discover: "I suspect it differed mainly from the noise of a land-fight by the addition of 'Avasts' and 'Belays' " (p. 235). Similarly, the " 'noise of driving cattle without,' " which also worries Lawrence, is "probably reduced to a 'Gee up' and a whip-crack or so." Barker supports his contention by reference to known eighteenth-century practice—thunder, lightning, and rain were all reproduced in the theatre, "but on drums or a metal sheet in the wings" (p. 235).

Lawrence spends a great deal of time discussing the use of traps on the Elizabethan stage, and Barker judges his research thorough and conclusions mainly right. However, Lawrence's discussion of the subject is full of traps "of more than one sort," and he amusingly illustrates those into which Lawrence falls. For example, Lawrence argues that the Ghost in *Hamlet* makes his first exit through a trapdoor six feet deep; Barker retorts by asking us to imagine the reaction of the audience when the ghost reappears, having just seen the actor fling himself down a six-foot trap in broad daylight. Barker does agree that the Ghost probably *did* "travel up and down a bit, and the final sinking at

> Adieu, adieu, adieu, remember me,

has all the warrant of dramatic suggestion." However, the suggestion is one of a somewhat less violent exit than the one Lawrence proposes (p. 237).

Barker's best example of the limitations of Lawrence's inductive skills is from *Romeo and Juliet:*

> Does he really wish us to think that Juliet in her tomb was below stage and out of sight, that Romeo lowered the dead Paris on the top of her, and addressed his farewell speech—to a hole? And all because, by one stage direction, "Juliet rises"! (Pp. 236–37)

As Barker admirably sums up, Lawrence "is shrewd and skilful at induction. But the theatre is inconsequence itself. It laughs at logic" (p. 236). Barker illustrates the obverse side of the coin as well: if one applies too rigid a rule of logic to the theatre, it becomes ridiculous, losing its own dramatic logic, as in the scene imagined above.[28]

Barker's next project was the revision of his prefaces to *The Players' Shakespeare;* they appeared between 1927 and 1947 as *Prefaces to Shakespeare* and are still generally regarded as the soundest dramatic criticism of Shakespeare's plays.[29] Not surprisingly, very little of this work is out-of-date despite several decades' advances in methods of production and schools of interpretation: Barker always rooted himself firmly within the play and the limits it set for itself. His discussions focus on what the play says and how best to express that dramatically, on what the play demands dramatically and how that reveals its meaning. His insistence on discovering dramatic truth makes valuable his insights (for example, into the effects of juxtaposing two scenes or characters) long after Bradley's psychological fleshing-out of characters appears an astute but pointless exercise. For Barker, a play is never a novel manqué.

Barker's general introduction to the *Prefaces* repeats the same points, often in the same words, of the earlier introduction.[30] However, his organization is much more systematic, the essay being divided into several sections: "The Study and the Stage," "Shakespeare's Stagecraft," "The Convention of Place," "The Speaking of the Verse," "The Boy-Actress," "The Soliloquy," "Costume," and

"The Integrity of the Text." Barker's concerns here are identical to those voiced in his previous essays; the new introduction does not substantially expand the ideas of the original. Its importance lies rather in its succinct and clear comprehensiveness; it serves as an index of Barker's views to date. About that rather ambiguous "character in action," for example, Barker now says simply: "All great drama tends to concentrate upon character; and, even so, not upon picturing men as they show themselves to the world like figures on a stage—though that is how it must ostensibly show them—but on the hidden man" (p. 7). His many points about the nature of Elizabethan place and the function of modern scenery are summarized in the following way:

> When we learn with a shock of surprise . . . [that Shakespeare's stage had no scenery], we yet imagine ourselves among the audience there busily conjuring . . . up [battlements, throne rooms, picturesque churchyards] before the eye of faith. The Elizabethan audience was at no such pains. Nor was this their alternative to seeing the actors undisguisedly concerned with the doors, curtains and balconies which, by the play's requirements, should have been anything but what they were. As we, when a play has no hold on us, may fall to thinking about the scenery, so to a Globe audience, unmoved, the stage might be an obvious bare stage. But are we conscious of the scenery behind the actor when the play really moves us? If we are, there is something very wrong with the scenery, which should know its place as a background. (Pp. 8–9)

Explaining his ideas about the relation of scenery, location, and actor, Barker uses the point he made about the Actium scenes of *Antony and Cleopatra* in his criticism of Chambers: "Had Shakespeare tried to define the whereabouts of every scene in any but the baldest phrases . . . he would have had to lengthen and complicate them; had he written only a labeling line or two he would still have distracted his audience from the essential drama. Ignoring whereabouts, letting it at most transpire when it naturally will, the characters capture all attention" (p. 10). He offers the sound advice that since Shakespeare's own practice was neither logical nor consistent, varying "with the play he is writing and the particular stage he is writing for [, the use of location] . . . will best be studied in relation to each play" (p. 8). The last sentence serves as a model of Barker's approach to every aspect of a play.

One point Barker does elaborate in this introduction is the dislike of modern-dress productions first voiced in his review of Barry Jackson's *Hamlet:* "It is a false logic which suggests that to match [the plays'] first staging we should dress them in the costume of ours. For with costume goes custom and manners" (p. 17). Barker recognizes that such costuming may heighten intimacy between actors and audience, but that the price paid is too high in terms of credibility: "Why . . . [should] a young man in a dinner jacket search . . . for a sword—a thing not likely to be lying about in his modern mother's sitting room—with which to kill Polonius, who certainly has window curtains to hide behind instead of [an] arras?" (p. 18). In this discussion, Barker makes explicit his belief that consistency in dress and speech is necessary for dramatic credibility—a belief he merely implies in his review of "*Hamlet* in Plus-Fours." He expands the importance of "the commonplace traffic of life" in Shakespeare's plays:

> However wide the spoken word may range, there must be the actor, anchored to the stage. However high . . . the thought or emotion may soar, we shall always find the transcendental set in the familiar. [Shakespeare] keeps this balance constantly adjusted; and, at his play's greatest moments, when he must make most sure of our response, he will employ the simplest means. The higher arguments of the plays are thus kept always within range, and their rooted humanity blossoms in a fertile upspringing of expressive little things. Neglect or misinterpret these, the inner wealth of Shakespeare will remain, no doubt, and we may mine for it, but we shall have leveled his landscape bare. (P. 20)

Barker's points are valid, both for the time he is writing and now, but their application has changed in regard to modern-dress productions. The audience's familiarity with Shakespeare in a contemporary setting leads to a willingness to suspend disbelief in the unlikely joining of sixteenth-century language and twentieth-century manners and dress; they must, however, be joined as tactfully as possible.[31]

Finally, besides stating once again that "the speaking of the verse must be the foundation of all study" (p. 12), Barker indicates the need to study ways of speaking it "in relation to the verse's own development":

> The actor must not attack its supple complexities in *Antony and Cleopatra* and *Cymbeline*, the mysterious dynamics of *Macbeth*, the nobilities of *Othello*, its final pastoral simplicities in *A [sic] Winter's Tale* and *The Tempest* without preliminary training in the lyricism, the swift brilliance and the masculine [sic] clarity of the earlier plays. . . . [W]ithout an ear trained to the delicacy of the earlier work, his hearers, for their part, will never know how shamefully he is betraying the superb ease of the later.

Barker's point about the need to train audience as well as actor is not a new one, but his recommendation that an actor not attempt delivery of Shakespeare's later verse without ample experience of the earlier marks a practical development of his theories about verse-speaking.

On Dramatic Method, the Clark Lectures for 1930, appeared in print the following year.[32] In this series of lectures for Trinity College, Cambridge, Barker explores the nature of drama and its successful expression. He very early declares himself against the formulation of dramatic rules; as a practicing playwright, he recognizes the stultifying effects of writing to convention. The only "laws" worth heeding are the theatre's own: a play should have vitality, and the audience should be able to respond to it spontaneously rather than cerebrally.

Barker devotes much discussion to the interpretation of character. He believes that the actor and dramatist must collaborate; that the actor must recreate character in terms of her or his own personality (pp. 20–21): a "fully achieved character . . . paradoxically enough . . . can be given a dozen different personalities and [be] interpreted from nearly as many different points of view, and yet remain essentially the same character" (p. 27). One example of such a character is Hamlet:

> It is said that no actor ever fails as Hamlet. . . . Shakespeare has somehow contrived to distil so much humanity into the fiction, that at a touch, at the lively speaking of a line, it wells up and overflows; he has shown so many sides of the man that no actor . . . can fail to reflect a few of them. (P. 27)

Barker, however, recognizes that no actor in a single performance can give us the whole of so complex a character.

His recognition leads to a slight reappraisal of Bradley. Barker feels his analysis of *Othello* is "masterly" and textually justified, but that his supersubtle interpretations of Othello and Iago are not conveyable on stage. Barker quickly adds that he does not mean a play can be too good for the theatre, but that one must accept drama's limitations as a means of depicting humanity; no one actor *can* convey the whole of a character. Conversely, if performance does not bring out the best in a play—and that "best" does not mean ideal or perfect, but what is realizable through the "imperfect medium of humanity", then the play itself is "useless". One must accept the imperfections inherent in the art of drama (pp. 28–29).

The part language plays in the realization of character forms a second theme in this lecture series. Good dramatic dialogue will tell the story, disclose character, and stimulate the audience's imaginations and emotions, thus precluding the need for reliance on formal artifice. Obviously, such dialogue must be skillfully written; as Barker asserts, the stage should never present casual conversation, but only the effect of it. And when "magic" is needed in speech, poetry will provide it.

Barker expands his ideas about poetry in drama by reference to Shakespeare. Making the point that poetry should be like music, graceful and easy to speak or sing, he turns to Shakespeare's uses of it. He emphasizes that Shakespeare never rhymes by rule, but always for an immediate effect; similarly, very few scenes are written wholly in verse. Taking *Romeo and Juliet* as an example, Barker discusses poetic function: Capulet's "fussings and bridlings" in blank verse established the "verbal backbone" of the scene, against which Romeo's rhyming "ecstasy at his first sight of Juliet" stands out. Shakespeare also uses rhyme to give "precision and importance" to Tybalt in this scene (p. 49). Turning to the first meeting of the lovers themselves, Barker explains how Shakespeare fits metrical form to dramatic use.[33] The sonnet the lovers exchange, fated in its "rounded completeness," is also formal, setting them apart from the rest of the characters and action: "All their innocence is in the manner, as the religion of their love is in the matter of it" (p. 49). The proportions of the sonnet are also balanced; Barker points out that each of the lovers speaks four lines, then one, after which Romeo, the wooer, speaks a couplet. The last couplet is shared, and the sonnet ends with a kiss (p. 50).

Besides being used for specific effect, poetry can also be used for characterization. Barker explains that verse is not dramatic when neither the sense nor the sound of the words tells us which character is speaking and what kind of person s/he is; for example, Benvolio and Montague, heralding Romeo's approach, are hardly distinguishable. On the other hand, the Nurse's speech is very characteristic; Barker details her curt syllables, monotonous meter "just saved from monotony by irregularities" (p. 69), favoring of one-syllable words, slurring of longer words, and use of regular meter for self-assertion. As he points out, Shakespeare's verse is most rich and free when his creation of character is most complete. When it is not, it usually does not matter, as in the example above where Benvolio and Montague speak the same kind of language. A dramatist like Marlowe, however, refuses to sacrifice the integrity of his poetry to the dramatic demands of the play; as Barker remarks, three-quarters of Tamburlaine's speeches, judged by style, could just as appropriately be spoken by any other character, while some, like the "marvellous threnody upon Zenocrate," do not suit him at all (p. 57). Such lack of distinctive speech inevitably leads to loss of dramatic life in the creation of character.

Barker glances at play after play, illustrating Shakespeare's organic, rather than formal, use of poetry. In *A Midsummer Night's*

Dream, it creates both character and the forest in which the action takes place (p. 72); in *Hamlet,* it is absolutely essential for revealing the "innermost of the man" (p. 88). Barker makes clear that successful verse must be absorbed into the purpose of the play, that it must be a "transparent" medium drawing attention not to itself but to the matter it embodies.[34] Obviously, such a demand calls for sensitive delivery; Barker points out, for example, that regularity of meter should be no guide to speaking it: "I am dying, Egypt, dying" will lose all its beauty and power if spoken according to its measured stresses (p. 109). Extending the argument about regularity to the form of Shakespeare's plays, Barker emphasizes that it is not formulaic construction that gives the plays their power, rather their variations in tone and pace, changes of scene, similarities and differences in characters, heightening and relaxation of tension, alternations of climax and anticlimax.

Barker's brief discussion of *Measure for Measure* is interesting. He regards the play as something of a failure because character is sacrificed to plot, and consequently, plot fails to convince; he adds that the reverse situation, of plot sacrificed to character, would matter little in terms of dramatic life: "Our passage [into a play's world] . . . depend[s] far more upon what the inhabitants authentically are than upon the things they do" (pp. 99–100). These few remarks show again how strongly Barker feels character to be the basis of all drama: a reflection of his own concerns as a dramatist rather than an uncritical acceptance of contemporary views.[35] Yet even here, Barker's own advice that it is risky to generalize about Shakespeare (pp. 111–12) must have helped him to sense that, in some plays, Shakespeare's main interest is the exploration of an idea or problem rather than of character: the play's "powerful concentration upon a theme counts for much; the play's purpose holds us." Despite his lack of full appreciation for the play, Barker is still ahead of his time in gauging Shakespeare's intent, in recognizing that *Measure for Measure* is the "beginning of a new [chapter]" for Shakespeare, just as *Hamlet* is the end of one (p. 100).

In 1930, Barker was elected president of the Shakespeare Association. His presidential address was delivered at King's College, London, in November 1931 and published the following year as *Associating with Shakespeare.*[36] Here, he sets his concern for discovering Shakespeare's stagecraft in the context of previous criticism:

> Coleridge, rescuing his ideal Shakespeare from the cavilling commonsense of the eighteenth century, set us all star-gazing. One cannot well overrate what his divination did for our possession of Shakespeare the poet. . . . [But f]rom Coleridge springs our En-

glish school of metaphysical closet-criticism, which . . . set . . .
Shakespeare the man of the theatre aside altogether. . . . (Pp. 9–
10)

Barker adds that sole concentration on Shakespeare the seventeenth-century playwright provides a necessary corrective to former
neglect, but that "the point of rest" between the two views is ultimately essential: one must understand Shakespeare both as poet
and as dramatist. And in order to concern oneself with the Shakespeare "who was more than seventeenth-century playwright," one
must remember the maxim that is the basis of all Barker's discussion:
separate the essentials from the accidentals of Shakespeare's stagecraft (p. 17).

The second "capital obligation" Barker lays down in the "search
for a method which will, as nearly as may be, restore the authentic
Shakespeare" to the theatre regards the audience; once more, he
stresses that the play must be presented in a way that enables the
audience to respond to it spontaneously. Barker comes to emphasize
more and more that spontaneity, the result of unself-consciousness
on the part of actors and audience, is a sine qua non of dramatic
enjoyment. If the actors cannot surrender themselves to the characters, nor the audience to the emotional impact, the play is no longer
living drama, but a museum piece (p. 18).

Barker, however, is not naive about the need to develop such
unself-consciousness in regard to noncontemporary plays: one must
cultivate "an historic sense of Shakespeare's art" in order "to respond, with sufficient spontaneity, to the kind of illusion upon which
it counts." Although Barker gives no specific examples, one can
readily imagine the Elizabethan conventions one must learn: the
impenetrability of disguise (Polixenes and Florizel) and the possibility of perfect concealment (Beatrice and Benedick, Sir Toby and
the other plotters) are two obvious examples. Once one attains this
knowledge, all that is necessary is "a readiness to respond" to the
plays themselves, and this "intimacy with the art of drama itself"
(p. 24) is more important than any knowledge.

The note on which Barker ends is a challenging one; besides
recognizing Elizabethan essentials and conventions, one must also
recognize inadequacies: "In what makes these plays great Shakespeare did outrun the resources of his theatre and . . . the certain
capacities of his actors."[37] Therefore, on this level alone, there is "no
mere demand for a reconstruction of the past . . . but new work for
a[n alert and alive] theatre" (pp. 26–27). In order to meet "Shakespeare's challenge to the future," a sensitive director should review
his staging methods—for example, armies should not march around

in puppetlike fashion and the savagery of Nature in *Lear* need not be
represented so visually. But even more important is the delivery of
the verse; if the "beauty and power . . . of the mysteriously dynamic
poetry of [the] later plays" were properly expressed, it would take
away concern for any "further illusion":

> Whatever may lie beyond this satisfaction—the mere mechanical
> part of the business, the staging and costuming—will prove . . . to
> be a simple affair. But give me this [delivery], and I will not
> complain if I get more. (P. 28)

Barker remained president of the Shakespeare Association for a
number of years, and during this time his office brought him into
close contact with G. B. Harrison, the Honorable Secretary of the
society. The two corresponded for a number of years about Shakespeare Association business and also jointly edited *A Companion to
Shakespeare Studies.* While Barker's letters to Harrison generally concern mundane administration of the Association, they do occasionally illuminate his preoccupations and concerns about the study of
Shakespeare.[38]

Barker was eager to establish a "comprehensive ten years programme" of pamphlets and lectures for the association; he suggests
planning should start with "a survey of what has been done and
(more particularly) what remains to be done to give us a complete
view of the drama and the theatre and its audience as these were
when alive, from the opening of the Theatre to the closing of the
theatres" (12.30.30). Such a "complete view" involves much more
than investigation only of the drama itself, as his letters and indeed
his own *Companion* make clear; Barker wanted to establish a broad
context for the study of drama, to discover as much background
information about its age as possible. Thus, he strongly supports
Harrison's plan to commission facsimiles of "a series of rare texts
illustrating life and thought in Shakespeare's England."[39] In all,
fifteen texts were reproduced between 1931 and 1938; they deal with
a number of subjects of contemporary interest, from witchcraft to
plague to tobacco. Some are discourses on the arts of fencing and
hunting; some deal with almost sociological subjects, such as the
status of servants and the life of an executed thief. Works of philosophy and of theatrical satire were also reproduced, as were news
pamphlets and ballads. Each text is accompanied by an introduction;
in the case of Silver's *Paradoxes of Defence,* a work about fencing, J.
Dover Wilson speculates in his introduction about the light it sheds
on the fencing match in *Hamlet.*

While this series was produced under Harrison's general editorship, it does reflect Barker's own approach to Shakespeare studies and had his full support. One project Barker himself tried very hard to initiate was a full-scale study of the Blackfriars Theatre, which would encompass an examination of the transition from outdoor to indoor staging in the period 1610 to 1640; he planned a book of approximately ten articles by various contributors, dealing with the Blackfriars company, playwrights, plays, stage, machinery, scenery, music, and audience. Staging was to be examined through an intensive study of plays written specifically for the Blackfriars Theatre and only performed there, together with plays adapted for its stage. Similarly, Barker hoped to show how the theatre worked not just in performance but in its wider life: what kinds of rehearsals were held; how often plays were performed, how often changed; whether actors memorized parts or were prompted; what the company's business considerations were; what changes occurred in actors' economic status (3.21.31; 7.26.31). Although Barker did not succeed in realizing this project, the plan itself witnesses the scope of Barker's ideal scholarship: one may focus on the play itself, responding to it on its own terms, but one must bring to the play both a deep knowledge of the theatre of the time and a wider appreciation of its place in society.

Barker's letters to Harrison clearly demonstrate his commitment to thorough scholarship. Time and again, he mentions the need to encourage young scholars, often suggesting specific people who might be commissioned to research certain projects; as often, he asserts the need to engage American scholars in the work being done in England. His attitude shows a real openness to varied approaches; he is committed to no party line on Shakespeare (12.30.30). Indeed, the preface to A Companion makes explicit his commitment to diversity of opinion: "The editors . . . have made no attempt to reconcile the opinions of their collaborators. . . . [T]he utmost agreement desired was upon this way of approach."[40]

The role of the Shakespeare Association, as Barker sees it, should be the provision of useful "tools" for students. Thus, he favors projects such as Harrison's facsimiles, the Blackfriars volume, and bibliographies of the works of scholars like W. J. Lawrence and E. K. Chambers. However, he does not feel the association should reprint its own lectures and papers, his own included: "Pleasant reading: but I don't feel that they are—unless very exceptionally—*tools* for the Shakespearean student" (6.28.35). He feels that the papers might properly belong in an annual, like the *Shakespeare Jahrbuch*, which England lacks, but given the work still to be done, such a book is not a priority. A record of the work done on Shakespeare each year is much to be preferred.

Barker emerges from these letters as a committed scholar, diffident about his own abilities and rigorous in his standards. His letter congratulating Harrison on his Penguin edition of *Hamlet* (4.24.35) is generous in its praise and yet almost niggling in its criticism. Having praised it as "*far* the best thing of its sort that has yet been done," Barker criticizes three points. First, as can be expected, he "carps" about the prominent display given the spurious act I heading and wishes a point had been made about act divisions existing only for reference purposes. Second, he criticizes Harrison's explanation of the nunnery scene. In a note to "Where's your father?" Harrison explains that Hamlet's jealousy of a supposed rival is confirmed when the arras moves; according to Ophelia, Polonius is at home, and thus Hamlet thinks "it must be the lover" behind the curtain. Barker criticizes this explanation not only because the text gives no support for it, but also because the actor would not be able to "give the slightest hint of it." Barker's final criticism, which he describes as "unimportant," regards fact: he writes that the play's act divisions were first completed in the Players Quarto of 1676 and not in the eighteenth century, as Harrison states; Barker's authority is "the latest (but one) important work on the play." The points Barker makes are worth noting: they show him as a stickler for thoroughness and accuracy, current in his reading of scholarship, aware of the relative unimportance of some of his fastidiousness but unapologetically critical when performance cannot confirm commentary. It is clearly wrong to view Barker as merely a producer's critic or a Bradleyan interpreter of character.

As has been mentioned, Barker's and Harrison's *Companion to Shakespeare Studies* reflects the broad range Barker believed necessary for the proper study of drama; their contributors produced essays on historical and social as well as theatrical background. An essay on Shakespeare's life restricts itself to facts, omitting popular conjecture about Shakespeare's dark and happy periods. Several essays deal with particular aspects of Shakespeare's art: his dramatic development, poetry, texts, sources. Other articles examine his achievements in their contemporary context: his use of language and of music, his relation to the drama of his time. In addition, there are short histories of Shakespearean criticism and scholarship, as well as of Shakespeare in the theatre. Appendixes provide chronological tables of contemporary books, plays, and important events, together with an explanation of prices in Shakespeare's time. In short, the volume aims to provide the contemporary background necessary to begin to understand Shakespeare, whether one is a specialist student or an interested playgoer. The volume's thoroughness is reflected by the fact that the *New Companion* follows this same pattern but brings it up to date.[41]

Barker's own contribution to the volume is an essay entitled "Shakespeare's Dramatic Art."[42] As one can surmise from the title, this essay does not contain many points not already found elsewhere in Barker's work; however, many of his cherished ideas about Shakespeare are here given a wider context. For example, his contention that Shakespeare established a new art of acting is discussed through a more thorough comparison of *Hamlet* to *Tamburlaine*, while Shakespeare's use of place is illustrated by reference to *Edward II* as well as to *Richard II*. Thus, Barker more forcefully indicates ways in which Shakespeare is a product of contemporary conventions and ways in which he transcends them.

The idea of poetic drama is also developed more fully in this essay than it has been previously. Barker virtually begins the essay by reference to it: the secret of Shakespeare's success

> lies . . . in the very conception and genesis of whatever idea is to find pervasive expression in the play. A poetic idea, dramatically conceived. The fruit of it . . . will be not drama written in the form of poetry, but something we can truly call poetic drama— which is a very different thing. (P. 46)

Barker later clarifies his belief that the dramatic idea generally concerns character:

> As [Shakespeare's] powers ripen, he turns them more and more to the elucidation of character and develops his stagecraft almost wholly to that end. . . .
> . . . His capital discovery . . . is that physical action in itself and by itself is the least effective thing upon [the] stage. . . . The why and the wherefore, what went before and what is to come after, those are what count. They are the fruitful stuff of drama. From which it soon follows that not rhetoric merely or mainly, nor what may be openly said, but the thing only thought or felt will need to be expressed. (Pp. 67–68)

Barker elaborates all the ways Shakespeare reveals such thoughts and feelings (p. 70); obviously, the soliloquy is one of them. Shakespeare also streamlines his writing, so that action or movement exists not for its own sake, but to express character or theme—for example, the frenzied movements of Hamlet between the end of "The Mousetrap" and his capture by the guards (pp. 70–71). Description, too, either merges into the action or expresses a character's mood; the opening of *Hamlet* with its "quick confused exchange between sentries" evokes "the hour and its darkness . . . [better than] a page of description of the chill, boding, [punctuation: *sic*] silence . . ." (p. 72).

Poetry also plays an important part in revealing character, as Barker has already written elsewhere. But here he emphasizes its integral function in the play:

> Form apart, here will be words wielding something like absolute power. It is true poetic drama, not merely drama in poetic form, that he is writing now. He can project a character in a single line. When Antony's Octavia says:
>
>> The Jove of power make me most weak, most weak,
>> Your reconciler,
>
> sense, tune and rhythm combine to reveal her to us. (P. 75)

Though Barker does not define "poetic drama" either here or at the beginning of the essay, his examples enable one to grasp his meaning. Poetic drama seems to be an organic union of character, idea, action, and language, each component so expressive of the next that separation is unthinkable, even impossible: thus the difference between poetic drama and drama merely written in poetic form. The resonance of this union gives Shakespeare's plays what Barker calls "the inner commerce of the scene," where so much more than external action is revealed (see pp. 75–76); the power this cohesion gives the play enables the audience to respond in the way Barker feels necessary:

> The art of the drama makes a primary demand upon us: to leave our armchair throne of judgment and descend into the mellay [*sic*] of contradictory passions—which the action of a play is—and submit for the while to be tossed to and fro in it. . . . [D]rama's first aim is to subdue us by submitting us emotionally to the give and take, the rough and tumble, of some illusion of life. (P. 86)

For Barker, this submission is a means of educating the human spirit—a point he makes clear in all his writing and most fully elaborates in his early book, *The Exemplary Theatre*.[43] This volume grew out of his commitment to the establishment of a national theatre; in it, he articulates his view that the theatre can, and should, be an "educational force" in the community (p. 1). However, Barker moves beyond the obvious value of drama in exploring current political and social ideas; he demonstrates that it can "produce a greater number of more fully and freely developed . . . and more cooperative human beings" (pp. 36–37).

Barker explains how the theatre's demand for collaboration—among dramatists, actors, and audiences—gives it its educative value (p. 73); as he points out, drama is an art where the "expression of the single self is inadequate," where egotism must be set aside (p. 48). For instance, the company must collaborate in determining the meaning of the play; actors must interpret their roles, striking a balance between imposing their own personalities on the characters and being wholly taken over by them (pp. 242 & 246); and the audience itself must be "highly attuned" (p. 253), ready to engage in the play's experience—with the actors and each other—rather than to watch it passively. Thus, drama aids both personal and social development: "Unity *in* diversity . . . must be our social ideal, and it is this that drama in its very nature does expound and, through the sympathetic power of impersonation, interpret" (p. 128). In other words, drama expands the narrowness of individual experience, giving us a "second self" (p. 129), as well as "vicarious experience that may almost stand for personal illumination" (p. 287). For Barker, then, plays are never mere artistic creations, technical achievements, or historical illustrations, but a shared experience which can

> evolve from the sentient mass a finer mind, responding to the fine fellow-mind of the poet, expressed in terms of a common experience through the medium of human beings, whose art has that significance that we find in the faces and voices of friends with whom we have come through the gates of understanding. This is the ideal, and towards it the paths are many. (P. 288)

One of these paths is, of course, poetic drama, and Barker returns to its exploration in *On Poetry in Drama;* here, he makes explicit what can be inferred from "Shakespeare's Dramatic Art."[44] The relationship between poetry and drama is an interdependent one: Barker can speak both of poetic drama and of dramatic poetry. For him, the poet is one who "deals always with the inwardness of things, treating appearances as the mere clothing for that. . . . [I]n the theatre, where so much can be made of externals, appearance will tend to be everything, unless the dramatist can contrive to give greater value to what should lie behind it. And the dramatist who can do this, by whatever means, is a poet" (pp. 11–12). Thus, for Barker, drama is poetic when it concerns inner being, when it deals "—as poetry in its essence does—with the things that are immortal" (p. 42).

Barker goes on to explain the importance of poetry in fulfilling this "poetic" function of drama. As he implies in "Shakespeare's Dramatic Art," drama has a "fourfold language . . . of words and action, situation and presented character" (p. 30), and the four are, or should be, inextricably linked:

> To consider verbal expression alone, we need some use of words of a more than rational power. Because with presentation of

character involved, it is a question not merely of what a man thinks he knows about himself (or whatever part of that, rather, he may be willing to disclose; and a very partial and misleading revelation this would be!), but, added to this, and by far the more important, the things about himself he does *not* know. All of which things, diverse and sometimes contradictory, must be expressed at one and the same time (for even comment by other characters must be justified by the character itself) and (lest illusion by broken) in one and the same fashion. We need a language, then, capable of expressing thought and emotion combined, and, at times, emotion almost divorced from thought. It is plain that a merely rational vocabulary and syntax will not suffice. (Pp. 33–34)

It is also plain how poetry provides the necessary suprarational language:

The poet knows how to work on his hearers by subtler ways; openly by the melody and rhythm of words, more powerfully by suggestion, association, by stimulating our imagination. He appeals, past reason, past consciousness often, to our entire sentient being. (P. 34)

Barker here goes beyond a formal definition of poetry to a functional one. The poetry he praises would not necessarily be recognized as such when removed from its context. For example, he commends the "significant and memorable phrase" that rivets together the play's "structure of idea and character"; in Shakespeare, this takes the form of connected images: *Hamlet*'s references to weeds and flowers, *Macbeth*'s to darkness, blood, and offended Nature (p. 35). (Such expressions also serve to "keep us in mind of characters who pass out of sight," who still exist though they are absent from the stage.) Similarly, Shakespeare uses phrases that can sum up an entire situation or reveal a whole character; Barker quickly points out, however, that these are neither isolated brilliancies nor epigrams but are "rooted in the soil of character or play" (p. 36). For example, Coriolanus's "I banish you," summing up his "fatal pride," is flung out "at the crisis of his fate, when he himself is striving to find expression for what he means unshakeably to be. Its dramatic validity and tremendous effect lie in that" (pp. 38–39). Poetry for Barker, then, is not merely verse, but the organic expression of character; only sometimes will such expression depend upon formal poetry.

Although Barker speaks of the "fourfold language of drama," it is by now clear that, for him, character and idea (or situation) are paramount; language and action are means of expressing the other two. Barker briefly discusses the importance of character patterns as another way of revealing a play's meaning:

Of [characters'] relations to each other[, the successful dramatist] will have learnt to make one sufficingly significant pattern—pattern of character being, incidentally, the most useful of all these dramatic patterns, since it is fundamentally effective. (Pp. 31–32)

He likens the character pattern to a painting's composition, "each figure doing double duty, to itself, and by setting off the others"; thus, such a pattern will be three-dimensional, "since both extent of action and depth of character are involved in it" (p. 32). He continues, citing *Othello* and *Macbeth* as examples: "Great plays will always . . . be balanced constructions of character" (p. 32).

With the exception of the *Prefaces*, which he continued to write until his death, *On Poetry in Drama* was Barker's last major work dealing with Shakespeare. From 1937 on, Barker's published work on Shakespeare was confined to broadcasts and to scholarly reviews, a combination which shows his dedication both to serious academic study and to popularization of Shakespeare. As has been mentioned, Barker saw drama as a means of educating, in the broadest sense, all those who produce, study, and view it; in *The Perennial Shakespeare*, he made it clear that the study and production of Shakespeare is valuable as a means of improving "the whole standard of our drama, old and new, in its writing and its acting." To this end, Barker spent much of his energy trying to organize a national theatre, for "a theatre organised for the production of masterpieces will bring quality of distinction to whatever it does" (p. 27).

Considering Barker's desire for wide appreciation of Shakespeare, it may seem strange that in a 1937 broadcast for the BBC, later printed as "Alas, Poor Will!" in *The Listener,* he criticized the adaptation of Shakespeare to film and radio. His position, however, does not proceed from the knee-jerk instincts of a purist—as Alfred Hitchcock intimates in a rebuttal—but from carefully thought-out and familiar reasons.[45]

Barker begins by recognizing the difference between Shakespeare in the cinema as it is and as "theoretically it might be" (p. 387), but questions whether Shakespeare's "medium and the cinema's have . . . [anything] that really matters in common" (p. 389).[46] He concludes that they do not:

The cinema must put its best foot forward. . . . That foot is picture-making. Shakespeare either does not want pictures; or, if he does, he makes them in his own fashion, which is not the cinema's. All question of quality apart, the two arts are in their nature and their methods, it seems to me, radically and fatally opposed. (P. 425)

Thus, the whole question of picturesque scenery and its adverse effects is once again raised: it duplicates the verse, distracts attention from meaning, and involves the adaptation of story and character to its own advantage (p. 389). The consequence "is the maximum of effort made for a minimum of dramatic result" (p. 388).

Such emphasis on the moving picture blunts the effects of the poetry and distorts the play's meaning, but also limits the audience's response:

> Shakespeare, by asking us to conjure up this picture [Macbeth's castle] in our mind's eye by aid of his poetry, is exercising our imagination upon simple things, so that later on he may make more important demands on it. And if we have not imaginatively responded to the simple demand, where shall we be when it comes to:
>
>> Pity, like a naked new-born babe,
>> Striding the blast, or heaven's cherubin, horsed
>> Upon the sightless couriers of the air . . .
>
> Will the film-producer of Macbeth try to help us out by an accompanying picture of *that?* (P. 425; ellipsis Barker's)

Barker concludes that "Shakespeare in the cinema will do—with Shakespeare left out": that is, films should steal Shakespeare's stories (p. 425) just as Shakespeare borrowed the plots of prose writers and shaped them to his own ends; he would, one feels, have approved the success of *West Side Story*.

Hitchcock's facetious assault on Barker, who sees only "words" where the cinema sees stage directions, is not persuasive; he dismisses Barker as "firmly convinced that the only thing that matters about Shakespeare is the poetry" (p. 448), which clearly misses the relevance of Barker's points. He rather lamely concludes that the cinema is, and should be, entertaining, and that it can therefore popularize Shakespeare. Barker, however, would question the value of popularizing a falsification.

Barker's position is nevertheless assailable, and from a quarter he himself partly foresaw: films need not concentrate on the moving picture where Shakespeare is concerned. For example, one of the most successful adaptations of play to screen is the version of Trevor Nunn's 1976 *Macbeth* filmed for television; like the stage production, its sole concern is the text. It makes use of no picturesque background whatsoever; the actors emerge from a placeless black, which together with a sensitive use of close-ups and varied camera angles achieves an intense intimacy that mundane live productions often fail to reach. But even a more conventionally realistic treatment of Shakespeare on the screen does not necessarily alter a play's essence; anyone who saw Zeffirelli's *Romeo and Juliet* is more likely to remember the poignancy of the lovers' situation and their youth than the background scenery. But Barker is right in seeing that the demands of the motion picture will often, though not necessarily, lead to scenic excess.

Barker's feeling about radio versions of Shakespeare is more complex, since this medium is "not . . . demonstrably at cross-purposes with Shakespeare" (p. 425); obviously, it offers no distractions to the spoken word and certainly suits some of the earlier plays that depend on "sheer beauty of speech" (p. 426). However, as Barker points out, "the physical absence of the actors . . . is more than a loss of the mere sight of them": it makes it harder to sustain interest in the characters, it makes it difficult to note the silent characters, and it deprives one of the shared emotion between actors and audience that, to Barker, is the basis of the theatrical experience (p. 425).[47] Actors, too, may be tempted to convey too much by voice alone, which can often lead to exaggeration, though Barker also recognizes an advantage in not having to play to a bad or demoralizing audience.

Barker's views on the limitations of radio and film presentations of Shakespeare once again demonstrate his concern for the integrity of Shakespeare's intentions; his objections are not the result of a thoughtless insistence on custom and convention but of a careful examination of ways in which a new form may or may not embody the spirit of the plays.

Barker's work on Shakespeare was recognized as important in his own lifetime. His early work is summarized in Augustus Ralli's *A History of Shakespearian Criticism* (1932), while the second series of the *Prefaces* were hailed by G. B. Harrison as "the most important contribution to Shakespearean criticism since Bradley's volume on the four great tragedies . . . appeared in 1904." Both Harrison and Hardin Craig affirm that Barker's work explores what was seen as one of the most worthwhile areas of scholarship at the time: a study of the text in relation to the stage; Craig also places Barker's *Players' Shakespeare* among the most notable editions. Only L. C. Knights in *Scrutiny* questions the value of Barker's approach; his review of *A Companion to Shakespeare Studies* criticizes the volume for its failure to relate Shakespeare's work to the present day, to explore its significance in living modern life.[48] Criticizing Barker on these grounds is rather like complaining that Shakespeare should have written novels; that is, it does not judge the work on its own terms.

The ten years or so after Barker's death did not see any radical reappraisal of his work. Hardin Craig once again pays generous tribute to Barker's approach in a discussion of the "Trend of Shakespeare Scholarship" for *Shakespeare Survey,* singling him out as a paradigmatic interpreter of Shakespeare:

> What great scholars do and have always done is to study Shakespeare so carefully and from so many sides and angles that he has to reveal his meaning; the lapse of time and the great alteration in the philosophy of intellectual life fail to obscure his meaning. . . . Such scholarship will deprecate both unjustified conservatism and the needless creation of new dogma.
> I should like to illustrate the painstaking labour I have recommended from the last complete essay [the preface to *Coriolanus*] of the late Harley Granville-Barker . . . [H]e studied the play from every possible point of view, let nothing escape him. The action, the source, the characters, the staging, the versification, the stage-directions, the text itself came in for the most detailed and patient scrutiny. . . . Granville-Barker's interpretation, arrived at by these honest means, I think may be described as triumphant, as the best study of *Coriolanus* ever achieved by a critic, and all the greater because it releases Shakespeare from the necessity of having some one definable purpose in mind. (P. 113)

Kenneth Muir, in another retrospective study of "Fifty Years of Shakespearian Criticism: 1900–1950" for the *Shakespeare Survey,* "fittingly conclude[s] [the section on critics who take account of the Elizabethan stage] with a discussion of Harley Granville-Barker's work":

> Granville-Barker's aim was to find the best method of presenting Shakespeare on the modern stage, with due regard to the technique and conventions of the Elizabethan stage, but also to the subtlest interpretation of Bradley and other critics, in order to advise a modern producer on the staging of the plays and on the acting of the parts. On the whole he succeeds brilliantly, and the improvement in stage productions of Shakespeare since 1910 is largely due to him. . . .
> . . . [I]f Granville-Barker's *Prefaces* might have been improved by the incorporation of the ideas of some of the critics we have been discussing, they are likely to remain unsurpassed in their kind; and, it may be added, they will always provide what may be a necessary antidote to the excesses of symbolic criticism.[49]

Yet Barker also anticipated the future trend of Shakespearean scholarship. Although she does not discuss Barker's work, Muriel Bradbrook, in examining a half-century of criticism of Shakespeare's style, indicates that while "exploration of theatrical conditions" dominated Shakespearean criticism from 1900 to 1930, "the exploration of language and style [e.g., imagery] has been gaining ground and now [in 1954] predominates."[50] Barker's *Prefaces*, as Muir, others, and this chapter point out, examine language and style as crucial elements in Shakespeare's characterization and meaning.

The past fifteen years or so have seen only slight disagreement about Barker's place in the critical hierarchy. Patrick Murray, in *The Shakespearian Scene: Some Twentieth Century Perspectives* (1969), dismisses Barker with a mere mention in his bibliography, where he credits him with "character criticism in the Bradley tradition," while Frank Kermode, in *Four Centuries of Shakespearian Criticism* (1965), credits Barker with leading "the theatrical revision of Bradleyism." Kermode thinks Barker's value as literary critic has been "overrated," and that his real contribution was his "[very great] impact on theatrical presentation of Shakespeare"—an impact made as much by the *Prefaces* as by his actual theatre work. As Kermode recognizes, Barker's "aim was not to controvert other critics, but to get Shakespeare sensibly back to the stage."[51] And here Barker succeeded brilliantly.

With this appraisal, all major critics seem to agree. Arthur Eastman, in his ambitious and comprehensive *Short History of Shakespearean Criticism* (1968), concludes that

> Granville-Barker, as no one else in the history of Shakespearean criticism, helps us to a sense of the stage actuality of a Shakespearean play. One cannot follow him and remain quite so contentedly in the Bradleyan closet or on the Freudian couch or in the anthropologists' realm of ritual and myth or in the new critical world of metaphorical analysis. Granville-Barker takes us back to the place where Shakespeare began, to "the play's acting in a theatre." (Pp. 334–35)

His contention that Barker is able to achieve this vital kind of reconstruction by "convey[ing] the emotional life of the scenes as well as their kind of action," often by focusing on Shakespeare's language (pp. 331–32), is echoed by Douglas Paschall, in his doctoral dissertation (1976) on Barker's plays and criticism: Barker is at his best, he writes, not in saying what something or some character means, but in "*how* it contrives to achieve, or fails to achieve, its intended significance in dramatic terms" (p. 311). J. L. Styan, in his finely detailed *Shakespeare Revolution* (1977), also agrees with these assessments, and adds that "nowhere did Granville-Barker attempt, or show any inclination, to say what the play 'meant.' His achievement was to track those experiential elements which would permit perception of meaning" (p. 116). More precisely, perhaps, Barker uncovers meaning, showing how the play's intentions are revealed in its form and language; he starts from the play, not from a premise.

These critics clearly agree with my assessment of the significance of Barker's criticism: its constant insistence on examination of the play itself, on discovery of meaning from the play's structure and language, mark a new respect for Shakespeare's art and craft. However, the question remains as to the influence of Barker's achievement on later Shakespearean work, both in criticism and in the theatre. Many critics have already indicated that no one has surpassed Barker's work in "descriptive dramative criticism,"[52] but whether this kind of criticism is still useful is a moot point. It appears, however, that Barker's work is still a force to be reckoned with, a kind of touchstone against which more abstract criticism can be tested; his *Prefaces* are still frequently cited by scholars. But even more importantly, Barker is responsible for critical recognition of the limitations of purely literary argument. Scholars now habitually tend to take account of how far their theories are realizable on stage, and arguments that have no relevance to performance are recognized as literary, or one-dimensional: no claim is made that the play's whole meaning is there revealed. Barker made potential performance a crucial consideration in determining the meaning of a text.[53]

Clearly, such an achievement will influence theatrical practice as well as scholarship, and several productions are specifically indebted to Barker's ideas. The 1940 *King Lear* at the Old Vic, the subject of the next chapter, was inspired by a reading of Barker's *Preface,* while Gielgud's next *Lear,* for Stratford in 1950, carried "acknowledgments to the late Harley Granville-Barker." T. C. Worsley, writing for the *New Statesman and Nation* in 1953, after the Lears of Gielgud, Wolfit, Olivier, and Redgrave, credited Barker with reviving interest in the play: "From being the least acted and least popular of the great tragedies, *King Lear* has recently been accepted into the repertoire as if it had never not had its place there. We owe this perhaps as much to Granville-Barker as to anyone. His authority as an actor and producer has weighed in the scales against those writers who for so long dominated Shakespearean criticism from the study." Similarly, as Muriel St. Clare Byrne relates, Barker's *Prefaces* inspired productions of *Antony and Cleopatra* in a Renaissance style, most notably by Harcourt Williams at the Old Vic in 1930 and by Bridges Adams at Stratford in 1931. The 1946 production by Glen Byam Shaw at the Piccadilly Theatre seized on Barker's pronouncement that "here is the most spacious of the plays"; while its modern architectural set proved too much for the audience, Byrne asserts that it nevertheless "gave the death blow to realistic pictorial scenery for this play."[54]

Less finitely, Barker's writings have influenced the very concept of Shakespearean stage production in this century. The chain of influence has been ably sketched by other scholars—the young actors whom Barker directed became producers themselves; drawing inspiration from Barker's criticism as well as from their actual work with him, they passed on his ideals and methods to a new generation of actors and directors. But even those who have only met Barker through his criticism have been shaped by it; Henry Hewes, whose 1957 survey of twenty-one successful Shakespeare directors measured the value of scholarship in theatre practice, found that the *Prefaces* were cited more than any other work as "most stimulating in the formation of [the director's] approach to Shakespeare."[55]

Unquestionably, the most dynamic forces in the English-speaking theater this century—John Gielgud, Barry Jackson, Tyrone Guthrie, Glen Byam Shaw, Harcourt Williams, W. Bridges Adams, Lewis Casson, George Devine, B. Iden Payne, Michael MacOwan, Peter Brook—all owe a debt to Barker. He did not provide rigid answers to the problems of dealing with a Shakespeare play, but he carefully laid out the flexible and individual approach to each play that has led to more coherent and more meaningful productions of Shakespeare than anyone would have thought possible eighty years ago. As Barker himself explains, "Only from a study of the craft will a right understanding of the art emerge; that, at least, is the belief of the school of criticism to which I am apprenticed" (*On Poetry in Drama*, p. 40).

4

King Lear: Preface and Production

BARKER, already retired from active theatre work, was briefly lured back in 1940 to direct *King Lear* at the Old Vic. He had always felt the play's challenge: Lear's universally acknowledged "unactability" made it the perfect vehicle for proving Shakespeare's case as a playwright. As early as 1910, Barker complained that in the twenty years of his involvement in the theatre, he had never had the chance to see it performed until an amateur company risked a production: "I had read *Lear* much and fondly, but I was electrified at things which actual performance threw into relief. I hardly suspected the wonderful craftsmanship of the scene between blind Gloucester and mad Lear, when the dialogue only reinforces the poignancy of that perfectly devised meeting."[1] Barker returns to the play again and again in his criticism, indicating the consummate stagecraft *within* which the admired poetic heights are scaled. But it is only in his *Preface to King Lear*, written in 1927 and partly revised in 1935, that Barker could devote his full attention to a detailed elaboration of the play's dramatic skill.

The *Preface* begins by tackling the critical tradition originating with Lamb: "'Lear is essentially impossible to be represented on a stage'"; Barker retorts that his "chief business . . . will be to justify . . . its title there."[2] Reviewing its theatrical history, he finds reason both for Lamb's opinions and for their wrongheadedness, but his main energy is spent in refuting that twentieth-century giant, Bradley. He begins his attack by quoting at length Bradley's argument that *Lear* is "'too huge for the stage'" and that its storm scenes there lose their essence. This essence is "'such poetry as cannot be transferred to the space behind the foot-lights, but has its being only in imagination.'" Thus, Bradley concludes, the play shows "'Shakespeare at his very greatest, but not the mere dramatist Shakespeare'" (pp. 8–9).

Barker then proceeds to dismantle Bradley's argument. First, he points out how distant Bradley's viewpoint is from the dramatic one that should apply to a theatrical work:

> To say of certain scenes that they were "immensely effective in the theatre" and add that they *lost* there "very little of the spell they have for the imagination" . . . [is] queer commendation. For in whatever Shakespeare wrote was the implied promise that in the theatre it would *gain*. (P. 9)

Bradley's mistake, Barker continues, is to start from the "standpoint of imaginative reader" and thus neglect the stagecraft that makes the scenes work on stage.

Bradley's complaint that the play lacks "dramatic clearness" is also misdirected. Barker argues that a great play does not "necessarily make all its points and its full effect, point by point, clearly and completely, scene by scene, as the performance goes along";[3] it should instead "produce a constant illusion of life" (p. 10). The clearness Bradley demands

> would cost . . . dramatist and actors their emotional, their illusionary, hold upon their audience. Lear's progress—dramatic and spiritual—lies through a dissipation of egoism; submission to the cruelty of an indifferent Nature, less cruel to him than are his own kin; to ultimate loss of himself in madness. Consider the effect of this—of the battling of storm without and storm within, of the final breaking of that Titan spirit—if Shakespeare merely let us look on, critically observant. . . . Shakespeare needs to give us more than sympathy with Lear, and something deeper than understanding. If the verity of his ordeal is really to be brought home to us, we must, in as full a sense as may be, pass through it with him, must make the experience and its overwhelming emotions momentarily our own.
>
> Shakespeare may (it can be argued) have set himself an impossible task; but if he is to succeed it will only be by these means. In this mid-crisis of the play he must never relax his emotional hold on us. And all these things of which Bradley complains, the confusion of pathos, humor and sublime imagination, the vastness of the convulsion, the vagueness of the scene and the movements of the characters, the strange atmosphere and the half-realized suggestions—all this he needs as material for Lear's experience, and ours. (P. 11)

And, of course, it is this plunging into another life that gives drama such value, as Barker reiterates throughout his criticism.

Furthermore, the illusion of life that Barker demands does not necessarily lead to incoherence or confusion; a playwright as skilled as Shakespeare knows how to give coherence to the action without turning it into a lifeless diagram. For instance, Barker indicates (and later elaborates) Shakespeare's use of a "raisonneur" to point out the significance of emotions that may not be clear to the characters themselves: "In this . . . play we detect him in the Fool, and in Edgar turned Poor Tom. But note that both they and their 'reasoning' are blended not only into the action but into the moral scheme, and are never allowed to lower its emotional temperature by didactics—indeed they stimulate it" (p. 10). Furthermore, a careful juxtaposition of characters illuminates the "vagueness and confusion" Bradley fears: "To whatever metaphysical heights Lear himself may rise, some character (Kent and Gloucester through the storm and in the hovel, Edgar for the meeting with the blinded Gloucester), some circumstance, or a few salient and explicit phrases will always be found pointing the action on its way". And as Barker rightly concludes, even if the significance of Lear's agony should escape the audience at moments, "memory [may] still make this clear" as it often does for "our own emotional experiences" (p. 11).

Having justified his disagreement with prevalent critical opinion, Barker begins the real business of the *Preface:* the examination of the stagecraft on which successful production depends. He ranges freely through all aspects of the play—characters, plot, dialogue, music, staging, and text, but his main focus (if not his organizing principle) is the interplay of character, situation, and speech. Without at all reducing the play to a diagrammatic pattern, as more recent criticism often does, Barker traces the subtle interrelationships that give the play its resonance.

The interplay that Barker points out takes varied forms: it exists, of course, between characters and between scenes, but also between different modes of speech and even within one character. It involves parallel and contrast, in both obvious and subtle forms, and sometimes juxtaposition. For example, in the storm scenes, "there are the two Lears in one: the old man pathetic by contrast with the elements, yet terribly great in our immediate sense of his identity with them" (p. 16). Shakespeare achieves this effect partly through Lear's own speech; as Barker explains,

Though the storm is being painted for us still—

> Rumble thy bellyful! spit, fire! spout, rain!
> Nor rain, wind, thunder, fire are my daughters:
> I tax not you, you elements, with unkindness;
> I never gave you kingdom, call'd you children,
> You owe me no subscription: then let fall
> Your horrible pleasure; here I stand, your slave;
> A poor, infirm, weak and despis'd old man.

—both in the sense of the words and the easier cadence of the verse the human Lear is emerging [from the apocalyptic one], and emerges fully upon the sudden simplicity of

> here I stand, your slave;
> A poor, infirm, weak and despis'd old man. (P. 14)

Nor is this an isolated instance; Lear repeatedly comes "down from the heights to such moments" (p. 26)—moments which sometimes involve more than speech. For instance, his

> Make no noise, make no noise; draw the curtains;
>   so, so, so.
> We'll go to supper i' the morning; so, so, so.

. . . brings us to the simplest physical actualities; Lear's defiance of the elements has flickered down to a mock pulling of the curtains round his bed. Later, when he wanders witless and alone, his speech is broken into oracular fragments of rhapsody; but the play of thought is upon actuality and his hands are at play all the time with actual things; with the flower (is it?) he takes for a coin, with whatever serves for a bit of cheese, for his gauntlet, his hat, for the challenge thrust under Gloucester's blind eyes. . . . And when Lear wakes to his right senses again, simplicity is added to simplicity in his feeling the pin's prick, in his remembering not his garments. The tragic beauty of his end is made more beautiful by his call for a looking-glass, his catching at the feather to put on Cordelia's lips, the undoing of a button. These things are the necessary balance to the magniloquence of the play's beginning and to the tragic splendor of the storm.[4]

Barker expresses the idea yet another way: "Shakespeare has . . . to carry us into strange regions of thought and passion, so he must, at the same time, hold us by familiar things" (p. 26).

But as Barker further explains, the union of what he calls the human and the symbolic Lear is not dependent only on "the swift descent . . . from magniloquence to simplicity" in speech and gesture (p. 16); it is also enhanced by the characters surrounding him. The Fool, for instance, answering Lear's "Blow, winds" speech (III.ii) with

> O nuncle, court holy water in a dry house
> is better than this rain-water out o' door.
> Good nuncle, in, ask thy daughters' blessing;
> here's a night pities neither wise men nor fools. [,]

. . . [helps] to keep the scene in touch with reality. Yet note that the fantasy of the Fool only *mitigates* the contrast, and the spell is held unbroken. (P. 13)

Barker later elaborates this "contrasting use of the Fool": "feeble, fantastic, pathetic, [he is] a foil to Lear, a foil to the storm—what more incongruous sight conceivable than such a piece of Court tinsel so drenched and buffeted!" (p. 37). Yet again the Fool is useful in terms of dramatic construction: his "snatches of song and rhyme [are a] . . . lyric lightening of the epic strength of these [heath] scenes" (p. 56).

Kent is another kind of foil both to Lear and to the action; before Lear's scenes on the heath, "the note of Kent [meeting the gentleman in III.i] is interposed to keep the play's story going its more pedestrian way and to steady us against the imaginative turmoil pending" p. 37). In the storm scenes themselves, Kent's "sober, single-minded concern for the King . . . [is] a necessary check to their delirium" (p. 54). Yet as Barker indicates, this "sound, most 'realistic' common sense, persuading [Lear] to the shelter of the hovel," is not admitted until "Lear's defiant rage, having painted us the raging of the storm, has subsided" (pp. 13–14); that is, it balances the madness of these scenes, rather than interferes with it.

Barker sees that "Edgar also is drawn into Lear's orbit; and, for the time, to the complete sacrifice of his own interests in the play. 'Poor Tom' is in effect an embodiment of Lear's frenzy, the disguise no part of Edgar's own development" (pp. 19–20). However, in later discussion, Barker touches on the relevance of Poor Tom to Edgar's own character; for example, Tom's ravings help us "detect . . . [Edgar's] misprision of the sensual life—of his father's life, is it?" (p. 65). Barker also shows how Poor Tom serves another function vis-à-vis Lear—as a "living instance of all rejection," he is

Lear's new vision of himself.

> What! have his daughters brought him to this pass?
> Could'st thou save nothing? Did'st thou give them all?

Side by side stand the noble old man, and the naked, scarce human wretch.

> Is man no more than this? . . . Come, unbutton here. (P. 39)

Although Barker's focus on the relationship of Poor Tom to Lear causes him to miss the disguise's role in Edgar's own development,[5] he does trace much of the remarkable web Shakespeare weaves between story, idea, and character. Edgar's disguise as Poor Tom is necessary to the plot and useful in revealing and developing his own character; it is also made relevant to the character of Lear, Edgar's feigned madness adding poignancy and pointed contrast to Lear's real insanity, Lear's vision of Tom indicating his own preoccupations.

Moreover, the nature of the disguise has an organic place in the evolution of the play's "moral scheme" or idea (which Barker elsewhere in the *Preface* distinguishes from the story):[6] it provides an instance for Lear's discovery of essential humanity and his share in it, for Lear's growing spiritual awareness which is the real subject of the play.

Barker also discusses Shakespeare's dramatic construction, showing the several ways in which one scene can play off another. For instance, the three storm scenes are separated by two short ones showing Edmund's treachery. By arranging the scenes in this way, Shakespeare manages to move the action of the subplot as well as of the main plot and at the same time highlights his theme: the scenes of Edmund's betrayal of Gloucester "in their sordidness . . . stand as valuable contrast to the spiritual exaltation of the others" (p. 20). Furthermore, as Barker elsewhere explains, these scenes help postpone Lear's entering the hovel, which "fits . . . with the agitated movement of the action" (p. 38 n); on a purely practical level, the "interweaving of the scenes concerning [Oswald and Gloucester as well as Edmund] saves the actor's energy for the scenes of the rejection and the storm" (pp. 18–19).

Barker gives many more examples of the resonance between characters and scenes. For instance, having pointed out that "Gloucester and his sons are opposite numbers . . . to Lear and his daughters" (p. 58), he explains the way in which Gloucester serves as Lear's counterpart in dramatic construction as well as in character: "The very violence and horror of [the dreadful blow to Gloucester] finds its dramatic justification in the need to match in another sort— since he could not hope to match it in spiritual intensity—the catastrophe to Lear" (p. 20). In turn, the "fantasy of Gloucester's imaginary suicide [is] an apt offset to the realistic horror of his blinding" (p. 21). A character can therefore be played off against itself, just as it can be against another: "The larger dramatic value of the [scene between mad Lear and blind Gloucester, the sensual man robbed of his eyes, and the despot, the light of his mind put out] can hardly be overrated" (p. 41). But as Barker points out, in these charged situations "no moral is preached to us. . . . [W]e are primarily to *feel* the significance." If we do not, Edgar's asides (for example, "O! matter and impertinency mixed,/Reason in madness!") will point the way to understanding.

Barker also highlights the echoes between scenes themselves. For instance, the scene between mad Lear and blind Gloucester, with Lear's speech on justice and authority (IV.vi.152ff.), is

the picture of the mock trial given words. But with a difference! There is no cry now for vengeance on the wicked. . . . [but]

compassion for sin as well as suffering[.] . . . [Shakespeare] has led [Lear] mad to where he could not hope to lead him sane (P. 43)

—just as Gloucester, blind, can see the truth of which, sighted, he was unaware. But the echoes do not die here—the mock trial scene is itself reminiscent of the opening:

> The chief significance is in the show. Where Lear, such a short while since, sat in his majesty, there sit the Fool and the outcast, with Kent whom he banished beside them; and he, witless, musters his failing strength to beg justice upon a joint-stool. Was better justice done, the picture ironically asks, when he presided in majesty and sanity and power? (P. 40)

In fact, Shakespeare's dramatic method is very like Barker's critical one: both point similarities and differences, inviting us to make comparisons and draw conclusions, hinting at significance and meaning. But just as Shakespeare never reductively states his meaning, so Barker refrains from pronouncing a final, or exclusive, interpretation: he lays the groundwork by which we can reach our own understanding.

Finally, Barker explores the interplay between different kinds of speech. In discussing the opening scene, Barker sees Shakespeare's intention to create an atmosphere of formality and grandeur embedded in the language:

> The producer should observe and even see stressed the scene's characteristics; Lear's two or three passages of such an eloquence as we rather expect at a play's climax than its opening, the strength of such single lines as

> The bow is bent and drawn, make from the shaft.

> with its hammering monosyllables; and the hard-bitten

> Nothing: I have sworn; I am firm.

> together with the loosening of tension in changes to rhymed couplets, and the final drop into prose by that businesslike couple, Goneril and Regan. Then follows, with a lift into lively verse for a start, as a contrast and as the right medium for Edmund's sanguine conceit, the development of the Gloucester theme. (P. 18)

Likewise, Barker points out the "effect of Goneril's appearance before her father, in purposed, sullen muteness" (in I.iv), and of her breaking into "the prepared formality of verse, as this verse will

seem, capping the loose prose of the scene and the Fool's rhyming"
(p. 33). And, of course, there are Lear's "ominously broken thoughts
and sentences at the end of the speech to Kent just before the hovel
is reached . . . ominously . . . set between connected, reasoned passages" (p. 38 n). Thus, Shakespeare's variations of speech help to
define and enhance character, mood, and situation.

Barker's discussion of Shakespeare's patterns of character, action,
and speech is not developed in any formal way; rather, his points are
scattered throughout discussions of various aspects of the play. Similarly, his hints about discovering and projecting character, although
concentrated in the section called "The Characters and Their Interplay," are also contained in other parts of the essay.[7] They will be
discussed later, in the section on the Old Vic production itself, to
avoid repetition.

Turning his attention to production, Barker rejects "anything
approaching [a realistic staging of the play]" (p. 72). First of all,
realistic staging would destroy meaning; for example, as Barker
writes time and time again, Lear must *be* the storm, and

> clearly the effect cannot be made by Lamb's "old man tottering
> about the stage with a walking-stick"; and by any such competitive
> machinery for thunder and lightning as Bradley quite needlessly
> assumes to be an inevitable part of the play's staging it will be
> largely spoiled. (P. 13)

Barker also asks whether any actor "in his senses . . . would attempt
to act the scene 'realistically'" (p. 13), for such representation will
cause "dissociation" in actor and audience alike: it will reduce the
characters to "mere matter of fact" and so compromise "the appeal
to our imagination" (p. 15).

Besides interfering both with significance and imaginative response, realistic staging would not suit the mode of the play;
Gielgud recalls that Barker

> declared that the much-held view that the first actor of *Lear* is
> impossible, that Shakespeare wrote a ridiculous story, was non-
> sense. He told us to think of it as something from the Old Testa-
> ment, or one of the great fairy stories . . . and it illuminated it for
> us all.[8]

Barker makes a similar point in the *Preface,* in his evaluation of
Gloucester's and Edgar's characters in relation to their trust of Edmund:

> We must not . . . appraise either [Gloucester's] simplicity or
> Edgar's, at this moment, with detachment—for by that light, no

human being, it would seem, between infancy and dotage, could be so gullible. Shakespeare asks us to allow him the fact of the deception, even as we have allowed him Lear's partition of the kingdom. It is his starting-point, the dramatist's "let's pretend," which is as essential to the beginning of a play as a "let it be granted" to a proposition of Euclid. (P. 59)

Barker is not the first critic to make such points, but his sensitivity rather than originality is the issue here. Barker's demand for non-realistic treatment accords with the demands of the play itself; it does not arise from blind adherence to Elizabethan modes of staging.

Barker remarks that the play's "prevailing atmosphere and accent is barbaric and remote" (p. 73) and feels that it should be costumed accordingly. In some minor characters and incidents, however, the "seventeenth century [is] patent":

Edmund's relationship to Iago may seem to us to give him a certain Italianate flavor, and Edgar's beginning suggests bookishness and the Renaissance. But clothe these two as we please, their substance will defy disguise. Oswald . . . is a topical picture; in the Ancient Briton he will be all but obliterated. That must be faced. Of the Fool, by shifting him back a dozen centuries, we lose little, because . . . we are bound already to lose so much [since he can never be to us what he was to Shakespeare's audience]. And if a Fool in a barbarous king's retinue seems to us an anachronism . . . , the fantasy of the part marks it out as the fittest note of relief from consistency. To consistency in such matters no dated play of Shakespeare can be submitted. Here our main losses by desertion of seventeenth century habit and manners will end. (P. 73)

However, Barker adds that "it is equally clear that archaeological accuracy profits nothing. Nor should the producer lose more than he need of such sophistication as Shakespeare himself retained."

The text of *Lear* receives much attention from Barker. Although in some instances he finds the Quarto's readings preferable, Barker feels that in general the Folio is "of better authority": it is "more carefully transcribed," cuts passages that are structurally extraneous, and tightens dialogue (p. 75). He recommends any producer of the play to use the Folio as foundation, but to show a "courageous discretion" (p. 78) between the two texts. Barker's judgment, at a time when the Globe text was still widely followed, has since been validated by the Arden edition of the play; Kenneth Muir, the editor, writes that "there is now fairly general agreement that the Folio text is not only more accurately printed, but also much nearer to what Shakespeare wrote, than that of the Quarto.[9] However, he adds that while his edition "is based on F, . . . since the F texts of other plays contain numerous errors and 'sophistications' . . . , we shall accept Q readings not only where the F readings are manifestly corrupt, but also where Q seems palpably superior" (p. xix).

In accordance with his demand for discretion, Barker recommends a number of major cuts, which he feels are textually and/or aesthetically justified. For instance, the Fool's soliloquy at the end of III. ii is incongruous, and so Barker believes, "spurious":

> Its offense against the dramatic situation disallows it. The very heart of this is Lear's new-found care for the shivering drenched creature at his side.
>
> > Come on, my boy. How dost, my boy? Art cold? . . .
> > Poor fool and knave, I have one part in my heart
> > That's sorry yet for thee.
>
> Shakespeare is incapable—so would any other dramatist in his senses be—of stultifying himself by dispatching Lear from the scene immediately after [this speech], and letting him leave the Fool behind him. (P. 58; ellipsis Barker's)

Barker also recommends that the Quarto's soliloquy for Edgar at the end of III. vi be cut. On dramatic grounds, it "lower[s] the tension of the action. . . . [which] may damage the scene of Gloucester's blinding, which follows immediately" (p. 77); its removal will also link Gloucester's "catastrophe . . . more closely to Lear's misfortunes" (p. 21 n). Furthermore, in terms of character,

> the chief purpose of the soliloquy . . . is to give Edgar a fresh start in his dramatic career. It is a quiet start, the effect of which the violent scene that follows must do much to obliterate. When the Folio, then, postpones it to the beginning of Act IV, it does Edgar a double service, as the Quarto doubles the disservice by making the second soliloquy . . . seem dramatically redundant. (P. 77)

With ample reason, then, one should "here follow the Folio text" (p. 77).

The Folio also omits act IV, scene iii, the conversation between Kent and a gentleman which "begins with a lame explanation of the nonappearance of the King of France; it goes on to a preparation for the reappearance of Cordelia and it ends with some unconvincing talk about Lear's 'burning shame' and Kent's disguise" (p. 78). Furthermore, it "contains as dramatically feeble an excuse for the delay in handing Lear over to his daughter's care, though it gives none for the devoted Kent letting the distracted old man out of his sight to roam the fields crowned with wild flowers" (pp. 19–20 n). Barker recommends therefore that the scene be cut, not only on the Folio's authority but "on the principle— . . . an excellent one in the theatre—of: 'Never explain, never apologize'" (p. 19 n). The audience will not worry about matters not brought to its attention.[10]

These, then, are the salient points of Barker's *Preface to King Lear,* representing his thoughts about the play in 1935. To explore the way he put these ideas into practice, the next section will consider the Old Vic production of 1940, examining how the *Preface's* ideas were realized dramatically or changed by the exigencies of performance. Fortunately, both the production and the extent of Barker's involvement in it are well documented. During rehearsals and performances, Hallam Fordham took extensive notes, which focused mainly on the portrayal of Lear, documenting movements, intonations, and other normally ephemeral dramatic information; they were intended for a book which was never published but the typescript of which is held by the Folger Shakespeare Library. John Gielgud, who played Lear, added valuable notes to this volume, besides publishing memoirs which contain his own recollections of the production and Barker's notes about the role.[11]

As they were written at the time of the production, I have relied most on Fordham's account and the notes Gielgud appended to it. Next in reliability is Gielgud's own *Stage Directions,* written in 1963 and reproducing in its appendix the notes he took while reading through Lear's part with Barker. Gielgud's *An Actor and His Time,* based on reminiscences recorded for BBC Radio in 1978 and published in 1979, is also useful, but because of its later date should not be trusted when it contradicts other sources. Purdom's biography of Barker does not provide much detail about the production; in regard to some facts, it is probably more reliable than Gielgud's reminiscences, but less so than Fordham's and Gielgud's contemporaneous accounts.

Barker's exact role in the production warrants some discussion. At the time, the program credited Lewis Casson with the direction, adding that the production was based on Barker's *Preface* and additional "personal advice." However, from studying the evidence, it seems clear that Barker was in fact the director and Casson his assistant. Fordham, who was present at rehearsals, writes in his notes to prospective publishers that the production "was directed in detail" by Barker, even though he did "not allow his name to be given on the program as the producer" (p. 2). Gielgud confirms this in *Stage Directions,* where he writes that Barker "accepted an invitation from Tyrone Guthrie and myself to direct a production of *King Lear* at the Old Vic" (p. 51). However, he adds that "Barker refused to have his

name officially announced as director, and only agreed to supervise
some rehearsals, using his own preface to the play as a foundation."
Purdom further confirms that Barker accepted Gielgud's offer only
"on condition that his name was not mentioned in connection with
the production, and that Lewis Casson . . . should be the acknowledged producer" (*HGB,* p. 261).

Clearly, Barker's refusal to be acknowledged as director does not
suggest dissatisfaction with the production; rather, it was a precondi-
tion for his participation in it at all. The reasons for his insistence are
nowhere spelled out, but are nevertheless accessible to those familiar
with his life. His second wife, whom he married in July 1918, detested the theatre and tried her best to separate him not only from
active theatre work but even from his theatrical friends. Barker
himself was quite ready to exchange directing for a writing career;
he had grown discouraged in his long fight to set up a national
repertory theatre that would challenge West End commercial considerations, and having had little formal education, he also seems to
have felt more respectable as a writer. In addition, he had been
suffering from ill health for a number of years, and since 1930, had
lived in Paris. Finally, he was still regarded as the paramount director of his time, and clamors for his return to the stage had never
stopped.[12]

These many factors illuminate Barker's reluctance to have his
active return to production trumpeted abroad; they also help to
explain why he was unwilling to take total responsibility for supervising the production from beginning to end. Perhaps what is now
unclear is why he ever agreed to be involved at all. But Barker was
irresistibly drawn toward the work he had left behind, work he had
left not because he cared too little but because he cared too much.[13]
Indeed, twelve days after the start of the Second World War, Barker
wrote to Gielgud that "if this war is to go on for long, something
should be done to save the theatre from falling into the pitiable state
. . . into which it fell during the last" (Purdom, *HGB,* p. 261). It is not
really surprising, then, that Barker responded positively to Gielgud's
invitation several months later.

Having done so, Barker came to London for preliminary work on
the production.[14] He met with Roger Furse, the designer, and Lewis
Casson, who with Tyrone Guthrie was to supervise rehearsals until
Barker arrived to work with the actors himself. The early details
established by these conferences as well as by letter included "a
ground-plan for the production, simple patterns of levels and entrances, diagrams showing how the furniture should be placed, and
so on"; Gielgud adds that "in all these matters he had shown a
masterly understanding of the scenic essentials that he felt to be

demanded by the text" (*SD,* p. 52), a judgment which suggests that
these early details remained fixed. During this time, Gielgud also
read the part through with Barker, who told him: "Well, you've got
two lines right. Of course, you are an ash and this part demands an
oak, but we'll see what can be done"; the actor thought the assessment "pretty shrewd."[15] Barker then went home to Paris, where he
"constantly" wrote letters to Casson which were later lost in the war
(Purdom, *HGB,* p. 261); he returned to London a few weeks later to
supervise rehearsals himself (*SD,* p. 52).

His arrival on the scene appears to have been a revelation to the
company, even though they had begun to rehearse with Casson and
Guthrie some days before his return (*SD,* p. 52). Gielgud writes that
these ten days of working with Barker "were the fullest in experience that I have ever had in all my years upon the stage" (*SD,*
p. 52)—a sentiment one discovers in the memoirs of many actors
who have been directed by him.[16] Gielgud writes that Barker did not
use notes, but sat "on the stage with his back to the footlights, a copy
of the play in his hand . . . quiet-voiced, seldom moving, coldly
humorous, shrewdly observant, infinitely patient and persevering"
(*SD,* pp. 52–53).

Gielgud also says in *An Actor and His Time* that when Barker
arrived he "changed everything [Casson and Guthrie] had done"
(p. 134), but whether this statement should be taken quite literally is
doubtful. Gielgud makes clear, both here and in *Stage Directions,* that
Barker had very definite ideas about the play, both during the
preliminary work and at the rehearsals themselves; he also makes
clear, in his notes on the production as well as in his reminiscences,
that Barker could be responsive to an actor's own understanding of a
role. Since the remark's context emphasizes how superbly Barker
was able to inspire his actors, I think it more likely that this is the
kind of change Gielgud means; a remark by Harcourt Williams, who
played Albany, also bears out this interpretation: Barker "was unable
to take command until the last ten days or so. Into that all too short
period he crushed a month's work. Fortunately, Casson's schooling
had put us all on the right road and Barker lost no time in whipping
us from a joyful trot into a canter" (*Old Vic Saga,* p. 163). Certainly,
Gielgud's account of the rehearsals does not suggest that Barker
found the company incapable of responding to his conception of the
parts or that he had changed his mind about them: Barker

> knew exactly what he wanted to say and do. He would take infinite
> plans to achieve what he thought necessary yet was always pre-
> pared to give an actor a certain amount of latitude. He was no
> sergeant-major, forcing us to adopt his own tones and inflections;

somehow he *implied* what he wanted. He was wonderfully percep-
tive musically; he knew just where the voice should rise, just where
it should be sustained or dropped.

To me he was like a masseur who forces you to discover and use
muscles you never knew you possessed. (*AHT*, p. 134)

Gielgud states elsewhere that Barker's "first concern was certainly
for the speaking of the verse and the balance of the voices," but this
was definitely not his only preoccupation; the actors "were constantly
dismayed . . . by the high standards he continually demanded of
them, and by the intense hard work to which he subjected them
without showing any appearance of fatigue himself. For, the moment they appeared to begin to satisfy him in one direction, Barker
was urging them on to experiment in another. Tempo, atmosphere,
diction, balance, character—no detail could escape his fastidious ear,
his unerring dramatic instinct and his superb sense of classic shape-
liness of line." Gielgud is also quick to point out that Barker

> was in no way old-fashioned. He was not afraid to have an actor
> standing downstage or with his back to the audience. On the other
> hand, he had none of the modern fear of clichés in the acting of
> Shakespeare—what is called "ham acting" when it is crudely ex-
> ecuted. He encouraged grand entrances and exits centre-stage, a
> declamatory style, imposing gestures. Only under his subtle hand
> these theatrical devices became classic, tragic, noble, not merely
> histrionic or melodramatic, because of the unerring taste and
> simplicity with which he ordered them. (*SD*, pp. 53–54)

Barker advocated a somewhat larger-than-life style of playing for
this larger-than-life play because it suited its intrinsic quality—so
much so that Gielgud used Barker's directions in other productions
of the play:

> I remember rehearsing the last scene of *Lear* one night very late
> and he stopped me on every two words to give me inflections and
> tones. And I thought that at any moment he would say "Now don't
> act any more, we'll work it out technically." But he never did. So I
> thought I had better stick it out and keep going if I could with full
> emotion. By the time I looked at my watch we had been at it for
> forty-five minutes and I had never stopped weeping and ranting,
> but he found me a way to do the speech which I have never varied
> since. (*AHT*, p. 134)

Clearly, the "declamatory style" Barker favors is not the speechifying
delivery of Victorian Shakespeare, but a natural one writ large.

It is in fact a necessary style; as Barker writes in the *Preface*,

Shakespeare's only means of "showing . . . Lear's agony, his spiritual death and resurrection" is through "his actors, their acting and the power of their speech" (p. 12). He adds that

> it is not a mere rhetorical power, nor are the characters lifted from the commonplace simply by being given verse to speak instead of conversational prose. All method of expression apart, they are *poetically conceived;* they exist in those dimensions, in that freedom, and are endowed with that peculiar power. They are dramatic poetry incarnate. (P. 12)

This conception of the characters goes some way in helping us to imagine the style of delivery Barker sought; as he puts it, again in the *Preface,*

> Give the character the transcendent quality of poetry, [and] the actor can no longer bring it within the realistic limits of his personality. He may—obtusely—try to decompose it into a realism of impersonation, decorated by "poetic" speech. It is such a treatment of Lear which produces Lamb's old man with a walking-stick, and, for Bradley, dissipates the poetic atmosphere. But what Shakespeare asks of his actor is to surrender as much of himself as he can—much must remain; all that is physical—to this metaphysical power. (Pp. 14–15)

However, Barker also says that "the exact combination of qualities that distinguishes the writing of *King Lear* we do not find again; nor indeed should we look to, since it is the product of the matter and the nature of the play" (p. 24). So Barker's recommendations here are not meant to be applied to all of Shakespeare's plays; as he himself makes clear, "There is no one correct way of speaking Shakespeare's verse and prose, for he had no one way of writing it" (p. 25).

To the dismay of the company, Barker left London after the first dress rehearsal.[17] Gielgud speculates that "he was no longer prepared to face the tedious anxieties of the last days before production" and that he had also stopped caring about audience reaction and critical opinion (*SD,* p. 54). However, Barker had not washed his hands of the production; Gielgud reports that

> for several weeks afterwards I kept receiving postcards and short notes from him, indicating improvements and suggesting details, showing that his mind was not entirely free of his work with us, and that it had even moved him to a reconsidered study of the play. (*SD,* p. 54)

Gielgud reprints three of these letters in appendix 1 of *Stage Directions;* they confirm Barker's constant search for ways to express the text fully. They also seem to indicate his continuing influence on the production even after he was no longer involved in supervising it personally; although there is no way of proving this point, Gielgud always quotes Barker with such approbation that it is difficult to believe he did not take his further advice to heart.[18] The very fact that he reprints the letters suggests he found them useful.

Nevertheless, Barker's absence from London after the dress rehearsal does raise the question of how far the finished production can really have been his own. It is impossible to tell at this date whether changes that he suggested after his return to France were implemented or whether changes that were made were done so with his approval. However, I have already indicated my belief that Gielgud did respond to Barker's further suggestions, and it also seems to me that the two changes occasioned by audience reaction were made in accordance with his principles, if not his direct advice; these details will be discussed later. On the whole, I think the production was Barker's own—not necessarily his ideal one, but Barker himself never expected ideal performances; he is always the first to admit the imperfection of the dramatic medium. Imperfections there were in this case, particularly in the storm scenes, but Barker nowhere dissociates himself from the production on such grounds.

Some reasons for imperfection readily present themselves: shortage of rehearsal time, probably due to the wartime conditions, and the wartime conditions themselves; the production was, in fact, the first at the Old Vic since the outbreak of war, and only one other followed it before a bomb fell on the theatre in mid-1941.[19] Barker himself, in a letter dated 27 October 1940, wrote to Gielgud about the rehearsals: "We were all doing our best, under the circumstances, and this meant many compromises and much that belongs to the occasion only" (quoted in Purdom, *HGB*, pp. 266–67). But to interpret "compromises" in its modern dramatic context, as a euphemism for tension and disagreement in the company, and so conclude that Barker repudiated much of the production would be misguided.[20] Barker himself continually emphasizes the need for collaboration in the production of a play; it is clear from Fordham's account that he responded positively to the one suggestion Gielgud made, and Gielgud himself emphasizes that Barker was no autocrat. Barker's further statement that much belonged only to the occasion also indicates his ad hoc approach to drama; he expected a play's production to change, according to cast, time, theatrical convention, and the numerous other circumstances attendant on live drama. Consequently, if in some ways the production failed to embody

Barker's intentions or disappointed his expectations, it was still the *Lear* Barker was able to produce "under the circumstances."

Such reasoning apart, Barker wrote to Gielgud the day before the play opened, saying "Lear is in your grasp" (*SD*, p. 129); it seems he was satisfied with the work they had done at least in this important respect. It should also be remembered that Gielgud and Casson had tried to engineer Barker's return to the stage for many years, and their success on this occasion was a great coup; furthermore, the inspiration to mount a production of *Lear* came from their admiration of Barker's *Preface*. Considering these circumstances, it is highly unlikely that the production did not reflect Barker's ideas in its essentials, at the very least.

King Lear opened on 15 April 1940; it was played from a "virtually complete text," making only those omissions Barker recommends and justifies in the *Preface*. Playing time was three hours and forty minutes, including a fifteen-minute interval after III. vi. The stage made use of a permanent set; there was a variable backdrop at the back of the stage and, in front of that, a raised platform with steps which was extended for III. iii. In front of this was the main stage, which had permanent arched entrances, with steps, at both sides; a forestage curtain hung just in front of these arches, and for several scenes, was closed halfway to reveal only one side of the stage. The forestage, apronstage, and stage extension together were about half as deep as the main stage. Two permanent box seats were placed in the center of the apron stage, slightly to stage right and stage left. There were steps up to the apron stage from each side.[21]

Analysis of the relationship between production and *Preface* will concern only the production's salient features, as Fordham's type-script offers a fairly full reconstruction of it. Also, rather than run through the play from beginning to end, the discussion will first deal with those scenes performed very much as the *Preface* recommends, with special attention being paid to the ways in which Barker's more abstract ideas were translated into stage reality; then the scenes that deviated from the *Preface* will be examined, with the reasons for change being established where possible.

Barker always stresses the importance of Shakespeare's opening scenes, and Lear's is "a magnificent statement of a magnificent theme" (*Preface*, p. 17). Consequently, it should have "a proper formality . . . [and] a certain megalithic grandeur," and Lear should dominate it. In this scene, the king is "formal and self-contained"; his speeches are variously "eloquen[t]," "hammering," and "hard-bitten," showing "grim humor" and an ironic sense besides pride (pp. 18, 30–31). Lear's character is "fully and immediately, . . . immi-

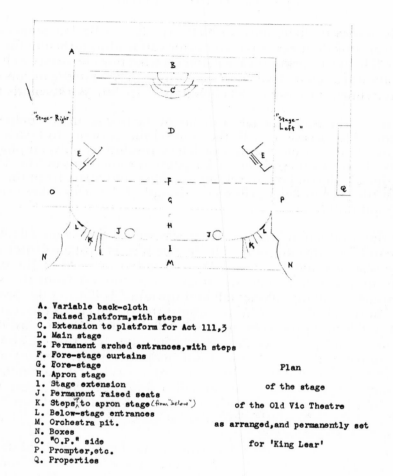

A. Variable back-cloth
B. Raised platform, with steps
C. Extension to platform for Act 111,3
D. Main stage
E. Permanent arched entrances, with steps
F. Fore-stage curtains
G. Fore-stage
H. Apron stage
1. Stage extension
J. Permanent raised seats
K. Steps to apron stage (from "below")
L. Below-stage entrances
M. Orchestra pit.
N. Boxes
O. "O.P." side
P. Prompter, etc.
Q. Properties

Plan

of the stage

of the Old Vic Theatre

as arranged, and permanently set

for 'King Lear'

Fordham's sketch of the stage plan for *King Lear*, Old Vic, 1940. Courtesy of the Folger Shakespeare Library.

nently and overwhelmingly set forth" (p. 29). As Barker points out, however, this definiteness of character can lead to difficulty for the actor: "He must start upon a top note, at what must be pretty well the full physical stretch of his powers, yet have in reserve the means to a greater climax of another sort altogether" (p. 30). Barker adds that

> here . . . the almost ritual formality of the first scene will help [the actor]. The occasion itself, the general subservience to Lear's tyranny (Kent's protest and Cordelia's resolution only emphasize this), Lear's own assertion of kingship as something not far from godhead, all combine to set him so above and apart from the rest that the very isolation will seem strength if the actor takes care to sustain it. (P. 30)

In the production, this first scene was set as a State Council taking place in Lear's throne room. The throne was set upstage center with three seats arranged semicircularly on either side. After the court made its procession onto the stage, Lear entered from the side, downstage, walking "alone, tall and upright." Following the procession, he reached center stage, where the other characters turned deliberately and proceeded upstage to their places. On his way to the throne, Lear spotted Gloucester; he paused, half-turned around, and impatiently struck the floor with his staff, commanding Gloucester to attend the suitors; the order was issued like "an irritable but half-humorous reminder of a duty neglected." Lear then ascended the throne, where he sat "with an accustomed ease" (*PA,* I.1.D2). Gielgud's notes show that at this point Lear is "Pleased. Happy" (*SD,* p. 120).

Such an entry marked a departure from the conventional staging of the scene, which had Lear emerge from the center; indeed, Gielgud recalls a complaint that Barker had in this way ruined Lear's first entrance (*AHT,* p. 135). However, he defends Barker's staging, explaining that "the whole scene was worked out in an absolutely symmetrical way" and that the throne had to be in the "dead centre" of the stage (*AHT,* p. 135). The notes that Gielgud appends to Fordham's account illuminate the rationale behind this staging; he explains that Barker

> continually urged that no great energy should be expended by the actor in this opening scene, which he had purposely arranged in levels and grouping so that Lear should dominate each moment by his position, his royal trappings, and the deference and awe which he inspired in everyone around him. (*PA,* I.1.JG2)

Barker's perception of Gielgud as an ash rather than an oak must have prompted this use of blocking to establish Lear's domination of

Opening scene. Lear's throne is surmounted by a canopy which is only partly shown; the two boxlike seats probably correspond to the "permanent raised seats" of Fordham's plan. Photo by Edwin Smith. Courtesy of The Raymond Mander & Joe Mitchenson Theatre Collection.

the scene; if Gielgud had started upon the "top note" Barker recommends in the *Preface*, he would have risked anticlimax in the storm scenes. Here, the effect Barker aimed at was achieved, while allowing the actor to keep his full power in reserve.

Even though Barker took such care to make the scene "a straightforward formal ceremonial, setting forth on the broadest possible lines the argument and the fable on which the rest of the play depends" (*PA*, I.1.JG1), it also helped to define character. Fordham's account compares the staging to that of Gielgud's previous appearance as Lear at the Old Vic and Sadler's Wells in 1931; that production featured a "more spectacular" first entrance: "Wearing a long white robe, Lear swept down a slope lined with scarlet spears and ascended a high throne on the opposite side of the stage." He addressed Gloucester formally, in keeping with the pictorial effect of the stage pageantry. Fordham feels that such staging was more "thrilling in its effect" but also kept Lear's character hidden; the economy of Barker's production, together with Gielgud's "surer touch," provided

a clearer definition of character . . . unblurred by emotion. . . . [W]e have a distinct impression of an old man who is yet alert and masterful; a testy martinet with nerves drawn taut, and great enough in himself to be reckoned with. (*PA*, I.1.A1)

The phrase "unblurred by emotion" may seem ambiguous, but the *Preface* affords a hint of what Fordham means. Barker writes there that "on his throne, . . . [Lear] showed formal and self-contained. . . . [After the abdication] he springs away; and . . . the whole play in its relation to him takes on a liveliness and variety" (p. 18). Obviously, the first scene was designed to show Lear in his state, but not at the expense of totally obscuring his character. Gielgud adds that Barker "emphasized continually in this scene the rhythmic, measured sweep of the verse and the importance of style and grandeur in the acting," and Fordham confirms that Gielgud treated the part not simply realistically, but "imaginatively and poetically" (I.1.JG2; I.1.A3).

Barker explains in the *Preface* that Shakespeare shows us Lear's might and genius not in anything he does, "but in every trivial thing that he is" (p. 31), which suggests that although we do not see Lear perform any great actions in these early scenes, we still recognize his greatness. The production achieved this effect in a number of ways. For example, when Lear demands "Give me the map there," Gielgud "without looking . . . half-extend[ed] his hands towards the chamberlain at his side" (*PA*, I.1.D2); such a small gesture helped to convey Lear's certainty of his power. Similarly, when Lear banished Kent with "take thy reward," Gielgud made a "swift, imperious" gesture with his hand, directing his chamberlain to record the sentence of banishment as he uttered it (*PA*, I.1.D4); the action further strengthened Lear's "By Jupiter, *this* shall not be revoked," which could then be delivered with a touch of ironic humor.

Several other points about the direction of this scene merit attention. Barker writes in the *Preface* that when Lear turns to Cordelia to bid her speak, there is a "hint of another Lear" (p. 31). This was marked in the production by a short pause, while Lear leaned towards Cordelia and called her his "joy": "The voice caresse[d] the words; the tone [was] vibrant, warm and tender. There [was] loving, joyful anticipation in the one word: 'Speak!'" (*PA*,I.1.D3). In order not to anticipate this effect, Barker departed from the practice, advocated by Poel, of having Cordelia enter with the king to show she is his favorite (*PA*,I.1.A1). Also, in the *Preface* Barker points out the drop from verse to prose when Goneril and Regan are left alone at the end of the scene (p. 18); in the production, the two "walked[ed]to and fro suggest[ing] a natural and business-like bridge between the tremendous grandeur and formality of the first previous action and the detailed events that are to follow" (*PA*,

I.1.A2). Finally, Barker's *Preface* stresses the importance Shakespeare attached to Lear's and Cordelia's kneeling to one another at their reconciliation (p. 44); in this scene he had Kent kneel to Lear's command "on thine allegiance hear me," with Lear in fact pointing to the foot of the throne on this line (*PA*, I.1.D4). When one remembers the kneeling pattern Barker established in his production of *A Midsummer Night's Dream*, it is likely that here he also meant to establish a pattern of meaningful action—a pointer of service and true devotion.

This production of *King Lear* also offers useful insights about Barker's approach to the interpretation of a role. Supposedly, J. M. Barrie once parodied Barker's method of stimulating actors' conceptions of their parts: "I want you to come on like a man whose brother has a chicken farm in Gloucestershire."[22] The parody is amusing, but the actual point it mocks is valid: it is Barker's call for collaboration between character and actor. In the *Preface*, he writes that the actor must

> make . . . himself . . . an intellectual and emotional instrument for [the] expression [of character]. . . . He must comprehend the character, identify himself with it, and then—forget himself in it. . . . [For example] very much as the storm's strength is added to Lear's when he abandons himself to its apprehension, so may the Lear of Shakespeare's poetic and dramatic art be embodied in the actor if he will but do the same. (Pp.14–15).

An illustration of what Barker means occurred at the end of this scene when Cordelia departs weeping. Gielgud recounts that

> many would suppose that Cordelia weeps at her father's cruelty towards her and because of her love for him which he has so monstrously repulsed. Granville-Barker finely suggested that it is her emotion at being kindly spoken of and finally asked in marriage by France that moves her to tears after her long ordeal of silence. Again, the cause may not be correctly interpreted by the audience; but what a significant and imaginative direction for the actress! (*PA*, I.1.JG2)

Just as in Gielgud's account of learning to do Lear's final speech, it is clear that the delivery of a merely technical performance does not interest Barker; the actor must understand the emotion behind the expression of it, even if the audience does not. In this case, he clearly wanted Cordelia's emotion to spring from the more noble cause of gratitude instead of from sorrow at being unjustly devalued.

Gielgud gives yet another example of this approach to the text.

Discussing the question of whether Lear's demand that his daughters speak their love comes as a surprise or is expected, he explains Barker's attitude:

> Curiously enough, important as this point may seem, as the fundamental crisis from which the whole tragedy springs, and much as it may affect the imagination of the individual actors as they enter the stage, the effect upon the audience will be very little heightened or dissipated whichever way the scene is taken. As a matter of fact, the lines were rehearsed both ways, and the final decision never actually dictated by the producer. . . . Events taking place off-stage or apart from the actual action of the play did not seem greatly to concern him. (*PA,* I.1.JG1)

Although it is unusual that Barker did not seek to reach a consensus with the company (perhaps another of the compromises due to shortage of time that he mentions in his letter), this anecdote once again illustrates Barker's concern for the actor's understanding of their roles, as well as his dismissal of offstage events as determinants either of meaning or of audience response.

Barker writes in the *Preface* that the next major scene involving Lear, the return from hunting, is designed to show Lear's greatness, again through trivial details: "All the action of [this] scene . . . , all [Lear's] surroundings are staged to this end" (p. 31), from the exchanges between Kent and Lear asserting the latter's "authority," to Lear's contretemps with Oswald, to the Fool's echoes of Lear's own whimsy. As Barker points out, Lear is not easy in this scene; Shakespeare does not "ask . . . our sympathy on easy terms for him" (p. 32). Yet the scene also marks a change in his character; when his knight mentions the "great abatement of kindness" towards him, the king gently answers: "I have perceived a most faint neglect of late; which I have rather blamed as mine own jealous curiosity, than as a very pretence and purpose of unkindness." He also responds—by not seeming to respond—to the thought of Cordelia; Barker quotes and interprets:

> But where's my fool? I have not seen him this two days.
> Since my young lady's going into France sir, the fool hath much pined away.
> No more of that; I have noted it well. Go you, and tell my daughter I would speak with her. Go you, call hither my fool. O! you sir, you sir, come you hither, sir!

—this last to the mongrel Oswald who has appeared again. . . . But the Fool's grief for Cordelia he has noted well. Lest it echo too loudly in his proud unhappy heart, with a quick turn he brings the old Lear to his rescue, rasps an order here, an order there and— takes it out of Oswald. (Pp. 32–33)

Lear's exchanges with the Fool that follow show him mentally alert but brooding, liable to snap even to a favorite, "Take heed, sirrah, the whip!" (pp. 32–33).

The production sought to put most of these ideas into practice. Lear's vitality was emphasized even before his entrance, with the sound of his laughing voice, together with those of his followers, heard before he "burst" through the central arch. "Flushed with exercise" and in good spirits, he threw off his outdoor clothes "in magnificent manner" (*PA*, I.4.D1-2). Barker took care to emphasize the difference between Lear's entrance in this scene and his previous exit; the "informal" and "domestic" Lear we are here shown helps to engage the audience's sympathy and admiration:

> The massive swirl of cloak and scarf, the sudden burst of his entrance, the ring of his voice and the freedom and breadth of his gestures all suggest a dynamic vitality. . . .
> Every detail . . . is contrived to show the [sic] Lear's inborn Kingship. The freedom with which he throws off hat, scarf and cloak bespeak the King accustomed to ready attendance; he has no need to look where the garments fall, for others will catch them.
> The little ceremony of the King's ablutions is also beautifully designed; the natural ease and yet fastidiousness with which he washes his hands and touches his brow and mouth with the water is eloquent of his station. After this ritual, with an almost unconscious flick of the hand he dismisses the servant who holds the bowl, and continues to dry his face and hands in the same manner with [a] small white towel. (*PA*, I.4.A1–2)

These details give one a good idea of the way Barker created business: there is nothing extraneous, nothing that does not embody the spirit of the text or amplify its meaning.

Lear's interaction with the Fool in this scene changed somewhat in its transposition from *Preface* to stage. As already mentioned, the *Preface* regards Lear's threat to the Fool as serious: "Take heed, sirrah, the whip!" is a warning snarled when his "sting goes too deep" (p. 33). However, Barker's preliminary notes to Gielgud annotate the line in a different way: "Not too fast. Encourage Fool to go on, buy it. This will be a good one I expect" (*SD*, p. 122). The performance itself emphasized the tender bond between Lear and the Fool in this scene; Fordham reports that Gielgud's voice took on a "special timbre, suggestive of understanding and affection," when-

ever Lear referred or spoke to him (I.4.A2). A description of the
action from the Fool's entrance will give a fuller idea of the interpretation: at "How now, my pretty knave," Lear goes to him "eagerly . . .
with outstretched hands," his voice expressing tender affection.
However, the Fool's remarks have a "bitter edge," and Lear's comment to Kent about the Fool's "pestilent gall" is assumedly casual, to
cover the hurt that has already flashed across the face. Anxious to be
entertained and also to show the Fool off to Kent, Lear questions
him in an eager, "almost childlike" way: "Why my boy? . . . No lad,
teach me." However, the barbs in the Fool's witticisms crush Lear's
"look of expectant joy" and he tries to hide his discomfort by reminding the Fool of the whip, "but there is no heart in his threats"
(*PA*, I.4.D3–4).

As one can see, the actual interpretation differs even from Barker's preliminary note. It is of course difficult to differentiate between the contributions of director and actor, especially in a play
produced over forty years ago, but one can assume that Barker
agreed with the interpretation even if he did not suggest it; his
preliminary note is itself a step toward this more complex interaction. Certainly, the abandonment of the *Preface*'s position is easy to
undertand: it adds nothing to our knowledge of Lear's character,
especially considering that his encounter with Oswald in the same
scene will sufficiently remind the audience of his temper. The note
Barker gave Gielgud suggests Lear's continuing good humor with
the Fool, but the final delivery adds greater richness to the portrayal:
it emphasizes not only Lear's bond with the Fool[23] but his inner
discomfiture at his treatment of Cordelia; it additionally parallels his
disappointment with her in the play's opening scene, pointing a
connection between his two "fools." Working this scene out with
actors, seeing the interplay between various aspects of Lear's
character, Barker must have realized the potential—and direction—
of the scene in a way difficult to achieve during academic study. Here
was yet another way of illustrating and developing the change he
had already noted in Lear.

Later in the scene, Lear quarrels with Goneril; the production
followed all of the *Preface*'s recommendations about its portrayal.
Goneril's "purposed, sullen muteness," as Barker describes it in the
Preface (p. 33), was emphasized on stage by her entrance: she sat with
her needlework at the opposite side of the room and took no note of
Lear. When she did speak, Lear in turn ignored her and continued
to feed scraps of food to the Fool. Only when her voice hardened was
"Lear's attention . . . arrested"; he then listened "in amazement and
repressed fury" (*PA*, I.4.D4). When Goneril finished speaking, Lear
sat silent for a moment; then he threw his napkin onto the table "like

"Are you our daughter?" Goneril sits with her needlework, ignoring Lear; the Fool lounges at his feet. Photo by Edwin Smith. Courtesy of The Raymond Mander & Joe Mitchenson Theatre Collection.

a gage." This bit of business shows wonderful economy on Barker's part: it was the same napkin brought to Lear at the beginning of the scene, held in his hand throughout the action, and before this occasion, used to strike Oswald "back and forth across the face" (*PA*, I.4.D3–4; I.4.A2). Thus, one prop alone served to illustrate Lear's kingship, contempt for Oswald, and rage at his daughter's treatment of him, while the challenge itself gave one of his later mad fantasies a context.

Gielgud also followed the *Preface*'s suggestion for the orchestration of Lear's reactions, which start with the irony of "Are you our daughter?," proceed to the explosion of rage in "Darkness and Devils!," dwindle to "senile self-reproaches," and culminate in the "slow, calm, dreadful strength . . . [with which Lear calls] down the gods' worst curse upon [his daughter]" (*Preface*, p. 33). Barker writes that

> the actor who will rail and rant this famous passage [Hear, Nature, hear! etc.] may know his own barnstorming business, but he is no interpreter of Shakespeare. The merely superficial effect of its

deadlier quiet, lodged between two whirlwinds of Lear's fury,
should be obvious. But its dramatic purpose far outpasses that[:]
. . . upon this deliberate invocation of ill . . . we pass into spiritual
darkness. (P. 34)

In the production, Lear spoke these lines in "grimly solemn, controlled tones," while looking up and "holding his hands in front of
him, palms upward in earnest supplication" (*PA,* I.4.D5). Gielgud
explains that this pose had two purposes: it suggested that Lear
receives heaven's curse upon his hands, and it also served as contrast
to his bowed head and body in the storm, humbly praying for good
(*PA,* I.4.JG1); two other "more obvious" supplications intervene between these, helping to form yet another link between them.[24]
Similarly, Gielgud emphasized the word *bastard* in Lear's taunt to
Goneril at line 262, and as Fordham points out in his analysis, "Great
effect is made with this expression, used so suddenly and with such
deadly venom, in contrast to the bandying of the word by Edmund
in scene 2" (I.4.A3). Through such gestures and emphases, Barker
helped the audience to make the connections between scenes, ideas,
and characters that he points out in the *Preface.*
    Although in this scene the production charted the same emotions
in Lear as the *Preface* does, the manner of arrival was somewhat
different. In the *Preface,* Barker seems to suggest—so Gielgud con-
strues it—that Lear deliberately dismisses the servants so that he can
call down the curse on Goneril; it is a solemn and terrifyingly
intimate occasion. It was such in the production as well,[25] but there it
was prompted by "Goneril's short outburst of contemptuous laughter as Lear first prepares to leave." Gielgud further explains that this
laugh

    was a piece of "business" invented by the producer after much
    experimenting. The precise moment during these lines at which
    the idea of the curse comes to Lear is the problem for the actor;
    Goneril's laughter was the final solution. (*PA,* I.4.JG1)

The idea was an appropriate one, even though not demanded by the
text: it did no violence to Shakespeare's conception of Goneril's
character, and it provided somewhat more justification for a father
who should appear to us as more sinned against than sinning. Lear's
second entrance in the scene also helped to effect this perception of
him: following the *Preface*'s suggestion, it was staged "as a deliberate
anti-climax" to the curse, countering the impression of strength
made by the invocation and also hinting at Lear's dangerously weak
physical and mental condition (*PA,* I.4.JG1).
    Barker explains in the *Preface* that Lear passes "from personal

grievance to the taking upon him . . . the imagined burden of the whole world's sorrow . . ." (p. 35); he achieves "this transition from malediction to martyrdom" partly by receiving "four quick shocks— his sudden recall of the outrage upon his servant, the sound of a trumpet, the sight of Oswald, the sight of Goneril"—which make him "face the realities arrayed against him" (p. 35). Barker writes that

> this must be made very plain to us. On the one side stand Goneril and Regan and Cornwall in all authority. The perplexed Gloucester hovers a little apart. On the other side is Lear, the Fool at his feet, and his one servant, disarmed, freed but a minute since behind him. Things are at their issue. (Pp. 35–36)

The production translated these shocks into a visible bombardment, almost a physical cornering of Lear. At the moment the trumpet call sounded from the right of the stage, Oswald appeared in the door-way on the left; Goneril then entered through the archway on the right, and Regan went upstage to greet her. As Fordham points out, Lear was left downstage center

> at the lowest point of the stage to take in the situation—with the audience. The other characters all dominate[d] him at this moment, yet he [was] in a perfect position for making his own effect, speaking half to them, half to the audience.[26]

Clearly, the blocking not only made Lear's situation plain both to him and to the audience, but also engaged the latter's sympathies further. Similarly, when Lear first speaks to Regan in this scene and describes Goneril's unkindness (II.iv.135ff.), Gielgud made complicated but meaningful movements: he passed diagonally from center stage to left front, then to right front at an angle, then again diagonally to upstage center, moving from one character to another (*PA*, II.2.A2). The pattern of movement suggested both Lear's agitation and his need to establish relationships with those who are rejecting him: indeed, at Regan's first approach to Lear, he had taken her hands into his (*PA*, II.2.D4).

Barker used stage movement very purposefully, and Fordham writes that in this production "the movement and grouping of the actors . . . [were] memorable." He explains that Barker

> used a simple, classic shape, employing broad right-angled and diagonal crosses for the actors, and continually weld[ed] the groups into pyramidal or triangular shapes, with the central character at the peak—usually to the centre of the stage, sometimes quite low down near the footlights. (II.2.A1)

Lear is cornered by "four quick shocks." Photo by Edwin Smith. Courtesy of Mrs. Edwin Smith.

However, Barker also diverged from this pattern, as in the second heath scene, when Lear and Edgar made a "circular sweep, at the back of the stage," and earlier in this scene, when Kent chased Oswald and finally caught him "by the scruff of his neck" (*PA*, II.2.A1; II.2.D1). These divergences not only provided variation but also helped to set the tone: the scuffle between Kent and Oswald would have seemed more anarchic in its departure from the classic groupings, and Lear's sweeping exit with his noble philosopher would have perfectly indicated the expansiveness of his freed mind.

Barker arranged the important speeches in a similarly classic way, "the supporting characters being turned upstage to give the protagonist the strongest possible position." However, Barker varied the "triangular grouping . . . with magnificent freedom" in the scene between Lear, Goneril, and Regan. He used almost every bit of the stage throughout the scene, and made the side arches an important focus: "like flanking attacks, . . . the grouping suddenly converge[d upon them] in a sensational but simple way" at significant moments, like Goneril's entrance, Lear's and Oswald's re-entrances, and Lear's exit to the heath (*PA*, II.2.A1). Thus, Barker's staging was neither static nor rigid, but a controlled expression of the text's meaning. At the same time, it never underscored a textual point at the expense of dramatic impact. For instance, Lear's exit was

One of the triangular groupings of the storm scene: Lear, Kent, and the Fool. Photo by Angus McBean. Courtesy of the Shakespeare Centre Library, Stratford-upon-Avon.

carefully designed to avoid anticlimax after the great speech of lines 266–88 ("O reason not the need"): after delivering his final curse, Lear walked backwards to the arch, and framed within it, cried to the Fool; the latter rushed to him and crouched at his feet. Then, with only two backward steps, both Lear and the Fool were able to disappear from the stage, avoiding an anticlimactic turn and long exit (*PA*, II.2.A3). In the *Preface*, Barker writes that this speech marks Lear's "abandoning of the struggle and embracing of misfortune" and is therefore both "a turning point of the play [and] a salient moment in the development of Lear's character"; as such, "its significance must be marked" (p. 36). Clearly, the production sought to do so by sustaining and heightening dramatic tension, rather than by treating the speech as a set piece or a still point in the action.

Such was the general plan of the scene on stage, but more detailed information exists about the way Gielgud played it. He himself writes that Barker

> demanded four contrasting emotions in this scene:
> 1. The actual progression of events which must be experienced by the actor—the deep moral indignation.
> 2. The "rash mood"—outbursts of uncontrollable fury, checked continually by reason and attempts at patience.
> 3. The physical strain on the body—expressed particularly at two points: "Hysterica passio" and "Oh me my heart! My rising heart," and gradually leading to the climax when Lear, beaten, sinks exhausted on to the seat [when he begs the gods for patience].
> 4. The knowledge of the toppling reason; the fear of going mad. To these must be added the task of miming old age in movement, pose and gesture. (*PA*, II.2.JG3)

Gielgud portrayed these emotions in various ways. At "hysterica passio," for example, the king swayed unsteadily, grabbing at his breast and speaking in strangled tones (*PA*, II.2.D3), while Barker's preliminary note for "O me, my heart" directs the actor to be "physical" and to use an "entirely new voice" (*SD*, p. 123). Lear's attempts at patience were marked by appropriate movement: after railing to Regan about Goneril's injustice and hearing her pretended concern that he will someday curse her too, Lear suddenly sat beside her in an attempt to establish some relationship and to prove his fears about this daughter wrong (*PA*, II.2.D5). He violently rose when reminded of the affront to his dignity ("Who stocked my servant?"), and his "You! did you!," when Cornwall acknowledges responsibility, was spat out with contempt (*PA*, II.2.D6; *Preface*, p. 36).

When Goneril enters and Lear suddenly realizes that his daugh-

Probably the conclusion of Lear's "O reason not the need" speech—"O Fool! I
shall go mad" (II.iv.288)—as he and the Fool are positioned for their dramatic
exit. Photo by Edwin Smith. Courtesy of Mrs. Edwin Smith.

ters are in league, Gielgud marked the moment by "stagger[ing]
back with arms outflung and then deliberately cover[ing] his eyes
with both hands" (PA, II.2.D5)—a gesture that underlines not only
Lear's feelings about Goneril but the painfulness of the truth he
learns and finally accepts. The gesture, initiated by Gielgud during
performance (PA, II.2.JG2), is reminiscent of Gloucester, who having failed to see the truth, is literally blinded, and, as Barker points
out in the Preface, still does not fully learn the lesson Lear does;
Gloucester's "agonized reflection" culminates only in

> The king is mad: how stiff is my vile sense
> That I stand up, and have ingenious feeling
> Of my huge sorrows! Better I were distract:
> So should my thoughts be sever'd from my griefs,
> And woes by wrong imaginations lose
> The knowledge of themselves. (Preface, pp. 60–61)

Not only does Gloucester misjudge the king's suffering, but as Barker comments, "The only thing, it seems, that the average sensual
man cannot endure is knowledge of the truth. Better death or
madness than that!" (Preface, p. 61). Lear's gesture in this scene
helped to mark, however subtly, the parallel between the king and
Gloucester, and through the parallel, the finer difference.

Lear's humiliation at his daughters' hands was marked by a similar gesture: having decided to go with Goneril, who will allow him twice the number of soldiers, Lear hid his face in his cloak, bowed his head, and approached her: "I'll go with thee" (*PA*, II.2.D6). When Goneril then demands to know why he needs even one soldier, Gielgud's Lear gave up the struggle, making a "fluttering, protective gesture of the hand" and answering her with "a new, defeated note in the voice" (*PA*, II.2.D6); he then collapsed onto a seat to pray for patience and anger. Afterwards he leapt up, fists clenched above his head, and cursed his enemies "with a final exertion of tremendous vindictive power." Groping toward the arch, Lear made his nameless threats, but was unable to sustain the effort. His tone of voice, as he called to the Fool, was completely and suddenly "helpless and pitiful." Gielgud held the Fool close as he voiced his fear of madness, the awful foreboding arresting him momentarily. Then the two figures rushed offstage (*PA*, II.2.D7). One can see how the careful orchestration of voice, gesture, and movement charted both Lear's wide-ranging reactions and the way in which they buffet him, preparing the audience for the breakdown that follows; there was no simple, straight descent to madness, but a lifelike portrayal of unendurably conflicting emotions.

Gielgud's notes on this act give some further clues to Barker's approach as a director. He stressed, for example,

the importance of starting off this scene on the same line and pace as the last in which Lear appeared [I.v]. This opening of each scene is particularly important in Shakespeare, when the scenes are so violently contrasted for this very purpose. Change of costume or make-up, and a "wait" of some minutes, may make the actor fumble in his approach to the scene in which he returns to the stage, whereas a certainty of pace, and style and attack will carry the actor briskly forward, besides marking freshly for the audience the exact style [stage?] of development at which the characters have arrived since they last appeared. (*PA*, II.2.JG1)

Gielgud also makes clear Barker's disapproval of gestures made merely for pictorial effect. Discussing his movements when Lear sees Goneril for the first time in this scene, he writes that he

had copied this "business" from an account of, I think, Macready's "Lear." In the 1931 production I had been complimented on its effectiveness, but at the rehearsals of this production I did not like to put it in, as it seemed contrary to the intention of the director to slow up the scene for a show effect at this point. In his view the climax was not reached until the next speech of Lear ["O reason not the need"].

As I grew more at home in acting the scene, however, I gradually dared to restore the action, although I modified it somewhat so as not to give an effect of finality, and so risk harming the passage which followed. (*PA*, II.2.JG2)

Gielgud here emphasizes the importance of the director in regulating such business: "There is always a danger, unless [such pieces of invention] are designed in conjunction with the main outline conceived by the director, that they will take undue significance and distort balance and values" (*PA*, II.2.JG2). He thereby provides additional confirmation that the production reflected Barker's conception of the play, even when he did not himself initiate business.

Gielgud's discussion of the scene between Lear and Kent in the stocks also provides insight into Barker's sure handling of the play; in this case, his lack of fear of the scene's inherent comedy. In the *Preface*, he writes of "the brusque familiar give-and-take which true authority never fears to practice with its dependents" (p. 34), but experience seems to have made him aware of further potential in the exchange between king and servant. Gielgud explains that

the audience laugh[ed] with Kent at Lear's expense. I resented this at first, then, realizing the value of the comedy, I tried to help the situation (contrary to the instructions of the director) by "feeding" with my lines at a quick, rallying pace. Later in the run, playing the scene with deeper sincerity, I gave the replies slowly, as if unaware of their comic effect. To my surprise the audience laughed more easily still. The comedy effect was obtained naturally, without stage trick, and the development of rage and indignation progressed more freely. (*PA*, II.2.JG1)

Unfortunately, neither Barker's nor Gielgud's understanding of the full value of the comedy is recorded, but Gielgud's last sentence suggests some of its usefulness: it serves as a powerful contrast to the rage that follows, making it seem all the stronger, and it also lulls the audience into a false sense of security, so that the rage breaks over them with greater effect.

The trial scene (III.vi) was also sensitively handled. In the *Preface*, Barker explains that the "lunatic mummery" is "pure drama"; that is,

it cannot be rendered into other terms than its own. Its effect depends upon the combination of the sound and meaning of the words and the sight of it being brought to bear as a whole directly upon our sensibility. The sound of the dialogue matters almost more than its meaning. Poor Tom and the Fool chant antiphonally; Kent's deep and kindly tones tell against the higher, agonized, weakening voice of Lear. (P. 40)

Kent in the stocks. The Fool sits at his feet; the two figures in the back are not identifiable. Photo by Angus McBean. Courtesy of the Shakespeare Centre Library, Stratford-upon-Avon.

The scene's main importance, Barker continues, is in the "show," in its visible reminder of the Lear who divided his kingdom and its implicit questioning of the justice of his judgment then.

The scene on stage showed an interior, bare and dimly lighted by a glowing brazier, set center forward; low stools stood on either side of the brazier and a rough couch at the back (*PA*, III.6.D1). The feeling conveyed was one of "weirdness and mystery," partially achieved by having all the characters speak softly, in contrast to earlier scenes (*PA*, III.3,4, and 6. A2; *SD*, p. 126). The disintegration of Lear's mind was suggested by his standing and staring "vacantly" ahead, with Poor Tom sitting on his left and the Fool crouching on his right (*PA*, III.6.D1). The picture obviously suggested a trio of the mentally incapacitated, Lear chief among them. (Note, too, that Edgar's disguise, as here it should be, is made subservient to Lear.)

Barker's preliminary note to Gielgud defines the action as beginning at "It shall be done," Lear's decision to arraign his daughter. To mark this on stage, he suggests a "sudden move," followed by his "swinging [the] stool in [his] hand" (*SD*, p. 126); more importantly, he advises that "equal value [be given] to real and imagined characters" throughout the scene. Thus, on stage Lear saw the escaping Regan in the stool he waved madly about his head (*PA*, III.6.D1), while the tame dogs turned against him were equally visible to him: he pointed at them, weeping miserably, feeling "rejected and alone," and only became calm when Tom pretended to scare them off (*PA*, III.6.D2).[27] In thus peopling Lear's madness with creatures both imaginary and misinterpreted, Barker managed to suggest its combination of fantasy and hallucination.

The scene also illustrates Barker's aptitude for devising business perfectly attuned to the words of the text. For instance, Lear's lines, "Then let them anatomize Regan, see what breeds about her heart. Is there any cause in nature that makes these hard hearts?," were spoken slowly and reflectively, in a changed, deep voice, after Lear had been holding a stool on his lap and fingering its hard surface (*PA*, III.6.D2); he only relinquished the thought when Kent gently removed the stool from his hand. The obvious connection between the object and the idea suggested the struggle in Lear's mind to make sense of the seemingly incomprehensible: it added richness both to the line and to the character. In the *Preface*, as previously noted, Barker writes that it is important to root Lear in the "simplest physical actualities," to have "his hands . . . at play all the time with actual things (p. 27); in seeing how Barker himself realized his suggestion, one further understands his point.

The scene of Gloucester's blinding was played very realistically; as Barker writes in the *Preface*, it provides a physical parallel to Lear's spiritual "catastrophe" (p. 20). Given this understanding of it, the need for realism is evident; although he gives no details, Fordham writes that the scene was effective enough to make some members of the audience, especially men, leave "with unbecoming haste" (*PA*, III.7.D2). One interesting point about its depiction, however, is that Cornwall gouged out Gloucester's eye with his thumb, while the text has him threaten to use his foot. It is unusual for Barker to have word and action so contradict each other, although Gloucester's sitting on a stool with his back to the audience perhaps enabled the actor playing Cornwall to apply make-up to the eye quickly; a Gloucester held down and stamped on would provide no such opportunity.

The Lear-Gloucester correspondence is also manifest in act IV, scene vi: Gloucester's arrival at Dover and his encounter with the mad king. One of the difficulties of production little commented on—so much do the storm scenes preoccupy critical attention—is Gloucester's supposed leap from the cliffs; it is a rare performance that does not elicit a few embarrassed giggles or outright laughter. Although no reviews of the production indicate whether its enactment was effective, Fordham's description, though not very detailed, suggests that it was: Gloucester, kneeling in prayer, then "[rose] quickly and, throwing his cloak up, over his face, [fell] to the ground, where he [lay] stunned" (*PA*, IV.6.D1). The fluttering of the cloak must have provided a sense of movement which helped the audience believe in Gloucester's illusion—an improbable response when an actor merely lurches forward and falls. It is this minor but telling detail that Barker was so skilled in devising.

Lear enters the scene, according to Barker's preliminary notes (*SD*, p. 127), as a "happy King of Nature." He has "no troubles," is "tremendously dignified," and carries a "branch in [his] hand, like [his] staff in [the] opening scene." In fact, Barker told Gielgud that "The entrance [should] be a caricature of the first entrance in the play, combined with a feeling of lightness and freedom; speaking aloud to the trees and birds" (quoted in *PA*, IV.6.JG1); he added that "the prevailing note must be kingly dignity; always, when in doubt, return to that."[28] Lear's appearance in this scene illustrated how much Barker wanted to remind the audience of Lear's kingship: autumn leaves were strung together, encircling Lear's head like a crown, while a garland took the place of his chain of office (*PA*, IV.6.D2). The audience could not help being aware of how much Lear has lost, how much gained since that first scene. Gielgud's interpretation, of course, further elicited this response: his gestures were "broad and fluid"; his expressions, such as unmotivated "fleeting smiles," indicated "a mind unrestricted by consciousness" (*PA*,

The "Happy King of Nature." The blind Gloucester sits on the right, while another figure holds Lear's staff. Photo by Edwin Smith. Courtesy of The Raymond Mander & Joe Mitchenson Theatre Collection.

IV.6.A1). Fordham writes that Lear's "Ay, every inch a king" was spoken "with quiet, unforced dignity . . . to himself rather than to Gloucester" (*PA*, IV.6.D3); such delivery seemed to suggest that, having lost his identity in losing his kingship, Lear now asserts something intransiently noble about his newfound identity. The overall impression Gielgud created was of "an intuitive balance between nobility and childishness, mental chaos and spiritual illumination."[29]

The production seems to have emphasized the reason in Lear's madness, delicately helping the audience to trace the connections he makes between thoughts. For instance, when Lear sees the field mouse and offers it a piece of toasted cheese, Gielgud bent to put it on the ground. The sight of his outstretched hand made him think about gauntlets thrown to the ground; he then mimed the removal of a glove, boasting his willingness to challenge a giant. The delusion gained a more pointed resonance, thanks to Barker's earlier use of the napkin thrown down as a gage in Lear's first confrontation with Goneril. The use and absence of certain props in this scene helped fulfill the *Preface*'s advice to show the imaginary and the real as equally present in Lear's mind: he took an imaginary coin from his pocket at "There's your press-money" (*PA*, IV.6.D2), but presented Gloucester with a leaf to read instead of a challenge (*PA*, IV.6.D5). He later tore up this leaf as he spoke, embodying the suggestion that Lear's hands should "play all the time with actual things" (*Preface*, p. 27) to balance the grandeur of the drama.

The performance of this scene was one of the highlights of the production. Gielgud writes that it caused him "the greatest possible apprehension in rehearsal" because of its intrinsic difficulties: redundant to plot, relevant to theme, it demands lengthy virtuoso interpretation (*PA*, IV.6.JG1; *Preface*, p. 44). However, he adds that because

> the direction was lucid, the "business" brilliantly and simply conceived, . . . to my great surprise, the final result was infinitely the most satisfactory, by general consensus of opinion, in the whole of my performance. (*PA*, IV.6.JG1)

The following scene, where Lear is reunited with Cordelia, receives little attention in the *Preface:* its

> simple perfection . . . one can leave unsullied by comment. What need of any? Let the producer only note that there is reason in the Folio's stage direction:

> *Enter Lear in a chair carried by servants.*

> For when he comes to himself it is to find that he is royally attired and as if seated on his throne again. It is from this throne that he totters to kneel at Cordelia's feet. Note, too, the pain of his response to Kent's

> In your own kingdom, sir.
> Do not abuse me.

> Finally, Lear must pass from the scene with all the ceremony due to royalty: not mothered—please!—by Cordelia. (P. 44)

The production took up these hints and elaborated them simply but effectively. Lear was dressed not only in new clothes but in regal scarlet, and the chair he sat in was placed sideways so that he was seen in profile (*PA*, IV.7.D1; *SD*, p. 127). Gielgud writes that this position was an unusual one for an important scene, but that it was "amply justified by the first picture of the King, sitting in profile, . . . and by the moment of the two kneeling to one another. . . . Played

The reconciliation of Lear and Cordelia. Photo by Angus McBean. Courtesy of the Shakespeare Centre Library, Stratford-upon-Avon.

in the Irving manner, on a couch, this scene must surely have lost enormously in its simple effect" (*PA*, IV.7.JG2).[30]

Although Gielgud does not explain why he found the profile view so effective, it seems that the silhouette-like effect of the two figures kneeling to each other must have emphasized its significance, etching the picture out in dramatic outline. Other resonances further increased the significance: the "throne" Lear slips from, no longer central but peripheral; the two proud characters competing now in humility; the echo of "our joy" in the triumphant pronouncement of Cordelia's name as the climax of Lear's hesitant speech—all these bring to mind that first scene, which seems now to be played out again to a happier, though poignant, conclusion.

The scene was carefully devised in other terms as well. Fordham writes that it was "played in an entirely different, far slower tempo than any preceding episode" (IV.7.A1) and adds that its "background of music enable[d] Gielgud to suspend the words and sustain the thought and language through pauses of unusual length, creating an atmosphere of pulsating stillness, of gentleness and yet of pain"; the actor's "gleaming far-away look" also contributed to this complex suggestion (*PA*, IV.7.D1). Gielgud further explains how Barker helped the actors avoid the danger of too much pathos and sentimentality swamping the strength of the scene:

Cordelia's tent. Photo by Edwin Smith. Courtesy of The Raymond Mander & Joe Mitchenson Theatre Collection.

The beauty of the King's pose, the poetry of the two kneeling figures, the slow, stately exit, the tenderness of the recognition— these were devised by the director in perfect harmony with the pathos of the poet's words. But the actors were told to play the scene for reality, simplicity, suspense [and to avoid using pathetic, noble voices]. . . . Cordelia must be moved, but still tongue-tied and almost brusque, just as she was before her father in the opening scene. "He wakes, speak to him"; but she cannot find words herself, and all she can trust herself to utter is the formal: "How does my royal lord? How fares your Majesty?," and the royal obeisance.

The doctor is important, as are all such small parts in Shake-speare. Practical and kindly, he acted apart from the emotion of the scene, and thus contributed valuable change and contrast whenever he spoke. (*PA*, IV.7.JG1–2)

The scene ended with Lear rising from his seat as if from a throne, and departing with Cordelia in royal dignity (*SD*, p. 128; *PA*, IV.7.D3).

The final scene of the play was, of course, just as carefully conceived, and it embodied many of the *Preface*'s ideas as well as Barker's later reconsiderations. Gielgud writes that his treatment of the "Come, let's away to prison" speech

was entirely based on Granville-Barker's original suggestion: "The speech must be like a polka," he said, "sung in every possible range and variety of tone, but lightly, like a boy of nine telling a story to a child of six." (*PA*, V.JG1)

Fordham confirms that Gielgud achieved this sense of innocent joy (V. A1) and details some of the nuances of his delivery: the reiterated "no" at the beginning of the speech "descend[ed] to a note of deep content" (*PA*, V.3.D1), while the word "come" in the following speech (V.iii.26) was "completely detached [from the rest of the speech, not in manner] and spoken with deep richness of feeling" (V. A1). Here was Barker's vision of a Lear who "has passed beyond care for revenge or success, beyond even the questioning of rights and wrongs" (*Preface*, p. 45), brought vividly to life.

The movements accompanying the speech were also recorded: Fordham writes that it was delivered "with a swinging, almost dance-like movement, as [Lear] walk[ed] down[stage] with Cordelia, swaying her arms in his and bending his head from side to side in beautiful, child-like happiness" (V. A1). Gielgud adds that this downstage position, right at the footlights, was "daringly inventive and superbly justified" (*PA*, V. JG1), and although he does not explain why, the reasons are easy to deduce: the position would have strengthened the feeling of their isolated contentment, the audience's sympathy with them, and perhaps even the sense of their danger; Fordham explains that the production showed "Cordelia's mistrust of their enemies and Lear's blindness to the possibility of future harm" (V. A1), and this blocking as well as the acting could have reinforced her misgivings and his obliviousness.[31] Certainly, movements were designed to give full value to speech and emotion: when Gielgud spoke the lines "Upon such sacrifices . . ." (V.iii.20–21), he released Cordelia's hands and walked a little past her, then turned around, his "face radiant," throwing "his arms wide open" for "Have I caught thee?" (*PA*, V.3.D1).

The *Preface* emphasizes "the likeness and the difference" of the first and last scenes of the play (pp. 23, 45–46). One similarity is that Lear is here "the same commanding figure; he bears the body of Cordelia as lightly as ever he carried robe, crown and scepter before. All he has undergone has not so bated his colossal strength but that he could kill her murderer with his bare hands" (p. 45). Barker ensured that this point was not lost in performance. Cathleen Nesbitt recalls that in rehearsal, the Captain recited his one line in rather a neutral way; Barker then took immense care to explain that "that is an extremely important line. You must let the audience *feel* you have seen a miracle—you *have*. . . . You have seen a thing that is not possible, yet you have seen it—you heart must beat faster when you say: 'Tis true, my lords, he did.' It must be with awareness that almost stops Lear's rage for a second—he must *feel* you there and turn to *you*. 'Did I not, fellow?' . . . Now go away and *think* about it" (quoted in *A Little Love,* p. 179). Such care over a single line and a minor character is not unrepresentative, but typical of Barker's approach to a play.

Barker found yet another way to achieve the effect of Lear's strength in performance: Gielgud carried Cordelia on one arm, "by means of a sling over the other shoulder, covered by a piece of drapery of the same colour as Lear's shirt" (*PA*, V.JG1). While Fordham reports that some people were distracted by its "artificial appearance," he himself felt it successfully depicted Lear's strength and also had the advantage of allowing the actor to gesture with one arm (*PA*, V.A1–2). Gielgud himself concludes that "there is no question that it made a nobler and more dignified picture than the usual entrance, with the body held out in both arms, and would have looked finer with a central entrance (which was planned in this production, but found to be impractical, owing to technical complications), and with an actor of greater girth and stature playing Lear" (*PA*, V.JG1). He values the dramatic effect of Lear's "appearance of massive strength . . . in this last tragic scene."

"Have I caught thee?" Lear and Cordelia stand downstage, unaware of Edmund's plotting upstage. Photo by Edwin Smith. Courtesy of Mrs. Edwin Smith.

The *Preface* suggests that Lear should enter mutely with Cordelia's body, while all "stand silent and intent around him" (p. 45). Lear "glar[es] blankly at them for a moment. When speech is torn from him, in place of the old kingly rhetoric we have only the horrible, half human 'Howl, howl, howl, howl!'" (pp. 45–46). In fact, in performance Lear entered from the side and advanced "slowly to [the] centre, his voice rising and increasing in volume with each deliberate cry" while everyone turned around in horror; only then did he look blankly at those present and accost them as "men of stones" (*PA*, V.3.D4).

Certainly, this procedure invested Lear's grief with more dramatic sense; as the *Preface* itself makes one realize, part of the scene's dramatic power comes from Lear's total abandonment of himself to Cordelia, in marked contrast to that first scene where he unsuccessfully contrives self-glorification, and from its coming too late: "All his world, of power and passion and will, and the wider world of thought over which his mind in its ecstasy had ranged, is narrowed now to Cordelia; and she is dead in his arms" (p. 46). This abandonment will be clearer if Lear does not seem to indulge in it for the sake of his silent audience. Moreover, as Fordham points out, Lear's entrance is preceded by Edmund's fatal wounding, which in this production was treated as "rank melodrama." Consequently, "the attention of the audience [had to be] cunningly distracted from his

**Lear's howling entry with the dead Cordelia on one arm. Photo by Edwin Smith.
Courtesy of Mrs. Edwin Smith.**

Edmund's death. Photo by Angus McBean. Courtesy of the Shakespeare Centre Library, Stratford-upon-Avon.

exit, surrounded by soldiers, to the sensational entrance, on the other side of the stage and at the back, of Lear with the body of Cordelia" (*PA*, V.A3). Lear's howl immediately commanded such attention from the audience as well as from those on stage.

Barker writes in the *Preface* that "the clue to the last scene [is] this terrible concentration upon the dead, and upon the unconquerable fact of death" (p. 46), and Gielgud's intent focus on Cordelia's corpse achieved this effect in the production (*PA*, V.3.D5). However, the *Preface* seems to call for Lear's attention to be directed unrelentingly at Cordelia: "Kent kneels by him to share his grief. Then to the bystanders comes the news of Edmund's death; the business of life goes forward, as it will, and draws attention from him for a moment. But what does he heed? When they turn back to him he has her broken body in his arms again. 'And my poor fool is hang'd . . .'" (p. 46). But what is Lear to do while attention is focused elsewhere? He can, of course, continue to hold Cordelia in his arms, but then his renewed mourning might sound too pat, too much like a response to the silence of others—in short, like an answer to a bald cue to speak, especially following Albany's "O! see, see!" There is also the danger that Lear may seem to compete with the news of Edmund's death. Far more effective, far less theatrically contrived, is the hint one may take from the text: that Kent's self-revelation momentarily distracts Lear from the unbearable fact, and then something forces it upon him yet again.

The production followed this hint. Lear seemed to recognize Kent for a moment; the two men sparred for a while, and then Lear seemed to remember, with a trace of anger, his banishment of Kent. His mind then wandered again, and he walked aimlessly away. At this point a messenger announced Edmund's death, but the news made no impression on the king. Then Lear suddenly noticed a soldier in the background holding the hangman's noose; he snatched it, came downstage carrying it in both hands, and burst out anew in grief: "And my poor fool is hang'd" (*PA*, V.3.D6). The dramatic and textual justification for this staging is self-evident: there is good reason for Lear's distraction from Cordelia, equally good reason for the pain of his renewed awareness, and even something—Lear's actions with the noose—for Albany to "see" and call attention to. Thus, the action achieved the *Preface*'s aim of "terrible concentration" on death, but through means more subtle than the *Preface* suggests.

Interestingly, the business with the rope was not devised by Barker, but by Gielgud,[32] and at first the director disapproved, saying it was

Lear's "terrible concentration . . . upon the unconquerable fact" of Cordelia's death. Photo by Edwin Smith. Courtesy of Mrs. Edwin Smith.

"too much like the sort of thing Tree did," but after a few moments he called out: "No, no, I'm sure its [*sic*] right. Try it, and the last speech must then be a keening: 'never, never, never, never, never' must wail all round the roof of the theatre" [instead of being spoken in the broken level tones Gielgud had been using]. (*PA*, V.JG1–2)

Gielgud writes that he achieved this effect at one rehearsal only: he "became self-conscious about [the scene] and only played it once or twice with any sense of real satisfaction" (*PA*, V.JG2). Fordham recounts that

at early performances the ["never" passage] . . . was delivered in an ascending voice, ending with the hands clutching at the neck on the final repetition, with a strangled tone. At later performances this line was spoken more simply [blankly, with a dead tone; the final word . . . detached, descending to a low, open note of absolute despair], and the idea of physical constriction presented separately. (*PA*, V.A2; V.3.D6)

He adds that Gielgud spoke all of Lear's repeated words—the howls, no's, and never's—"with great technical skill and beauty, with constant variety of rhythm and tone" (*PA*, V.A2).

The *Preface* agrees with Bradley that Lear dies of joy, thinking that Cordelia is still alive (p. 46 n), and Gielgud managed to make this clear in performance: turning to look at Cordelia after having his button undone, he "suddenly exclaim[ed] with an ecstasy of joy . . . 'Do you see this?'"; his expression was "radiant" (*PA*, V.3.D6).

Although this analysis has necessarily focused mainly on the production's depiction of Lear, equally careful thought was given to other characters and effects; some examples will illustrate Barker's characteristic sensitivity and attention to detail. Regan, for example, entered the last scene "looking pale and ill . . . [and] helped by an attendant," who provided a stool for her to sit on (*PA*, V.3.D2). This minor preparation for the news of Goneril's having poisoned her sister ensured that the audience did not miss the revelation when it came; given the dense action of this last scene, such a loss of spoken information is possible if no preparation is made for it.[33]

Barker also invented an interesting bit of business for Regan in act IV, scene v: he had her sit at her dressing table, dressed in mourning for the dead Cornwall, but holding a mirror and making up her face as she talked to Oswald. Gielgud remembers that she was conceived "as a kind of cold pussy-cat," and the way in which this unostentatious action illuminated her character—its vanity, callousness, and egotism—is admirable.[34] Nesbitt adds that Barker "made the parts of Regan and Goneril interesting to play" because he "somehow brought out the odd impulse of humanity in the monsters," Edmund included. Recognition of the play's potential humor was one way in which Barker avoided superficial characterization in these parts; for example, Edmund's kiss left Goneril swooning, so that when she turned to "her fussy, timorous, elderly husband, her sigh of 'Oh, what a difference of man to man!' [*sic*] made the audience laugh so much that they almost felt a wave of tolerance towards her" (*A Little Love*, pp. 179–80).

As for effects rather than characters, the battle scenes, which Fordham describes as "usually so muddled and difficult to follow," were lucidly presented by means of "simple and significant groupings, the clear arrangements of entrances and exits, and the masterly use of the stage-space" (*PA*, V.A2). No attempt was made to suggest an army, nor was one necessary: "The effect of battle and violent action [was] sufficiently indicated by the strong delineation of the principal characters and their purposes."

So far only those scenes that have either transposed the *Preface*'s precepts into stage action or followed its general advice in ways differing only slightly from its recommendations have been discussed. However, some parts of the production strikingly deviated from Barker's published principles or specific directions. Reasons for change can be definitely stated in a few cases, but in most are subject to informed conjecture.

Some of the changes were quite minor. For example, in a note

following the *Preface* proper, Barker writes that the stage need not
be cleared between II. ii and II. iii, respectively the scene of Kent in
the stocks and Edgar's soliloquy. Barker remarks that "curtains
might be drawn before Kent in the stocks, but he may as well sit
there asleep while Edgar soliloquizes. On an *unlocalized* stage I doubt
its puzzling even a modern audience if he does; it certainly would
not have troubled Shakespeare's" (p. 79). When it came to the production, Barker either did not trust his audience or felt that the stage
was too localized: on one side was an arched entrance and on the
other a doorway to Gloucester's house (*PA*, II.1.D1). In any case,
the forestage curtain was used to separate the two "scenes" (*PA*,
II.2.D2).

Barker also strongly believed in the effect of having Goneril's and
Regan's bodies onstage at the finale, as the text demands; he explains
in the *Preface* that this last scene assembles all "the same company [as
the first] . . . or all but the same, and they await [Lear's] pleasure."
There is Cordelia,

> dumb and dead, she that was never apt of speech—what fitter
> finish for her could there be? What fitter ending to the history of
> the two of them, which began for us with Lear on his throne,
> conscious of all eyes on him, while she shamed and answered him
> by her silence? . . . Even Regan and Goneril are here to pay him a
> ghastly homage. (Pp. 23–24)

Clearly, the presence of Goneril and Regan is necessary for Barker's
underlining of the echoes between the first and the last scenes of the
play, but it had to be abandoned in deference to audience response.
Fordham explains that the bodies were brought out on a bier, but
"the spectacle was not sufficiently impressive" and caused laughter;
the incident was therefore cut (V.A3). He is sure, however, that "with
more time and expenditure this effect could have been striking and
effective, and have heightened the drama of the final episode." It is
not known whether Barker was consulted about the change, but his
own critical position would have advocated the abandonment of
theory in favor of experience.

Another change that did not drastically alter Barker's vision of the
play although it did depart from the *Preface*'s instructions involved
the close of III. vi and the placement of the interval. The scene
ended with the Fool and Kent about to bear the sleeping Lear away
as the forestage curtain fell; Edgar then delivered his soliloquy to
the audience, after which the proscenium curtain fell for the interval
(*PA*, III.6.D3). The *Preface*, of course, calls for its placement after
the end of act III (scene vii) and for the omission of Edgar's soliloquy
here. Given that the break was moved up a scene, one can under-

stand why Barker reinstated the speech: it provides a winding-down point, a rounding-off of the action;[35] furthermore, placed before the interval, it no longer runs the danger of lowering tension before the blinding of Gloucester (*Preface*, p. 77). It is, in fact, harder to understand why Barker moved the interval, as he cogently argues in the *Preface* that

> to this point [the end of act III] the play is carried by one great impetus of inspiration, and there will be great gain in its acting being as unchecked. . . . [T]he strain should not be excessive upon either audience or actors. Shakespeare's stagecraft—his interweaving of contrasted characters and scenes—provides against this, as does the unity of impression and rapidity of action, which his unlocalized staging makes possible. (P. 17)

One can only guess at Barker's reasons for the change but many present themselves to mind. For one, the blinding of Gloucester is a counterpart to Lear's going mad, and postponing the former until after the interval may link the two halves of the play more firmly, if subconsciously, in the audience's mind; separating it from the emotionally draining scenes of Lear's madness will also give it more impact. For another, III. vii introduces the "close-packed" action of the latter half of the play; Barker explains in the *Preface* that act III marks the relaxation of tension in the Lear plot, and that from here on "the producer therefore must give his own best attention to Albany, Goneril and Regan and their close-packed contests, and to the nice means by which Edgar is shaped into a hero" (p. 21). Therefore, he may have deemed it wise to end the first section of the play with Lear's "conveyance . . . out of the main stream of the play's action" (p. 20); the change does not interfere with the momentum of the heath scenes and starts the second half of the play on a similarly charged pitch. In any case, the decision he actually took makes as much textual, thematic, and dramatic sense as the suggestion in the *Preface*.

The production also deviated from the *Preface* in the matter of setting. The latter calls for a primitive background, although, as the early part of this chapter demonstrates, it recognizes the many Elizabethan elements in the play. However, the program credited Roger Furse with designing a Renaissance production. It is not difficult to see why Barker changed his mind; as Robert Speaight notes, the *Preface* itself "puts up quite a convincing case for the Elizabethan interpretation" even though it discards it.[36] That Barker did sanction the change seems unquestionable; as previously recounted, he met with Furse while making preliminary arrangements and Gielgud suggests that these scenic details remained fixed. Critical response to the setting and costumes was somewhat mixed, however, and it is unfortunate that no material has been uncovered to suggest whether Barker ultimately regretted or approved his reconsideration of the *Preface*'s position.

The greatest challenge to Barker's translation of theory into practice must have been act III with its storm scenes; as champion of the scenes' stageworthiness, he must have given them the particular care and concentration that he devotes to them in the *Preface* and other critical writings. The extent to which their depiction on stage faithfully embodied Barker's theoretical positions about them will be made clear in the following analysis.

In his criticism, Barker indicates that preparation is necessary for the storm scenes proper; as already noted, for example, in "Shakespeare and Modern Stagecraft," he explains that the first scene of act III "gives [the] audience the cue to the dramatic effects which are to follow, bids them to look for the old King, striving

> . . . in his little world of man to outscorn
> The to-and-fro conflicting wind and rain." (Pp. 721–22; ellipsis Barker's)

The production treated the scene as such a preparation. The forestage was darkened and the sound of the storm raged; then Kent entered, head and body wrapped in his cloak for protection against the violent weather (*PA*, III.1.D1). Not only was the anonymous gentleman he meets also "shrouded in his cloak," but the two figures were bent by the force of the storm and even swayed in their effort to remain upright; they had to shout above the wind and thunder. Clearly, Barker devised this preliminary scene to give a realistic picture of the storm—one too dangerous to give in conjunction with Lear, for as he notes in the *Preface*, the actor must create the storm himself: in the first place, "the shaking of a thunder-sheet will not greatly stir us" in these scenes; in the second, "the storm is not in itself . . . dramatically important, only in its effect upon Lear." The only way "to give it enough magnificence to impress him, yet keep it from rivaling him [is] . . . by identifying the storm with him, setting the actor to impersonate both Lear and—reflected in Lear—the storm" (p. 12).

The speech that opens scene ii, Lear's "Blow, winds, and crack your cheeks!," achieves this union. As Barker writes in the *Preface*,

> This [speech] is no mere description of a storm, but in music and imaginative suggestion a dramatic creating of the storm itself; and there is Lear . . . in the midst of it, almost a part of it. Yet Lear himself, in his Promethean defiance, still dominates the scene. (P. 13)

As explained in the early part of this chapter, Barker believes that in the storm scenes the human Lear is mostly submerged in what he calls the symbolic, peeping out only at moments like "here I stand, your slave" and in conjunction with the Fool; the production naturally sought to achieve this effect. Fordham writes that Gielgud's presentation here was more symbolic than real; he deliberately treated the first great speeches in a "detached and unrealistic" way, both in gesture and delivery; his detailed account reveals that

> the verse [was] spoken with the greatest power that the actor [could] command, with the full sweep of elevated speech. The postures [were] statuesque and broad, each change of attitude being made deliberately and held for a time according to the structure of the speech.
> . . . The signs of age and mental instability in Lear [were] suggested sufficiently but with economy, and the acting never degenerate[d] into a naturalistic characterisation, but rather delineate[d] the progress of a mind. (*PA*, III.3, 4, and 6.Al)

Barker's preliminary notes to Gielgud give some further clues about Lear's manner of speech in this scene; they suggest that Lear speak in a "low key" with "every word impersonal" (*SD*, p. 124). Furthermore, the Fool spoke in a "high, contrasting voice" (*PA*, III.2.D1), which further emphasized Lear's difference.

Lear dominated the scene not only by acting style but also by position. The whole stage was dark, except for a beam of light which descended to reveal Lear and the Fool "on a raised plane far back in the centre." Lear stood upright, in a "statuesque pose," with his "arms extended and face lifted upward" in defiance of the elements; the Fool crouched at his feet, looking miserable.[37] The sight of the Fool beaten by the storm must have powerfully evoked both Lear's defiance of and identification with the raging elements. However, the production's depiction of the storm was not wholly nonrealistic. Fordham explains that while no attempt was made to depict a real wind ruffling hair and clothes, there was "the conventional-realistic sound of thunder and wind"; he adds that this was "super-imposed with unfortunate effect, since it result[ed] in a confusion of styles and tend[ed] to detract from audibility" (III.3, 4, and 6.Al.) Obviously, the sound effects were not merely token. Gielgud also mentions "the general opinion . . . that the first [storm] scene in particular was neither completely stylised nor treated realistically." He continues:

> It was thought by some that the figures were placed too far back on the stage, by others that the stillness of the grouping and the

Storm scene. The Fool crouches at Lear's feet; both are on a small raised platform. Photo by Angus McBean. Courtesy of The Raymond Mander & Joe Mitchenson Theatre Collection.

conventional poses were belied by the accompanying wind and thunder effects, which seemed to ask for realistic, wind-blown hair and garments, and broken, crouching attitudes to make the scene convincing. No doubt further experiments and rehearsals for lighting, sound-effects and movements were badly needed, but time and money were lacking, and therefore this scene was probably never carried out to the producer's satisfaction. (*PA*, III.3, 4, and 6.JG1)

Gielgud makes clear, however, that despite these unsatisfactory concessions to realism, Barker intended the voice "to convey the main feeling of the storm," and to do so, he bade the actor use his "full range."

It is at first difficult to reconcile Barker's use of sound effects with the position he seems consistently to maintain in the *Preface,* and elsewhere, against the use of such realistic devices. However, it is possible that the *Preface* does not condemn mechanical storms out of hand, but only the use of them in a way competitive to Lear. Barker writes that

by any such competitive machinery for thunder and lightning as Bradley quite needlessly assumes to be an inevitable part of the play's staging [the effect of Lear's creation of the storm] will be largely spoiled. (P. 13)

A note further elaborates that

Bradley argues in a footnote that *because* Shakespeare's "means of imitating a storm were so greatly inferior to ours" he could not have "had the stage-performance only or chiefly in view in composing these scenes." But this is, surely, to view Shakespeare's theater and its craft with modern eyes. The contemporary critic would have found it easier to agree that just *because* your imitation storm was such a poor affair you must somehow make your stage effect *without* relying on it. (P. 13 n)

Thus, Barker in fact seems not to demand a total absence of storm effects; rather, he simply suggests that they be used but not depended on to create the necessary effect—that is, they must not compete with Lear's creation of the storm. In this case, one can understand Barker's decision to use them in a manner complementary to Lear, and accept Gielgud's verdict that they were mismanaged because of lack of time. Furthermore, given Barker's earlier pronouncement about lack of scenery being as distracting to modern viewers as too much, he may very well have hesitated to present the audience with a totally imaginary storm; Barker's first concern is never to get in the way of audience response to Shake-speare's intention. If this conjecture is right, Barker's own intention backfired; his conception of the storm's depiction may have been clear, but its execution was confused and confusing.

Although his intention to show Lear as the embodiment of the storm was only partly fulfilled, Barker ensured the depiction of his more human elements in this first storm scene. His notes to Gielgud direct that "Here I stand, your slave" should be "simpler. Voice down, then up"; that "Let the great gods" be given "full value" and that Lear should "point to the audience" while it is spoken, thus including them in his experience; that Lear should "listen tenderly to the Fool" (*SD*, p. 125). This last point indicates a change in Lear, an abandonment of his solipsism, and to further illustrate it, Barker had Lear remove his cloak and kneel down—the kneeling always a significant gesture—to put it around the Fool. Moreover, the tone of Gielgud's voice managed to suggest that Lear's interest in finding shelter is for the Fool's sake alone (*PA*, III.2.D2). Finally, not forget-ting to give the audience a hint of the madness to come, Barker directed Gielgud to leave the stage "on a high, unfinished note" (*SD*, p. 125; *PA*, III.3, 4, and 6.JG1). He exited, incidentally, "with his arm placed protectively round the Fool" (*PA*, III.2.D2), thus embod-ying the *Preface*'s suggestion that the Fool should not be left to speak his soliloquy and so destroy the dramatic effect of Lear's change.

The second heath scene marks a further development in Lear; Gielgud, echoing Barker's preliminary note, writes that he "now lives in a purely metaphysical world, distant and dignified, with a burst of vision and horror in the speech in which he remembers the agony and grief to which he is a prey" (*PA*, III.3, 4, and 6.JG1; cf. also *SD*, p. 125). The scene opened onstage with Kent, Lear, and the Fool entering "from the back, at one side of the raised level"; Kent, who was leading, turned around to see Lear standing "rapt, above." The king's appearance showed the emotional crisis he had undergone since his last appearance: he had been crying and looked physically and mentally exhausted; his hair was disheveled, making him look both wild and pathetic. His demeanor, however, was "gentler," no longer suggesting "the outward grandeur of defiance, but the inner struggle" of the soul (*PA*, III.4.D1). When Lear spoke, it was with "a strange, detached note in his voice." Barker's preliminary note to Gielgud also suggests that Lear should use a "Strange Walk" here (*SD*, p. 125).

In the *Preface*, Barker writes of Lear's progress during this scene from patience, to thankfulness for his simple humanity, to humility and "gentle dignity," but says that "the crowning touch of all" comes in "I'll pray, and then I'll sleep" (pp. 37–38). To mark this moment in the production, Lear knelt in the mud, completely sincere; he bowed his head, clasped his hands in prayer, and beat his chest in contrition. Unlike his cursing posture, he dropped his hands "in front, palms outward, in a gesture of complete resignation to suffering"; his whole bearing showed the resolution of the struggle he has undergone (*PA,* III.4.D2). Gielgud writes that Barker also directed Lear to cross himself before beginning the speech "Poor naked wretches"; however, the actor found he had to omit this business

> after a few performances, as many people complained of its inconsistency with the emphasis on Pagan gods throughout the play. I bowed to their opinion, not wishing to confuse the emotional effect of such an important dramatic moment in the play by any extraneous action which should distract or offend, and so draw away the attention of certain members of the audience. But I still think the idea a very legitimate and effective one, giving the idea of prayer, and solitude in an oratory—very moving at such a moment on the wind-swept heath. . . . The beating of the breast was part of the same idea, and was, to my mind, more suggestive when it was preceded by the crossing. (*PA,* III.3, 4, and 6.JG1–2)

It is surprising that so many members of the audience were disturbed by the anachronism, especially given the fact that the costumes and scenery were of the Renaissance. As the production stood, Barker would have approved of Gielgud's omission on the grounds the actor himself gives; one has only to remember his remarks about the unprofitable distraction Shakespeare's bawdy sometimes occasions. In any case, Lear's entire posture still provided a stark and significant contrast to that which he assumed to call down the curse on Goneril.

Because this scene also marks Lear's final loss of his tenuous hold on sanity, Barker gave much thought to its presentation on stage. In his preliminary notes to Gielgud, he says simply that "the Fool's scream [when he finds Poor Tom in the hovel] turns [Lear] off his head"; to mark the moment, the actor should "lean . . . back on knees. Look through cage—fingers in front of face" (*SD,* p. 125). But Barker rarely felt perfectly satisfied with an idea; one of his most valuable critical faculties was his openness, his refusal to make fixtures of his responses and opinions.[38] So, here, Barker continued to develop his conception of the scene even after he had returned to France; he wrote to Gielgud, offering further suggestions:

> April 29, [1940]
> 18, Place des Etats-Unis

My dear Gielgud. Did we ever agree as to the precise moment at which Lear goes off his head?

I believe that Poor Tom's appearance from the hovel marks it. The "grumbling" inside, the Fool's scream of terror, the wild figure suddenly appearing—that combination would be enough to send him over the border-line. Do you mark the moment by doing something quite *new*? Difficult, I know, to find anything new to do at that moment. But something queer and significant of madness, followed (it would help) by a dead silence, before you say (again in a voice you have not used before)

Didst thou give all . . .

I don't doubt you have devised something. But thinking over the scene this struck me—ought to have struck me before; perhaps we *did* agree to it—so I drop you this line. . . . [last ellipsis mine]

April 30, morning.
I think I have it:—see next sheet.

. . . *shows the heavens more just.*
   Lear remains on knees at end of prayer, head buried in hands.
Edg: *Father . . . poor Tom.*

make much of this; don't hurry it; give it a "Banshee" effect, lilt and rhythm.
At the sound Lear lifts his head. Face seen through his outspread fingers (suggestion of madman looking through bars).
The Fool screams and runs on: business as at present. This gets Lear to his feet. He turns towards the hovel watching intently for what will emerge.

Dialogue as at present.

Edgar's entrance and speech: *Away . . . warm thee,* much as now. And Lear immensely struck by it. cf. Hamlet-Ghost. Just as it is finishing (Edg. not to hurry it) stalk him to present position for *Didst thou . . .*

and, as he turns for the speech, at B, we see that he is now quite off his head.

N.B. Once Edgar is on, he Kent and Fool must keep deadly still so that these movements of Lear may have their effect. Translate the Hamlet-Ghost business into terms of Lear and it will about give you the effect.

I believe this may be right. Worth trying anyhow. (*SD*, pp. 131–32)

These slight changes show Barker at his meticulous best. Instead of the Fool's screams providing the final, crude jolt to Lear's senses, it is the otherwordly wailing of Poor Tom that arrests Lear's attention; he lifts his head, not crazed with fright, but strangely drawn. Then, with his back to the audience as Barker directs, the actor is allowed space to let his eyes register Lear's change.

Fordham does not mention Gielgud's articulation of these new ideas, but what appears to be the original staging of the scene; its details confirm that it lacked the subtlety of Barker's afterthought (cf., for instance, the simple difference between Lear's rising in concern for the Fool above and the rather aimless—but not significantly so—action of the original staging: after praying, Lear

> remain[ed] silently in this position for one moment, radiating a new beauty of soul. Suddenly a wild voice [was] heard from the hovel. . . . The Fool rush[ed] out with a piercing, terrified scream and [clung] to Kent. The sudden, confused sound [broke] in on Lear's new-found peace with a fatal violence. Still kneeling, he raise[d] his hands, pressing clenched fists against his forehead in an agonised attempt to control his wits. But his eyes show[ed] that the turning point ha[d] been reached and that the mind ha[d] at last failed. (*PA*, III.4.D2)

Lear then rose "abstractedly," and only then did Tom emerge from the hovel and engage his fascination. From this point, however, one can assume that Fordham's descriptions illustrate Gielgud's portrayal of Lear's madness in either version: his gestures, now that the mind was "released from . . . struggle," became "free and ample," full of kingly courtesy. His speech was limpid and pitched higher than usual. His eyes ranged "without control," showing mental instability, while his lower jaw hung slackly, demonstrating that he no longer had full control of his faculties (*PA*, III.4.D3).

Barker's staging of this scene in terms of movement was both imaginative and evocative. Fordham relates that when Lear tried to cast off his "lendings,"

> Kent and the Fool rush[ed] to prevent him, and the three figures grapple[d] together for a moment, swaying in one mass in the semi-darkness. Kent [was] behind and the Fool in front of Lear, with Lear's head forming the apex of the weird triangle.
>
> At this moment Gloucester enter[ed]. . . . Lear's arm [shot] out from the mass, pointing wildly down at the approaching figure: "What's he?"
>
> Lear's mind [was] now distracted from its first impulse and he [was] left to stand alone again. (*PA*III.4.D3)

The triangular grouping of course demonstrated the close relationship between the three characters, and most particularly, the

concern of Kent and the Fool for Lear. But its grappling and swaying motion must also have suggested the hallucinative aspect of
Lear's mind, and the rapid succession of poses, its disjointedness.
Fordham also writes that Poor Tom's madness was partly embodied
in "his circular running round the stage" (III.3,4, and 6.A2); the fact
that he and Lear, at the end of the scene, circled the back of the stage
during their conversational pacing (*PA*, III.4.D4) must have further
strengthened the audience's perception of Lear's insanity, especially
when one considers that such movement diverged from the production's normal pattern. Lear finally left the stage, not understanding
the need for silence, but accepting it "like a child, placing his finger
to his lips and uttering a sibilant sound," while his companion, Poor
Tom, recited "a mad jingle" (*PA*, III.4.D4).

The management of the storm scenes, then, involved much more
than mere adherence to or rejection of Barker's earlier advice. While
the first scene between Kent and the anonymous gentleman simply
transposed the *Preface*'s points onto the stage, the scenes involving
Lear himself were more complicated: speech, gesture, and blocking

**The toppling of Lear's reason; Gielgud's eyes register the change Barker sug-
gested. Photo by Edwin Smith. Courtesy of Mrs. Edwin Smith.**

a.

b.

c.

d.

e.

Lear's interaction with Poor Tom; Fordham assigns the following lines to each photo:

a.

   Edgar (within): "Away, the foul fiend follows me . . ."

b.

   Lear: "What hast thou been?"

c.

   Lear: "Is man no more than this?"

d.

   Lear: "To have a thousand with red burning spits . . ."

e.

   Lear: "the little dogs, and all . . ."

Photos by Edwin Smith. Courtesy of The Raymond Mander & Joe Mitchenson Theatre Collection.

"Off, off, you lendings!" The grappling figures of Kent, Lear, and the Fool, with Poor Tom as onlooker. Photo by Edwin Smith. Courtesy of Mrs. Edwin Smith.

were orchestrated in a way that allowed Lear to embody the storm himself, as the *Preface* suggests, but the mechanical storm interfered with the full achievement of the intended effect because it both competed with the actors' voices and clashed with the stylized acting. The action of Lear's second heath scene, on the other hand, was refined to allow a more telling interpretation of Barker's original aim: to signify the final blow to Lear's mind.

Before moving on to a final assessment of the production's successes and failures, it is worth discussing the staging of act I, scene v. The scene receives no mention in the *Preface*, but in the production was interpreted differently by director and actor. When Gielgud had previously played this scene, the emphasis had been "on the mental processes in Lear and the Fool, and particularly on the mutual compassion of the two characters"; here, the emphasis was on "Lear's consuming impatience to escape from Goneril and press forward towards Regan." Consequently Lear paced restlessly while the Fool remained still, and Fordham judges that this "perpetual movement and noise tended to distract attention from the more subtle interplay

Storm scene sequence: Lear, Poor Tom, Kent, and the Fool. Six consecutive shots from one performance. Photos by Edwin Smith. Courtesy of Mrs. Edwin Smith.

of emotion" between the two characters (I.5.A1). But Gielgud himself writes understandingly of Barker's intention:

> The Producer interpreted this whole scene as representing—con-
> ventionally, for the purposes of the theatre—Lear's journey from
> Goneril to Regan. In demonstrating this idea, the combination of
> physical and mental weariness, impatience, despair and ap-
> prehension were completely welded in a simple and moving pat-
> tern by the genius of the producer. . . . (PA, I.5.JG1)

However, despite his understanding of Barker's purpose, Gielgud
found that the memory of his previously successful, and different,
approach to the scene hampered his commitment to Barker's interpretation, and furthermore, that the "rapid and continual walking"
was "almost impossible" to fit into his idea of the king's movements
(I.5.JG1). It is doubtful that Barker knew of Gielgud's hesitation
about this interpretation;[39] if he did, it is equally unlikely that he
would have insisted on it had Gielgud not understood its rationale:
as the actor himself writes, Barker did allow actors a certain latitude
in interpretation. However, Barker also felt that the director should
ensure a production's unity; the staging of the scene in this way
undoubtedly contributed to the pace and rhythm of the play, while
the relationship between Lear and the Fool was emphasized
elsewhere. Nevertheless, the unresolved differences of approach
seem to have interfered with the scene's successful depiction on
stage.

   The preceding account of the production shows that it successfully embodied many of the finer points of Barker's Lear, but
whether it fulfilled critical and audience expectation is another matter. The subjective nature of dramatic criticism is nowhere more
apparent than in comparing opinions of the same performance: on
the one hand, George W. Bishop of the Daily Telegraph and Morning
Post admired the "strength and . . . remarkable assumption of over-
powering physique in the Blake-like figure Mr. Gielgud presented,"
while on the other, James Agate of the Sunday Times lamented that
although "Mr. Gielgud composes a noble head for the part, it is . . . a
little less grand than Blake would have drawn." Such personal preferences aside, the production as a whole was greeted favorably,
although several aspects of it received some negative criticism.[40]

   The production was generally praised for the conception and
execution of the main part. Although Agate complained that the
ashlike Gielgud lacked the booming voice the part requires, suggested petulance instead of anger, and failed to make the critic feel
his danger of madness, he concluded that "with the necessary corrections, Gielgud's performance is a thing of great beauty, imagina-

tion, sensitiveness, understanding, executive virtuosity, and control. You would be wrong to say—this is not King Lear! You would be right to say that this is the King every inch but one."[41] Several other reviewers commented on the youthful quality of Gielgud's voice, although not all felt it a defect, given his expressive delivery. Many others commended his effective portrayal of Lear's madness, his cursing of Goneril, and his entry with the dead Cordelia in his arm, points that had all received especial attention from Barker. The *Times* critic praised Gielgud's performance in detail, concluding that its "particular strength . . . rest[ed] upon the boldness—the bold recognition from the first that in this tragedy we are borne through realms of fantasy in which cold reason cannot find satisfaction. To this, he added his appreciation of the way in which the actor "sketche[d] in [the details of the old King's corporal infirmities] lightly and adequately . . . not suffer[ing them] to become a load fettering him to the realistic plane." Clearly, Gielgud's Lear went beyond the realistic, successfully embodying the superhuman "portent" Barker reveals in the *Preface*.

The balance of the production and its ensemble playing also received universal acknowledgement; even Derek Verschoyle of the *Spectator*, who maintained that the play was a "ridiculous" one to put on stage, admitted that the acting and the "brilliance of the production concealed many of [the play's] absurdities." Many reviews praised nearly all of the cast members individually, Jack Hawkins's Edmund being especially remarked as both electrifying and engaging. In addition, several critics noted the individuality of Cathleen Nesbitt's Goneril and Fay Compton's Regan, which avoided easy "Ugly Sister-ish" caricature *(Daily Mail);* the *Illustrated London News* added that their parts, instead of being cut and then filled by second-rate actors, were "made really exciting and imposing."

Such careful attention to every part of the play was characteristic of the production: David Fairweather of *Theatre World* found it "difficult to imagine [one] more powerful or finely balanced," adding that "interest is not riveted on the tragic king to the exclusion of the other characters"; The *Times* praised its "large mould and controlled momentum." This praise was echoed by Ivor Brown in the *Observer:* "You see 'King Lear' in trim and in proportion. The scholars have got it wrong and now Mr. Granville Barker and Mr. Casson and a glorious company have put it right." Desmond Mac-Carthy, whose review for the *New Statesman and Nation* echoed the judgment of other critics, explained how the balance was achieved and how it affected one's perception of the play: the production had the "great merit of taking the play straight through . . . [and] this has the effect of welding the sub-plot of Gloucester and his sons and the

tragedy of Lear and his daughters together in the manner Shakespeare intended." He added that "the production also gives what I
have never seen before, due emphasis to the scene of Gloucester's
eyes being scooped out. If this strong horror is not allowed proper
place after Lear's storm and madness scene [,] an emotional anticlimax is apt to be felt by the audience while the moving reunion
with Cordelia is preparing and the double story continued." Here is
the point from Barker's *Preface,* not stated theoretically but felt in
performance; however, its similarity to Barker's wording might indicate that MacCarthy was already influenced by the *Preface* before he
ever saw the production.[42] Nevertheless, in either case, his comments show that the points Barker makes in his criticism are dramatically achievable.

This universal praise turns to almost universal disappointment
with the storm scenes. Bishop, for one, felt the production gave
Lamb the lie until the first one; then, a good start was ruined by the
subsidence of both the real and the internal storms. Ivor Brown
agreed that "the Storm Scene fell short of expectation: there was,
perhaps, a fault of lighting or too much of the stage-managerial
wind-machine. Lear *is* the storm here—and somehow was not." The
News Chronicle and *Bystander* also commented that Gielgud's words
were sometimes lost because of sound effects. On the other hand,
the *Times* reported that Gielgud "trust[ed] the verse and his power to
speak it, as a solitary silver figure in the dark loneliness, he [spoke]
the storm, and his trust [was] never at any vital point betrayed."
MacCarthy, to cite yet another view, made no mention of the mechanics of the storm, but felt that the scenes "need[ed] much subtler
orchestration than they have received [in regard to] the voices of
Lear, Poor Tom and the Fool." He, in fact, found Gielgud's changes
in pitch and note throughout the play too various, and therefore
distracting. On the other hand, Ashley Dukes complained that the
scenes were played too far back, making Lear seem "remote" and the
other characters "shadowy," and thus interfering with the audience's
empathy for them. Nevertheless, David Fairweather felt Lear's agony
in the storm to be one of the outstanding moments of the production, while the *Daily Sketch* reviewer simply could not believe that
"the storm scene . . . has ever been better played. . . ."

The difference in critical opinion about the cause of the storm
scenes' failure suggests that the failure was not complete; certainly,
the tone of the comments quoted above is one of disappointment
rather than condemnation. Most of them imply that if only this
element, or that, had been more fully worked out or adjusted, the
scenes would have come right, thus bearing out Gielgud's own judgment that more time, money, and experimentation could have made

the scenes succeed. While it is unfortunate that Barker could not fully prove his case against Lamb in the crucial test of performance, it is arguable that he still managed to prove Lamb wrong; no one felt that the scenes had been performed in the best way possible and still fell short; rather they glimpsed the possibility of successful performance through the partial failure. Barker would have brilliantly won his case if audiences had felt "It's finally been done!"; as it was, he made them feel "It wasn't done here but I can see how it could have been." That itself is a far cry from Lamb's attitude that it cannot be done at all. Indeed, many of the reviews recognized, whether explicitly or implicitly, that this production *had* proved Lamb wrong: "Those who declare the part is unactable should learn wisdom from [Gielgud's] latest portrayal of it, which in the tempest scene rises to tragic heights which are positively dizzy, and in the mad moments is very, very mad" *(Daily Mail);* "Gielgud acts the unactable excellently, giving dignity to the king even in his maddest moments" *(Evening Standard);* "It has been the opinion of some authorities that Lear may be pictured in the brain but not realized on the stage. [However,] John Gielgud's fine presentation is certainly a powerful impressive creation" (the *Stage*); and finally, "Lamb might have retracted his assertion about 'King Lear' being unactable had he seen the noble performance [of] John Gielgud . . ." (the *Star*). The reviewers' praise was validated by audience response: halfway through its wartime run of six weeks, the *Bystander* reported that performances were still packed, even though, by Ashley Dukes's estimation, London had by then "lost two-thirds of its playgoers" ("The English Scene," p. 470). Dukes himself, attending a performance some time into the play's run, could only obtain standing room in a theatre crowded with 1,350 other spectators (p. 467).

Despite such enthusiastic response, the storm scenes may not have been the only deficient aspect of the production; it is difficult to determine whether Barker managed to strike the right balance in setting and costume. Bishop wrote that the production's "Tudor period" setting was effective, while Dukes's response was qualified: he commented that "Elizabethan [or any other] treatment . . . could have been satisfying . . . if the elemental character of the drama was still preserved. . . . But . . . this neo-Tudor style [was] weak in conception, effeminate in detail" ("The English Scene," pp. 467–68); therefore, it was only effective until the storm scenes, when a more pagan and elemental atmosphere is felt.[43]

Thus far, the program's straightforward description of the Renaissance setting is verified, even though its complete appropriateness is questioned. But Ivor Brown received an impression of mixed intentions, which he described in his *Observer* review:

Mr. Furse's decoration attempted a mixture of the primitive and Renaissance elements in the text, and that must mean something of a mess. The yellow background to the cliff scene was sheer pain to the eye, and almost destroyed the acting in front of it, although that acting contained the grandest fragments of Lear's crumbling mind . . . projected beautifully by Gielgud.

Perhaps Barker and Furse deliberately tried to incorporate both possible settings into one background, or, more likely, the primitive element was a figment of Brown's imagination; all other reviews mentioned an Elizabethan, neo-Tudor, or Tudor setting, and the *Daily Mail, Reynolds News,* and the *Stage* actually commented on the effective use of curtains and simple settings. Given Barker's commitment to the harmonious design of a production, it is hard to imagine he would countenance a confused and confusing presentation of period.

The portrayal of the Fool came in for some of the severest criticism; hardly one critic found anything good to say about his performance, although some conceded the difficulty of the part. The failure of Stephen Haggard in this role points to yet another reason for the possible failure of some of Barker's ideas; they are only realizable through a human medium, which Barker himself stresses is a fallible one. If an actor is incapable of realizing a particular conception of a role, it does not mean that the conception itself is faulty. Cordelia, too, was criticized by the *Tatler* and *Bystander* for being merely competent in her role, a complaint that gives some idea of the very high standard of playing; the *Illustrated Sporting and Dramatic News* made the more damning comment that she spoke "in a large theatre as if it were the village institute at Little Peddlington."

But these are nevertheless minor points. The contemporary appraisals of the production as a whole have been validated by later theatre historians. Maynard Mack reports that "from all accounts [it was] the greatest performance of our time," while Robert Speaight says it "remains among the glories of the Shakespearian stage" and feels "quite sure that its equal has not been seen in our time." Gielgud himself, arguably the finest actor of his generation, believes that he only ever touched Lear in this production, and in playing the role subsequently, acknowledged Barker's continuing influence on his interpretation. Comparison with some subsequent productions bears out these evaluations.[44]

Peter Brook's *Lear* of 1962 provides a useful contrast. In the first place, it worried over matters already solved by Barker thirty years before; Charles Marowitz, who was assistant director and kept a "Lear Log," writes that he and Brook spent hours discussing Edgar's

Curtain detail. Probably Lear's second departure from Goneril's house. Photo by Edwin Smith. Courtesy of Mrs. Edwin Smith.

disguise as Poor Tom, puzzling over the way it fit into his whole character development. As Barker admirably demonstrates in the *Preface,* the disguise at times relates not to Edgar at all, but to Lear. Brook and Marowitz attacked the play from a consistent psychological angle, and thus failed to see some of the role's point.[45]

In the second place, they tried to fit the play into a "Beckettian" view of life, citing as "germinal" Gloucester's suicide attempt at Dover, which is a "metaphysical farce which ridicules life, death, sanity and illusion" (Marowitz, "Lear Log," p. 104). This may be an element in the play, but again in search of consistency, they reworked scenes that did not fit their conception: the servant who defends Gloucester during his blinding was omitted, and those who aid him afterwards were replaced by rude, busy servants who shove and collide with the pathetic old man. This was done, Marowitz writes, "to remove the tint of sympathy usually found at the end of the Blinding Scene." Similarly, the play ended with a dull, rumbling noise, suggestive of the storm but more ominous than it (Marowitz, "Lear Log," p. 114).

Last but also important, Lear's stature was belied by his actions. The "Log" relates how improvisation led to Lear's knights breaking up Goneril's hall at his command, and the sequence was kept in the film version of the production.[46] Here, Lear looks and acts like a legendary berserk, as he and his men smash benches, hurl tables from a balcony into a courtyard below, and generally terrorize Goneril's household. It is an odd *Lear* that justifies his daughters' comments and behavior and a dubious distinction for its directors. Furthermore, as Maynard Mack points out in his response to the scene, one was left with the impression that with such a force at his command, Lear could seize control of the kingdom again at any time; one wondered why he felt so vulnerable ("King Lear," p. 32).

By all accounts, other Lears have been equally lacking. Both Mack and Speaight describe Charles Laughton's at Stratford in 1959 as a Father Christmas figure, one who captured the human Lear at the expense of the "apocalyptic." Donald Wolfit's Lear of 1943 was well received, but according to Speaight was part of an "inadequately supported" production. Herbert Blau's 1961 production for the San Francisco Actors' Workshop focused on the subtextual "nothing" to the exclusion of all else—a fault of "directors' theatre" whose shortcomings Mack succinctly demonstrates.[47]

More recent productions have been more successful, but to trace the history of *Lear* since Gielgud's portrayal is beyond my brief; the references to subsequent productions are not meant to be exhaustive but to help define, by contrast, Barker's achievement. His production was not perfect, as he himself admits, and it failed for many viewers in the crucial test of the storm scenes. Nevertheless, it let its audience glimpse a Lear who was symbolic as well as human, and made strong the connection between plot and subplot. It refused to reduce the play to any one of its elements, finding space for its humor as well as its tragedy. It illuminated the actability of the storm scenes despite its own failure there, and seemed to make the audience as well as the actors feel that they "were having the experience of [their] lives."[48] Quite simply, as the *Times* pointed out, Barker trusted "the play's stagecraft . . . to a company whose accomplishment collectively and individually [was] equal to every demand made upon it." He presented, that is, not Barker's *Lear*, but Shakespeare's.

5

Conclusion

As I hope I have demonstrated, Barker's influence on the modern understanding and performance of Shakespeare's plays has been crucial and pervasive. The way the plays are staged and many of the ways they are considered ultimately derive from his practice and instruction, although some of the lessons he taught have still to be fully learned.

Those who today attend a performance of a Shakespeare play have certain expectations about its presentation. They will not expect to see a realistic picture framed by a proscenium arch, but a suggestive background, if there is one at all, on an open stage or on the floor of a small studio theatre. Their presence as an audience will be noted by the actors on stage, who will direct asides and soliloquies to them. They will most likely hear the virtually complete text of the play spoken naturally and briskly, and only the music that the text demands. Scene changes will be minimal: the slight rearrangement of an architectural setting, the suggestive use of lighting or props, or nothing at all. Therefore, they will expect the performance to last only two-and-a-half to three-and-a-half hours, with a single interval of fifteen minutes.

Their expectations derive from the precedents set by the Savoy Shakespeare. Certainly, as I have indicated, Barker's was not the only voice calling for reform of the Shakespearean stage, but his was the most influential. As a practical and respected man of the theatre, he was better placed to influence custom through his reforms than Poel or Craig, the one regarded as an eccentric pedant and the other as an impractical genius.[1] Barker's all-round experience of the theatre, as actor and playwright as well as director, sharpened his sensitivity to dramatic construction and portrayal and gave authority to his written criticism.

Because of the regard in which Barker was held, his influence extends well beyond the details of production; it has affected attitude as well. The audience described above will visit the theatre not primarily to hear beautiful poetry spoken well, but to see a good play; Shakespeare's case as a playwright no longer needs proof. They will probably come with an understanding of the conventions of Shakespeare's theatre, ready to accept the stage as any place it needs to be and obvious disguise as impenetrable; if they do not, staging practice will quickly teach it. Modern production has achieved the compromise between the seventeenth and the twentieth centuries that Barker advocated.

Barker's approach to the stage interpretation of a play has also had its effect, although not as much as one could sometimes wish. As I have illustrated, Barker approached each play individually, taking it on its own terms; his view, whether considering character, atmosphere, meaning, or any other element of the play, was never one-dimensional. Thus, he can see Edgar's disparate functions as a character in his own right and as a foil to Lear in the course of the play. He could join the varied elements of *The Winter's Tale* into a coherent whole without subjecting it to a rigidly consistent treatment of period. He could allow humor into tragedy and take an ad hoc approach to character, understanding that Leontes's jealousy is functional and Othello's thematic; that is, he understood that Leontes's jealousy is not the subject of the play but the catalyst of its action and, as such, needs no psychological context or plausible motivation. His approach, put most simply, was eclectic, refusing to define precisely time, place, and character when such definition would interfere with the life and meaning of the play.

In the best modern performances, his approach is followed, but all too often Shakespeare's plays have become hobbyhorses for directors to ride. Sometimes this takes the benign form of finding parallels between the play and later historical events; for example, a *Richard II* set in Russia with Richard as Tsar and Bolingbroke as Lenin.[2] No violence is done to the play itself, though one may find oneself wondering, like Barker at seeing Hamlet in plus fours, why this Russian Gaunt apostrophizes England. But put away that thought and one is struck anew by Shakespeare's insight into political conflict; history becomes not past event but a mirror of our own time.

More damaging is the production that wrenches Shakespeare's play into the director's vision at the expense of the playwright's own meaning; Peter Brook's *Lear*, described in the preceding chapter, is an obvious example of such interference. The need to express a definitive and idiosyncratic view of a play's meaning is the modern contribution to theatrical distortion of Shakespeare, a distortion that is also reflected in criticism of the plays—a point to which I will return. Barker's influence here could be salutary: his insistence on the need for performance to bring a play to life involves the recognition that no performance is definitive, no production the final statement of a play's meaning. His whole emphasis on the need for collaboration—between scholars and directors, directors and actors, actors and characters, actors and audience, audience and play—implies multifaceted meaning. To Barker, the play is like a crystal and the production light which picks out certain sides and colors; the whole is always there but is never seen at once or in the same way. The image is not the vital one Barker himself would choose but it serves to illustrate his approach. A play to Barker is always a living organism, never the organized illustration of a principle.

Barker's emphasis on character in action as the basis of drama is an integral part of this approach and can provide a safeguard against modern reductive tendencies. As the discussion of *King Lear* has shown, Barker approaches meaning through the subtle interplay among characters and between facets of one character; his attitude that theme is embodied in character leads to a more subtle understanding of the ideas informing a play than the opposite approach: deciding on the theme of a play and then turning the characters into cardboard illustrations of it, distorting them and the action where necessary. Because he approached it through character, Barker's emphasis on theme, both in his productions and in his criticism, was never an exclusive one; he never said, "*This* is what the play means."

And here modern criticism can also learn from Barker. Norman Rabkin, in *Shakespeare and the Problem of Meaning* (1981), outlines the critical tendency a decade ago to reduce each play's meaning to a central theme; reaction against a multiplicity of "central" themes for each play has now led to a refusal to find any meaning at all in the plays.[3] Barker represents a midpoint between these procrustean and nihilistic views, sanely illustrating that the humanity and vitality of Shakespeare's plays lead to valid multiple meanings, that the plays are spacious reflections of life and not tightly argued disquisitions. Furthermore, his own productions and prefaces demonstrate that flexible treatment of a play does not preclude a coherent conception of it.

This openness to meaning is one area where Barker's lesson still needs to be taken to heart, but some other of his ideas have already had a profound influence on criticism. Most importantly, scholarship now habitually takes account of stage performance; even Wilson Knight, who favors a symbolic interpretation of the plays and is at the other end of the critical spectrum from Barker, so recognized the importance of stage presentation that he devoted much of his career to giving dramatic recitals and directing productions.[4]

This idea alone—of the text-as-score—has assured Barker's continuing effect on the way criticism approaches the plays; recognition of the validity of emotional responses to disparate productions of the same play, responses that cannot be ignored now that performance is an accepted element of the play's existence, has led to increasing calls to "free Shakespeare." This demand is exemplified in John Russell Brown's book of that name, in which he argues for "the freeing of Shakespeare's plays from restrictive presuppositions and the limitations of inherited procedures" and asks questions about "what the plays do in particular circumstances, not with what they always are." He mentions that Barker's "good sense is still acclaimed by both scholars and directors," and in fact, Barker's own criticism and productions would have satisfied Brown's demands, many of which were made by Barker himself half a century ago.[5]

To conclude, Barker's ideas about Shakespeare are not just important for the influence they have already had but for the answers they may still give us about critical and theatrical interpretation. Certainly, Barker's work is liable to some historical limitations; advances have since been made, for example, in the textual and Elizabethan theatre studies on which he relied. But if one may adapt his own phrase, these are incidental rather than essential limitations; even his conception of character is based on an understanding of dramatic interaction rather than on the contemporary novelistic premises of critics like Bradley. His emphasis on character in action as the expression of dramatic idea sometimes leads him to misjudge plays like *Measure for Measure,* but on the whole it brings him closer to the truth and enduring values of the plays than many of our contemporary critics ever reach. His sure sense of the theatre safeguards him from abstraction, from a disposition to sum up, which some critics might regard as a deficiency but others consider a constructive reticence: a desire to make the play itself, rather than an individual view of it, accessible to audiences and readers.

Most important of all perhaps, Barker's work, both practical and written, insisted on the vitality of Shakespeare's plays. He demanded that they take their rightful place on our stage, not as museum pieces but as mirrors of life, at once capable of producing spontaneous enjoyment and provoking better knowledge of ourselves and others. He demonstrated that they did this not through any naive appeal but through skillful dramatic construction, and he demonstrated this both in theory and actuality. Changes would have eventually occurred without Barker, but his presence on the Shakespearean scene from 1912 until his death in 1946 undoubtedly redirected the course of Shakespearean production and criticism in this century. John Gielgud, writing in 1952, lends his own authoritative voice to this assertion when he calls Barker's "example . . . so powerful that I unhesitatingly consider him to have been the strongest influence I have known in the theatre. . . ."[6] Certainly, Granville Barker has been not only the strongest but the most benign influence we have yet felt in the restoration of an authentic Shakespeare to his modern audience and readers.

Appendix 1
Cast Lists for the Savoy Productions and *King Lear*

SAVOY THEATRE.

Licensed by the Lord Chamberlain to
Mr. G. A. Richardson (Secretary Savoy Theatre and Operas, Ltd.), Savoy Hotel, W. C.

Lillah McCarthy   **Granville Barker.**

SATURDAY, SEPTEMBER 21st. 1912, AT 8 P.M., AND
EVERY FOLLOWING EVENING AT 8.15,

SHAKESPEARE'S

The Winter's Tale

PRODUCED BY GRANVILLE BARKER.

Time	HERBERT HEWETSON
Leontes	HENRY AINLEY
Mamillius	ERIC RAE
Camillo	STANLEY DREWITT
Antigonus	GUY RATHBONE
Cleomenes	FREDERICK CULLEY
Dion	FREDERICK MORLAND
Polixenes	CHARLES GRAHAM
Florizel	DENNIS NEILSON-TERRY
Archidamus	FELIX AYLMER
Mariner	FRANCIS ROBERTS
Old Shepherd	H. O. NICHOLSON
Clown	LEON QUARTERMAINE
Autolycus	ARTHUR WHITBY
A Servant	ERIC LUGG
Another Servant	J. P. TURNBULL
A Gaoler	HERBERT ALEXANDER
An Officer of the Court	JOHN KELT
The Court Poet	H. B. WARING
A Lord	GEORGE BURROWS
Another Lord	FRANK CONROY
Paulina's Steward	NIGEL PLAYFAIR
Hermione	LILLAH McCARTHY
Perdita	CATHLEEN NESBITT
Paulina	ESMÉ BERINGER
Emilia	ENID ROSE
Mopsa	JANET ROSS-JOHNSON
Dorcas	EFGA MYERS
A Lady	MARY DEVERELL
Another Lady	VERA DYER

DECORATION OF THE PLAY BY NORMAN WILKINSON.
THE COSTUMES DESIGNED BY ALBERT ROTHENSTEIN.

THERE WILL BE ONE INTERVAL OF 15 MINUTES.

[ORIGINAL PROGRAM.]

205

SAVOY THEATRE.

Licensed by the Lord Chamberlain to
Mr. G. A. Richardson (Secretary Theatre and Operas, Ltd.) Savoy Hotel, W.C.

Lillah McCarthy.   **Granville Barker.**

FRIDAY, NOVEMBER 15TH, 1912 AT 7 P.M., AND EVERY
FOLLOWING EVENING AT 8.15 P.M.

SHAKESPEARE'S COMEDY

Twelfth Night

PRODUCED BY GRANVILLE BARKER.

Orsino.. ARTHUR WONTNER
Sebastian.. DENNIS NEILSON-TERRY
Antonio... HERBERT HEWETSON
A Sea Captain.. DOUGLAS MUNRO
(By arrangement with MISS HILDA TREVELYAN AND MR. EDMUND GWENN)
Valentine.. COWLEY WRIGHT
Curio.. FRANK CONROY
Sir Toby Belch.. ARTHUR WHITBY
Sir Andrew Aguecheek....................................... LEON QUARTERMAINE
Malvolio... HENRY AINLEY
Fabian.. H. O. NICHOLSON
Feste.. C. HAYDEN COFFIN
Priest... EDGAR PLAYFORD
1st Officer... FRANCIS ROBERTS
2nd Officer.. HERBERT ALEXANDER
Servant.. NEVILLE GARTSIDE
Olivia... EVELYN MILLARD
Maria.. LEAH BATEMAN HUNTER
Viola.. LILLAH McCARTHY

Lords, Guests, Sailors, Officers, Musicians, Attendants.—Messrs. Geo. Burrows, Maurice
Tosh, Gilbert Chalmers Colona, Felix Aylmer, William Moore, Harold French, Eric Lugg,
H. B. Waring, Reginald Garnett, Cecil Apted, J. Burrows, S. Belinfante.
Mesdames Margaret Bruhling, Vera Dyer, Enid Rose.

DECORATION OF THE PLAY AND COSTUMES DESIGNED BY NORMAN
WILKINSON.

There will be Two Intervals of 10 minutes.

[ORIGINAL PROGRAM.]

SAVOY THEATRE, STRAND, W. C.

Licensed by the Lord Chamberlain to
Mr. G. A. Richardson (Secretary Savoy Theatre and Operas, Ltd.), Savoy Hotel, W.C.

Lessee and Manager .... H. B. IRVING.

Lillah McCarthy   **Granville Barker**

EVERY EVENING AT 8 P.M.

SHAKESPEARE'S COMEDY

A Midsummer Night's Dream

Produced by GRANVILLE BARKER.

Theseus... BALIOL HOLLOWAY
Hippolyta.. EVELYN HOPE
Egeus... RALPH HUTTON
Hermia.. LAURA COWIE
Lysander.. E. ION SWINLEY
Helena.. PHYLLIS RELPH
Demetrius... GUY RATHBONE
Philostrate... HERBERT HEWETSON
Quince.. ARTHUR WHITBY
Snug.. NEVILLE GARTSIDE
Bottom.. NIGEL PLAYFAIR
Flute... LEON QUARTERMAINE
Snout... STRATTON RODNEY
Starveling.. H. O. NICHOLSON
Oberon.. DENNIS NEILSON-TERRY
Titania... CHRISTINE SILVER
Puck.. DONALD CALTHROP
A Fairy... GEORGE BURROWS
Peas-Blossom.. ODETTE GOIMBAULT
Cobweb.. MARJORIE COULSON
Moth.. EILEEN JOWETT
Mustard-Seed.. SHEILA O'BRIEN

Attendant on Titania—	*Attendant on Oberon—*	*Attendant on Theseus—*
Olive Alexander, Elsie Averill, Gladys Blume, Margot Brigden, Margaret Dean, Jean Gregor, Winifred Tappings, Valentine Savage, Gladys Wiles	Eileen Desmond Deane, Olive Elton, Iris Fraser Foss.	Dorothy Warren, Beatrice Drury, Elaine Temple, Manora Thew, Mary Ross-Shore, Angela Colenso, Sybil Graham, Tomara Richards.
Gerald Jerome, Horace Taylor.	D. Cooper, Alex. Fortescue, M. Hogan, P. Madgewick, M. Neville, C. Stock, E. Warburton, H. Woodward.	Cecil Brymer, E. C. Francis, Charles Melling, Eric Messiter, J. H. Moore, Edmund Phelps, C. Shepherd Smith, G. West, H. P. Templeton.

The Decoration of the Play by NORMAN WILKINSON.
The Music and Dances by CECIL SHARP.

The Management owes many thanks to VICTOR MACLURE for painting the Scenery; to MISS DOROTHY CARLTON SMYTH, MRS. OWEN and MR. SAVAGE for making the Dresses, to R. & G. MANNING PIKE for painting many of them; to MR. CLARKSON for Wigs; to MR. GAMBA for Shoes; and indeed to many others whom it is impossible to mention.

There will be one interval of 5 minutes and one inverval of 15 minutes.

With the indulgence of the Audience, no calls will be taken by the Actors until the end of the Play.

[ORIGINAL PROGRAM.]

THE OLD VIC THEATRE, LONDON

APRIL 15 TO MAY 25, 1940 (38 PERFORMANCES)
(MATINEE ON SATURDAYS; NO PERFORMANCES ON MONDAYS)

SHAKESPEARE

King Lear

Lear, King of Britain	JOHN GIELGUD
King of France	ALAN MACNAUGHTEN
Duke of Burgundy	BASIL COLEMAN
Duke of Cornwall	ANDREW CRUICKSHANK
Duke of Albany	HARCOURT WILLIAMS
Earl of Kent	LEWIS CASSON
Earl of Gloucester	NICHOLAS HANNEN
Edgar, son to Gloucester	ROBERT HARRIS
Edmund, bastard son to Gloucester	JACK HAWKINS
Curan, a courtier	CHARLES STAITE
Old Man, tenant to Gloucester	FRANK TICKLE
Doctor	CHARLES STAITE
Fool	STEPHEN HAGGARD
Oswald	JULIAN SOMERS
A Captain, employed by Edmund	JAMES DONALD
A Herald	JOHN McCALLUM
Goneril)	CATHLEEN NESBITT
Regan) daughters to Lear	FAY COMPTON
Cordelia)	JESSICA TANDY

SCENERY AND COSTUMES, OF THE RENAISSANCE PERIOD,
BY ROGER FURSE
MUSIC ARRANGED BY HERBERT MENGES

THE PRODUCTION BY LEWIS CASSON,

based on Harley Granville-Barker's 'Preface to King Lear',
and his personal advice besides.
Played from a virtually complete text.
Actual time of playing; from 7.30 p.m. to 11.10 p.m.
(including one interval of fifteen minutes after Act III, Scene 6.)
[REPRINTED FROM HALLAM FORDHAM'S "PLAYER IN ACTION."]

Appendix 2
Barker and the Forum Scene
from *Julius Caesar*

In 1911, Barker was invited by Beerbohm Tree to direct the Forum Scene from *Julius Caesar* as part of the latter's Coronation Gala at His Majesty's Theatre on 27 June. His attempt to do so deserves discussion, as it is in many ways representative of his approach to Shakespeare. However, the nature of the occasion and the production of an isolated scene, together with the uncertainty of whether Barker's version was actually performed, place it outside the mainstream of his work.

Barker's planning of the scene is characteristic of his thorough approach to production. He printed a 24-page pamphlet of detailed stage directions for the 239 actors, many of them distinguished, who were assembled to make up the crowd. The plan divides them into identifiable factions of senators, lictors, women, old men, Caesar's old soldiers, knights, republicans, and commoners; these groups are identified by a letter of the alphabet and the actors in them by numbers. Barker outlines the attitude of each group (the soldiers' anger, the republicans' triumph, the women's wariness, the commoners' ignorant excitement) and then further characterizes them, assigning all odd-numbered commoners, for example, a murmur of protest at Antony's mention of Caesar. He also individualizes the members of these groups, denoting specific gestures, actions, and lines for particular actors (always identified by letter and number). For example, he has two commoners attempt to storm the platform when Antony addresses the crowd as "Romans."

The whole scene is worked out with immense care for the orchestration of mood; here Barker's concern for plausible motivation and behavior is very much in evidence. Instead of depicting the crowd simply as a mindless mob swayed first by Brutus and then by Antony, Barker makes Caesar's old soldiers loyal to him throughout the action and only cowed into conforming silence. Moreover, by careful manipulation of small groups, he is able to show how tentative and scattered response, first to one orator and then to the other, is gradually transformed into overwhelming mass emotion: members of the crowd discuss the speeches amongst themselves, agreeing, disagreeing, arguing, and finally, being persuaded.

Similarly, Barker carefully plots the levels of vocal response in the scene, avoiding obvious and artificial manipulation of volume. Instead, he varies from the opening general hum of conversation (earnest, rapid, but not loud), to cheers and hoots, to silence when Brutus explains why he has killed Caesar, a silence only broken when Brutus concludes he has offended no one; then the approval of the crowd erupts in crescendoing sound. The arrival of Caesar's body still does not silence them, and with the departure of Brutus and the senators they become more rowdy; only now do they abandon themselves to shouting. When Antony attempts to speak, he is greeted by the soldiers' cheers and the far greater howls and shouts of protest from the rest of the crowd; these are eventually prolonged for forty seconds at "Countrymen" and force Antony to wait for silence. Gradually, the crowd quietens, until Antony's mention of Brutus sets off a drowning shout of approval. This ebb and flow of sound, sometimes diminishing to silence, continues throughout the scene.

Such is Barker's plan on paper, though it is difficult to ascertain whether his version was actually performed at the gala. The program credits him with production of the scene, and a review in the *Bystander* (5 July 1911) describes action similar to that in Barker's stage directions; for example, one member of the crowd tried to climb up to the rostrum to scuffle with Antony at the beginning of his speech, and later, Antony was "interrupted by a storm of wild cheers" when he mentioned Brutus. However, the reviewer for the *Times* indicated that "it was really impossible to tell" if Barker's plan "was carried out as designed. . . . The Forum crowd has always been wonderfully life-like at His Majesty's, and there was no very perceptible difference in the total impression last night" (28 June 1911, p. 12). Hesketh Pearson, who was himself a member of the crowd, writes in *The Last Actor-Managers* (London: Methuen & Co., 1950), p. 76, that Barker's detailed action required more rehearsal time than was available. Barker tried to supervise two or three rehearsals with the help of a "powerful bell," but they were "chaotic" and ineffective. Tree therefore "scrapped" Barker's pamphlet and adopted the "simple method . . . of letting the rabble do what they liked when given free rein, while attending in dead silence to Antony [played by Tree] whenever he was orating." His account is substantiated by the *Times*'s reviewer, who reported that during the dress rehearsal on 26 June Tree "could be heard whispering instructions to the crowd" even though he was "in the midst of his most impassioned flights of oratory" (27 June 1911, p. 8).

The plan itself in some ways departs from Barker's usual practice. The difficulty of coordinating 239 actors (the number of names listed in the program) may explain the anomaly of Barker's working out such detailed action, contrary to the principles of directing that he espoused (see chapter 2). In addition, it is not clear how much freedom Barker had in determining some aspects of production—for example, it is unlikely that he actually requested the presence of 239 extras. Finally, it should be remembered that the circumstances of production, geared to once-only performance for a special occasion, did not make Shakespeare or theatre its priority; as the *Times*'s reviewer recognized, "the nature of the performances" could be summed up in the word "vehicular" (28 June 1911, p. 12). However, his feeling that the Forum Scene somehow transcended the occasion by virtue of its "rhythm and movement, and cumulative force," as well as his complaint about its "strictly symmetrical arrangement" of the crowd around the center-stage rostrum, suggests that Barker's plan strongly influenced, even if it did not dictate, the details of production.

A copy of Barker's pamphlet, printed for him by Warrington & Co., London, and dated 16 June 1911, can be found in the Beerbohm Tree Collection, University of Bristol Theatre Collection. Copies of the Coronation Gala program and reviews of the occasion (including that from the *Bystander*) are held by the Theatre Museum, London, currently housed in the Victoria & Albert Museum.

Notes

Preface

1. Two other shorter studies have recently been published: Manmohan Mehra, *Harley Granville-Barker: a critical study of the major plays* (Calcutta: Naya Prokash, 1981) and Elmer W. Salenius, *Harley Granville Barker* (Boston: Twayne, 1982). Dennis Kennedy's *Granville Barker and the Dream of Theatre* (Cambridge: Cambridge University Press, 1985) appeared while this book was in production.

Chapter 1. Forerunners of Barker: Poel and Craig

1. For much of the material included in this discussion, I am indebted to Allardyce Nicoll, *Early Nineteenth Century Drama 1800–50*, vol. 4 of *A History of English Drama, 1660–1900*, 2d ed. (Cambridge: Cambridge University Press, 1955), pp. 58–78 for information about the quality of nineteenth-century drama, and to J. L. Styan, *The Shakespeare Revolution: Criticism and Performance in the 20th Century* (Cambridge: Cambridge University Press, 1977), pp. 11–29 for information about Victorian Shakespeare and the theatres in which it was performed.

2. George Nash, *Edward Gordon Craig 1872–1966* [Exhibition catalogue for the Victoria and Albert Museum] (London: HM Stationery Office, 1967), p. 7.

3. Quoted in Robert Speaight, *William Poel and the Elizabethan Revival* (London: Heinemann, 1954), pp. 25 and 32.

4. Speaight, *William Poel*, p. 80.

5. See William Poel, *Shakespeare in the Theatre* (London and Toronto: Sidgwick & Jackson, 1913), pp. 120–21; on pp. 179–80 he criticizes an Anglo-Saxon production of *King Lear*. Further references to this book, hereafter cited as Poel, appear in the text. Styan, *Shakespeare Revolution*, p. 21, recounts the famous anecdote regarding the nineteenth-century search for authenticity: Kean not only set his production of *The Winter's Tale* in Bithyria (since Bohemia has no coastline), but also cut out Autolycus and the English shepherds for reasons of accuracy.

6. John Addington Symonds, quoted in Poel, p. 9.

7. Edward M. Moore, "William Poel," *Shakespeare Quarterly* 23 (Winter 1972):33–34.

8. William Poel, "Shakespeare's 'Prompt Copies': A Plea for the Early Texts," letter to the *Times Literary Supplement*, 3 February 1921; reprinted by the London Shakespeare League as a broadsheet, BL 1865. c 3 (162); Speaight, *William Poel*, pp. 66–67.

9. Sir Lewis Casson, "The Influence of William Poel on the Modern Theatre," BBC Broadcast Script in Birmingham Central Library, pp. 8–9. This radio talk later appeared as "William Poel and the Modern Theatre" in *Listener*, 10 January 1962, pp. 56–58.

10. *William Poel and his Stage Productions 1880–1932* [London, 1932], n.p.

11. Quoted in Speaight, *William Poel*, p. 264.

12. Concerning Craig's compromise between pedantry and detail, see The Review of the Week, 11 August 1900, quoted by Edward Craig, *Gordon Craig: The Story of his Life* (London: Gollancz, 1968), p. 124; concerning Craig's lighting, see Denis Bablet, *Edward Gordon Craig*, trans. Daphne Woodward (1962; translation, London: Heinemann, 1966), pp. 37 and 39. Bablet notes that this bridge lighting had not yet appeared in Germany, whence it eventually spread elsewhere.

13. The first quotation in this paragraph is from Gordon Craig, *A Living Theatre* (Florence,

1913), p. 3; the second from *On the Art of the Theatre* (London: Heinemann, 1924), p. 109; the last from *The Theatre Advancing* (London: Constable, 1921), p. 124. Despite Craig's condemnation of his methods, Poel served on the International Committee for Craig's School for the Art of the Theatre, according to *Living Theatre*, p. 75.

14. Gordon Craig, *The Art of the Theatre* (Edinburgh and London: Foulis, 1905), pp. 18 and 54.

15. The quote is from Edward Craig, *Gordon Craig*, p. 233. The information about Craig's chessboard stage comes from p. 234, and from Bablet, *Edward Gordon Craig*, p. 118. In 1972 I saw several productions using the segmented stage. Richard David, *Shakespeare in the Theatre* (Cambridge: Cambridge University Press, 1978), p. 143, writes that it was first used in 1972; it seems finally to have been removed in 1976 (p. 215), having not been used since 1973.

16. I am indebted to Edward Craig, *Gordon Craig*, pp. 239 and 254, and to Bablet, *Edward Gordon Craig*, p. 119, for the preceding information. Craig writes that among those who rejected his father's methods were Beerbohm Tree and Joseph Harker; see pp. 254 and 263.

17. Kessler quoted in Janet Leeper, *Edward Gordon Craig: Designs for the Theatre* (Harmondsworth: Penguin, 1948), p. 8; Beerbohm quoted in Styan, *Shakespeare Revolution*, p. 80. The program for the production is in the Raymond Mander and Joe Mitchenson Theatre Collection, London; Christopher Innes, *Edward Gordon Craig* (Cambridge: Cambridge University Press, 1983), p. 132, also remarks that the play became almost a masque because of the number of dances and songs added.

18. William Poel, "Scenery and Drama," letter to the *Nation* 10 (14 October 1911):97; Roger Fry, "Mr. Gordon Craig's Stage Designs," the *Nation* 9 (16 September 1911):871.

19. The first quotation is from Craig, *Art of the Theatre*, p. 22, and the second from *On the Art of the Theatre*, pp. 119–20.

20. Quoted in Laurence Senelick, *Gordon Craig's Moscow "Hamlet," A Reconstruction* (Westport, Conn.: Greenwood, 1982), p. 66. I am indebted to Senelick for the following discussion of Craig's *Hamlet;* see pp. 24–25, 63–64, 76, 87, 150.

21. *My Life in Art,* quoted in Senelick, *Gordon Craig's Moscow "Hamlet,"* p. 110.

22. Some mention should be made of the possible influence of Max Reinhardt on Barker as well. Barker visited several German theatres in 1910 and reported his impressions as a "special correspondent" to the *Times* in two articles called "The Theatre in Berlin" (19 November 1910, p. 6, and 21 November 1910, p. 12); C. B. Purdom, *Harley Granville Barker: Man of the Theatre, Dramatist & Scholar* (London: Rockliff, 1955), p. 118, confirms that Barker actually met Reinhardt during this visit. Barker's articles show that he was especially impressed by the vitality of the German theatre and its imaginative use of scenery; he complains, however, about the often crude acting.

How far Reinhardt's ideas may actually have influenced Barker is difficult to determine: he seems to have been impressed by the German director's staging of *Comedy of Errors* (19 November), but he disliked his *Dream* because of its treatment of the lovers and disregard for the play's "lyric beauty" (as he recalled in "Alas, Poor Will!", *The Listener* 17 (3 March 1937): 387). I think on the whole that Reinhardt may have opened Barker's mind to certain possibilities in staging and design, but Barker's techniques are not copied from Reinhardt or from anyone else; they are too original and consistent in their whole design to be a mere pastiche of other people's good ideas. The whole question is put into perspective when one remembers that Reinhardt himself was greatly influenced by Craig's ideas.

Chapter 2. Barker's Savoy Productions

1. The quote is from A. C. Sprague and J. C. Trewin, *Shakespeare's Plays Today: Some Customs and Conventions of the Stage* (London: Sidgwick and Jackson, 1970), p. 108. For more information about Barker's life and achievements, readers should consult Purdom, *Harley*

Granville Barker (hereafter cited as *HGB*), and Eric Salmon, *Granville Barker: A Secret Life* (London: Heinemann, 1983).

According to reviews of Barker's *Two Gentlemen,* the text was rearranged although given virtually complete, the verse well-spoken, and the scenery pictorial but simplified. See the *Morning Post,* 9 April 1904, p. 7; *Daily Mail,* 9 April 1904, p. 5; the *Observer,* 10 April 1904, p. 6; the *Daily Telegraph,* 9 April 1904, p. 10; the *Sunday Times,* 10 April 1904, p. 6. W. Bridges Adams, in his review of M. St. Clare Byrne's foreword and illustrations for a new edition of the *Prefaces, Theatre Notebook* 18 (Winter 1963/64): 63, calls it "modestly scenic."

2. Desmond MacCarthy, *The Court Theatre 1904–1907: A Commentary and Criticism* (London: A. H. Bullen, 1907), p. 123.

3. Shaw's claim is from George Bernard Shaw (hereafter cited as GBS), "Granville-Barker: Some Particulars," *Drama* n.s. no. 3 (Winter 1946): 14. Regarding Behrend's influence, both Purdom, *HGB,* pp. 13, 21, and 164, and Sir Lewis Casson, "Granville Barker, Shaw and the Court Theatre," in Raymond Mander and Joe Mitchenson's *Theatrical Companion to Shaw* (hereafter cited as *TCS*) (London: Rockliff, 1954), p. 288, comment on it.

In discussing Shaw and Barker as directors, I am indebted to the following sources: GBS, *The Art of Rehearsal* (New York: Samuel French, 1928); GBS, "Shaw's Rules for Directors," *Theatre Arts* 33 (August 1949):6–11; GBS, "Bernard Shaw, Producer," in *TCS,* pp. 6–10; GBS, "Granville-Barker: Some Particulars"; Sir Lewis Casson, "GBS at Rehearsal," pp. 16–18, and "Granville Barker, Shaw and the Court Theatre," pp. 288–92, both in *TCS;* Archibald Henderson, *GBS: Man of the Century* (New York: Appleton-Century-Crofts, 1956); G. W. Bishop, *Barry Jackson and the London Theatre* (London: Arthur Barker, 1933); Lillah McCarthy, *Myself and My Friends,* with "An Aside" by GBS (London: Thornton Butterworth, 1933); Harley Granville Barker (hereafter cited as HGB), "Notes on Rehearsing a Play," *Drama* 1 (July 1919):2–5; HGB, "The Heritage of the Actor," *Quarterly Review,* no. 476 (July 1923): 53–73; HGB, *The Exemplary Theatre* (London: Chatto & Windus, 1922); Alan S. Downer, "HGB," *Sewanee Review* 55 (1947): 627–45; Anthony Jackson, "HGB as Director at the Royal [*sic*] Court Theatre, 1904–1907," *Theatre Research* 12 (1972): 126–38; Souvenir of Complimentary Dinner to Mr. J. E. Vedrenne and Mr. HGB at the Criterion Restaurant, 7 July 1907; Sir Lewis Casson, "Foreword," in Purdom, *HGB,* pp. vii–viii; correspondence between Shaw and Prof. Alan Downer, now in the Burgunder Shaw Collection, Cornell University Library.

4. For Shaw's views, see also *The Art of Rehearsal,* p. 5, where Shaw advises directors to "be on the stage, handling your people and prompting them with the appropriate tones . . ." and GBS, *Bernard Shaw and Mrs. Patrick Campbell: Their Correspondence,* ed. Alan Dent (London: Gollancz, 1952), p. 205, where he tells her "I should have liked half a dozen rehearsals seated round a table, books in hand, to get *the music* right before going onto the stage. But as that was impossible through lack of time, I have had to depend on the usual mechanical routine and start with the business and words, leaving the unfortunate victims to find out later what they are all about" [letter of 29 January 1920 re *Pygmalion*]. For correspondence regarding the production of Shaw's plays, see *Bernard Shaw's Letters to Granville Barker,* ed. C. B. Purdom with commentary & notes (London: Phoenix House, 1956), pp. 31–40; hereafter cited as *Letters.*

5. GBS, "Shakespear: A Standard Text," reprinted in *Shaw on Theatre,* ed. E. J. West ([London]: Macgibbon & Kee, [1960]), pp. 138 and 148 respectively.

6. See Cathleen Nesbitt, *A Little Love and Good Company* (Owings Mills, Md.: Stemmer House, 1977), pp. 51 and 177, and Harcourt Williams, *Old Vic Saga* (London: Winchester Publications, [1949]), p. 163.

7. The first two quotations are from Casson's "Foreword," in Purdom, *HGB,* p. vii, and the next two from his "Granville Barker, Shaw & the Court Theatre," in *TCS,* p. 290.

8. The first quotation in this paragraph is from GBS, *Our Theatres in the Nineties,* vol. 1, rev. ed. (London: Constable, 1932), p. 24; hereafter cited as *OTN.* Shaw's remark about the Bastille comes from *Ellen Terry and Bernard Shaw: a correspondence,* ed. Christopher St. John (1931; reset, London: Reinhardt & Evans, 1949), p. 136; for his advice not to perform Shakespeare,

see for example his letter to Ellen Terry of 1 November 1895, p. 16, and of 3 August 1907 to HGB, pp. 97–98 in GBS, *Letters.*

That Shaw regarded Poel as both his and HGB's mentor in regard to Shakespearean staging is made clear in a questionnaire he completed for Professor Downer, now in the Burgunder Shaw Collection, Cornell University Library. Asked whether he had himself influenced Barker in this regard, Shaw replied that they had "both agreed that William Poel's movement to restore the Elizabethan stage and play Shakespeare without the execrable mutilations of Irving and Daly . . . should be followed up, and the plays given in their entirety" (© 1986 The Trustees of the British Museum, The Governors and Guardians of the National Library of Ireland, and the Royal Academy of Dramatic Art). He doubted whether Barker had ever read his Shakespeare criticisms, as he was too young when they first appeared and they had not yet been reprinted when he embarked on the Savoy productions.

9. Concerning the *Twelfth Night* production, Lillah McCarthy, Barker's first wife, also writes in *Myself and My Friends*, p. 157, that the play had "a very good run—for Shakespeare!" Helen M. Kelly, "The Granville-Barker Shakespeare Productions. A Study Based on the Promptbooks" (Ph.D. diss., University of Michigan, 1965), p. 154, records that it ran for 139 performances.

Theatre historians generally accept Barker's establishment of modern staging practices. For example, Robert Speaight, "The Pioneers," *Shakespeare Jahrbuch* 93 (1957):170, credits Barker and Poel together with "establish[ing] a clear break between the fashions of the late nineteenth century and the prevailing vogues"; Muriel St. Clare Byrne, "Fifty Years of Shakespearian Production: 1898–1948," *Shakespeare Survey* 2 (1949):4, 7–8, & 15, writes that the Savoy productions "marked the birth of a new tradition" (p. 15); and J. C. Trewin, *Shakespeare on the English Stage 1900–1964: A Survey of Productions* (London: Barrie & Rockliff, 1964), p. 184, documents Barker's influence on subsequent stage history. More recently, Eric Salmon, *GB: A Secret Life*, p. 320, acclaims him as the originator of a "whole school of Shakespearean production."

10. HGB, "The Golden Thoughts of Granville Barker, Author, Mime, and 'Producer,'" *The Play Pictorial* 21, no. 126 [January 1913]: iv.

11. HGB quotation from the *New York Times*, 26 July 1914, quoted in Styan, *Shakespeare Revolution*, p. 82. See also Norman Marshall, *The Producer and the Play* (London: Macdonald, 1957), p. 55, and Marion Trousdale, "The Question of HGB's Shakespeare on the Stage," *Renaissance Drama*, n.s. 4 (1971): 21. Trousdale notes that Barker saw language as the determinant of a play's worth, both on and off stage, and that this view becomes "increasingly explicit" in his work.

12. For my description of the stage I am indebted to the following sources: Marshall, *Producer and the Play*, p. 153; Styan, *Shakespeare Revolution*, p. 84; Trewin, *Shakespeare on the English Stage*, p. 52; Byrne, "Fifty Years," p. 8; and Gary Jay Williams, "A Midsummer Night's Dream: The English and American Popular Traditions and HGB's 'World Arbitrarily Made,'" *Theatre Studies*, no. 23 (1976/77): 42.

13. W. Bridges Adams, *The Lost Leader: W. Bridges Adams on HGB* (London: Sidgwick & Jackson, 1954), p. 8.

14. Albert Rutherston, "Decoration in the Art of the Theatre," *The Monthly Chapbook* 1 (August 1919): 19. Originally a lecture given at Leeds University, February 1915. The following quotations are also taken from this article, p. 19. (Rutherston is sometimes known as Rothenstein; he changed his name during World War I.)

15. Trewin, *Shakespeare on the English Stage*, p. 53. Speaight makes the same point in reference to *The Winter's Tale* in *Shakespeare on the Stage: An illustrated history of Shakespearian performance* (London: Collins, 1973), p. 142.

16. See Trewin, *Shakespeare on the English Stage*, p. 53, for Poel's abolition of footlights; I have already mentioned Craig's. Some theatre historians (as well as contemporary reviewers) wrongly regard HGB as the initiator of this practice.

The quote regarding Barker's hygienically bright lighting is from Bridges Adams, *Lost Leader*, p. 12. His comment is supported by the *Stage*, 26 September 1912, which generally disliked all of Barker's Savoy productions and here found the reflections of the actors on the backcloth "disconcerting" and too "aggressively" black, pp. 21–22. Bridges Adams's comment is nevertheless something of an exaggeration, as the promptbooks for both *Twelfth Night* and the *Dream* indicate Barker's use of blackouts, dimming up and down, and shadowy light when appropriate. The drinking scene in *Twelfth Night*, for example, started in darkness, the circle arcs coming up slowly as candles were lit on stage; they gave "just enough light to see faces and cover the people at table" (prompt copy, electric plot). Generally, though, the stage seems to have been well illuminated.

17. Except where specifically noted, the following sources (as well as those already cited in this context) have provided details of, and critical comments on, Barker's production of *The Winter's Tale*: "A Fine Production," the *Daily Telegraph*, 22 September 1912, p. 11; the *Illustrated London News*, 141 (28 September 1912): 449, 460, and photos, and (5 October 1912), photos on p. 496; the *Morning Post*, 23 September 1912, p. 8; H.W.M., "Shakspere [sic] Come Again," the *Nation* 11 (28 September 1912): 935–37; P. C. Knody, the *Observer*, 22 September 1912, pp. 9–10; P. P. H., "Shakespeare at the Savoy-I," the *Outlook* 30 (5 October 1912): 452–53, and "Shakespeare at the Savoy-II," (12 October 1912): 488; John Palmer, "Shakespeare's *The Winter's Tale*," the *Saturday Review* 114 (28 September 1912): 391–92; E. F. S. (Monocle), the *Sketch* 79 (2 October 1912), p. 402, and Supplement, pp. 4–7 (photos); the *Stage*, 26 September 1912, pp. 21–22; J. T. Grein, *The Sunday Times*, 22 September 1912, p. 7; the *Times*, 23 September 1912, p. 7; Leonard Inkster, "Shakespeare and Mr. Granville Barker," *Poetry & Drama* 1 (March 1913): 24.

Besides these contemporary sources, there is Helen M. Kelly's unpublished doctoral dissertation, "The Granville-Barker Shakespeare Productions," mentioned in note 9 above. While this dissertation meticulously reconstructs the productions of *Twelfth Night* and the *Dream* and provides useful information regarding length of runs, intervals, etc., it has not contributed significantly to the contents of this chapter. Nor has Karen Greif's "'If This Were Play'd upon a Stage': HGB's Shakespeare Productions at the Savoy Theatre, 1912–1914," *Harvard Library Bulletin* 27 (April 1980): 117–45, which did not come to my attention until I had written this chapter. Trewin, Styan, and Speaight have also provided useful information on the productions, in books already cited.

18. The "cut-out" comment is from Hugh Hunt, "Granville-Barker's Shakespearean Productions," *Theatre Research* 10 (1969): 47. (Originally a paper delivered in Budapest 25 September 1967.) Hunt provides other useful details that I have not specifically noted.

19. Regarding cutting of the text, sources vary; anything from 6 to 20 lines were cut. Styan, *Shakespeare Revolution*, p. 87, and Kelly, "Granville-Barker Shakespeare Productions," p. 116, say there were three cuts totalling 11 lines; Purdom, *HGB*, p. 139, and Hunt, "Granville Barker's Shakespearean Productions," p. 46, that there were 6 lines omitted; the critic of the *Outlook* that 14½ lines were excised because of obscurity and unhelpful bawdiness. Trousdale, "Question of HGB and Shakespeare," p. 23, cites Stanley Wells's documentation of cuts of 20 lines.

20. Bridges Adams, "Granville Barker and the Savoy," *Drama* n.s. no. 52 (Spring 1959): 29, considers that Barker's limitations were due to his rationalism; Inkster, "Shakespeare," p. 26, calls him "cold and intellectual."

21. Quote from Edward Dent, "The Musical Interpretation of Shakespeare on the Modern Stage," *Musical Quarterly* 2 (1916): 536.

22. Except where specifically noted, the following sources have provided details of, and critical comments on, Barker's production of *Twelfth Night*: the *Daily Telegraph*, 16 November 1912, p. 12; the *Illustrated London News* 141 (23 November 1912): 780; the *Morning Post*, 16 November 1912, p. 11; H. W. M., "The Charm of Shakspere," the *Nation* 12 (23 November 1912): 351–52; P. C. Knody, the *Observer*, 17 November 1912, p. 7; the *Outlook* 30 (23 November 1912): 693–94; B. W. Findon, ed., the *Play Pictorial* 21, no. 126 [January 1913]; John Palmer,

"Twelfth Night," the *Saturday Review* 114 (23 November 1912): 637–39; the *Sketch* 80 (27 November 1912): 226, (photos) 240, and Supplement: 1, 8–9 (photos); the *Stage*, 21 November 1912, p. 22; J. T. Grein, the *Sunday Times*, 17 November 1912, p. 6; the *Times*, 16 November 1912, p. 10.

23. HGB, "*Twelfth Night* prompt copy." The Department of Rare Books and Special Collection, The University of Michigan Library. I have also used the Library's prompt copy of HGB's *Midsummer Night's Dream*. Both copies are in Val Gurney's handwriting.

24. The quotations are from the *Outlook;* the description derives from *Play Pictorial* photos, which also provide the details of Malvolio's, Viola's, and Sebastian's costumes.

25. According to the promptbook, the following lines were cut: I. iii. 68–71, Maria's joke about the buttery bar and Andrew's questioning of her metaphor; I. iii. 100–1, Toby's wish that a housewife would take Andrew between her legs to spin his hair off; I. iii. 126, Toby's comment that he would even "make water" while performing a sink-a-pace if he were Andrew; I. v. 5–16, Feste and Maria's play on "I fear no colours"; III. i. 55–56, Feste's hope that "The matter . . . is not great" and comment that "Cressida was a beggar": IV. i. 14–15, Feste's fear that "this great lubber, the world, will prove a cockney." (All references are to the Arden edition.) Clearly, Barker only cut those lines that are hopelessly obscure and those that he felt would make the audience unprofitably uncomfortable.

26. HGB, Preface to *Twelfth Night: An Acting Edition* (London: Heinemann, 1912), pp. vi, vii. Reprinted in HGB, *Prefaces to Shakespeare*, vol. 6, ed. Edward M. Moore (London: Batsford, 1974), pp. 28–29.

27. Terry Hands's production for the Royal Shakespeare Company (RSC), which opened at the Royal Shakespeare Theatre, Stratford, on 6 June 1979 and at the Aldwych Theatre, London, on 8 April 1980.

28. See especially the *Daily Telegraph*, the *Observer*, the *Nation* ("the eye is pleased and held, not gorged, as in the commonplace spectacle, while the ear, the fancy, and the intelligence are given their proper food," p. 352), and the *Times* ("great beauty . . . of line and colour, posture and movement," p. 10); Inkster, "Shakespeare," p. 25, denies this.

29. Hunt, "G-B's Shakespearean Productions," p. 47; he also provides the information about the audience's unfamiliarity with the play.

30. Except where specifically noted, the following sources have provided details of, and critical comments on, Barker's production of the *Dream:* the *Daily Telegraph*, 7 February 1914, p. 12; Karl Schmidt, "How Barker Puts Plays On," *Harper's Weekly* 55 (30 January 1915): 115–16, and an unsigned editorial, p. 99; the *Illustrated London News* 144 (14 February 1914): 248–49, and (28 February 1914): 330, and Supplement (11 April 1914): 602–3 (with photos); the *Morning Post*, 7 February 1914, p. 9; "A New Fairy Convention," the *Nation* 14 (14 February 1914): 825–26; Desmond MacCarthy, "A Midsummer Night's Dream," the *New Statesman* 2 (21 February 1914): 629–30; the *Observer*, 8 February 1914, p. 9; P. P. H., "Mr. Barker's Fairies," the *Outlook* 33 (14 February 1914): 204–5; John Palmer, "Mr. Barker's Dream," the *Saturday Review* 117 (14 February 1914): 202–3; the *Sketch* 80 (11 February 1914): 168–69 (photos), and (18 February 1914): 206 (review by E. F. S. [Monocle]), and *Sketch Supplement* (25 February 1914): 4–6 (photos); the *Stage*, 12 February 1914, p. 26; J. T. Grein, the *Sunday Times*, 8 February 1914, p. 6; the *Times*, 7 February 1914, p. 8; George C. D. Odell, *Shakespeare from Betterton to Irving* (1920; reprint, London: Constable, 1963), 2: 168.

Besides these contemporary sources, three modern critics have provided useful information on this production: Charles M. Barbour, "Up Against A Symbolic Painted Cloth: *A Midsummer Night's Dream* at the Savoy, 1914," *Educational Theatre Journal* 27 (December 1975): 521–28; Trevor Griffiths, "Tradition and Innovation in HGB's *A Midsummer Night's Dream*," *Theatre Notebook* 30 (1976): 78–87; and Gary Jay Williams (see note 12 above). Williams provides much information about the curtains.

31. Griffiths, "Tradition and Innovation," p. 80. See Marshall, *Producer and the Play*, p. 161, and Speaight, *Shakespeare on the Stage*, p. 143, who also note the contrasts.

32. HGB, "A Midsummer Night's Dream" (Preface to the *Acting Edition*, published by

arrangement with Heinemann), *Saturday Review* 117 (24 January 1914): 106; the next quotation is from p. 107. Reprinted in HGB, *Prefaces*, vol. 6, ed. Moore, pp. 35 and 38.

33. Comet description from Walter P. Eaton, *Plays and Players* (Cincinnati, 1916), quoted in Williams, "Midsummer Night's Dream." p. 45. Barker to William Archer, 14 February 1914, British Library BM 45290 fol. 133.

34. The first quote is from the *Nation*, p. 826, which, together with MacCarthy, pointed out that this Puck was no Ariel. The next two quotations are from MacCarthy; the following two from the *Nation*.

35. The promptbook directs Theseus (in his speech beginning "Thrice blessed they that master so their blood") to speak "To the audience—Big." Barbour, "Up Against a . . . Cloth," p. 525, also notes this, but concludes not that Barker intended to underline the play's theatricality but "to stress situation." He draws the same inference from Helena's playing part of her soliloquy of II. ii ("O that a lady of one man refused,/Should of another therefore be abused") directly to the audience.

36. Barbour, "Up Against a . . . Cloth," p. 527, quoting Barker's *On Dramatic Method*.

37. Barbour argues that Theseus jumps when Pyramus stabs himself and so concludes that "Barker takes the workers and their play very seriously indeed" ("Up Against a . . . Cloth," p. 528). I agree that Barker emphasized the meaning of the play-within-the-play, but not with the point Barbour makes from a careless reading of the promptbook. Theseus's jump is clearly indicated between the two "no's" and not at Pyramus's suicide.

38. First quote from Barker, Preface to *Acting Edition, Saturday Review*, p. 106; HGB, *Prefaces*, vol. 6, ed. Moore, p. 34. Palmer disagreed that the mechanicals need no comic exaggeration. He complained that "Bottom was intellectually presented as an artist craving for opportunities of self-expression. It was quite a pleasant surprise for all of us when he condescended at last to a bergamask, his only other lapse of the evening being a call for the tongs and bones." Palmer's criticism reflects his general dislike of the whole production and does not seem accurate, given other accounts of the performance. Following quotes from William Shakespeare, *A Midsummer Night's Dream, The Players' Shakespeare*, vol. 4 (London: Ernest Benn, 1924), pp. xlii–xlvii. Reprinted in HGB, *Prefaces*, vol. 6, ed. Moore, p. 130. For Barker's discussion of Bottom and the mechanicals, see also pp. 125–29.

39. Griffiths, "Tradition and Innovation," p. 84, quotes Percy Fitzgerald's remark that Tree's "Bottom . . . spread himself over the whole play with a resulting 'lack of proportion and disturbance, the rest being dwarfed in consequence'" (*Shakespearean Representation*, London, 1908, p. 74).

40. However, the same critic complained of Oberon's "sing-song whine" as sounding peevish. Perhaps this mode of speech, like the jerky movements, was used to differentiate the fairies from the mortals, as the *Nation* notes that Puck's "elaborately harsh elocution" was a feature of his characterization. Or perhaps Barker was the first producer to note the unattractive side of Oberon's character.

41. Williams, "Midsummer Night's Dream," p. 49, discussing the New York production, mentions the performance time. Barker's comment from Preface to *Acting Edition, Saturday Review*, p. 107; *Prefaces*, vol. 6, ed. Moore, p. 39.

42. The first two quotes are from HGB, Preface to *Players' Shakespeare* edition of the play, p. xx; *Prefaces*, vol. 6, ed. Moore, p. 105. The comment about Sharp's music is from the *Times;* the review continues: "More quaint than tuneful . . . but somehow or other . . . [i]t goes quite well with the gold." However, the reviewer also joked that, given the costumes, Stravinsky would have been appropriate. It should be noted that Barker and Sharp disagreed about the use of Elizabethan music for Shakespeare's plays: Barker felt it would be effective and Sharp that it would be distracting; see HGB's Preface to *Players' Shakespeare* edition, pp. 105–8, and Sharp's *The Songs and Incidental Music Arranged and Composed for Granville Barker's Production of A Midsummer Night's Dream at the Savoy Theatre in January 1914* (London: Simpkin, Marshall, Hamilton, Kent, 1914), pp. 10–11. Barker did agree that folk music was appropriate for the *Dream*, if not for other plays by Shakespeare.

43. HGB, Preface to *Acting Edition, Saturday Review*, p. 107; *Prefaces*, vol. 6, ed. Moore, p. 39.

44. HGB, Preface to *Players' Shakespeare* edition, pp. xxiii–xxiv; *Prefaces*, vol. 6, ed. Moore, pp. 108–9.

45. For Barker's actors turned directors, see, for example, David, *Shakespeare in the Theatre*, pp. 56–57, 61–62, and M. St. Clare Byrne, Introduction to HGB's *Prefaces to Shakespeare*, vol. 2 (London: Batsford, 1963), p. xlii.

46. Glenn Loney, ed., "Ronald Bryden: A Drama Critic Introduces Peter Brook," in *Peter Brook's Production of William Shakespeare's "A Midsummer Night's Dream": Authorized Acting Edition* (Chicago: The Dramatic Publishing Company, 1974), p. 20. This acting edition, besides containing the prompt script, property and cast lists, etc., includes previously published articles about the production, as well as new interviews conducted by Loney. It will hereafter be cited as *Acting Edition;* if no author is named, Loney is the compiler/author/interviewer.

47. Karl Schmidt, "How Barker Puts Plays On" (interview with Barker during New York run of the *Dream*), *Harper's Weekly* 60 (30 January 1915): 115.

48. Quoted in "MSND at the Drama Desk" (question and answer session with Brook, cast members, and critics, 25 January 1971), *Acting Edition*, pp. 25 & 32.

49. Quoted in "Sally Jacobs: Designing the Dream—From Tantras to Tunics," *Acting Edition*, p. 47 (first ellipsis mine).

50. Irate critic quoted in "Lloyd Burlingame: Lighting the Empty Space for 'The Dream's' New York Run," *Acting Edition*, p. 73.

51. For quotations, see John Kane, "Plotting with Peter," *Acting Edition*, p. 57, and "Barbara Penny: Perils of a Deputy Stage Manager on 'The Dream's' World Tour," *Acting Edition*, p. 97.

52. "Introduction: Filling the Empty Space with a Daring New Dream," *Acting Edition*, p. 13 (quoting Bryden's *Observer* review), and "Bryden," p. 17.

53. "Introduction," *Acting Edition*, p. 11 (quoting Marowitz's *New York Times* review).

54. "Jacobs," *Acting Edition*, pp. 47–48. Also described in "Introduction," p. 11.

55. Details of costume and its rationale are taken from *Acting Edition:* "Bryden," p. 17; Kane, p. 55; and "Jacobs," p. 50, who stresses her concern to find "absolutely *timeless*" costumes.

56. Peaslee quoted in "Richard Peaslee: Creating 'Organized Noise for Peter Brook's Dreams,'" *Acting Edition*, p. 70. See *Acting Edition*, Brook at "Drama Desk," p. 31, re mortals; "Burlingame," p. 73, re lighting. The quotation following is from Bryden's *Observer* article/program note, reprinted in "Bryden," *Acting Edition*, p. 17.

57. See critics Marowitz and Wardle, quoted in "Introduction," p. 11; "Bryden," p. 19; Brook at the "Drama Desk," pp. 31–32, all in *Acting Edition*. Specifically, Brook credits Jan Kott's essay, "Titania & the Ass's Head," in *Shakespeare our Contemporary*, trans. Boleslaw Taborski (1964; reprint, New York: W. W. Norton, 1974), with revealing the "dark and powerful currents of sensuality running through" the *Dream* ("Drama Desk," *Acting Edition*, p. 32); however, he disagrees with Kott's view that the play is "without any joy, any gaiety, and any sparkle." Brook's emphasis on acrobatic physical activity was precursed by Meyerhold's "bio-mechanic" type of theatrical training (see John Russell Taylor, ed., *The Penguin Dictionary of Theatre*, rev. ed. [Harmondsworth: Penguin, 1974], p. 186), while his recognition of the ritual nature of drama was influenced by Grotowski and Artaud ("Bryden," *Acting Edition*, p. 19). Bryden also reports that Brook invited Grotowski to work with the cast of another of his productions.

Chapter 3. Barker's Shakespeare Criticism

1. In this context of dealing with particulars of Barker's productions, some of these prefaces have been quoted in the preceding chapter. This quotation is from the Preface to *The Winter's Tale: An Acting Edition*, reprinted in HGB, *Prefaces*, vol. 6, ed. Moore, p. 19. Further references appear in the text.

2. Cf., for example, Barker's discussion of the Clown as countryman in the preceding chapter.

3. HGB, Preface to *A Midsummer Night's Dream: An Acting Edition*, reprinted in *Prefaces*, vol. 6, ed. Moore, p. 37. Further references appear in the text.

4. Douglas D. Paschall, in "A Study of the Plays and Criticism of HGB" (D. Phil. diss., University of Oxford, 1976), convincingly demonstrates that Barker, as playwright and critic, is concerned with the revelation of inner being.

5. *Essays by Divers Hands* (Transactions of the Royal Society of Literature of the United Kingdom), n.s. vol. 3, ed. F. S. Boas (London: Oxford University Press, 1923), pp. 17–38. First read on 7 June 1922. Further references appear in the text.

6. The *Spectator* (19 April 1940), p. 556.

7. "I maintain that [the] solution [to the problem of the appropriate presentation of Shakespeare] is the master key to the general appreciation of his art and to its preservation as a living force" (p. 29).

8. See, for example, Norman Rabkin, *Shakespeare and the Problem of Meaning* (Chicago: University of Chicago Press, 1981) for a fine discussion of modern reductive tendencies.

9. Barker again broaches this subject in one of his last critical essays, a review of Una Ellis-Fermor's *The Frontiers of Drama* published in *English Studies* 22 (April 1946): 144–47. He takes issue with her argument that *Troilus and Cressida* is a masterpiece of Shakespeare's philosophy; if one judges Shakespeare as dramatist rather than philosopher, Barker argues, the play is not great: it lacks the "life" of the great plays, and its characters do not engage our sympathy or interest. Barker complains that this treatment of Shakespeare as "the centre of a philosophy" blurs one's recognition of his real achievements as a dramatist.

10. His changes are mostly stylistic; Barker moves toward greater preciosity in language in his later work, a point also made by Trousdale, "Question of HG-B," p. 33. The most dramatically altered preface is that to *Cymbeline*.

11. HGB, Introduction to *The Players' Shakespeare*, reprinted in *Prefaces*, vol. 6, ed. Moore, p. 43. Further references appear in the text.

12. In the letter to William Archer cited previously, Barker makes a similar point: "I do agree with what you say about the dead lines, and if I felt that the non-cut, play-straight-through battle was really won I should have been tempted to take out a few; but it is not and we have nailed Shakespeare un-cut to the mast. Also it is a tricky business to cut. One is so apt to take things out because they don't suit you, because you can't understand them."

13. Shaw to Mrs Patrick Campbell, 22 December 1920, in *Bernard Shaw & Mrs. Patrick Campbell: Their Correspondence*, p. 217.

14. Barker explicitly makes the point about the platform stage in his Introduction to the *Prefaces:* "If we solve the physical side of [the problem of the soliloquy] by restoring, in essentials, the relation between actor and audience that the intimacy of the platform stage provided, the rest [i.e., ease of actor and audience] should soon solve itself." *Prefaces to Shakespeare*, vol. 1 (London: Batsford, 1968), p. 17.

15. I have found this to be true of my Shakespeare students at Ithaca College, London, many of whom have little previous experience of live theatre, let alone Shakespeare.

16. John Barton's production at the Royal Shakespeare Theatre in Stratford-upon-Avon, with Michael Pennington in the title role. First performance: 25 June 1980.

17. Toby Robertson's production of *Antony and Cleopatra* for the Prospect Theatre Company at the Old Vic, London, starred Barbara Jefford and John Turner. First performance: 17 June 1977, with Dorothy Tutin and Alec McCowan. First performance with Jefford and Turner: 21 February 1978. Program notes indicate that the costumes were inspired by Tiepolo's paintings.

Peter Brook's production of the same play for the Royal Shakespeare Company starred Glenda Jackson and Alan Howard. First performance at the Royal Shakespeare Theatre, Stratford-upon-Avon: 4 October 1978; at the Aldwych Theatre, London: 12 June 1979.

Trevor Nunn's production of *Macbeth* for the Royal Shakespeare Company starred Ian McKellen and Judi Dench. First performance at The Other Place, Stratford-upon-Avon: 4 August 1976; at the Warehouse, London: 20 July 1977.

18. In his later Introduction to the *Prefaces*, vol. 1, p. 12, Barker explains that Leontes's "confusion of thought and intricacy of language is dramatically justified. . . . We parse the passage and dispute its sense; spoken, as it was meant to be, in a choky torrent of passion, probably a modicum of sense slipped through, and its first hearers did not find it a mere rigmarole."

19. For other discussions of the *Prefaces*, see, for example, Styan, *Shakespeare Revolution*, pp. 112–21, and Arthur M. Eastman, *A Short History of Shakespeare Criticism* (New York: W. W. Norton, 1974), pp. 322–35.

20. HGB, "From *Henry V* to *Hamlet*" (British Academy Annual Shakespeare Lecture, 1925), in *Prefaces*, vol. 6, ed. Moore, pp. 135–67. Further references appear in the text.

21. HGB, "Shakespeare and Modern Stagecraft," *Yale Review* 15 (July 1926): 703–24; further references appear in the text. This article also exists in a shorter version as "The Stagecraft of Shakespeare," *Fortnightly Review* NS vol 120 (July 1926): 1–17.

22. HGB, "Hamlet in Plus Fours," *Yale Review* 16 (October 1926): 205. The article appeared too late to be included in the article cited above. Jackson's production opened at the Kingsway Theatre, London, on 25 August 1925.

23. Barker reiterates this point later in his career, in the twentieth of the Broadcast National Lectures (13 October 1937), which was later published as "The Perennial Shakespeare," in *The Listener* 18 (20 October 1937): 823–26, 857–59, and as *The Perennial Shakespeare* (London: BBC, 1937). In a section dealing with improvements necessary to the modern theatre, Barker argues that "the shock tactics of eccentric staging and costume, though these may seem to win a momentary victory, do harm, not good, since the victory is not the play's own. A play's interpretation lies in its acting and in nothing else that matters" (p. 24).

24. See HGB, "A Note upon Chapters XX. and XXI. of *The Elizabethan Stage*," *Review of Engliish Studies* 1 (January 1925): 60–71. Further references appear in the text.

It is interesting to note that in a letter to G. B. Harrison dated 14 September 1931 (The Department of Rare Books and Special Collections, The University of Michigan Library), Barker remarks that his "heart does not warm to Edmund [Chambers] either." He finds Shakespeare an odd choice for so much of Chambers's work, given his dryness. Once again, Barker indicates how much he believes in the vitality of Shakespeare's plays and the necessity of a full response to them—a response capable of informing one as a total human being rather than merely as an intellect.

25. Barker repeats many of the same criticisms in his much later review of John Crawford Adams's *The Globe Playhouse*, a typed ms. dated February 1944, now in the possession of the Humanities Research Center in Austin, Texas. In it, Barker again condemns overreliance on the Swan drawing; he also emphasizes the lack of boundary between inner and outer stage, the desirability of moving the action to the outer stage as soon as possible, the limited use of the upper stage, and the distinction between the stage fiction and the stage itself. Given Barker's continued insistence on the fluidity of the Elizabethan stage, it is interesting to note that he seems to have held different opinions before sending William Archer proofs of his *Players' Shakespeare* prefaces to *Macbeth* and *Cymbeline*. In a letter of 21 June 1923, Archer instructs Barker that the Elizabethan stage was not three stages, but one with two extensions, and adds that no substantial action took place on the inner and upper stages, as Barker seems to have thought (British Library, BM 45290, fol. 133).

26. HGB, Review of W. J. Lawrence's *The Physical Conditions of the Elizabethan Public Playhouses* and *Pre-Restoration Stage Studies, Review of English Studies* 4 (April 1928): 229–37. Further references appear in the text. In another letter to Harrison (28 June 1935), Barker remarks that Lawrence sometimes "dogmatises pure rubbish," but adds that "he *has* thrown more light on the mechanics of the S[hakespearean] stage than anyone else and, moreover, shown people *how* to study it."

27. See p. 233. Barker again makes this point in his review of Adams's *The Globe Playhouse;* see note 25 above.

28. There is one point about which Barker is not entirely fair to Lawrence: he accuses him of tautological reasoning about the upper stage and its use. Having established that one upper

stage was twelve feet above the lower and that this was a common jump, Lawrence deduces the acrobatic nature of Elizabethan actors, according to Barker, by "the mere crediting them with such feats." Barker's own position is that the distance was not so great (pp. 231–32). However, Lawrence himself recognizes that twelve feet, which was the height of the Fortune's gallery, is rather high—too high to assume that this was the "normal elevation" of the upper stage; *The Physical Conditions of the Elizabethan Public Playhouses* (Cambridge: Harvard University Press, 1927), p. 77. I can only assume that Barker read this section of Lawrence carelessly, as he nowhere else distorts the position of another scholar.

29. HGB, *Prefaces to Shakespeare* (1930 [1927–47]; reprint, London: Batsford, 1968–71), 5 vols. The *Prefaces* have run through several editions; all quotations will be taken from this edition and will appear in the text.

30. HGB, Introduction, *Prefaces*, vol. 1, pp. 1–23.

31. See, for example, chapter 5 of Richard David's *Shakespeare in the Theatre*, in which he favorably contrasts Buzz Goodbody's very successful modern-dress *Hamlet* at the Roundhouse, London (February 1976) with Peter Hall's more traditional production for the National Theatre (NT), London (May 1976, at the Lyttleton). David criticizes the NT production on many of Barker's grounds: for example, the general background clashed with Albert Finney's style of playing. His discussion of Goodbody's success illustrates the opportunities sensitive direction can give to modern-dress productions.

32. HGB, *On Dramatic Method* (Clark Lectures, 1930) (London: Sidgwick & Jackson, 1931. References will appear in the text.

33. Barker also makes the point that prose too is used for dramatic ends. See pp. 77 ff., where he discusses the prose of *Henry IV, Part 1*; *Henry V*; *As You Like It*; *Twelfth Night*.

34. See p. 107. Barker also recognizes the existence of a subtext; he refers the reader to Maeterlinck's preface to his translation of *Macbeth* and paraphrases it in this way: "There is . . . the dialogue by which the immediate action is carried on, but beneath it there is another which we unconsciously hear, and which paints upon our minds the tragic atmosphere and the mysterious influences that externalize Macbeth's conscience" (p. 110).

35. One could argue that Barker's dramatic concern with character itself reflects contemporary preoccupations. But it is the way in which Barker uses and sees character as a means of exploring theme that distinguishes him from those preoccupied merely with character analysis.

36. HGB, *Associating with Shakespeare* (London: Shakespeare Association, 1932). Presidential address for the Shakespeare Association, 25 November 1931. Further references appear in the text.

37. See p. 26; Barker, however, does not suggest that Shakespeare should be blamed for the avant-garde nature of some of his plays: "These greater plays were written by a master-dramatist and a very practical man" (p. 27).

38. Barker's letters to Harrison are in the possession of The Department of Rare Books and Special Collections, The University of Michigan Library, which supplied me with photocopies. The dates of the letters are given in parentheses in the text.

39. Shakespeare Association advertisement on end pages of texts.

40. HGB and G. B. Harrison, eds., *A Companion to Shakespeare Studies* (Cambridge: Cambridge University Press, 1934), p. x.

41. Kenneth Muir and S. Schoenbaum, eds., *A New Companion to Shakespeare Studies* (Cambridge: Cambridge University Press, 1971). In their preface, Muir and Schoenbaum state that one of their main differences from the parent volume is the inclusion of articles by American scholars (p. v); Barker's letters to Harrison show that he himself wished to include such articles in the original volume.

42. HGB and Harrison, *A Companion*, pp. 45–88. Further references appear in the text.

43. HGB, *The Exemplary Theatre* (London: Chatto & Windus, 1922). Further references appear in the text.

44. HGB, *On Poetry in Drama* (London: Sidgwick & Jackson, 1937). Further references appear in the text.

45. See the *Listener* 17 (3 March 1937): 387–89, 425–26 (further references appear in the text), and Alfred Hitchcock and Val Gielgud, "Shakespeare: Much Ado about Nothing?," the *Listener* 17 (10 March 1937): 448–50 for two rebuttals under one title (Hitchcock addresses the question of film adaptation and Gielgud of radio).

46. Barker mentions having seen only two Shakespeare films: Reinhardt's *Dream* and MGM's *Romeo and Juliet.* He criticizes them on pp. 387–88.

47. Regarding the problem of silent characters, at the discovery of Duncan's murder, for example, "it is the sight of [Macbeth and Lady Macbeth] as they stand listening to the horrified protests around them that counts" (p. 426).

48. References are to Augustus Ralli, *A History of Shakespearian Criticism*, vol. 2 (London: Oxford University Press, 1932), pp. 562–64; G. B. Harrison, "Literary History and Criticism," *London Mercury* 22 (June 1930): 184–85 (written before or at the commencement of Harrison's acquaintance with HGB); Hardin Craig, "Recent Shakespeare Scholarship," the *Shakespeare Association Bulletin* [New York] 5 (April 1930): 39–54; and L. C. Knights's review of *A Companion, Scrutiny* 3 (December 1934): 306–14.

49. Hardin Craig, "Trend of Shakespeare Scholarship," *Shakespeare Survey* 2 (1949): 113; Kenneth Muir, "Fifty Years of Shakespearian Criticism: 1900–1950," *Shakespeare Survey* 4 (1951): 17–18. Muir criticizes Barker for being too realistic and not appreciating the deliberate artificiality of the early verse, but it seems from my reading that Barker is in fact sensitive to and appreciative of Shakespeare's varied styles; Eastman, *A Short History*, p. 334, supports my view. F. E. Halliday, *Shakespeare and His Critics*, rev. ed. (London: Duckworth, 1958), p. 33, also commends Barker as responsible for much of the improvement in the staging of Shakespeare this century.

50. M. C. Bradbrook, "Fifty Years of the Criticism of Shakespeare's Style: A Retrospect," *Shakespeare Survey* 7 (1954): 8.

51. Patrick Murray, *The Shakespearian Scene* (London: Longmans, Green, 1969), p. 174; Frank Kermode, ed., *Four Centuries of Shakespearian Criticism* (New York: Avon Books, 1965), p. 26.

52. Styan, *Shakespeare Revolution*, p. 121. The fact that so many critics have to paraphrase Barker's points also supports this contention.

53. See M. St. Clare Byrne's Introduction to HGB, *Prefaces*, vol. 2 (London: Batsford, 1963), pp. xxv and xli. Consider, too, the increasing importance of practical theatre work to scholarship; the *Shakespeare Quarterly* and *Shakespeare Survey* now regularly devote whole issues to stage productions, interviews with actors and directors, etc.

54. See John Gielgud, *An Actor and His Time* (London: Sidgwick & Jackson, 1979), p. 130; Byrne, Introduction to HGB, *Prefaces*, vol. 2, photo 19 (caption); Styan, *Shakespeare Revolution*, p. 116; and Byrne, Introduction to HGB, *Prefaces*, vol. 2, pp. xxii, xxiii, and xxxi.

55. For HGB's influence on actors, see especially Styan, *Shakespeare Revolution*, pp. 105–6, and Byrne, Introduction to *Prefaces*, vol. 2, pp. xxii, xxxii, xlii–xliii. For the *Prefaces'* influence on directors, see Henry Hewes, "How to Use Shakespeare," *Saturday Review* [New York], (13 July 1957): 10. Hewes also remarks on a shift in interest from reading the plays and criticism to seeing them performed and notes directors' preferences for a flexible stage giving audience intimacy (pp. 10–11).

Chapter 4. *King Lear: Preface* and Production

1. HGB, "The Theatre: The Next Phase" (A Lecture given on 9 June 1910), *English Review* 5 (July 1910): 635–36.

2. *Preface to King Lear*, in *Prefaces to Shakespeare*, vol. 2 (1930; reprint, London: Batsford, 1970), p. 7. Further references are to this edition and appear in the text.

3. Barker continues: "For the appreciation of such a work as *King Lear* one might even demand the second or third hearing of the whole, which the alertest critic would need to give to (say) a piece of music of like caliber" (p. 10).

4. HGB, *Preface to King Lear*, p. 26–27. One could argue that Lear's coin and bit of cheese are entirely imaginary, but it would not do to ignore a director as experienced as Barker. It would probably be easier for the actor to use the flower Barker suggests than to mime handling a coin, and furthermore, it adds another depth to his madness: Lear not only sees things that do not exist, but cannot identify things that do.

5. I am grateful to Professor Lester Beaurline of the University of Virginia for pointing out Edgar's disguise as an attempt to magnify his own suffering.

6. Barker writes that "the meeting of mad Lear and blind Gloucester . . . is, of course, most germane to the play's idea—a more important thing to Shakespeare than the mere story—but it checks the march of the story" (p. 21n). Cf. also Barker's similar discussion of the mock-trial scene, pp. 34–44, and of the relation of Poor Tom and the Fool to Lear, p. 10, discussed earlier in this chapter.

7. Barker usually calls this section "The Characters" in his prefaces; obviously, the idea of interplay and interrelationship was exceptionally important to him in this play—perhaps as a way of demonstrating stageworthiness, for Barker was always alive to dramatic patterns. I do not mean to suggest, however, that he ignored such patterns in the other prefaces.

8. John Gielgud, *An Actor and His Time*, p. 135; hereafter cited in the text as *AHT*. See also the *Preface*, p. 17, where Barker wrote that the first scene's "probabilities are neither here nor there."

9. Barker writes of the Pied Bull and Butter quartos as one; see the *Preface*, p. 75n. Quotes from William Shakespeare, *King Lear*, ed. Kenneth Muir, 8th ed. with corrections (New York: Vintage Books, 1963), p. xvi.

10. Gielgud reports a similar worry in *AHT*, p. 135, and in Hallam Fordham's "Player in Action" (cited below). He had asked Barker how, on his reentry at I. iv. 302, Lear knows that half his followers have been dismissed; Barker replied: "What happens off-stage is not important. Realistic detail of time and circumstance did not concern Shakespeare. Such accuracies belong to the school of dramatists of our modern theatre, beginning with Ibsen. With Shakespeare it is the theatrical effect to display concentrated action and character in action which is important" (I.4.JG2).

11. Hallam Fordham, "Player in Action. John Gielgud as 'King Lear'" (ca. 1940), The Folger Shakespeare Library, Washington, D.C., catalogue no. T.b.17. The typescript consists of Fordham's description of each scene, followed by his analysis of it and further notes by John Gielgud. Since the pages are unnumbered, my references are to its sections. Thus, II.2.D3 refers to the third page of description of II. ii; II.2.A3 to the third page of analysis of the same scene; and II.2.JG3 to the third page of Gielgud's commentary on it. The title is abbreviated *PA* in the text.

It seems that the book was never published because Barker objected to his role in the production being made so public and because he did not want to "'go on record'" in a book for which he was not himself responsible; see his letter of 27 October 1940 to Gielgud, reprinted in Purdom, *HGB*, pp. 266–67. For Gielgud's memoirs, see Sir John Gielgud, *Stage Directions* (hereafter cited as *SD*), (1963; reprint, London: Heinemann, 1979), pp. 51–55, and Appendix 1, pp. 120–32, and *AHT*, pp. 130–35.

12. For discussion of Helen Granville-Barker's dislike of the theatre, see Purdom, *HGB*, pp. 187–89, 195, 226–28, 253, and Robert Speaight, "The Actability of King Lear," *Drama Survey* (Minneapolis) 2 (Spring 1962); 49. Hesketh Pearson, *GBS: A Postscript* (London: Collins, 1951), pp. 159–61, recounts Shaw's attempt to lure Barker back to stage work, and Purdom, *HGB*, p. 80, discusses his attraction to a writing career. For other biographical details, see Purdom's index.

13. Pearson, *GBS*, p. 161, recounts that Barker was tempted to return to acting to play the Grand Inquisitor for Gabriel Pascal's projected filming of *Saint Joan*, but his wife disapproved. Purdom, *HGB*, gives countless examples of Barker's being drawn back to theatre work; for example, he advised Gielgud on *Hamlet* in 1939 (p. 259).

14. Gielgud writes in *SD*, p. 51, that Barker came for a weekend, and in *AHT*, p. 134, he suggests it was only for one day; Purdom, *HGB*, p. 261, writes that it was for two weeks. I

would tend to trust the biographer in this matter; the inconsistency in Gielgud's two accounts suggests he was relying on memory, and since he had also received help from Barker on *Hamlet* during a weekend in 1939, he may be conflating the two occasions. Purdom, however, may be thinking of the two weeks Barker spent supervising rehearsals. (Incidentally, Barker also insisted that there be no publicity before he advised Gielgud on *Hamlet;* see *AHT*, p. 131).

15. Quote and comment in Gielgud, *AHT*, p. 134. James Agate's review of the production for the *Sunday Times*, "The Old Vic Reopens," 21 April 1940, p. 3, coincidentally begins by complaining that Lear is an oak and Gielgud an ash.

16. Cathleen Nesbitt, *A Little Love*, pp. 180–81, writes that everyone who "has worked with Barker is apt to become a bore on the subject"; she adds that of all the plays in which she has acted, she has vivid memories only of the two directed by Barker, memories in which she can still hear the cadences of Ainley's and Gielgud's voices.

17. Barker was still in London on 14 April, the day before the play opened, as he wrote to Gielgud from the Athenaeum on that day (*SD*, p. 129); he must have taken the play right up to the opening.

18. In a letter to Gabrielle Enthoven dated 5 May 1940, now in the Enthoven Collection of the Victoria and Albert Museum, Gielgud remarks that he has achieved "some of the range and gradual ebb and flow" of Lear because of "Barker's wonderful guidance."

19. Ronald Hayman, *John Gielgud* (London: Heinemann, 1971), p. 128. Appendix A of Williams's *Old Vic Saga* (pp. 217–22) also hints at the difficulties of production during the war: in the 1938–39 season, the Old Vic company presented eight productions; 1940, 1941, and 1942 saw only two productions a year. Not until 1948–49 was the company again able to mount eight productions a season.

20. One "compromise" is readily identifiable; Gielgud writes that Barker believed "in reading the play round a table for a week or more, but on this occasion there was no time for that" (*SD*, p. 53).

21. Information from the program and from a "Plan of the stage of the Old Vic as arranged and permanently set for 'King Lear'" (both reproduced in *PA*), as well as from Fordham's own descriptions. His description of I. ii indicates the use of half-curtains: "The fore-stage, half-curtained. In the archway at one side is the entrance to the house, with a large stone seat set before it" (I.2.D1).

22. Quoted in Margery M. Morgan, *A Drama of Political Man: A Study in the Plays of Harley Granville Barker* (London: Sidgwick & Jackson, 1961), p. 31.

23. And yet the bond suggests no equality: at Goneril's appearance, Lear was feeding the Fool with scraps of food while encouraging him to beg like a dog (*PA*, I.1.D4).

24. Lear prays for patience, "with outstretched arms," in the stocks scene: "O Heavens! If you do love old men . . ." and "You Heavens, give me patience, patience I need" (*PA*, I.4.JG1).

25. For Lear's motivation, see HGB, *Preface*, p. 33, and Fordham, *PA*, I.4.JG1. Regarding the production, Lear's solemnity has already been described, but Goneril's has not; she "dropped her needlework during the curse, while she tried to ward off Lear's words." Afterwards, she walked about, "trying to control her agitation" (*PA*, I.4.D6).

26. Fordham, *PA*, II.2.A2. Barker's notes to Gielgud suggest that "I gave you all" should be played "very big. *To the front.* Bewildered. Not as fast as their speeches" (*SD*, p. 124; italics mine). Clearly, Barker even here had an appeal to the audience in mind.

Incidentally, although in the text this act comprises four scenes, in the production II. 2 combined the text's II. ii, iii, and iv and followed II. i without a break.

27. Later in the scene, Lear closed imaginary bed curtains and then poked his head out between them (*PA*, III.6.D2; *SD*, p. 126).

28. The need for dignity in this scene was emphasized by Andrew Robertson's 1982 production for the Young Vic; Lear entered wearing a floppy Paddington Bear-style hat, which made him appear a harmless and silly lunatic rather than a tragic figure.

29. Fordham, *PA*, IV.6.A1. Gielgud writes that "Lear by this time may be tired physically, and [but?] mentally lightened and freed" (*PA*, IV.6.JG3).

30. Bradley also makes this point about the importance of Lear's chair in Note W, "The

Staging of the Scene of Lear's Reunion with Cordelia," *Shakespearean Tragedy* (Greenwich, Conn: Fawcett Publications, n.d.), pp. 386–89.

31. Fordham seems to contradict himself in describing Lear and Cordelia's exits: "The two figures walk across the stage and out of sight in a silence which is lit by the loving gaze between Lear and Cordelia. They take no notice of Edmund throughout the scene, and we are made to feel that nothing in the world matters to either of them except their joy in each other" (*PA*, V.A1).

32. However, according to Barker's preliminary notes (*SD*, p. 128), Lear should "wander about at the back of stage. Find the body again. The rope round her neck." It seems then that the idea of Lear's attention being drawn away from and then back to Cordelia and of his focusing on the rope was Barker's own; Gielgud must have suggested that the soldier have the rope.

33. Cf. Frank Dunlop's 1981 production for the Young Vic; a healthy-looking Regan came on stage, behaved normally throughout most of her scene, suddenly grasped her stomach, was removed offstage, and eventually announced as dead.

34. Gielgud's description from *AHT*, p. 135. Fordham also notes this business (IV.5.D1).

35. In a footnote to the *Preface*, p. 21 n, Barker writes that Edgar's first soliloquy "forms a 'considering point.'" Incidentally, the production also retained Edgar's soliloquy of IV. i to give him "a fresh start in his dramatic career" (*Preface*, p. 77) and to build up his stature in the second half of the play.

36. Speaight, "The Actability of King Lear," p. 53; in *Shakespeare on the Stage*, p. 224, Speaight mentions Barker's change of mind about the setting.

37. Fordham, *PA*, III.2.D1. Later, in his analysis, Fordham writes that "the lighting [of these scenes was] purely atmospheric, the limits of the stage being shrouded in darkness and the figures picked out with diffused lights from an invisible source" (III.3,4, and 6.A1).

38. Purdom, *HGB*, explains how Barker constantly cut and rewrote his plays (p. 211) and how he revised his criticism, even starting a reconsideration of his *Hamlet* preface a few months before his death (pp. 233–34). He also quotes G. B. Harrison, who says that Barker rewrote and polished his work "right up to the page-proof stage and even beyond" (p. 229).

39. The only suggestion Gielgud seems to have made at rehearsals involved the business with the rope at the end of the play; Hayman, *John Gielgud*, p. 127, writes that the actor "was too overwhelmed by the genius who was directing him to put forward any other ideas of his own." His comment suggests that Gielgud never discussed his discomfort with the interpretation of I.v.

40. See George W. Bishop, "John Gielgud's King Lear: Old Vic's Brilliant Reopening," *Daily Telegraph & Morning Post*, 16 April 1940, p. 5, and James Agate, *Sunday Times*, 21 April 1940, p. 3. Besides those already quoted, the following reviews have been consulted: Ivor Brown, the *Observer*, 21 April 1940, p. 9; Ashley Dukes, *Theatre Arts* (New York) 24 (July 1940): 469; David Fairweather, *Theatre World* 33 (May 1940): 104; Herbert Farjeon, the *Bystander*, 8 May 1940, pp. 164–65; Desmond MacCarthy, *New Statesman and Nation* 19 (n.s.) (20 April 1940): 527–28; Derek Verschoyle, the *Spectator*, 19 April 1940, p. 556; *Daily Herald*, 16 April 1940, p. 10; Philip Page, *Daily Mail*, 16 April 1940, p. 9; *Daily Sketch*, 16 April 1940, p. 18; *Evening News*, 16 April 1940, p. 2; *Evening Standard*, 16 April 1940, p. 10; *Illustrated London News*, 4 May 1940, pp. 606 & 608; *Illustrated Sporting & Dramatic News*, 26 April 1940, pp. 124–25; *News Chronicle*, 16 April 1940, p. 8; *Reynolds News*, 21 April 1940, p. 10; the *Stage*, 18 April 1940, p. 7; the *Star*, 16 April 1940, p. 5; *Sunday Dispatch*, 21 April 1940, pp. 124–25; the *Tatler*, 24 April 1940, p. 125; the *Times*, 16 April 1940, p. 4.

41. Once again, subjectivity is an issue. Bishop admiringly recounts that "in [Lear's] wrath in the unreasonable encounter with Cordelia there was a touch of incipient madness": where one critic sees petulance, another sees anger and insanity. Cf. too Bishop's judgment that the production "moves quickly and catches the vigour of the play," while Ivor Brown thought the rate of speech should have been brisker; in this opinion he is alone, as many reviewers commented on the fast pace of the production.

42. Many of MacCarthy's points seem to echo the *Preface;* for example, besides mentioning the importance of Gloucester's blinding, he also refers to the need to orchestrate the voices in the storm scenes.

43. Speaight summarizes Dukes's position in this way, in *Shakespeare on the Stage,* p. 224.

44. See Maynard Mack, *King Lear in Our Time* (London: Methuen, 1966), p. 27; Speaight, *Shakespeare on the Stage,* p. 224, and "The Actability of King Lear," p. 50; and Trewin, *Shakespeare on English Stage,* p. 186. In an interview with the *Times* in 1959, Gielgud said that his rehearsals with Barker "seared into my brain and I follow that interpretation still" (quoted in Byrne, *Prefaces,* vol. 2, as a caption to a photograph facing p. 82).

45. See Charles Marowitz, "Lear Log," *Tulane Drama Review* 8 (Winter 1963): 104–5. Admittedly, the role of Poor Tom does seem to cause problems for the audience; many reviewers of Barker's production commented that credibility was lost upon his arrival. The modern imagination seeks psychological plausibility despite characters, and pointers, to the contrary. The *Preface* sees the disguise as giving *some* clues to Edgar's nature (e.g., the "notion . . . would not come . . . to a commonplace man," p. 65), but its main emphasis is on the disguise's relationship to Lear.

46. Marowitz, "Lear Log," p. 113; the film was directed by Brook and faithful to the stage version.

47. Mack, *"King Lear,"* pp. 27, 40–41; Speaight, "The Actability of King Lear", pp. 51–52.

48. Stephen Haggard, who played the Fool, quoted in Trewin, *Shakespeare on English Stage,* p. 186.

Chapter 5. Conclusion

1. M. St. Clare Byrne also makes this point about Poel in her Introduction to vol. 1 of the *Prefaces;* she remarks that Barker made acceptable in three months what Poel had advocated for three years (p. ix).

2. The Young Vic mounted such a production, directed by Robin Lefèvre, in 1981. My comments about the production are based on my own students' reactions to it; Shakespeare's idea of the cyclical nature of history was suddenly crystallized for them.

3. Rabkin, *Shakespeare & the Problem of Meaning.* See, for example, pp. ix, 8, 12–13, 19–21, 23, 25, 63, 113–14, 140.

4. See, for example, G. Wilson Knight, *Shakespearean Production* (London: Faber & Faber, 1964), and *Shakespeare's Dramatic Challenge* (London: Croom Helm; New York: Barnes & Noble, 1977).

5. Speaking of performance as an element of a play's existence, Rabkin makes a similar point: "The dominant evasion [is] the redaction of the play to a theme which, when we understand it, tells us which of our responses we must suppress" (p. 8); he adds that "one may profitably ask how so much brain power in the most sensitive and highly trained critical audiences has produced so little that can't be punctured simply by watching one's own responses to details of a play" (p. 19). See also John Russell Brown, *Free Shakespeare* (London: Heinemann, 1974), pp. 4, 113, and 6 respectively.

6. *John Gielgud: An Actor's Biography in Pictures,* compiled and described by Hallam Fordham with personal narrative by John Gielgud (London: John Lehmann, 1952), p. 56. Gielgud's view of 1952 still holds; John Miller, who taped eighteen hours of interviews with Sir John for the BBC in January 1978, mentioned in a phone conversation with me (23 March 1982) that Barker is Gielgud's "great hero."

Bibliography

For unsigned reviews, please see notes.

Agate, James. "The Old Vic Reopens." The *Sunday Times,* 21 April 1940, p. 3.

Bablet, Denis. *Edward Gordon Craig.* 1962. Translated by Daphne Woodward. London: Heinemann, 1966.

Barbour, Charles M. "Up Against A Symbolic Painted Cloth: *A Midsummer Night's Dream* at the Savoy, 1914." *Educational Theatre Journal* 27 (December 1975): 521–28.

Barker, Harley Granville. "Alas, Poor Will!" *The Listener* 17 (3 March 1937): 387–89, 425–26.

———. *Associating with Shakespeare.* An address delivered at King's College, London, on 25 November 1931. London: Humphrey Milford for the Shakespeare Association, 1932.

———. "The Casting of *Hamlet.* A Fragment." *London Mercury* 35 (November 1936): 10–17.

———. *The Exemplary Theatre.* London: Chatto & Windus, 1922.

———. "From *Henry V* to *Hamlet.*" British Academy Annual Lecture, 1925. In *Prefaces to Shakespeare*, vol. 6, edited by Edward M. Moore, pp. 135–67. London: Batsford, 1974.

———. "The Golden Thoughts of Granville Barker, Author, Mime, and 'Producer.'" *Play Pictorial* 21, no. 126 [January 1913]: iv.

———. "*Hamlet* in Plus Fours." *Yale Review* 16 (October 1926): 205.

———. "The Heritage of the Actor." *Quarterly Review,* no. 476 (July 1923): 53–73.

———. *Julius Caesar: The Forum Scene.* London, 1911. Beerbohm Tree Collection, University of Bristol Theatre Collection.

———. Letter to William Archer. BM 45290, fol. 133. British Library, London.

———. Letter to *Daily Mail,* 26 September 1912, p. 4.

———. Letters to Alan Downer. Bernard F. Burgunder Collection, Department of Rare Books, Cornell University Library.

———. Letters to G. B. Harrison. The Department of Rare Books and Special Collections, The University of Michigan Library, Ann Arbor.

———. *"A Midsummer Night's Dream" prompt copy.* The Department of Rare Books and Special Collections, The University of Michigan Library, Ann Arbor.

———. "A Note upon Chapters XX. and XXI. of *The Elizabethan Stage.*" *Review of English Studies* 1 (January 1925): 60–71.

———. "Notes on Rehearsing a Play." *Drama* 1 (July 1919): 2–5.

———. *On Dramatic Method.* London: Sidgwick & Jackson, 1931.

———. *On Poetry in Drama.* London: Sidgwick & Jackson, 1937.

———. "The Perennial Shakespeare." *Listener* 18 (20 October 1937): 823–26, 857–59. The text of "The Twentieth of the Broadcast National Lectures delivered on 13 October 1937" was also published in pamphlet form as *The Perennial Shakespeare.* London: The British Broadcasting Corporation, 1937.

———. Introduction to *The Players' Shakespeare.* London: Ernest Benn, 1923. Reprinted in *Prefaces,* vol. 6, ed. Moore, pp. 43–59.

———. Preface to *A Midsummer Night's Dream: An Acting Edition.* London: Heinemann, 1914. Reprinted in *Prefaces,* vol. 6, ed. Moore, pp. 33–42.

———. Preface to *A Midsummer Night's Dream, The Players' Shakespeare,* vol. 4. London: Ernest Benn, 1924, pp. ix–lii. Reprinted in *Prefaces,* vol. 6, ed. Moore, pp. 94–134.

———. Preface to *Twelfth Night: An Acting Edition.* London: Heinemann, 1912, pp. iii–xi. Reprinted in *Prefaces,* vol. 6, ed. Moore, pp. 26–32.

———. Preface to *The Winter's Tale: An Acting Edition.* London: Heinemann, 1912, pp. iii–x. Reprinted in *Prefaces,* vol. 6, ed. Moore, pp. 19–25.

———. *Prefaces to Shakespeare.* 1930 [1927–47]. Reprinted in 5 vols. London: Batsford, 1968–71. Vol. 6 (1974), edited by Edward M. Moore, contains miscellaneous articles and prefaces to the acting editions.

———. *Prefaces to Shakespeare.* 1930 [1927–47]. Reprinted in 4 vols. Introduction, illustrations, and notes by Muriel St. Clare Byrne. London: Batsford, 1963.

———. "A Review of *Designs by Inigo Jones for Masques and Plays at Court.* With Introduction and Notes by Percy Simpson and C. F. Bell." *Review of English Studies* 1 (April 1925): 231–35.

———. Review of *The Frontiers of Drama,* by Una Ellis-Fermor, *Review of English Studies* 22 (April 1946): 144–47.

———. Review of *The Globe Playhouse,* by J. C. Adams. February 1944. TS, Humanities Research Center, Austin, Texas.

———. Review of *The Physical Conditions of the Elizabethan Public Playhouses* and *Restoration Stage Studies,* by W. J. Lawrence. *Review of English Studies* 4 (April 1928): 229–37.

———. "Shakespeare and Modern Stagecraft." *Yale Review* 15 (July 1926): 703–24.

————. "Shakespeare's Dramatic Art." In *A Companion to Shakespeare Studies,* ed. Harley Granville Barker and G. B. Harrison, pp. 45–87. 1934. Reprint. Cambridge: Cambridge University Press, 1959.

————. "Some Tasks for Dramatic Scholarship." *Essays by Divers Hands,* n.s. 3 (1923): 17–38.

————. Souvenir of Complimentary Dinner to Mr. J. E. Vedrenne and Mr. Harley Granville Barker at the Criterion Restaurant, 7 July 1907. British Library.

————. "The Stagecraft of Shakespeare," *Fortnightly Review,* n.s. 120 (July 1926): 1–17. [A variant of "Shakespeare & Modern Stagecraft."]

————. "The Theatre in Berlin." *Times* (London), 19 November 1910, p. 6, and 21 November 1910, p. 12.

————. "The Theatre: The Next Phase." Lecture given on 9 June 1910. *English Review* 5 (July 1910): 631–48.

————. *"Twelfth Night" prompt copy.* The Department of Rare Books and Special Collections, The University of Michigan Library, Ann Arbor.

————. *The Use of the Drama.* London: Sidgwick & Jackson, 1946.

Barker, Harley Granville, and G. B. Harrison, eds. *A Companion to Shakespeare Studies.* 1934. Reprint. Cambridge: Cambridge University Press: 1959.

Bishop, George W. *Barry Jackson and the London Theatre.* London: Arthur Barker, 1933.

————. "John Gielgud's King Lear: Old Vic's Brilliant Reopening." *Daily Telegraph and Morning Post,* 16 April 1940, p. 5.

Blau, Herbert. "A Subtext Based on Nothing." *Tulane Drama Review* 8 (Winter 1963): 122–32.

Bradbrook, M. C. "Fifty Years of the Criticism of Shakespeare's Style: A Retrospect." *Shakespeare Survey* 7 (1954): 1–11.

Bridges Adams, W. "Granville Barker and the Savoy." *Drama,* n.s. no. 52 (Spring 1959): 28–31.

————. *The Lost Leader: W. Bridges Adams on Harley Granville Barker.* London: Sidgwick & Jackson, 1954.

————. Review of M. St. Clare Byrne's Foreword and illustrations to *Prefaces to Shakespeare. Theatre Notebook* 18 (Winter 1963/64): 62–64.

Brown, Ivor. "At the Play." *Observer,* 21 April 1940, p. 9.

————. "The World of the Theatre." *Illustrated London News,* 4 May 1940, pp. 606–8.

————. *Shakespeare and the Actors.* London: Bodley Head, 1970.

Brown, John Russell. *Free Shakespeare.* London: Heinemann, 1974.

————. "Originality in Shakespeare Production." *Theatre Notebook* 26 (Spring 1972): 107–14.

Byrne, Muriel St. Clare. "Fifty Years of Shakespearian Production: 1898–1948." *Shakespeare Survey* 2 (1949): 1–20.

Casson, Sir Lewis. "William Poel & the Modern Theatre." *Listener* (10 January 1952): 56–58. Published version of "The Influence of William Poel on the Modern Theatre," broadcast on the Third Programme, 31 December 1951. BBC Broadcast TS. in Birmingham Central Library.

Cooke, Katharine. *A. C. Bradley and his Influence on Twentieth-Century Shakespeare Criticism.* Oxford: Oxford University Press, 1972.

Craig, Edward. *Gordon Craig: The Story of his Life.* London: Gollancz, 1968.

Craig, E. Gordon. *The Art of the Theatre.* Edinburgh and London: T. N. Foulis, 1905.

———. *A Living Theatre.* Privately published in Florence, 1913.

———. *On the Art of the Theatre.* London: Heinemann, 1924.

———. *The Theatre Advancing.* London: Constable, 1921.

Craig, Hardin. "Recent Shakespeare Scholarship." *Shakespeare Association Bulletin* [New York] 5 (April 1930): 39–54.

———. "Trend of Shakespeare Scholarship." *Shakespeare Survey* 2 (1949): 107–14.

David, Richard. *Shakespeare in the Theatre.* Cambridge: Cambridge University Press, 1978.

Dent, Edward. "The Musical Interpretation of Shakespeare on the Modern Stage." *Musical Quarterly* 2 (1916): 523–77.

Downer, Alan S. Correspondence with Harley Granville Barker, 1944–45, and with George Bernard Shaw, 1947–48. Bernard F. Burgunder Collection, Department of Rare Books, Cornell University Library.

———. "Harley Granville Barker." *Sewanee Review* 55 (1947): 627–45.

Dukes, Ashley. "The English Scene." *Theatre Arts* [New York] 24 (July 1940): 467–70.

Eastman, Arthur M. *A Short History of Shakespearean Criticism.* New York: W. W. Norton, 1974.

Fairweather, David. Review of *King Lear. Theatre World* 33 (May 1940): 140.

Farjeon, Herbert. "Mr. Barker Gets Reinhardtitis." *Theatreland* 1 (11 October 1912): 14–15.

Findon, B. W., ed. *Play Pictorial* 21 [January 1913]. The entire issue is devoted to *Twelfth Night.*

Fordham, Hallam. "Player in Action. John Gielgud as 'King Lear.'" Ca. 1940. TS, cat. no. T.b. 17. Folger Shakespeare Library.

Fry, Roger. "Mr. Gordon Craig's Stage Designs." *Nation* 9 (16 September 1911): 871.

Gielgud, Sir John. *An Actor and His Time.* London: Sidgwick & Jackson, 1979.

———. "Granville-Barker's Shakespeare." *Theatre Arts* [New York] 31 (October 1947): 48–49.

———. *John Gielgud: An Actor's Biography in Pictures.* Compiled and described by Hallam Fordham with personal narrative by John Gielgud. London: John Lehmann, 1952.

———. Letter to Gabrielle Enthoven, 5 May 1940. Enthoven Collection, Theatre Museum, Victoria & Albert Museum.

———. *Stage Directions.* 1963. Reprint. London: Heinemann, 1979.

Glick, Claris. "William Poel: His Theories and Influence." *Shakespeare Quarterly* 15 (Winter 1964): 15–25.

Greif, Karen. "'If This Were Play'd Upon a Stage': Harley Granville Barker's Shakespeare Productions at the Savoy Theatre, 1912–1914." *Harvard Library Bulletin* 27 (April 1980): 117–45.

Grein, J. T. Review of *The Winter's Tale. Sunday Times,* 22 September 1912, p. 7.

———. Review of *Twelfth Night. Sunday Times,* 17 November 1912, p. 6.

———. Review of the *Dream. Sunday Times,* 8 February 1914, p. 6.

Griffiths, Trevor. "Tradition and Innovation in Harley Granville Barker's *A Midsummer Night's Dream." Theatre Notebook* 30 (1976): 78–87.

Guthrie, Tyrone. *A Life in the Theatre.* London: Hamish Hamilton, 1960.

Halliday, F. E. *Shakespeare and His Critics.* Rev. ed. London: Duckworth, 1958.

Harrison, G. B. "Literary History and Criticism." *London Mercury* 22 (June 1930): 184–85.

Hayman, Ronald. *John Gielgud.* London: Heinemann, 1971.

Henderson, Archibald. *George Bernard Shaw: Man of the Century.* New York: Appleton-Century-Crofts, 1956.

Hewes, Henry. "How to use Shakespeare." *Saturday Review* [New York], 13 July 1957, pp. 10–13.

Hitchcock, Alfred, and Val Gielgud. "Shakespeare: Much Ado about Nothing?" *Listener* 17 (10 March 1937): 448–50.

Hunt, Hugh. "Granville-Barker's Shakespearean Productions." *Theatre Research* 10 (1969): 44–49. A paper originally delivered in Budapest, 25 September 1967.

Inkster, Leonard. "Shakespeare and Mr. Granville Barker." *Poetry and Drama* 1 (March 1913): 22–26.

Innes, Christopher. *Edward Gordon Craig.* Cambridge: Cambridge University Press, 1983.

Jackson, Anthony. "Harley Granville Barker as Director at the Royal [sic] Court Theatre, 1904–1907." *Theatre Research* 12 (1972): 126–38.

Kelly, Helen M. T. *The Granville-Barker Shakespeare Productions: A Study Based on the Promptbooks.* Ann Arbor, Michigan: University Microfilms, 1965.

Kermode, Frank, ed. *Four Centuries of Shakespearian Criticism.* New York: Avon Books, 1965.

Knight, G. Wilson. *Shakespearean Production.* London: Faber & Faber, 1964.

———. *Shakespeare's Dramatic Challenge.* London: Croom Helm; New York: Barnes & Noble, 1977.

Knights, L. C. Review of *A Companion to Shakespeare Studies. Scrutiny* 3 (December 1934): 306–14.

Kott, Jan. *Shakespeare our Contemporary.* 1964. Translated by Boleslaw Taborski. New York: W. W. Norton, 1974.

Lawrence. W. J. *The Physical Conditions of the Elizabethan Public Playhouses.* Cambridge: Harvard University Press, 1927.

Leeper, Janet. *Edward Gordon Craig: Designs for the Theatre.* Harmondsworth: Penguin Books. 1948.

Loney, Glenn, ed. *Peter Brook's Production of William Shakespeare's "A Midsummer Night's Dream": Authorized Acting Edition.* Chicago: The Dramatic Publishing Company, 1974.

MacCarthy, Desmond. *The Court Theatre 1904–1907: A Commentary and Criticism.* London: A. H. Bullen, 1907.

———. "The Production of Poetic Drama." *The New Statesman, A Weekly Review of Politics and Literature* 2 (14 February 1914): 597–98.

———. "A Midsummer Night's Dream." *New Statesman* 2 (21 February 1914): 629–30.

———. "Lear at the Old Vic." *New Statesman* 19, n.s. (20 April 1940): 527–28.

McCarthy, Lillah. *Myself and My Friends.* With "An Aside" by G. Bernard Shaw. London: Thornton Butterworth, 1933.

Mack, Maynard. *King Lear in our Time.* London: Methuen, 1966.

Mander, Raymond, and Joseph Mitchenson. *Theatrical Companion to Shaw.* London: Rockliff, 1954.

Marowitz, Charles. "Lear Log." *Tulane Drama Review* 8 (Winter 1963): 103–21.

Marshall, Norman. *The Producer and the Play.* London: Macdonald, 1957.

———. Review of John Fernald's *Sense of Direction: The Director and his Actors. Theatre Notebook* 23 (Summer 1969): 161–62.

Mazer, Cary M. *Shakespeare Refashioned: Elizabethan Plays on Edwardian Stages.* Theater & Dramatic Studies, no. 5. Ann Arbor: UMI Research Press, 1981.

Meisel, Martin. *Shaw and the Nineteenth-Century Theatre.* Princeton: Princeton University Press, 1963.

Moore, Edward M. "William Poel." *Shakespeare Quarterly* 23 (Winter 1972): 21–36.

Morgan, Margery M. *A Drama of Political Man: A Study in the Plays of Harley Granville Barker.* London: Sidgwick & Jackson, 1961.

Muir, Kenneth. "Fifty Years of Shakespearian Criticism: 1900–1950." *Shakespeare Survey* 4 (1951): 1–25.

Muir, Kenneth, and S. Schoenbaum, eds. *A New Companion to Shakespeare Studies*. Cambridge: Cambridge University 1971.

Murray, Patrick. *The Shakespearean Scene: Some Twentieth-Century Perspectives*. London: Longmans, Green, 1969.

Nash, George. *Edward Gordon Craig 1872–1966*. London: H. M. Stationery Office, 1967. Exhibition catalogue from the Victoria and Albert Museum.

Nesbitt, Cathleen. *A Little Love and Good Company*. Owings Mills, Md.: Stemmer House, 1977.

Nicoll, Allardyce. *A History of English Drama, 1660–1900*. 2d ed. Vol. 4. Cambridge: Cambridge University Press, 1955.

Odell, George C. D. *Shakespeare from Betterton to Irving*. Vol. 2. 1920. Reprint. London: Constable, 1963.

Palmer, John. "Mr. Granville Barker's Inheritance." *Saturday Review of Politics, Literature, Science and Art* 114 (14 September 1912): 325–26.

———. "Shakespeare's 'The Winter's Tale.'" *Saturday Review* 114 (28 September 1912): 391–92.

———. "Twelfth Night." *Saturday Review* 114 (23 November 1912): 637–39.

———. "Mr. Barker's Dream." *Saturday Review* 117 (14 February 1914): 202–3.

Paschall, D. D. "A Study of the Plays and Criticism of Harley Granville Barker." D.Phil. diss., University of Oxford, 1976.

Pearson, Hesketh. *GBS: A Postscript*. London: Collins, 1951.

———. *The Last Actor-Managers*. London: Methuen, 1950.

Poel, William. "Scenery and Drama." *Nation* 10 (14 October 1911): 97.

———. *Shakespeare in the Theatre*. London and Toronto: Sidgwick & Jackson, 1913.

———. "Shakespeare's 'Prompt Copies': A Plea for the Early Texts," *Times Literary Supplement*, 3 February 1921. Reprinted by the London Shakespeare League as a broadsheet. BL 1865. c. (162). British Library.

———. *What is Wrong with the Stage*. London: George Allen & Unwin, 1920.

[Poel, William ?] *Notes on some of William Poel's Stage Productions*. London: A. W. Patching & Co. for the Shakespeare Reading Society, 1933.

Purdom, C. B. *Harley Granville Barker: Man of the Theatre, Dramatist and Scholar*. London: Rockliff, 1955.

Rabkin, Norman, ed. *Reinterpretations of Elizabethan Drama: Selected Papers from the English Institute*. New York and London: Columbia University Press, 1969.

———. *Shakespeare and the Problem of Meaning*. Chicago and London: University of Chicago Press, 1981.

Ralli, Augustus. *A History of Shakespearian Criticism*. Vol. 2. London: Oxford University Press, 1932.

Rutherston, Albert. "Decoration in the Art of the Theatre." *Monthly Chapbook* 1 (August 1919): 7–27.

Salmon Eric. *Granville Barker: A Secret Life.* London: Heinemann, 1983.

———. "Shakespeare on the Modern Stage: The Need for New Approaches." *Modern Drama* 15 (December 1972): 305–19.

Schmidt, Karl. "How Barker Puts Plays On." *Harper's Weekly* 60 (30 January 1915): 115–16.

Senelick, Laurence. *Gordon Craig's Moscow Hamlet, A Reconstruction.* Westport, Conn: Greenwood, 1982.

Shakespeare, William. *King Lear.* Edited by Kenneth Muir. 8th ed. with corrections. New York: Vintage Books, 1963.

———. *A Midsummer Night's Dream.* Edited by Harold F. Brooks. London: Methuen, 1979.

———. *Twelfth Night.* Edited by J. M. Lothian and T. W. Craik. London: Methuen, 1975.

———. *The Winter's Tale.* Edited by J. H. P. Pafford. 4th ed. rev. 1963. Reprint. London: Methuen, 1978.

Sharp, Cecil. *The Songs and Incidental Music Arranged and Composed for Granville Barker's Production of A Midsummer Night's Dream at the Savoy Theatre in January [sic], 1914.* London: Simpkin Marshall, Hamilton, Kent, 1914.

Shattuck, Charles H. *The Shakespeare Promptbooks, A Descriptive Catalogue.* Urbana: University of Illinois Press, 1965.

Shaw, George Bernard. *The Art of Rehearsal.* New York: Samuel French, 1928.

———. *Bernard Shaw and Mrs. Patrick Campbell: Their Correspondence.* Edited by Alan Dent. London: Gollancz, 1952.

———. *Bernard Shaw's Letters to Granville Barker.* Edited by C. B. Purdom, with commentary and notes. London: Phoenix House, 1956.

———. *Ellen Terry and Bernard Shaw: a correspondence.* Edited by Christopher St. John. 1931. Reset. London: Reinhardt & Evans, 1949.

———. "Granville-Barker: Some Particulars." *Drama,* n.s. no. 3 (Winter 1946): 7–14.

———. Letter to Alan S. Downer and reply to a questionnaire, 1947–48. Burgunder Shaw Collection, Cornell University Library.

———. *Our Theatres in the Nineties.* Standard ed. 3 vols. London: Constable, 1932.

———. *Shaw on Theatre.* Edited by E. J. West. [London]: Macgibbon & Kee, [1960].

———. "Shaw's Rules for Directors," *Theatre Arts* 33 (August 1949): 6–11.

Speaight, Robert. "The Actability of King Lear: Reminiscences of thirty years of performances." *Drama Survey* 2 [Minneapolis] (Spring 1962): 49–55.

———. "The Pioneers." *Shakespeare Jahrbuch* 93 (1957): 170–74.

———. *Shakespeare on the Stage: An illustrated history of Shakespearian performance.* London: Collins, 1973.

———. *William Poel and the Elizabethan Revival.* London: Heinemann, 1954.

Sprague, A. C., and J. C. Trewin. *Shakespeare's Plays Today: Some Customs and Conventions of the Stage.* London: Sidgwick & Jackson, 1970.

Styan, J. L. *The Shakespeare Revolution: Criticism and Performance in the Twentieth Century.* Cambridge: Cambridge University Press, 1977.

Szyfman, Arnold. "*King Lear* on the Stage: A Producer's Reflection." *Shakespeare Survey* 13 (1960): 69–71.

Taylor, John Russell, ed. *The Penguin Dictionary of Theatre.* Rev. ed. Harmondsworth: Penguin Books, 1974.

Trewin, J. C. *The Edwardian Theatre.* Oxford: Basil Blackwell, 1976.

———. *Shakespeare on the English Stage 1900–1964: A Survey of Productions.* London: Barrie & Rockliff, 1964.

Trousdale, Marion. "The Question of Harley Granville-Barker and Shakespeare on the Stage." *Renaissance Drama,* n.s. 4 (1971): 3–36.

Verschoyle, Derek. "The Theatre." *Spectator,* 19 April 1940, p. 556.

William Poel and his Stage Productions 1880–1932. [London, 1932].

Williams, Gary J. "A Midsummer Night's Dream: The English and American Popular Traditions and Harley Granville-Barker's 'World Arbitrarily Made.'" *Theatre Studies* [Ohio State University Theatre Research Institute], no. 23 (1976/77): 40–52.

Williams, Harcourt. *Four Years at the Old Vic: 1929–1933.* London: Putnam, 1935.

———. *Old Vic Saga.* London: Winchester Publications, 1949.

Youngs, Olive, comp. *Theatre Notebook 1945–1971: An Index to Volumes 1–25.* London: The Society for Theatre Research, 1977.

Index

Abbey Theatre, 26
Agate, James, 192
Ainley, Henry, 54, 56
Androcles and the Lion (Shaw), 35–36
Antony and Cleopatra, 95, 105–6, 127; Barker on, 95, 100–101, 105–6
Archer, William, 63, 221 n.25
Arden Shakespeare, 90, 137
Artaud, Antonin, 82
Asphaleia System, 26

Barbour, Charles M., 58, 69–70
Barker, Harley Granville: on *Antony and Cleopatra*, 95, 100–101, 105–6; and Archer, 63, 221 n.25; on audiences, 99, 110, 114, 120; and Bradley, 85, 89, 111, 126, 129–31; "character in action," 97–98, 109, 118; on Coleridge, 113–14; on collaboration between scholarship and theatre, 89, 99, 104; at the Court Theatre, 31–36, 44; and Craig, 31–32, 39; on theatrical credibility, 94–95, 100, 103; critical appraisal of, 124–27, 199–203; on criticism, 87, 89–90, 114; on cutting, 91–92, 138–39; on *Cymbeline*, 100; as director, 32–36, 37–77, 140–42, 143, 144, 145–92; on Elizabethan staging and stage directions, 104–8 (*see also* Barker, Harley Granville: on staging Shakespeare); established as *Lear* director, 139–40, 144; on educational force of theatre, 119–20; on film and radio Shakespeare, 122–24; and Gielgud (*see* Gielgud, Sir John); on Gielgud as Lear, 141; on *Hamlet*, 87–88, 100, 111; on Harrison's *Hamlet* edition, 117; influence of, 77, 82–83, 125, 127–28, 145, 199–203; on "interpretative acting," 98, 104; on *Julius Caesar*, 98; on *King Lear*, 98, 101–2, 129–31, 131–32, 136, 137, 138–39, 143–44, 145–90, 200; on Lamb, 129; letters to Gielgud on *Lear*, 143–44, 145, 185–86; letters to Harrison, 115–18; on *Macbeth*, 101, 105; on *Measure for Measure*, 113; on *Midsummer Night's Dream*, 62–63, 70–71, 85–86; on modern-dress Shakespeare, 102–3, 109–10; national theatre, commitment to, 31, 119, 122; on performance, importance of, 86–87, 201–2; and Poel, 31–32, 35, 37–38, 39, 43, 63, 88–89, 95; on poetic drama, 118–19, 120–21; Preface to *King Lear* compared to Old Vic production, 145–90, 192; refusal to state meaning reductively, 135, 201; on rigidity, dangers of, 100, 106, 107, 111; role interpretation, approach to, 150 (*see also* Gielgud, Sir John; Nesbitt, Cathleen; Williams, Harcourt); on *Romeo and Juliet*, 100, 112; and Shakespeare Association, 113, 115–16; on Shakespeare texts, 90, 137; on Shakespeare's use of language, 85–86, 111–13; and Shaw, 32–36, 93; on speech delivery, 35, 142–43; on staging Shakespeare, 37–38, 87–89, 91–96, 101, 105–6, 109 (*see also* Barker,

237

PR
2972
.G7
D9
1986

88-1704

PR   88-1704
2972
.G7/D9/1986

AUTHOR
Dymkowski
TITLE
Harley Granville Barker

DATE DUE	BORROWER'S NAME

Gramley Library
Salem College
Winston-Salem, NC 27108